FLIGHT

FLIGHT

BRIAN GALLAGHER

POOLBEG

Published 2002
Poolbeg Press Ltd.
123 Grange Hill, Baldoyle,
Dublin 13, Ireland

Email: poolbeg@poolbeg.com
www.poolbeg.com

© Brian Gallagher 2002

The moral right of the author has been asserted.

Copyright for typesetting, layout, design
© Poolbeg Group Services Ltd.

1 3 5 7 9 10 8 6 4 2

A catalogue record for this book is available from the British Library.

ISBN 1 84223 092 1

Cover designed by Slatter-Anderson
Typeset by Patricia Hope in Palatino 10/13.5
Printed by
Omnia Books Ltd, Glasgow

ABOUT THE AUTHOR

Brian Gallagher was born in Dublin. He is a full-time writer whose plays and short stories have been produced and published in Ireland, Britain and Canada.

He has written extensively for radio and television and is one of the script team on RTE'S successful drama series *Fair City*.

He collaborated with the composer Shaun Purcell on the musical *Larkin*, for which he wrote the book and lyrics.

His debut novel *Invincible* won widespread praise, and he is currently writing a new novel, *Payback*.

Outside of writing, his interests include travel, tennis, music, and inland waterways. He lives with his family in Dublin.

Also by Brian Gallagher

Invincible

ACKNOWLEDGEMENTS

I'd like to record my gratitude for the assistance I received in researching this novel, particularly to Chief Inspector Kenneth Eccles for his patience in explaining police procedures – any deviation from standard operating procedures stems from artistic licence on my part rather than any lack of explanation on his.

I would like also to thank sincerely the following: Gaye Shortland, my editor, Freda Hogan, Pat Moylan, Alison Walsh and Mary Rooney for reading the manuscript and sharing their thoughts with me; and for technical assistance on a range of issues I am indebted to Glenn Meade, Shane Lynch, Paul Kelly, John Mc Cullen, Anne Hughes, Microfeech Data, Frank Clonan, Tommy Dwyer, Tom O'Reilly, Clare Dowling and Anne Fahey.

Finally thanks to my family, Miriam, Orla and Peter, whose support has been unwavering.

To my parents – in memory of my father, John, and for my mother, Mona.

Prologue

Browsdale Research Centre, Yorkshire

May 1993

Gatenby screwed the silencer onto the gun, pleased at how steady his hand was. He had never killed before, never even fired a shot in anger. If everything went to plan he wouldn't have to now either, but it was vital to have the option. Gatenby had seen the unexpected derail operations before – he was determined it wouldn't happen today.

He glanced at the clock on his office wall. 3.04 p.m. One more minute. He had chosen the time carefully. Even in a high-tech weapons research centre the tea break remained an institution, with most of the workforce adjourning to the canteen for fifteen or twenty minutes at three o'clock.

He slipped the gun into the inside pocket of his jacket, breathed deeply to calm himself, then looked again at the clock. Thirty seconds to go, after which his actions would make him the most wanted man in Britain. He watched the second hand move round to twelve, then rose from his desk and unlocked the office door.

Despite his preparations he was struck by the enormity of what he was going to do. He tried breathing deeply again and thought of his future if the plan worked – no, he corrected, *when* the plan worked. No more English winters, no more money worries – instead a life of ease and endless sunshine, of palm-fringed beaches and bronzed young women. By this time next month his life would be devoted entirely to pleasure. Strengthened in his resolve, he picked up his briefcase and opened the office door.

He walked down the corridor and turned into the open office area of the Data Section. "Afternoon, Jill," he said, approaching the clerk at the desk.

"Good afternoon, Mr Gatenby."

"Ellen at tea break?"

"Yes, sir, holding the fort for her . . ."

He forced a smile as he signed the entry book for the limited-access area in the rear office. "Mustn't miss the tea break – great British institution . . ."

"No indeed, sir," answered Jill with a smile as she activated the electronic device that opened the door.

"Shan't be too long," he said walking through, then he closed the door behind him. The room he entered had rows of neatly filed computer discs, microfiche film and conventional paper files, but as Deputy Director of Security Gatenby knew that the really top secret documents were stored in the wall-mounted safe in the alcove.

He moved quickly, inserting a key in a socket hidden behind a desk, then he keyed in the correct digits to neutralise the light-beams covering the approach to the safe. A second key in a similarly hidden socket enabled him to deactivate the pressure pads built into the floor. Finally he produced two more keys with which he switched off the movement detectors and heat sensors. With the interior alarm system nullified, he quickly crossed to the safe and keyed in the combination known only to himself and the Director, then opened the safe door.

He reached inside and sorted through the files until he came to one marked SMORTAR – TOP SECRET. He opened the file, confirmed the presence of the rows of microfiche film, then transferred it to his briefcase. He closed the safe, reactivated the alarm systems and emerged from the office.

His heart was thumping, but he was pleased at how casual his voice sounded as he nodded to the secretary. "Cheers, Jill."

"You're welcome, Mr Gatenby."

He walked down the corridor, entered his office and locked the door. Moving swiftly, he crossed to a bank of filing cabinets and manhandled two of them forward, revealing a hole about two feet square knocked into the wall.

He had known that no classified documents could be taken through the front and only entrance to the building without triggering an alarm, and so he had organised weekend construction work in the storage area adjoining his office, necessitating the switching off of the trembler switches. While the work was going on he had knocked the hole in the wall and immediately camouflaged it on both sides.

Now he crouched down, reached through the wall and shoved aside a wooden box that covered the hole from the other side. He took the briefcase and squeezed behind the filing cabinets and through the hole, emerging in a huge, dimly-lit storage area. He put the wooden box back in place, then climbed over a series of similar boxes, jumped down onto the floor and dusted off his suit. He was now in the central aisle of the weapons storage area, another high-security zone with which he was acquainted through his role as Deputy Director of Security.

The main loading bay was at the far end of the building, but Gatenby crossed to a small fire exit, a heavy side-door secured on the inside with four strengthened steel bars. He carefully removed the bars, placing each one noiselessly on the floor, then pulled a lever and swung the door inwards.

Sunlight flooded in, and to his amazement he found himself face to face with an armed guard. The startled soldier had been standing in the outside alcove of the door, a cigarette shielded in his hand. Gatenby was first to regain his composure and quickly went on the offensive. "Corporal! What the hell do you think you're at?"

"Sir?"

"Smoking? Smoking in an explosives storage area!"

The soldier immediately extinguished the cigarette. "I'm sorry, sir. I – "

"Sorry? Have you any idea how serious this is?"

"Yes, sir. But . . . but I was on the outside, sir."

"I should hope so! Your C/O will hear of this.

Meanwhile, get on with your patrolling." He nodded dismissively.

"Yes, sir." The man looked troubled. "Mr Gatenby?"

"What is it?"

The soldier looked at him a moment before speaking.

"Well?"

"May I ask, sir, what you were doing in a restricted area?"

Gatenby felt his stomach tighten, but camouflaged his fear with a show of outrage. "Are you taking leave of your senses? I find you smoking outside a high-explosives area, and instead of pleading for leniency you've the cheek to question the Deputy Director of Security?" He watched the man carefully, but the soldier wasn't wilting. He had the sort of stocky, thickset build that Gatenby associated with aggression, and although the soldier's words were courteous Gatenby sensed an innate willingness for confrontation in the man.

"I'm sorry, sir, but the area's always sealed except at agreed opening times. And we've had no notice of an opening."

"I'm telling you now, Corporal. I was carrying out a spot check."

"Yes, sir, but the rules state that anybody found . . ."

"Enough!" Gatenby cried angrily. "I'll have no more of this nonsense. We run the security here – the army simply supplies the manpower. Now get on with your duties!"

There was a long pause while the soldier looked at

him, then the man spoke politely but with no indication of backing off. "I'm sorry, sir . . . it's still my duty to ask you to explain being in a restricted area outside specified times."

Gatenby felt a tremor of fear run through him as the bull-necked soldier looked him in the eye. He forced himself to maintain eye contact. "I've told you it was a spot check," he said with conviction. "I *am* Deputy Director . . ."

"Even the Head of Security doesn't go in without notification, sir." The soldier glanced at Gatenby's right hand. "And I'm afraid, sir, I'll have to ask you to open your briefcase."

Jesus! thought Gatenby. He'd have to use the gun, he realised, and the thought made his knees tremble. He paused, then breathed out as though in resignation. "You're right, of course, Corporal." He gave the soldier a wry smile. "I suppose I should be pleased our security is so tight. All right," he said, taking a step back into the warehouse. He undid the catch and opened the briefcase, which he held out. "Here we are . . ."

The corporal approached, took the briefcase and bent slightly to examine it in the gloomier light. Gatenby watched as the soldier's attention was taken with the SMORTAR file and its Top Secret marking. Now was his chance. He swallowed hard, swiftly drew the pistol, placed it at the back of the soldier's head and fired twice.

The corporal fell to the floor, dropping the briefcase. Gatenby fought back his distaste at the bloody mess of the man's shattered skull and forced himself to check for certain that the soldier was dead. Despite the gruesomeness of his task he felt a thrill at the ruthless efficiency of what he had done. Satisfied that the soldier was dead, he pulled the fire door shut and looked about for a place to hide the body.

He swiftly dragged the limp form behind some of the wooden crates, stacking the boxes so only a definite search would reveal the body. That still left a clear trail of blood that would have to be obliterated. But how? He felt a stab of panic but forced it down. Thinking clearly at this stage could be the difference between success and failure. He scanned the area, then crossed to the fire extinguishers. In addition to the chemical and water extinguishers there were two old-fashioned fire buckets.

He quickly scattered a sprinkling of sand from one of the buckets onto the floor to camouflage the blood, then replaced the bucket, slid the steel bars from the door under a crate and reviewed the scene. In the low-wattage gloom the blood wasn't evident, and the sand would probably only be seen by someone actually looking for it. It wasn't ideal, but it was the best he could do. He took out a handkerchief and wiped the briefcase free of some small bloodstains, then exited through the fire-door, closing it behind him.

The warm May sunshine made him blink but he moved briskly towards his car, a silver BMW. He had parked it purposely at the end of the car park nearest the storage area and now he unlocked the boot, inserted the briefcase and got into the car unseen.

He started the engine and drove towards the exit,

careful to keep to his normal speed. The remote
Yorkshire valley housing the Weapons Research centre
was bathed in soft hazy sunshine, the nearby hills
purple in the afternoon light, but Gatenby was blind to
their beauty as he drove towards the exit.

He nodded casually to the soldier manning the
barrier, and the man saluted smartly and raised the
boom. Careful not to let any relief show, he drove
through and started down the narrow approach road.

1

Dave Walker thought the end would never come. He sat at the back of the conference-room listening with irritation to the speaker's droning voice. This, the final item on the agenda, was described in his programme as the "Keynote Address by T J Lawrence, General Manager, United Advertising, Northern Region".

He reckoned that only Trevor Lawrence would be pretentious enough to describe himself as General Manager, Northern Region, at a conference exclusively for the staff of United Advertising's Northern Region. Dave had been tempted to speak to Lawrence about it when the programme was being written, but instead had held back, reasoning that he had enough trouble keeping Lawrence from interfering with his copywriting team without fighting unnecessary battles.

Dave looked down the room now to where Lawrence was declaiming how important it was to increase their market share. Why did the man always have to labour the obvious? Since moving to the North two years previously as Creative Director, Dave had had to work with Lawrence, and he had grown to dislike everything about him, from his weak chin to his habit of stating a cliché as though it were an original insight that he, Trevor Lawrence, was generously sharing. Of course it was foolish to blame someone for the shape of his chin, yet it seemed to Dave an appropriate flaw for one who, despite his air of go-getting vigour, was in fact weak in character.

Lawrence droned on, full of contrived enthusiasm for business expansion. He extolled the opportunities offered by United Advertising's recently acquired Ministry of Defence contract, under which the agency would design an important recruitment campaign. Wonderful chance for spin-off business, both military and governmental, enthused Lawrence.

Yeah, thought Dave sarcastically, it would be great to make contacts with the armaments industry – maybe they'd get the Defence Export Services Organisation contract and help them streamline their roadshow for selling weapons to Third World countries. Still he mustn't be too bitchy, mustn't be too holier-than-thou. The MOD contract was significant, he just felt uneasy about a link to the world of militarism and its associations with arms dealing and clandestine operations. Noting a change in the cadence of the speech, Dave looked up and realised that the end was finally being reached. His relief was tempered by anxiety, for he feared that when the address was over Lawrence would approach him for a lift.

As the conference was being held in Carlisle, Dave

had been looking forward to the drive over the Pennines on the way home to Harrogate. In fact his love of the Yorkshire peaks had been an important factor in leaving London to accept his job as Creative Director with United Advertising's Leeds branch. His journey through the Dales today however would be an endurance test if Trevor Lawrence presented himself as a passenger. It was a habit of Lawrence's not to drive to conferences but instead to travel with senior staff and discuss company business. So far Dave had avoided this intrusion, but he feared that his turn might come today.

A sudden round of applause marked the end of the speech, and he clapped politely, then the staff were bade a safe journey home. Suddenly the room was full of movement, and people rose, eager to savour the hot May sunshine streaming through the hotel windows.

Dave got up quickly, slipped his papers into his briefcase and was making for the door when Lawrence intercepted him.

"David, my boy, what's the big hurry?"

"No big hurry, Trevor, just a long drive ahead."

"Yes, indeed. Wanted a word about that. No point in letting the old tempus fugit unproductively, is there?"

Dave felt his heart sink.

"Thought we might put our heads together on the way back."

"That might be dangerous if I'm driving, Trevor."

"Always a kidder, always a way with the words," said Lawrence, punching him playfully. "But seriously. No point wasting time looking at fields and hedges flying past. We could have a chat about this new ReadyBurger account . . ."

Dave looked down at the smaller man's upthrust face. He realised that it had probably never occurred to Lawrence that anyone might not wish his company – might actually enjoy driving alone through some of the finest scenery in England. Or if it had struck him it made no difference; he was the boss and what he wanted was what mattered. And suddenly Dave knew that he wouldn't take him along. Two hours cooped up with Lawrence and his foul-smelling cigars, overpowering aftershave and inane conversation was too much.

"I'm afraid we'll have to leave our chat till tomorrow, Trevor," he said, keeping his tone light.

"Why?"

"I'm visiting my aunt on the way home . . ."

Lawrence looked searchingly at him, and Dave felt that perhaps the improvisation was not sufficiently convincing.

"I promised her I'd visit," he added. "She'd be very disappointed if I didn't . . ."

"*I'm* disappointed now. I wanted to discuss the ReadyBurger campaign."

"We can discuss it in the office tomorrow."

"Not for two hours without interruption, we can't . . . and we need to talk about the MOD account."

Dave shrugged. "Sorry, Trevor. Duty calls. Family ties and all that . . ."

Lawrence looked him coldly in the eye. "I never knew you'd an aunt up here."

"Well, I suppose it didn't feature on my CV," said Dave with a smile.

"Where does she live?" Lawrence asked, his tone cold.

"In the Pennines."

"Whereabouts?"

"Hawkley."

"Hawkley?"

"Yes."

"Where's that?"

"Near Browsbrook."

"Where exactly is Browsbrook?"

"What's this, Twenty Questions?" said Dave lightly.

There was a pause, then Lawrence answered with an edge to his voice. "No, just interested in your aunt. Seeing as she's so important to you."

"Well, now you know . . ."

"Yes", said Lawrence meaningfully, "now I know. We'll talk tomorrow."

"Fine. See you then."

Lawrence nodded coolly, then Dave walked out to the lobby and collected his suitcase. He made for the car park; the hotel garden was a mass of bright green foliage bathed in sunshine, but the warmth of the afternoon had been clouded for Dave by the exchange with Trevor Lawrence. The General Manager was not a person to overlook a slight easily, and Dave knew there would be a reckoning for this afternoon.

To hell with that he thought as he put his luggage in the car boot and slammed the door. He was a damn good copywriter – head of the creative team at only thirty-five years of age; if the worst came to the worst he could always get another job. So let Trevor Lawrence be offended if he chose to be. Besides, confronting Lawrence was for tomorrow, and today he had his trip across the Dales to look forward to. It was a glorious drive and he would stop at one of the peaks and ring Mary.

At the thought of his wife his mood lightened further, and starting the car, he put United Advertising from his mind and headed south into the heat of the summer afternoon.

Gatenby drove carefully down the valley from the research centre. Reaching a fork, he ignored the right-hand turn for the main road that would have taken him towards his house outside Darlington and instead turned left.

He travelled along a narrow road, the Yorkshire countryside in blossom all around. He kept the air-conditioning on full blast against the heatwave that had bathed the Dales in uncharacteristic, sweltering heat and also against the sweat induced by the tension he had felt since taking the microfilm thirty minutes previously.

To his relief he encountered nobody on the roadway, the only creatures visible being the sheep that stood huddled in groups as they sought shade beneath trees and hedgerows.

A couple of miles further on he turned off the road onto a winding lane that led to a large wooden barn. He got out of the car and crossed to the double doors of the barn. After the air-conditioning of the BMW the hot still air felt like a furnace, and he quickly withdrew the key to the padlock and unlocked the barn doors. The sweat trickled down his back, and he was struck by how uncomfortable strong heat was in a British environment – as opposed to the attraction of year-round sunshine in the new life he had planned for himself.

He pulled aside the doors and stepped into the cooler interior of the barn. Parked there was a cream van. He drove it out, and left the engine running while he concealed his own car in the barn. He took the briefcase and a small holdall from the boot of the BMW, locked the double doors, entered the van and drove back down the winding lane.

The van's interior felt unpleasantly warm by comparison to the air-conditioned BMW and Gatenby opened the window, allowing in a stream of air. The cooling torrent of air dried the sweat on his face, and as he drove his spirits rose. Even if the worst came to the worst the authorities would be looking for a man in a silver BMW – by which time he would have driven the cream van to Manchester airport and left the country on his false passport. It was going well, he felt. Despite the problem with the guard he was still on schedule. Feeling both excited and pleased with himself, he drove on carefully through the sunlit Yorkshire Dales.

Mary Adams walked angrily across the car park of the BBC Radio Centre in Leeds. The sun beat down from a clear blue sky but even the prospect of a settled spell of glorious weather wasn't enough to cheer her. She got into her car, slamming the door. Despite being parked in the shade the car's interior was hot, and Mary turned on the engine and put the fan on full. She knew the car would cool more quickly if she were driving, but first she needed to get her thoughts in order.

Playing an eighteen-year-old virgin while almost eight months pregnant and thirty-four years old would be impossible for most actors, yet Mary knew she had been convincing in her role back in the studio. It was one of the advantages of radio acting that the voice was all-important, and Mary still sounded youthful enough for roles such as her present part as Cecily in *The Importance Of Being Earnest*. Since emigrating to England in her late teens her mild Irish accent had been largely replaced with an English tone and with her flair for mimicry she could convincingly do most regional accents.

Now however her youthful-sounding voice had caused a problem. Arnold Beazley, another freelance actor, had been sniping at her all week. Beazley was a florid middle-aged man given to wearing cravats and adopting the world-weariness he thought appropriate to a sophisticate. Together with a habit of noisily sucking Turkish Delights through his decaying teeth it made him a tiresome colleague, yet she had tried to be pleasant to him.

In return he had patronised her, with frequent sardonic references to her being "heavy with child". Mary had been puzzled initially at his niggling during rehearsals until it had been suggested that Beazley was jealous at her being allowed to play a part younger than her years. He, by contrast, had been cast as the middle-aged Canon Chasuble when he had wanted to play the leading but youthful role of Jack.

Things had come to a head in a flaming row several minutes previously when Beazley had made one comment too many about Mary's pregnancy. Her patience had finally snapped and she had rounded on him, letting him know what she thought of his pretentious demeanour, his blackened molars and his Turkish Delights. The Producer had discreetly wound up rehearsals for the day and, thinking back to the reaction of the other actors, Mary consoled herself that she would have their support. The incident might actually have its benefits, she reflected. Perhaps now that she had marked his cards Beazley would leave her alone. On the other hand she might have made a lasting enemy. And somehow she sensed that that was more likely. Well, no point fretting further about it. In half an hour she would be relaxing at home in Harrogate, and tonight Dave would be back from his conference. Comforted by the thought of his return, she started the engine and drove out of the studio car park.

His imaginary aunt would be Aunt Gwen, Dave decided, as he drove through the mountains. The name had a certain ring to it. He could even picture her as a character in one of his ads. Aunt Gwen's . . . *Aunt Gwen's Home Preserve.* *"Aunt Gwen's – it's got to be good!"*

He smiled, aware of how ludicrous it was to be thinking in catch phrases as he drove through such magnificent scenery. Occupational hazard, he thought. One of the side effects of working at copywriting was a tendency towards flights of fancy, and summarising people and situations into catchy headlines. *"Trite Trevor – thinks he's clever!"* had been his diary entry on first meeting Trevor Lawrence. Taking in the majesty of the sunlit mountains now, however, he was glad he had fobbed Lawrence off today. There was a stillness in the air and the soaring peaks seemed to shimmer in the heat-haze.

He drove on, appreciative as ever of the constantly unfolding new vistas. Bathed in sunlight and with a backdrop of clear blue sky, the peaks looked inviting and benign.

Which was misleading, he knew. There was nothing benign about these mountains where four years previously he had been in danger of losing his life. He had gone hill-walking with Simon Kingsley, a colleague from United Advertising's London office, Mary being away for a few days shooting a TV commercial. It had been a crisp autumn day and the bright conditions that had lasted until mid-afternoon had suddenly turned to drizzle. With a swiftness that was alarming, low cloud and fog had enveloped them and the temperature had dropped. They had been on an exposed peak only a couple of miles from where Dave now drove in sunshine, and they had opted for an immediate descent, before darkness fell.

The visibility had worsened however and in their

haste to get down from the peak Simon had fallen badly and broken his ankle. Dave had realised instantly how serious their situation was. Simon was unable to put any weight on his foot and, with a long, steep descent to negotiate, Dave knew that carrying his colleague was out of the question. Yet all his instincts rebelled at the notion of abandoning his injured partner. Nevertheless he could see that Simon was in shock and he knew that decisive action was called for. He had got Simon to shelter in the lee of a stone wall and had made him drink some hot, sweet tea before giving him some of his own spare clothes to keep him warm. He had ensured that Simon had his torch and whistle, then he had set off at speed.

He had known it was a race against time if he was to get down from the mountain before darkness fell and he had descended the fog-enshrouded peaks at high speed, stumbling and slipping numerous times, but suffering no serious injury. Although it was nerve-wracking, part of him had found the situation exhilarating. There was something about pitting himself against the elements in a situation of real risk that excited an adrenaline-fuelled response that surprised him.

In the event, he had reached safety with nothing worse than scratches and bruises, and Simon had been airlifted in time to save him from the dangers of exposure.

Dave had found himself cast as a hero but at Mary's suggestion had played things down, refusing a considerable fee offered by a tabloid newspaper for his story. Mary had argued that the tabloid would

sensationalise everything about the incident and that
the intrusion into their private lives wouldn't be worth
the hassle and the loss of privacy. On reflection he had
agreed with her and said no to the newspaper. He
knew that he was sometimes too gung-ho in his
responses and Mary's sound advice was frequently the
ballast that counterbalanced his flights of fancy and
kept his feet on the ground.

He smiled now as he thought of how Mary would
react to his latest creation, Aunt Gwen. She'd get on
well with Auntie Gwen, he thought, especially as Aunt
Gwen had been created to outfox Trevor Lawrence,
whom Mary disliked.

He would ring her from the next lay-by, he decided,
then he drove on through the mountains, where once he
had gambled with his life and won.

Barbra Streisand played on the tape deck, filling the van
with music. Gatenby sang along tunefully, occasionally
even going into harmony as he drove along through the
Dales.

The song was *Guilty*, the title track on the album and
one of his favourite tunes. The irony of the title wasn't
lost on Gatenby but he felt no guilt over what he had
done. Quite the opposite. He had been daring enough
to act decisively to secure his future, something his
time-serving colleagues would have been too timid to
attempt.

For choice he wouldn't have killed the soldier who
had surprised him but he had had no choice. And, once

having decided that the man had to die, he had acted with a coolness and professionalism that still thrilled him almost an hour after the event.

There would, of course, be an enormous hue and cry, but he had worked out his moves in detail, and the financial rewards he would soon reap would make the risk worthwhile. Not for Gatenby a life of calculated moderation; he wouldn't be like his boring colleagues calculating their pensions and saving to supplement them from carefully husbanded nest eggs.

What had originally galvanised him into action had been his sister Penelope inheriting most of the family fortune on the death of their mother. It wasn't so much that he begrudged Penelope the money – she had after all nursed their mother through her final illness. But, damn it all, he couldn't live in the style he desired solely on his salary. He had been counting on a bigger share of the family estate.

In a Thatcherite Britain in which looking after number one had become quite acceptable, he had simply taken that philosophy to its ultimate conclusion. If no citizen was responsible for any other citizen, why should anyone be responsible for anything else either? And if military secrets had a market value why shouldn't he exploit his ability to capitalise on that?

It had taken a long time to set up the necessary contacts for the coup he had carried off today but it would all be worthwhile when his life was one of luxury and indolence. As it would be this time next week, when he would be in South America.

He thought about Penelope. She would hate the

scandal, he had no doubt, but he knew she wouldn't really miss him – any more that he would miss her. He wouldn't miss anyone. Not when he could afford excellent Latin company in his new home . . .

He was smiling at the thought, still gently tapping out the rhythm of *Guilty*, when the engine suddenly spluttered. He felt a stab of fear, then the engine caught again and continued to run. Gatenby started to breathe out in relief, when the engine misfired again. Gatenby revved the accelerator, but the engine spluttered for another second or two, then died. The van shuddered and Gatenby shifted the gearstick into neutral. He tried starting it as it coasted along but all he got was a coughing sound from the ignition. He could feel a tightness in his chest as all his former tension returned but he concentrated on the road and brought the van to a halt at the grass verge. He held his breath, then turned the key in the ignition. Again the engine coughed but failed to ignite. He tried several times more but the engine simply wouldn't start. Gatenby quickly got out of the van and opened the bonnet. He had little flair for things mechanical, but there was just a chance that it might be something simple like a loose spark plug or a broken fan belt.

A quick inspection, however, showed it was neither of these. On finding that the carburettor cap was firmly in place, Gatenby had exhausted his list of easy solutions. He tried starting the engine several times more but still it failed to ignite. He cursed the backstreet garage that he had paid to service the rented van, knowing even as he did that his anger was useless.

He got out of the van again, beads of perspiration forming on his forehead, but he fought back his panic and tried to think rationally. The dead soldier probably hadn't been found yet. But once he was found all hell would break loose. And there was no denying what would happen then. It wouldn't be long before they came looking for Nigel Gatenby . . .

2

Mary lay on the garden sofa, unable to relax despite her surroundings. The hot summer air carried the scent of roses and the only sound was the song of the birds, but the incident with Beazley and the sniping leading up to it still rankled. In fifteen years of acting Mary had encountered both generosity of spirit and a fair deal of pettiness and begrudgery but Beazley's goading had left her feeling untypically disgruntled.

She knew she was neither timid nor thin-skinned – she had emigrated while still in her teens and would never have been successful in a competitive, over-crowded profession without an inner toughness – yet somehow Beazley had gotten to her. Perhaps it was because it related to her unborn child, she thought, a subject on which she knew she was vulnerable. Three years after her marriage she had decided with Dave to have a child, but their delight on her becoming pregnant had turned to heartbreak when she had suffered a miscarriage.

The pregnancy had been a troubled one, and she had been told that the miscarriage was nature's way of responding to a problem, but she had been devastated by the loss. They had just settled in Harrogate at the time and to try to channel her anger and sorrow she had thrown herself into re-establishing her career.

Although she had always been slightly plump, she knew she was attractive, with thick blonde hair, light blue eyes and a face that was pretty and friendly. Her looks enabled her to play glamorous roles, and with her natural ability and her flair for accents it meant that she was soon getting work with the local Harrogate Theatre and the West Yorkshire Playhouse. She had also gained a toehold freelancing with the BBC in Leeds.

Now, a year and a half later, she was almost eight months pregnant with a perfectly healthy baby. She also had a husband she loved, a fine house with a beautiful garden and a workshop where she could relax doing her stained glass – so why let Arnold Beazley make her unhappy? She would just have to snap out of it, she decided; he wasn't worth fretting about.

As she made her resolution the mobile phone on the garden table rang, and she reached out and took it without rising. "Hello?"

"Is that the lovely Mary Adams?"

"Yes," she answered with mock coyness, "this is she."

"Hello, Ms Adams. David Walker calling"

"David Walker? The name is familiar . . ."

"A handsome devil, five feet eleven, brown hair, slim build, last seen wearing a blue suit, married to the world- famous actress Mary Adams."

"Oh, that David Walker. How are you?"

"OK. More to the point – how are you?

"I'm fine."

"And the heir to the Walker fortune?"

"Fine too, kicking his mother at regular intervals."

"That's my boy – or girl, as the case may be."

"How was the last day of the conference?"

Dave groaned. "Same as the first day. Boring, costly and a waste of time."

"I missed you," said Mary.

"I missed you too. Although I did have an exciting offer."

"Oh yes?"

"Propositioned by Trevor Lawrence."

"Pardon me while I'm ill."

Dave laughed. "He wanted a lift home. Very put out when I couldn't take him because of Auntie Gwen."

"Who?"

"I've been an orphan too long, so I acquired Aunt Gwen."

"Dave!"

"Had to visit her in the Dales. Mind you, I don't think Lawrence really bought it . . .

"I'm not surprised!"

"So there'll be trouble at mill, as they say."

"Talking of which . . ."

"What?"

"I'd a spot of drama myself."

"Oh?"

"With Arnold Beazley. I told you he'd been needling me – today I really let him have it."

"Good for you! Blackened teeth all over the floor?"

"Not quite."

"Hung by his own cravat? Poisoned Turkish Delights?"

Mary laughed. "You are an idiot, Dave. I'll tell you the details later. What time will you be home?"

"Eh . . . ten past four now . . . should be back in about an hour and a half."

"Where are you anyway?"

"On a little mountain road beneath Langstrathdale."

"I know you and those mountains; you'll be gazing for ages. Don't dally too long. I've missed you."

"Me too. I'll get going. See you about half five."

"OK."

"And Mary?"

"Yes?"

"I love you."

"I love you too. Bye."

"Bye."

She lowered the phone and lay back on the sofa. The sun shone on her face, the birds sang in the trees and just at that moment all seemed well with the world.

Dave switched off his car phone, looked about, and wondered what he was doing working in advertising. The bright greens of the mountainsides seemed to glow in the heat of the afternoon and he savoured the splendour of the hills and the wonderful sense of isolation.

Much as he enjoyed the creative aspects of his work,

he wished at times that he were employed in the type of environment spread before him. Up here things took on a different perspective and the daily politics of office life seemed foolish and petty. How wonderful it would be to farm or do forestry work in such a spectacular setting, he thought, then he chided himself wryly for dreaming. There was no point in kidding himself. He had a highly paid job and a very comfortable lifestyle, and soon he would have the responsibility of being a father. That was reality; rural bliss was just a fantasy. He would simply have to enjoy the Dales at weekends and get on with his career.

He started the engine and pulled out onto the narrow road, but he couldn't quite shake off his sense of dissatisfaction. The incident with Trevor Lawrence had rankled and he suspected that Lawrence would now press even harder – notwithstanding the lucrative MOD account – to introduce short-term contracts for the staff in his department. It was something Dave had opposed, arguing that his staff deserved some security of tenure, and he hoped now that he hadn't put anyone at risk by his action in spurning Lawrence's company. He thought about it as he drove, recognising that fighting his corner tooth and nail mightn't be enough – he would need a well-thought-out strategy as well.

He had been driving for some time, his mind on the internal politics of United Advertising, when rounding a bend he saw the man up ahead.

He was the only walker Dave had seen in this isolated area and at first glance something seemed wrong. As he drew nearer he realised it was the man's attire. He wasn't wearing hiking gear, but a business suit, and he carried a briefcase and holdall rather than a rucksack.

A breakdown seemed the likely answer, yet Dave hadn't passed any parked cars for miles, the only vehicle being a cream van, and the figure ahead didn't look like a van driver.

The man had turned on hearing the car approach, and now he flagged Dave to a halt. He looked to be about forty, wore dark glasses and was expensively dressed, but the sheen of sweat on his brow and his overweight appearance suggested that he was not a walker by choice.

"Good afternoon," he said, as Dave stopped and rolled down the window.

"Good afternoon. You're a little off the beaten track . . ."

"My car broke down. I started to walk when I couldn't get it going again."

"Afraid I can't help you there; engines aren't my strong point. Where did it happen?"

"About a mile or so back."

"I didn't see a car . . ."

"Eh, no, I pushed it into a field – didn't want to block a mountain road. I wonder if I might ask you for a lift?"

Dave's instinct was to say "of course", yet as he looked at the man he felt an unease. There seemed something familiar about him, something he couldn't quite place. He also sensed a tension beneath the man's apparently innocent answers. And would someone whose car had broken down really push it into a field?

"I'd be most awfully grateful to you, I have a rather urgent business appointment."

The atmosphere was somehow wrong, yet Dave felt he couldn't leave the man stranded. "I'm going to Harrogate," he replied, "but I can drop you in Grassington. You'll be able to arrange transport or a mechanic there." He opened the passenger door.

"Thank you so much," answered the man, then he entered the car.

A smile played about Mary's lips as she stretched out comfortably on the garden sofa. Aunt Gwen indeed! Where did Dave get these characters? She knew her husband would create a whole world around this Aunt Gwen and she couldn't help but be amused by his zany enthusiasm. But then humour had been one of the attractions from the first time she had met him, when his quirky humour had reminded her of her brother Tom.

Although Tom was five years older than Mary they had always been close, partly because, like Dave, Tom could always make her laugh, and also because they had been the only two children in the family at a time when families of five and six children were the norm in Mayo.

That all seemed so long ago now and she could smile indulgently looking back, but in reality her teens had been characterised by a series of rows with her arch-conservative father. The clashes had been frequent and sometimes bitter, and despite the affection she had felt for Tom and her mother, she had left home soon after she turned eighteen.

Ever after Mary had always been amused when she heard the theory that women married men like their fathers. Part of the reason she had fallen in love with Dave was because he was funny, and liberal, and generous – the opposite of her father in many respects.

So let Dave indulge his daft Aunt Gwen fantasies, she thought; she would never lose sight of how good it was to have a lively, warm-hearted partner. Soon they would be together again and she would tell him the details of her clash with Beazley, he would tell her of his clash with Lawrence, and Aunt Gwen would, no doubt, be launched on an unsuspecting world. She smiled again at the notion, then closed her eyes and lay back contentedly on the garden sofa.

Driving in silence, Dave tried to pinpoint what it was about the passenger that caused his unease. There was still a nagging hint of familiarity about his appearance but Dave simply couldn't place it. There was also an underlying but discernible tension about the man.

"Wonderful scenery," the passenger ventured after a while.

"Yes, breathtaking." Why wasn't he talking about his car, Dave wondered. Surely most people would after a breakdown.

He decided to probe a little. "Where is your appointment?"

"Eh . . . Leeds. The Queen's Hotel at six."

"If you like I can take you to Harrogate Station. You could probably still make Leeds for six – the Queen's is

31

right beside the station." Glancing across at the man, Dave noticed the tiny beads of sweat that had re-formed despite the passenger having mopped his brow.

"Eh, no . . . no, thank you," the man answered. "Grassington will be fine. I want to arrange a mechanic, then I can get a taxi."

"If you're sure . . ."

"Yes, indubitably . . ."

Indubitably . . . indubitably . . . the word echoed through Dave's head. *Indubitably . . .* he hadn't heard it said in that tone for so long. Not since schooldays in St George's College. He had been fourteen, and his parents and sister had been killed in a car crash. His aunt, with whom it had been decided he would live, had agreed to keep him in the same school but as a boarder now, the distance from her home in Chichester being too far for commuting as a day pupil.

There had been a tradition of new boarders being subjected to initiation rites by the older boys and Dave had overheard a group of them discussing him. It had been suggested that in the circumstances he should be excused. Opinion had been divided, and Nigel Gatenby, the cruellest and most vindictive of the prefects, had been asked if he thought the initiation should go ahead. "Indubitably," he had replied, using one of his favourite words, "indubitably . . ."

It seemed like a lifetime ago, yet when Dave glanced over at him now he knew – despite the dark glasses and the fleshier face – this was the same man.

"Tell me this," said Dave, keeping his tone casual, "have you bullied anyone lately?"

"Sorry?"

"Have you picked on someone? Abused somebody weaker?"

"I don't know what you're talking about."

"You're Nigel Gatenby, aren't you?"

The man started, his face a mixture of surprise and confusion.

"Yes, I thought so," continued Dave.

"There must be some . . ."

"There's no mistake. David Walker ring a bell? St George's College?"

"I . . . I can't remember you . . ."

"No? Well, perhaps not. You probably bullied so many of the younger boys it's a blur."

"Look here . . . I . . . it was schooldays. Ages ago. We were probably all beasts."

"Some more than others."

"I'm sorry if there was . . . unpleasantness . . ."

"Oh, I wasn't your worst victim. Not by any means. After I shot up in height you never bothered *me* again . . ." Realising his passenger's uneasiness, Dave let an uncomfortable silence lie between them as he drove. Once more he was surprised at the depth of his own feelings, but he decided to let the other man sweat a bit.

He wondered if Gatenby had recognised him when he had stopped the car. It would explain the air of tension he had sensed about the man, yet Gatenby's claim not to remember Dave had seemed genuine. So why had the atmosphere felt strained? Before he could figure it out, Gatenby broke the silence.

"Pull over up ahead," he said.

"I don't take orders any more – you're not a prefect these days."

"Just stop the car."

"Trip down Memory Lane upset you?" Dave replied, then he slowed the car to a halt. "Well, parting is such sweet sorrow, Nigel, but the walk to Grassington will do you good. You're looking a bit too well-fed."

"I'm not walking anywhere," said Gatenby, unlocking his briefcase. "You're going to drive carefully till we see a track into the forest, then you turn off."

"Into the woods? I'm not that kind of guy, Nigel – you should remember that."

Gatenby pulled a gun from the briefcase and pointed it at Dave. "Listen, you stupid prick, and listen well. I've no time for your silly games and I won't have the slightest hesitation using this if you give me trouble. Now move!"

Dave stared at him dumbfounded. He could hardly believe that Gatenby had actually pulled a gun on him, yet there was no doubting the other man's conviction when he had spoken of using it. Looking at Gatenby's face, he felt a stab of fear.

"I said *move!*"

Dave put the car into gear, his hand trembling as he did so. He pulled away and drove automatically along the winding road, his mind reeling. This was beyond belief, like something from a nightmare.

"Slow down!" said Gatenby. "Up ahead, on the right, pull in there."

Dave slowed the car, then turned off the road onto a

forestry track. The track bordered a reed-fringed tarn, its waters sparkling in the sunlight, and after bumping along for about seventy yards, Dave slowed down as the track broadened into a clearing.

"Pull in over on the right," barked Gatenby.

"Look, this is ridiculous . . ." started Dave.

"Shut up!"

Dave stopped the car and turned in his seat. "What the hell is this? What do you want from me?"

"You wanted to relive old times, Walker – that's what we're going to do. You'll do as I decide, just like old times."

There was an unnerving, manic quality in Gatenby's voice but Dave sensed that he ought to stand his ground somewhat. He looked Gatenby in the eye and spoke softly. "Is that so?"

"Yes, it is so. Nice car you've got, Walker – I think I'll just take it."

"Look, this whole thing is really . . ."

"Shut it! Shut your mouth!" cried Gatenby. "One more word – one more *word* – and I'll blow your brains out. Now slowly, very slowly, open the door and step out of the car."

Dave gingerly undid his seat belt, opened the door and got out.

"Turn around," said Gatenby, and Dave obeyed. "Now, legs apart and hands on your head. Do it!"

Dave followed the instructions, his mouth dry with fear. He could hear the briefcase being closed, then there was a squeaking metallic noise. He risked a glance around and saw Gatenby screwing a silencer onto the gun. Dave's blood ran cold. If Gatenby only wanted to steal the car he didn't need a silencer.

He felt a cold sweat break out on his forehead but tried not to panic. Supposing he made a run for the trees? The sweet-smelling pines were closely packed; if he made it to them perhaps he could lose Gatenby in their midst. *If he made it to the trees.* He tried to gauge his chances but as he did so the passenger door slammed and he heard Gatenby walk round behind him.

"Keep your hands on your head and walk slowly towards the trees."

Dave turned gradually, so as not to panic his captor, then faced him directly. "Look, just take the car. Park it – park it in Leeds or wherever. Just leave me here . . ."

"I intend to. Now move . . ."

"Look, there's no need . . ."

"Move to the bloody trees, Walker!"

"No."

"You can either walk to them, or I can blow off your kneecaps and you can crawl to them."

Dave looked into his eyes. He had the look of a man capable of anything.

"Turn around and walk," shouted Gatenby, pushing him forward.

Dave started to walk, hesitantly, his stomach growing sickeningly tight. He tried to fight down the terror, yet he knew his life could end right here. In seconds he could be dead. He would never see his unborn child, never see Mary again. All his plans, all his dreams would end here. The feeling of loss was terrifying, yet the most awful part was the sheer pointlessness of being shot to death in a remote forest, for no apparent reason. He stopped, his back still turned to Gatenby, and spoke. "I have to know why."

"I told you to keep moving."

"I know you're planning to – to kill me," he said, his voice shaky. "It makes no sense. Please, just leave me and take the car. Please – "

"Get moving."

"There's no need for this – "

"There is. Start walking."

"Please. Tell me why – just tell me why!"

There was a pause, then Gatenby spoke. "I need transport urgently, I don't want to leave a trail and frankly, I don't like your manner."

Dave felt a sudden rush of anger. This bastard, this overgrown bully felt entitled to kill him because he didn't like his manner! He felt a push in the back as Gatenby propelled him towards the trees.

"Now get moving."

Dave walked slowly, his mind racing. Whatever happened, he wasn't going to accept meekly a bullet in the head. Gatenby was several feet behind – too far to try anything – but as Dave approached the trees an idea formed in his mind. "Where to?" he asked in a voice made deliberately shaky to keep Gatenby assured of his shocked acceptance.

"Keep going. I'll tell you when to stop."

Dave moved on, hands still on his head, pushing the branches aside with his elbows, then he heard Gatenby following him. Thank God for that, he thought. He moved forward, forcing back a large cone-laden branch, then he suddenly dropped his elbows and the branch swung back forcefully, catching Gatenby.

Dave immediately lunged backwards, slamming into the other man while he was off balance. The impetus of Dave's dive knocked Gatenby off his feet and both of them fell to the forest floor.

Despite being taken off guard, Gatenby hadn't dropped the gun. He swung it now towards Dave, who immediately slammed his opponent's hand onto the ground. Gatenby cried out in pain but still held onto the gun as they wrestled.

Dave held the gun-hand in his grip, and as they rolled towards the stumps of recently-felled trees he brought the hand down hard onto a sharpened stump. Gatenby screamed and dropped the gun into the undergrowth. Although several stones lighter than his opponent, years of hill-walking had made Dave fit and muscular, and he began to pin Gatenby down. Suddenly he felt a searing pain in his ribs as Gatenby managed to strike him with a piece of deadwood. Punching blindly, he landed a blow to Gatenby's stomach. Gatenby swung violently away, one hand grabbing Dave's lapel and pulling him down an incline in the forest floor.

Locked together, they tumbled over each other, and Dave felt the other man's fingers close around his throat. He pushed with all his strength and swung Gatenby backwards just as they reached the bottom of the incline. There was a resounding thud, then Dave felt the other man's body go limp. Crawling off him, he saw that Gatenby's head had smashed into another pointed tree-stump.

Blood was already staining the stump and Dave watched, horrified, as a small trickle dribbled from Gatenby's mouth. He shook him but there was no response. He looked at the closed eyes, then felt for a heartbeat, but there was none. Weak with shock, he leaned against a tree. He wished it were all a bad dream but he knew it was not. He had killed a man. He had been fighting for his life, he knew, but looking at the body he still felt sickened. Yet what else could he have done? He had had no choice; the police would surely understand that.

He stared at the body for a long moment, then, moving shakily, he headed back towards the clearing. He would call 999 on the car phone, the police would know how to handle everything.

He thought about Gatenby as he reached the car and got into the driver's seat. What on earth had got into the man? It could hardly have been simply a response to being goaded over bullying. He had also wanted the car. And then there was the gun. Why had he got a weapon? It was illegal to carry a gun . . . unless one had a permit – or was a police officer.

Dave felt a sudden chill. Could Gatenby conceivably have been a policeman, albeit a psychopathic one? Surely not. Yet if he had been, would Dave be believed when he said Gatenby had threatened his life? His eyes rested on the briefcase, and thinking to discover more about his victim, he reached over and opened it.

There was a large folder inside marked TOP SECRET in red. Puzzled, Dave took it out and opened it. SMORTAR MARK ONE it read. Inside was row after row of microfiche film. What the hell was Gatenby doing with this? Could he have been some kind of Intelligence officer? That would explain the gun, but what would an Intelligence Officer be doing with top secret documents on a mountain road? And why would he steal a car and kill a civilian? Perhaps to ensure no witnesses if he were going to show the documents to someone else – or steal them himself?

It was a possibility and it did seem to fit the facts. Dave put the folder back into the briefcase. Whatever the explanation, he knew he had stumbled onto something important. He was out of his league here and it scared him badly. Supposing the police thought *he* was somehow involved? The notion made his blood run cold and he sat unmovingly, his heart pounding and his mouth dry, and wishing fervently that he had never laid eyes on Nigel Gatenby.

3

Detective Constable Penny Hart looked apprehensively again at her new boss. Tackling him was not going to be easy. Part of the problem was that in many ways she liked what she saw. In speech, manner and even appearance, Detective Chief Inspector Jack Thompson reminded her of her father. They were both well-built men in their early fifties, both had unmistakable Yorkshire accents, and although it was too soon to be sure, Penny suspected that Thompson might well share her father's vigorous approach to life – an approach lightened by a droll sense of humour.

She knew too that she was lucky to be seconded to work with Thompson, who was regarded as one of the best detectives in the region. Office gossip had it that he could be a Chief Superintendent by now – even a Deputy Commissioner – were it not for his manner, which was deemed to be not suitably deferential to superiors, nor politically sensitive enough for really high rank. No one disputed his effectiveness however, and the word was that both Thompson and his superiors were happy to have him operate as a detective in the field, where he was at his most productive.

Penny had been delighted when her request for CID training had been approved, particularly when she realised that without leaving her native city of Leeds she could work with a man of Thompson's reputation.

At twenty-three her ambition was unlimited and she knew that her secondment to study Criminal Procedure was an opportunity to be grasped. All of which made her present position rather difficult. She hated the idea of having to rock the boat, yet she had always felt it was important to start as you intended to continue.

Glancing up from her notes, she looked across the office to where Thompson sat going through some charts. He had been welcoming and friendly to her, yet all of that could quickly change if she confronted him now. But now was the moment, she knew, when the room was untypically quiet.

She fiddled with her pen, trying hard to get her nerve up, then suddenly she put the biro down, rose from her chair, and crossed to Thompson's desk.

"I . . . I'm sorry to disturb you, sir . . ."

"That's all right . . ." Thompson laid the charts aside and looked at her quizzically. "What's bothering you?"

"Is it that obvious?"

"I am a detective, you know. Very important, reading a face . . ."

"I hate to – to cause problems. I'm really pleased to be here at all, but . . ."

"Come on then. Best have it out . . ."

"Well, we're going to be working together, and I want us to get off on the right foot, so . . ."

Thompson nodded encouragingly. "So?"

"So I'd really appreciate it if – if you wouldn't call me 'love'. Or 'lass' or 'dear' . . ." She looked at Thompson, unsure from his face whether or not he was taking offence.

"Which, presumably, I've done?"

"Yes, sir."

"I see," said Thompson.

"You wouldn't say it to a male officer, sir . . ."

"I should bloody well hope not!"

"Then I'd just like to be treated like my male colleagues. I'm sure no offence was meant but I don't think I'll be taken as seriously if people here call me 'love'."

Thompson looked her directly in the eye. "So you wanted to put me straight from day one, is that it?"

"Well . . . it's just something I feel strongly about, sir, and I thought I should . . . apprise you." She held her breath as she awaited Thompson's reply.

Suddenly he laughed. "By gum, it's not every day a chief inspector's ticked off by a constable! But you're right to do it. Mind you, you were right also about no offence being meant."

Thompson indicated for her to sit, and she felt a flood of relief.

"You see, I've got two daughters at home," he continued, "about your age, and I call them 'lass' or 'love'. Being a young woman I thought of you as being similar to them – but I shouldn't have. When you're on duty you're a constable. You're quite right there."

"I'm not out to be a fly in the ointment, sir. But . . . well, sometimes it's a struggle to be treated as an equal. You have to stand up for yourself."

"Aye, I daresay. Well you're not lacking in gumption, I'll give you that."

"Thank you, sir."

"While we're getting our lines clear, I'm not a great one for standing on ceremony – so you can ease off on the 'sirs'."

"Fair enough," said Penny.

"I'll call you DC Hart in front of outsiders, of course, but I usually call my detectives by their first names." He looked at her mischievously. "You won't feel obliged to tick me off for that, I hope?"

She smiled. "No, Penny's fine. What should I call you?"

"You don't call me Jack, if that's what you're thinking! I don't hold with formality but I'll not be cheeked either!"

There was just a hint of self-mockery in the man's tone, and recognising it, Penny sensed that he was a person she could grow to like a lot. "How shall I address you, then?"

"'Chief' is what most of them call me – to my face anyhow."

"'Chief' it'll be then."

The phone on his desk rang, and the inspector picked it up immediately. "Thompson . . ."

Penny saw his mood change as he listened.

"I see," he said. "Whereabouts?" He gave a low whistle. "Who discovered it . . . ? Right, tell them to touch nothing. We're on our way." Thompson pressed the receiver down but retained the phone in his hand as he turned to Penny. "Your timing is good," he said.

"How's that?"

"You wanted to study criminal investigation – how does a murder on your first day sound?"

Penny was about to say "wonderful", but it struck her as an inappropriate word. "I'm sure it will be instructive, Chief," she responded.

But Thompson had already dialled an internal number. "Frank? Jack here. We've got a murder up in Browsdale Research Centre. Organise a squad to get up there fast. No, I'm leaving now. I want Forensic there as quickly as possible, everyone you've got. What? I don't care what the bloody memo said about overtime – I want forensic evidence before they start playing silly buggers! Right, see you up there."

He quickly swung round in the chair. "And what are you smiling at then?"

"I'm sorry, Chief. It's just when you said about playing 'silly buggers'. My Dad's a football fanatic – if a Leeds defender tries something stylish he'll shout 'Don't play silly buggers, lad. Kick it away!'"

"Quite right too," said Thompson rising with a wry smile and quickly donning his jacket. "Well, if you're finished ticking me off and comparing me to your father, we've a murder to investigate."

"I'm ready."

"Then let's get up the Dales," he said, making for the door.

"You won't find what I'm going to tell you in any textbook – but it's good advice nonetheless," said Thompson.

Penny listened attentively as he drove speedily along the sunlit country roads leading to the research centre.

"In a case like this it's important to get to the scene quickly – first if possible – and establish it's a police matter. Mark my words, before you can say Jack Robinson, you'll have M15, Special Branch and the bloody Army all wanting to put in their tuppence worth. Probably would have tried to keep us out altogether if the chap who discovered the body hadn't dialled 999."

Thompson slowed down as they approached the entrance to the research centre and Penny could sense him moving into investigative mode. They were obviously expected at the entrance barrier, which was quickly raised when he flashed his ID. A second car carrying Detective Sergeants Annesley and Bryant, and Constables Wallace and Goodge followed and parked alongside them near the entrance to the Administration block.

Without waiting for his team, Thompson immediately made for the entrance door, with Penny right behind him.

An army officer in his early thirties approached. "Chief Inspector Thompson?"

"Yes. "

"I'm Captain Sainsbury." They shook hands and the man looked at Penny.

"This is Detective Constable Hart," said Thompson.

"How do you do," said Penny, shaking hands with the officer who held her gaze just a fraction too long. With her shiny black hair, olive skin and large hazel eyes she knew that men found her attractive, but she hoped the soldier wouldn't flirt with her, particularly in front of her new boss.

"If you could bring us through," said Thompson, with an edge to his voice. "This is the rest of my team," he added, indicating the approaching detectives.

"Follow me, please," said Sainsbury, leading them past reception and along a corridor between offices. At the end of the corridor they reached a reinforced metal door marked NO ADMITTANCE, underneath which it said ABSOLUTELY NO SMOKING. The door was guarded by two soldiers who stood aside at a nod from Sainsbury.

The group passed through and into a huge dimly-lit warehouse containing row after row of wooden boxes. They followed the officer until they came to a section that was cordoned off and guarded by three troopers.

"This is it, I'm afraid," said Sainsbury. He indicated the body, covered by a heavy blanket.

"Has anyone moved the body or anything around it?" asked Thompson.

"Just the packing cases that hid it."

"Not the body itself?"

"No, not when we realised the corporal . . . was dead."

47

"I know it must be upsetting, losing one of your men," said Thompson, "but this must come off." He crouched down and removed the blanket.

Penny balked on seeing the pool of blood and the shattered skull, but Thompson regarded the body closely, then nodded. He looked at the ground all around, stopping as something caught his eye. Taking from his pocket a pair of white cotton gloves, he donned them and reached under a wooden pallet. He carefully withdrew a steel bar and showed it to Sainsbury. "Any idea what this is?"

"Yes, actually – it's one of the inside locking bars of the fire-escape door."

"Are the others missing too?"

Sainsbury paused briefly. "I'll have that checked." He turned to one of the on-looking soldiers. "Dobbs, see if the other bars are off the fire door."

"Yes, sir."

"Just a second," said Thompson. "If you don't mind, Captain, I'll have one of my own men check it."

The officer raised an eyebrow.

"It's a police matter now. I don't want anyone – anyone at all – touching potential evidence." Thompson turned to the waiting Dobbs. "If you'd be kind enough to show Detective Sergeant Annesley to the fire door."

The soldier looked at his officer and Sainsbury nodded.

Penny smiled to herself, aware of what Thompson was doing.

Thompson turned to the other detectives. "Right, lads, rope it off. No one in or out till Forensics get here." He turned back to Sainsbury. "You've kept the chap who was loading for questioning, I presume?"

"Of course."

"I'll need an office, if you'd be so kind."

"An office?"

"In which to question him and run the investigation."

There was a slight pause. "Right," said Sainsbury.

"May I ask what steps you've taken already, Captain?"

"I've sealed off the Centre, doubled the perimeter guard, instructed all staff to remain here and notified the relevant people."

"Right. And who has overall responsibility for security?"

"The personnel are Army, commanded by myself – the Director of Security and his assistant are civilian. Mr Mathieson and Mr Gatenby."

"Where are they?"

"Mr Mathieson has been paged at home. We're expecting him any moment . . ."

"And Mr Gatenby?"

"Can't be found, so far."

"Hasn't he been paged?"

"Yes, but there's no answer."

It was Thompson's turn to raise an eyebrow. "That's rather odd, surely?"

"Yes, it is, rather."

"Has he left the premises?

"Yes, he was logged at the exit gate at three thirty and his office was locked, which suggests that he doesn't plan to return today."

Thompson thought a moment. "Anyone else leave here this afternoon?"

"An oil delivery truck – left at two minutes past four."

"No one else?"

"No."

"Let's see inside Gatenby's office then."

"I'm afraid it's still locked."

"Surely you've a master-key?"

"Not for the Security Personnel office. Only Mr Mathieson has that."

"Right, we'll break it down. I'm not hanging about waiting for Mr Mathieson. Can you organise a sledgehammer straight away?"

Sainsbury looked uneasy. "Actually, I'd rather not. In retrospect it might be seen as . . . exceeding authority – especially with Mr Mathieson due any moment."

"I'm investigating a murder, Captain. That gives me the authority. If you're worried about covering your back, I'll take full responsibility."

The officer was about to protest but Thompson spoke forcefully. "Let's get it open, shall we?"

Sainsbury paused briefly, weighing up his options, then he shrugged. "As you wish . . ." He turned to one of the waiting soldiers. "Fetch a sledgehammer from the tool cupboard and bring it to Mr Gatenby's office."

"Yes, sir."

"If you'd care to follow me," said Sainsbury.

Penny sensed a degree of tetchiness as the officer strode ahead. "I think his nose is out of joint," she said softly, as they followed him back through the warehouse.

"Pity about him," answered Thompson. "Afraid to do anything that's not in the book. Typical army . . ." he swallowed a word, not completing the sentence.

"Bullshit?" suggested Penny.

Thompson looked at her. "Well, yes, if you want to put it crudely."

"I thought you did."

"What?"

"I thought you wanted to put it crudely but were sparing me. It's OK – I won't be offended if you say bullshit."

"Cheeky young bugger, aren't you?" he said wryly.

"I've heard it said, Chief."

He smiled briefly, then glanced at her appraisingly. "What do you think happened here?"

"Well, Gatenby sounds suspicious but of course it could have been done by one of the staff still here."

"Why no word from Gatenby then?"

"Faulty bleeper, fallen asleep at home, heart attack even?"

Thompson nodded approvingly. "You're right to keep an open mind."

"This office here," said Sainsbury, as they passed from the warehouse into the corridor.

The soldier who had been dispatched for the sledgehammer approached carrying it, and after trying the handle of the wooden door Thompson indicated the lock. "Right, let's have it down."

Sainsbury nodded to the soldier who swung the sledgehammer enthusiastically. On the second blow the door burst inwards, and Penny, Thompson and Sainsbury entered the room. The office was unexceptional but for two of the filing cabinets being at a somewhat odd angle to the wall. Penny squeezed in behind one, then saw the open brickwork.

"Chief! In here!"

The two men looked at the hole in the wall. "My God, Gatenby had his own access," said Sainsbury with obvious shock.

"So it seems," said Thompson.

Just then a tall lean man in his late forties stepped through the shattered door. "Captain Sainsbury? What's going on?" he asked in an upper-class drawl.

The officer turned around, slightly flustered. "We . . . we had to break in . . ."

"I authorised it," interjected Thompson. "I'm heading the murder investigation. Detective Chief Inspector Thompson . . ."

"I'm Mathieson, Director of Security."

"Let me show you something," said Thompson, leading him to the filing cabinets and indicating the hole. "Unauthorised access for Gatenby to a restricted area, a murder in that area and Gatenby incommunicado." Mathieson was still staring at the hole as Thompson turned towards the door. "If we move quickly we might still nab him."

"Where are you going?" asked Mathieson.

"To the car radio. Roadblocks and a general alert might catch him."

"Just a second, Inspector. I'm not sure if police action is quite the thing here."

"Meaning what?"

"There's obviously been an intelligence breakdown – might be something we should handle ourselves."

"There's been a murder here, Mr Mathieson. I'm quite happy to liaise and keep you briefed, but it is a police investigation."

Mathieson looked at him, weighing up the detective. "The work done here is very sensitive, very sensitive indeed. I need to check what may have been taken, but we can't have it on the evening news."

"I take your point, Mr Mathieson, but we're losing time. While you check on what may have been taken, I'll put out an alert; Captain Sainsbury can describe Gatenby for me. We needn't name the centre here, and there's no need to go public yet on the killing, but I want a bulletin out straight away to head off this man."

Mathieson thought a moment. "He's a trained intelligence officer, presumably armed. I'd strongly suggest no heroics."

"Right, I'll make that clear. We'll speak again when you've checked what's missing. Now let's get to the radio. You can describe him as we go, Captain."

"Five foot nine," said Sainsbury, falling into step with Penny and Thompson. "Rather plump, dark hair, very well groomed. Last seen wearing a grey suit, white shirt and red tie. Drives a silver BMW, Registration number K489EYK."

"Note the number please, Constable."

"I have it, Chief. K489EYK," said Penny, jotting it into her notepad.

"Thank you very much, Captain," said Thompson, striding towards reception. "We'll speak to you later . . ."

"As you wish . . ."

"You've started with a big one, Penny," said Thompson, as they left the building. "You're going to be very busy."

"Yes, sir. Is there anything you'd like me to do?"

"Write off next weekend for a start," answered Thompson as they crossed the car park, "but first we get a message out to bottle up the Dales."

"Seal the entire area?"

"Roadblocks on every approach road. Who knows, our man could still be in the area. And if he is, we might just nab him . . ."

4

Mary wondered why Dave was late. He had said he would be home in about an hour and a half but that had been over two hours ago. Normally he was very dependable; in fact his reliability had been one of the qualities that Mary had found attractive during their courtship – making as it did for a change from the unreliability of theatrical life.

Rinsing dishes now at the sink as the evening sun filled the kitchen with warmth and light, she thought of ringing him, then dismissed the idea. It wasn't as though a meal were overcooking in the oven, she reasoned – they were just having a salad. Anyhow, he was only a little over half an hour late. Perhaps he had had a puncture or was stuck in traffic.

Besides, she had been determined when she became pregnant again to continue living normally – she wasn't going to start worrying and foostering and demanding extra attention. In reality it had been Dave who had worried his way through this pregnancy, thrilled that she was expecting their baby, yet terrified of another miscarriage.

When they had passed the chief danger zone of the first three months he had been exuberant and had produced books and articles on babies and foetal development. Mary smiled now as her eye fell on the wall chart he had stuck up in the kitchen. He had ticked off each stage of development as the baby's hands, fingers, eyes and so on had formed.

Looking at the chart, she thought how much she loved this man. And how their happiness would be complete when the child arrived. She hadn't revealed to him just how much the baby meant to her in case she might have another miscarriage, but the pregnancy had been perfectly normal.

Just then the baby kicked, and she experienced a surge of joy. So what if Dave were a little late, she thought. It was foolish to worry over trifles when they had been so fortunate. Instead she finished the dishes, then lowered herself into her easy chair and waited for the sound of her husband's car approaching.

The golden evening light reflected off the crockery and highlighted the sheen in Mary's blonde hair, but Dave was oblivious to his surroundings as he sat at the kitchen table. His pulses raced and his breathing was shallow as he looked guiltily at his wife's horror-struck face.

"But why, Dave?! Why didn't you just ring the police?!"

"I . . . I was in shock – so I followed my gut reaction."

"But you'd acted in self-defence. You could have explained that to the police!"

"They mightn't have believed me. It would have come out that there'd been bad blood between myself and Gatenby. Plus they could take a very unsympathetic line – the police are notoriously down on anyone who kills one of their own."

"But you don't know that Gatenby was a policeman."

"Maybe not a normal policeman, but – I don't know . . . Special Branch, Military Police, M15 – some kind of law enforcement; and I'd killed him."

"Jesus, Dave! That's – that's not reason enough not to report it!"

"It wasn't *just* that. There's also the Ministry of Defence thing."

"What?"

"United Advertising's just landed a big Ministry of Defence contract. Trevor Lawrence is leaning on me enough as it is – how do you think it would be if I turned out to have killed an official with MOD links?"

"Christ, Dave, this is way too serious to take second place to your career prospects!"

"It's not just my career. Others would suffer if Lawrence had that kind of leverage over me. There'd be job-shedding, short-term contracts, all sorts of stuff."

"But, Dave, we're talking about killing someone!"

"It was an accident! I didn't mean to!"

"I know, love. I know. But your reasons – they're not strong enough for not ringing the police."

"There were other reasons too."

"Like what?"

Dave breathed out deeply, then looked her in the eye. "I'd – I'd considered not telling you anything of what happened . . ."

"What?"

"I was afraid . . . with the baby and all . . . I thought maybe the shock . . ."

"We don't keep secrets, Dave! We never have!"

"I know. It was . . . confused thinking. I thought it might be for the best – but as soon as I saw you I knew I couldn't lie. But I had been thinking of you . . ."

"OK . . . OK. But, look . . . it's not too late, you can still ring the police and explain."

"And say I split open a man's skull – but it was an accident? Say I'm innocent but I weighed down his body with stones and sank it in a mountain tarn because I don't trust the authorities?"

"They'd still understand."

"Would they? On the way to Carlisle I listened to a radio programme about the Birmingham Six – six innocent men went to jail for sixteen years because the West Midlands police needed a scapegoat."

"That was 1974, Dave!"

"So?"

"This is different. There'd been a dreadful bombing then. The police were under enormous pressure to convict."

"Maybe there'll be enormous pressure here too. Espionage is a dirty business. The National Interest can cover all kinds of expediency – I don't want to be someone's scapegoat."

"I understand that," said Mary, her voice sympathetic, "but you're being . . . paranoid."

"Maybe I am. But I don't trust governments and I want to see our child being born. I want to watch it growing every day. I don't want to risk being stitched up for something that wasn't my fault. We've waited a long time for this baby, Mary. I couldn't bear not to be free to enjoy it."

Mary bit her lip and Dave felt guilty for painting such a bleak scenario, yet he felt he had to outline his fears.

Mary leaned forward at the table, breathing out and running her fingers through her hair; then she looked up, her expression anguished. "Why the hell couldn't you have just gone to the police?!"

"I've told you why – it was a spur-of-the-moment thing. I had to choose."

She gazed at him, her face etched with worry, then she spoke softly. "You chose wrong, Dave."

"I wouldn't be so sure."

"I would. You're going to have to go to the police."

"And throw myself on their mercy?"

"Yes. I know it will be messy in all sorts of ways but it's the lesser of two evils."

Dave slowly shook his head. "What I've done so far would sound really suspicious. Better to keep our heads down and let things blow over."

"Blow over? Murder investigations don't 'blow over'!"

"But it won't be a murder, not without a body. It'll be a missing person case."

"Will it? What about his abandoned car?"

"What about it? Even if it's found and traced to Gatenby-"

"If?!"

"He mightn't have been using his own car, Mary."

"Supposing he was?"

"Then they'll find it eventually – but it'll be miles from where his body is. It'll still be a missing person case. For all they know Gatenby could have skipped the country."

"You can't rely on that."

"Look, no one saw me dump the body, and – "

"How can you be sure?" interjected Mary.

"It was a really isolated spot; there were no other people about; the tree-cover ran right up to the edge of the tarn – believe me, no one saw what I did."

"It's – it's not right, Dave."

"Neither is being stitched up by the police!"

"You're obsessed with being stitched up."

"Because it's a possibility. It could happen, Mary, and I'd go out of my mind if I were locked in jail. This is the big bad world and nasty things happen to innocent people."

"Nastier things will happen if you *don't* go forward and then they catch you."

"How can they catch me? No one knows what happened – no one ever will."

"It won't be that simple. The police aren't stupid. They'll . . . I don't know, look for tyre marks, question anyone who drove within miles of the place . . ."

"There'll be no tyre marks. It was too dry. And I'll

post the microfilm back anonymously. That should help take the heat off. Nobody will ever know I met him."

Mary ran her hand through her hair again, and Dave hoped that perhaps he had shaken her instinctive conviction to turn to the police in times of trouble.

"This way at least we take our destiny into our own hands," he said persuasively.

"God, Dave," she snapped, rising from her chair," I can't believe what you're saying!" She crossed to the window and stood there, breathing unevenly.

Dave rose and followed her. "It's better than leaving things to Fate."

"How can you say that?"

"Because Fate is cruel and not to be trusted. When you lose your parents and sister at fourteen years of age it makes you reluctant to trust in Fate."

"Oh, Dave . . ." Mary reached out and touched his face. "Oh, Dave . . ." she whispered.

He saw her eyes moisten and he reached out and held her. They clung together a moment. Then she looked up. "You don't deserve to have this happen to you," she said.

"No, honey, it's you who doesn't deserve this. I'm so, so sorry to have landed it on you."

She kissed him lightly and shook her head. "It wasn't your fault, Dave. Whatever happens let's . . . let's always be agreed on that . . . killing him wasn't your fault."

"OK," he replied. "OK . . ." He looked at her, desperately wanting to make everything all right. "We'll pull through, Mary. We'll pull through."

"No," she answered quietly, "we won't, Dave. What we'll do is go to the police together . . ."

"No!"

"Yes. Listen, love, just for a second. We go to the police immediately, because the longer we wait the worse it seems. We go and we explain."

"No!"

"We have to."

"We don't have to! Can't you see the nightmare we'd enter if we did that?"

"It's a nightmare anyway!"

"But it's *our* nightmare, controlled by us."

"What the hell is that supposed to mean?"

"It means that *we* make the decisions. Our fate isn't at the whim of police and lawyers and judges."

"For Christ's sake, Dave, be realistic!"

"I am being realistic. This time your advice is wrong. And I'm not going to see my new-born child through the bars in some prison."

"That's exactly what *will* happen if you don't own up and get caught later."

"I won't get caught, not if you help me, not if we row together."

"*Row together?!* What do you think this is, some sort of game?"

"No. It's a matter of life or death – literally. And I'm counting on you to help me."

"Well, don't – because I won't be a party to this. I'll back you one hundred per cent with the police. No matter what happens I'll stand by you. But I won't be party to this."

Dave looked at her, his emotions a bewildering mixture of guilt at forcing this situation on his wife six weeks before she was due to deliver their child, anger, and a sense of betrayal. "Don't help then," he said softly. "I'll handle it myself – unless you're planning to shop me to the police."

Mary looked angrily at him, opened her mouth to speak, then bit her lip and, turning abruptly, walked out of the room.

Dave heard the distant bedroom door slamming, then he sat at the table and slowly, despairingly, lowered his head into his hands.

5

High above the Potomac River, in an office overlooking the George Washington Parkway, Bob Reinholdt waited restlessly. To a casual observer he would not have seemed worried. Reinholdt had always carried himself with an easy confidence, and although his curly brown hair was peppered with grey his trim physique and air of youthfulness belied the fact that he was approaching fifty.

He didn't look worried, yet he was; for he sensed that his meeting with the CIA's Deputy Director of Operations could be a pivotal one in his career. His rise through the ranks of the Company had been fast, and for the past two years he had been Chief of Station for the CIA's London office. Janet and the kids had become accustomed to the good life in England and he reckoned that the trappings that went with his rank just about compensated for the long hours and disrupted family life of which his wife frequently complained. But a sideways move or demotion to an unglamorous posting would put a strain on his marriage that he feared might not be sustainable.

There was no reason why he should suddenly fail now, he told himself, yet the phone call last night had shaken him. His source in British Intelligence had woken him to report a major security breach. Top secret SMORTAR data had been stolen from Browsdale Research Centre, and Nigel Gatenby, an M15 operative with responsibility for site security, was missing. Reinholdt had carefully considered the consequences, then taken the first flight from Heathrow to New York.

He had worked out his approach on the way to CIA Headquarters in Langley, and he was thinking through his presentation again when the secretary approached.

"Mr Reinholdt . . . if you care to go in, Mr Krucowski will see you now."

"Thank you."

He rose, then walked across the thick-piled carpet and into the inner office of the Deputy Director.

"Bob, good to see you. Take a chair," said Krucowski without rising from behind his desk.

"Thank you, sir. Good to see you again." Reinholdt smiled at the other man who, although only twelve years his senior, clearly belonged to a different generation.

Krucowski was a squat grey-haired man, dour in personality and appearance, but his outstanding track record pointed to a greater subtlety than his manner suggested. Reinholdt had served with him in Beirut, shortly after joining the Agency, and he knew not to underestimate the older man nor to mistake his bluntness for lack of thought.

"So what brought you hightailing it to Washington?" asked Krucowski.

"I'm sorry to bother you, sir, but when I heard Jim Beull was hospitalised I thought I'd better report directly to you."

"What's up?"

"It's something with the potential to be very worrying . . ."

Krucowski leaned back in his chair, his eyes attentive.

"As you know the British have developed a new weapons system called SMORTAR. Yesterday a set of manufacturing drawings, test procedures and operational instructions for it was stolen."

Krucowski raised an eyebrow. "That was . . . careless . . ."

"Very."

"The Limeys didn't tell you this themselves . . ."

"No, we have a source in their Military Intelligence."

"Who stole the data?"

"The theft seems to have been by a British agent . . ."

"Goddamn! Here we go again . . ."

"Of course the real question isn't who stole it but who he stole it for"

"And who's that?"

Reinholdt shrugged. "We don't know yet. The problem is, it's a terrorist's dream-come-true."

"Some kind of advanced mortar, isn't it?"

"A so-called 'smart' mortar – hence the name SMORTAR. It's fitted with an extremely accurate electronic directional device that's activated after its launch, but it can be fired from an ordinary mortar."

"So?"

"So if a terrorist parked a van, say half a mile from the White House, and fed in accurate co-ordinates, he could land a SMORTAR bang on target – in the President's garden, onto the main portico, wherever he choose."

"Jesus . . ."

Reinholdt stayed silent, allowing Krucowski to absorb the implications.

"These drawings, how much technical know-how would be required to produce the weapon from them?"

"A good deal," answered Reinholdt, "but a terrorist group with links to a sympathetic government would be a major concern."

"Have you a government in mind?"

"Not yet. The fundamentalist Moslem regimes would be a worry. Some of them have quite advanced technology; add that to a plethora of fanatical anti-American groups and it becomes a serious risk."

Krucowski turned in his chair and looked out pensively towards the river, but Reinholdt resisted the temptation to say more, knowing he had to let the Deputy Director digest it for as long as it took.

After a moment Krucowski swung slowly back around. "This conjures up Beirut '83."

"The bombing of the Marine barracks?"

Krucowski nodded. "I saw our casualties first-hand. I practically waded through the carnage. And when I looked around that slaughterhouse I swore something. *Never again.*"

"So . . . ?"

"We'll have to act on this," said Krucowski. "Are the British likely to inform you about it through normal channels?"

"I doubt it, or at least not until they've gone into action themselves."

"We can't sit on the fence waiting for that."

"No, sir. At the same time it's their country and they're our allies, so we can't be too overt."

"It may be their country, but if this SMORTAR gets into the wrong hands, you can bet your ass it's an American embassy, or an American barracks or an American statesman who'll be hit."

"I agree."

Krucowski looked at him searchingly. "Are you recommending we don't step on their toes or that we take direct action?"

"I think there's a way of doing both. We could use someone who's very effective but isn't Company. That way we can act to find out who's behind this, but if there are objections later we can say he wasn't CIA."

"Who do you have in mind?"

"There's a South African we've used before. Jan Visser."

"Visser?!"

"You know him?"

"He was in 'Nam, sixty-five, sixty-six . . . the guy was a psycho."

"He's become more sophisticated. We've used him in Chile, Angola, couple of other spots . . ."

"I don't know . . ." Krucowski looked thoughtful. "I saw some of his handiwork at Da Nang . . ."

"I know he's not exactly Ivy League, sir, but these days he's more discreet. He's also highly effective."

"It's not his effectiveness that worries me. He got more out of captured VC than any other interrogator, but we're talking about England. You don't strap someone to a chair in Piccadilly Circus and stick electrodes into them."

"Of course not, sir. But being a British operation I could keep a check on him. And time may be of the essence here . . ." He left the sentence hanging and watched the older man's rugged face as he considered the problem.

Suddenly Krucowski leaned forward, his decision made. "OK, use him, but emphasise the need to be discreet. And no ties to us. We still have to live with the Brits when this is over."

"Absolutely, sir."

"Where's Visser now?"

"He has a place in Bangkok. He lives there between jobs."

"Is he there at present?"

"I rang when I landed at Kennedy, and again from Dulles, but he wasn't in." Reinholdt glanced at his watch. "Mind you, right now in Bangkok it would be nine on a Friday night, so that's not surprising."

"Does he have an answering machine?"

"Yes but I didn't want to say anything on a tape machine."

Krucowski nodded. "Right, get our embassy in Thailand onto it. Have them leave a message for him to contact them immediately . . ."

"He mightn't listen to his messages immediately," interjected Reinholdt.

Krucowski looked at him in irritation. "I was also going to say have the embassy ring every fifteen minutes."

"Sorry, sir."

"Tell them ring right through the night if necessary . . ."

"Where do we patch the call through to?"

"Not this office," answered Krucowski. "The fewer people involved in this the better. Tom Travis is in Managua. Borrow his office and you can take the call there yourself."

"Right . . ."

"Stay tight on this one, Bob. I don't like the sound of it."

"Sure thing."

"Once you contact our man, run it personally from London. The priority is to find out who's involved, then we can decide how to play it. Keep me informed on a confidential basis."

"Via the Acting Head of Europe Division?"

"No, I haven't replaced Jim Beull yet – report directly to me."

"Right . . ."

"Let's keep this really quiet. No memos, nothing in writing – not when we're using Visser."

"I understand."

Krucowski nodded in dismissal. "Good luck, Bob."

"Thank you, sir," said Reinholdt, rising and making for the door. He understood all right. No phone call patched through to Krucowski's office, no memos, the operation run from London. If anything went wrong

Krucowski wouldn't be involved – it would be Bob Reinholdt's operation.

Of course, if it went well it could give a boost to his career, but if it backfired . . . he thought of Janet and their shaky marriage and he resolved not to lose what he had. It *wouldn't* backfire, he told himself. He couldn't afford it to.

He walked down the corridor, determination in his stride as he went to ring the embassy.

The young Thai couple at the brothel had been well worth the money – youthful, innocent-looking, yet thoroughly depraved and willing to perform any act he had ordered. Jan Visser considered himself an authority on brothels and he had long since decided that for a man of exotic tastes, Bangkok was hard to beat. Not the Bangkok of the tourists who flocked to the red-light district of Pat Pong, but the city where the more unusual pleasures that Visser enjoyed were to be had in a number of plush and select establishments.

He had sampled a new one tonight and it had been highly satisfactory. Sated after the evening's pleasure, he walked contentedly homewards, the hot tropical air touched with the scent of jasmine. He had left behind the city centre with its ceaseless din of criss-crossing *tuc-tucs*, blaring horns, and choking exhaust fumes, and the walk through his own quiet suburb brought home to him his good fortune. He savoured the fact that to afford peace and quiet in a city like Bangkok cost money – and he, Jan Visser, had money. In fact, his fees were such that by living in Thailand he could afford a life of considerable affluence.

It had not always been the case. Growing up in a poor white suburb of Johannesburg during the nineteen-fifties, life had been a constant struggle. His father's wages as a factory worker had been squandered on drink and gambling, and at an early age Visser had decided never again to be poor, never again to live in a household devoid of music and books.

On leaving school he had studied telecommunications by night while working for the telephone company by day, but his real break had come during his national service with the South African Army.

He had shown a natural flair for interrogation, and his ruthlessness, allied to his inventive use of electric shock treatment, had loosened the tongues of many ANC suspects. He had enthusiastically extended his range to include other forms of torture once he had relished the wonderful feeling of power to be had in breaking a prisoner, and the authorities had come to rely on the softly spoken youth who could always be counted upon to extract information from even the most intransigent prisoners.

He had stayed in the army after his national service ended, honing his skills and developing his reputation, before departing for the conflict in Vietnam.

It was in Vietnam that he had launched his career as an agent/interrogator par excellence, and for the next twenty-five years he had freelanced around the world, being handsomely paid for work that he would have done for pleasure, in Baghdad, Santiago, Angola and a score of other trouble spots.

It meant that at forty-nine years of age he could now live in luxury between assignments, in a city that catered readily for his needs.

He walked home contentedly, softly humming a Bach cantata as he crossed the bridge over the narrow, lily-edged *klong* that ran before his house. He thought again about the brothel as he opened his gate and entered the scent-laden garden. Perhaps next time he would hire the stunning-looking mother and daughter he had been offered tonight – it would be amusing, he thought, to have them inflict pain on each other. He was enjoying the notion when the sound of a phone ringing inside the house disturbed his thoughts and he quickly made for the front door, unlocked it, and picked up the phone. "*Sawadee*?"

"*Sawadee*," answered a voice with an American accent. "Is that Jan Visser?"

"Who wants to speak to him?"

"Are you Visser?"

"I said who wants to speak to him?"

There was a short pause, then the man answered. "Duty Officer McLeod, United States Embassy."

Visser thought a moment. "He'll ring you back in five minutes."

"Hold on," started the American, but the line had already gone dead.

Visser put the phone back on its cradle and left the house immediately. He walked briskly through the moonlit garden, unconscious now of the scented tropical flowers, recrossed the bridge and headed in the direction of the city. His earlier mood of relaxation was gone and his mind was racing. A call from the Americans probably meant an assignment, and if that were the case he would not discuss any aspect of it on his own phone.

Instead he stopped at a public telephone booth, looked up the number of the embassy, and dialled. The phone was answered on the second ring.

"United States Embassy."

"I'd like to speak to Mr McLeod."

"Whom shall I say is calling, sir?"

"That won't be necessary. He's expecting me."

"Just a moment." There was a short pause. "Putting you through now, sir . . ."

"McLeod speaking."

"You wanted to talk to me."

"Mr Visser?"

"Yes."

"Mr Jan Visser?"

"Yes."

"I'm to patch you through to Washington. Hold on a moment please."

There was static on the line, followed by a high-pitched electronic sound, then a strong American voice came clearly down the line. "Mr Visser?"

"Yes."

"I'm calling from Virginia . . ."

CIA in Langley, Visser realised. "I'm speaking from a public booth," he answered.

"OK, my line is clean here; nevertheless we'll be discreet."

"Of course."

"You did some consultancy work for us a while back. In Marseilles . . ."

"Yes, I remember that." He remembered it fondly – he'd used a blowlamp to persuade a drugs dealer to discuss a shipment of heroin.

"You recall me then?" asked the American.

"Very well indeed." Reinholdt, Bob Reinholdt. He looked like a football player but was actually quite a senior CIA man.

"I have some more consultancy work."

"Whereabouts?"

"London."

"I see. When did you have in mind?"

"Immediately."

"Hmm. I did have some other plans."

"And you'll want to be compensated for dropping them, right?" said Reinholdt.

"Well, yes."

"You always say that. I've checked."

"If you've checked, you'll know I always deliver the goods."

"That's why I rang you. We can discuss your fee in London. I'm sure we can make it worth your while."

"Very well."

"How soon can you be there?"

Visser thought a moment. "4.00 or 5.00 p.m. GMT. There's a seven-hour time difference; if I take the first flight in the morning I can get there late afternoon."

"Right, let's meet at 9.00 p.m. local time tomorrow night."

"OK. I take it this is a job of some proportion?"

"You take it correctly. Where will you be staying?"

"I haven't decided yet," answered Visser. He certainly wasn't going to meet Reinholdt in a hotel room; he had never believed in public contact with clients. "I'll be hiring a car. Let's meet in the car park in Brewer Street."

"Brewer Street?"

"Yes, it's in Soho. You enter the top floor, alone and on foot, and carrying a rolled newspaper. I'll be in a parked car."

"How do I know which one?" said Reinholdt.

"I'll flash the headlights."

"OK. Tomorrow night at nine."

"You'll make sure you're not . . . *accompanied* in any way?" asked Visser.

There was an edge to the American's voice. "I'm a long time in business and when I attend a meeting alone, I attend it *alone*."

"Of course, of course – forgive me." Visser's tone was placatory. "It's just that one's learnt the importance of caution."

"All right. See you tomorrow night."

"Tomorrow night then."

The line went dead and Visser put down the phone. He felt gloriously alive, as he always did at the start of a mission. He started for home, thinking that a spell in London might be enjoyable, especially with the Thai monsoon due in a week or two.

As he retraced his steps the scent of tropical flowers hit him and reminded him again of the perfumed brothel. It was a pity about the mother and daughter.

He had been looking forward to working on them. Still, an assignment usually provided similar opportunities for pleasure and pain, except that he wouldn't be paying for them. He would be getting paid.

He walked eagerly homewards, already feeling the first stirrings of the thrill of the chase . . .

6

Chief Inspector Thompson was in surprisingly good form for a man who had been up since dawn. Penny had thought he might be disappointed at the roadblocks yielding nothing, but instead he moved about the Incident Room that had been set up in Leeds, encouraging the members of his team.

Along one wall a bank of computers had been installed, and there was a constant toing and froing as the Receiving Officer sorted all the incoming paperwork, while the detectives were given their individual investigative roles by the Action Allocater.

Despite the early hour and the gravity of the crime there was a certain amount of banter, which Thompson didn't seem to mind. In fact as he approached Penny now there was a humorous air of irony in his voice. "Everything to your satisfaction, DC Hart?"

"Yes, Chief." She indicated the activity about them. "Actually, it's – well, it's rather exciting."

"Yes, I suppose it is. Of course, you wouldn't be familiar with HOLMES, would you?"

"Not personally, Chief."

"Not personally?"

"No." She lowered her voice conspiratorially. "But I once had a summer job with a girl called WATSON."

Thompson laughed and shook his head in mock dismay. "I can see I'm going to have to keep you on a tight leash."

Penny smiled. "I know HOLMES is Home Office Large Major Enquiry System, but I've no personal experience of it."

Thompson indicated the typists at the keyboards. "Every scrap of information, no matter how small, is fed into the HOLMES system and retained. It's a spin-off from what we learnt on the Yorkshire Ripper case."

"You were on that?"

Thompson nodded grimly. "Learnt our lessons the hard way there. *Every* piece of information is kept with HOLMES. Nothing that should be investigated, however minor, slips through the net."

"It sounds good."

"It is. It's also portable and we can tie into computers in other police forces to exchange information."

"Right . . ." Penny nodded approvingly

"It's only a tool, though. Crimes like this are solved by detectives thinking for themselves, using their initiative to spot some tiny slip-up the villains make. Always remember that."

"OK, Chief."

"Jack!" Inspector Powell, the Office Manager on the case, called to Thompson as he approached. "Mr Mathieson and Mr Carrow to see you. Interview Room One."

"Cloak and Dagger time," said Thompson wryly. "Come on, Penny. You have the map and the vehicle reports?"

"Yes, Chief."

"Let's go then."

They left the bustle of the Incident Room and crossed to a much quieter office across the corridor. The two men were waiting, already seated at a large table.

"Good morning, gentlemen," said Thompson as he entered the room.

Both men returned the greeting and Mathieson smiled at Penny, having met her the previous evening at Browsdale. He was quite handsome, with dark hair despite being in his late forties, and he had a pleasant if slightly old-fashioned manner; yet she sensed that behind the courteous demeanour and languid upper-class tones was a man who could take decisive and perhaps ruthless action.

The other man, Chief Superintendent Carrow of Special Branch, was new to her. She had been at the questioning of the loading operative the previous night when Carrow had flown up from London and he had already gone into conference with his Special Branch officers by the time she had resumed working with Thompson.

The man looked at her now with an irritatedly quizzical air.

"This is DC Hart," explained Thompson. "Chief Superintendent Carrow," he added to Penny.

"How do you do, sir," she said.

Carrow nodded curtly, then turned questioningly to Thompson.

"DC Hart has been seconded to CID – she's acting as my personal assistant on this case," said Thompson easily, then he indicated for Penny to sit and did so himself.

Carrow was a big-featured, heavy man of about fifty, with ginger hair combed straight back, and his well-cut tweed suit and brogues suggested a country squire image.

"I take it you're fully conversant with the Official Secrets Act?" he asked.

"Yes, sir," answered Penny.

"This is all highly confidential – *highly so* – you understand?"

"Absolutely, sir." She felt herself taking a dislike to this man. It wasn't just his dead-fish eyes and aggressive manner but his voice too. She recognised a Yorkshire accent that had been modulated in an attempt to sound upmarket. Probably dreams of being Master of the local hunt, she thought.

"So," added Carrow, "don't go chattering to your boyfriend about any of this . . ."

Penny felt a flash of anger and was about to respond, but Thompson got in ahead of her.

"All right, Mr Carrow," he said firmly. "I think the point's been made. Let's get down to the case, shall we?"

"Right," answered Carrow.

"Received Gatenby's personnel records from London, have you?" asked Mathieson.

"Yes, thank you," answered Thompson. "Very helpful – we're exploring his background in detail."

"My people are already running computer checks on his friends and acquaintances," said Carrow. "What we need to identify though is what exactly we're dealing with here."

Thompson looked at him. "Well, initially we're dealing with the murder of the guard, very probably committed by Gatenby."

"Yes," agreed Carrow, "but what are we dealing with when Gatenby left? A straightforward defection? A hit? A kidnapping? Double-crossing by his backers?"

"Have we established anything on the abandoned van yet?" asked Mathieson.

"Traced to a backstreet garage in Darlington," answered Thompson, "and rented by a man answering Gatenby's description."

"Well now . . . in that case whether it genuinely broke down or was left as a red herring becomes crucial," mused the Intelligence Officer.

"We had it towed away for examination," answered Thompson. "Penny?"

She took out some files, then addressed the others. "The technical report says the problem with the van's engine was a faulty condenser."

"Do they think it a genuine breakdown or induced?" asked Mathieson.

"Probably genuine, they say – it'd be difficult to

stage it breaking down just where you might choose."

"Unless you picked your spot, took out the good one and put back in a dud," said Carrow.

"Good point," acknowledged Thompson, "but would a man fleeing a murder halt and start disassembling an engine?"

"He might if he was cool enough," said Carrow.

Thompson looked at Mathieson. "He was your colleague. Would he have been?"

"Wouldn't have thought so. But then I wouldn't have thought him a murderer either."

Carrow nodded. "What about fingerprints on the van?"

"None whatsoever," answered Penny. "The report says the steering column and door handles must have been wiped."

"What about his own car?" asked Mathieson.

"No sign yet," Thompson replied. "The assumption being he's hidden it."

"You're searching for it, of course?" said Carrow.

"Of course." He nodded to Penny who indicated another list.

"We've run off the names of every lock-up and storage facility within a thirty-mile radius, sir," she said. "They're being contacted as we speak."

"I'm sure it will turn up," said Mathieson. "Question is, where's Gatenby? He obviously wanted to travel incognito to evade detection."

"We've alerted every airport and ferry linc," said Thompson. They have recent pictures of him, and a tight watch will be maintained."

"He could have left in disguise," suggested Carrow.

"He could," answered Mathieson, "but I suspect he hasn't."

"What do you base your suspicions on?" the Special Branch man asked.

"Nothing more substantial than hunch, but just assuming I'm right, it boils down to two things. If he *wasn't* intercepted he's still out there somewhere – and we've got to locate him. And if he *was* intercepted we've got to find out by whom. The information he has could be lethal in the wrong hands."

"What about the killing of the soldier. Can we go public on that yet?" asked Thompson.

"Mustn't link the two incidents," insisted Mathieson. "The official story's that the guard met with an accident."

"It was murder," snorted Thompson.

"I know. And you may be able to charge it as such when we catch Gatenby. Meanwhile National Security's involved, and we want to keep very discreet about what happened in Browsdale."

"All right," agreed Thompson reluctantly.

"What's the position on the radio appeals?" asked Carrow.

"They started broadcasting them last night. Going out again this morning," answered Thompson. "Hopefully we'll get a response as the morning goes on."

"Exactly what locations did the messages refer to?"

Thompson nodded to Penny. "The map, please."

Penny took a large-scale map of the Yorkshire Dales and spread it on the table.

"This is where the van was found," said Thompson, pointing. "The first message was a description of Gatenby – last seen touring in the Dales, missing persons approach, anyone who saw him to please contact the police. The second one was more specific." He indicated an area on the map. "Anyone within a ten-mile radius of this area on Thursday between three-thirty and five to please contact us. Serious crime in the vicinity, we need their assistance urgently."

"Let's hope it pays off," said Mathieson.

"Indeed," answered Thompson. He indicated for Penny to remove the map, then looked at the others. "Naturally we'll comb the area thoroughly and continue investigating every aspect of Gatenby's life. Meanwhile we'll follow up what our radio messages bring in. And then let's see if we can't tighten the net a little . . ."

7

Any minute now, thought Dave, as he glanced out his office door. Trevor Lawrence would be back in United Advertising from his breakfast meeting, and Dave knew that some sort of confrontation was inevitable, given his rejection of Lawrence's proposed car trip from Carlisle. Could that really have been only yesterday, he thought – it seemed like his whole world had since changed. Yet twenty-four hours previously he had been at the conference and Nigel Gatenby had been just a bad memory from schooldays.

Dave thought of Lawrence's suggestion to travel back together and felt a sharp pang of regret at not having agreed to it. If only Lawrence had been with him, he thought, then immediately he forced the notion from his mind. No use wasting energy on wishful thinking, he had more than enough real problems to deal with.

He had tried for a reconciliation with Mary the previous evening, but despite her further entreaties he had refused to contact the police and Mary, claiming exhaustion, had taken a sleeping pill and gone to bed early. He had gone for a long, restless walk around Harrogate, trying desperately to put his thoughts in order. Although he saw no way of being linked to what had happened to Gatenby, he had sensed that it might still be wise to establish his whereabouts during the evening, and so he had called briefly into the Tennis Club and a local shop before returning home.

Despite following Mary's example and taking a sleeping tablet, he had found it hard to get asleep, and then had slept badly, with images of Gatenby's fractured skull, the body slipping beneath the waters of the tarn, and Mary giving birth in a prison cell all mixed in a disturbing sequence of dreams.

He had had a strained breakfast with Mary, then they had driven together into Leeds. A police appeal for witnesses had come over the car radio and their fragile truce had been broken when Mary had insisted that it still wasn't too late to make a clean breast of things. Usually he valued her advice and tended to follow it, but this morning he had refused adamantly. Why couldn't she see that, awful as the incident with Gatenby was, now that the damage was done the lesser of two evils was to hold their nerve and lie low?

It grieved him to cause her so much worry when she should have been looking forward to the birth, but all his instincts had told him it would be better if he stuck to his guns and rode out the storm. He had dropped her off at the BBC studios, a palpable tension between them despite their kissing each other goodbye.

Since coming into the office he had tried hard to stop

his thoughts from going round in circles but he found it almost impossible to think about copywriting and advertising campaigns. Yet he must try to behave normally today. An innocent man would appear relaxed and involved with his work, and lest any investigation might for whatever reason point in his direction, it would be important that he had appeared normal and on top of his job this morning.

His reflections were disturbed by a movement in the outside open-plan office, and looking out, he saw the copywriting staff perk up as Trevor Lawrence entered the room. The last thing he wanted right now was trouble with Lawrence, but their relationship had never been a comfortable one. He suspected that despite all his bluster Lawrence was insecure at heart and perhaps felt threatened by Dave's success as Creative Director. They had once been co-participants on a leadership skills course subscribed to by United Advertising and held over a long weekend at a country manor. Dave had done really well on the course, inventively tackling the problems they had been given in sub-groups after each lecture, and being very much to the fore in the outdoor team-building tasks set each afternoon in the grounds of the manor.

Lawrence, by contrast, had been unpopular in the problem-solving sessions due to his dictatorial style, and had been particularly inept at the stream-crossing and raft-building tasks at which Dave had excelled.

Although there had been no tests or examinations at the end of the course Dave had nonetheless sensed that Lawrence felt he had been outshone, and with the General Manager being so fiercely competitive Dave had feared that there would be subsequent antagonism and point-scoring from him.

His fears had proved well-founded, and his relationship with Lawrence, though apparently amiable on the surface, was nevertheless a strained one. He would have given a lot right now to be spared a contretemps with Lawrence, but the General Manager approached and without knocking entered the office, his pungent aftershave detectable at a range of five yards.

"Morning, David," he said briskly, closing the glass-panelled office door behind him.

"Morning, Trevor."

"Needed a pow-wow. I've told June to hold all your calls."

"OK."

Before Dave could invite him to sit, Lawrence lifted a chair, swung it flamboyantly and placed it down beside the desk.

"So, how was your breakfast meeting with Mc Queen's?" asked Dave.

"Messy. Took a while to straighten things out."

"They've always been difficult."

"Had to give them a bit of a barracking," said Lawrence, nodding his head in apparent agreement with his own tactics. "Let them know that we want the business but not at any cost. Bit of a rough and tumble but I sorted them out in the end."

"Good."

"Now," said Lawrence, fixing a piercing gaze on Dave. "You and I need to discuss ReadyBurger, seeing as we couldn't yesterday due to . . . your aunt . . ."

"Yes," answered Dave non-committedly.

"All well in Hawksley?"

"Sorry?"

"Found your aunt all right?"

"Oh – yes . . ."

"Hidden away in the Dales . . ."

"Yes . . . she was glad to see me."

"I daresay. Pity it cost us hours of valuable time."

"Yeah . . . well, we're both here now, Trevor, so . . ."

"So let's get on with it." Lawrence leaned back in the chair, taking out a cigar. "Right, what have you in mind for ReadyBurger?"

Dave glanced at the no-smoking sign on the wall but said nothing as Lawrence lit up.

"Well?"

"I was thinking of giving the campaign to Gary Miller," said Dave.

"To Gary?"

"He's an excellent copywriter, getting better all the time. His lager ads have been first-class."

"Granted. But he's young and inexperienced. This could grow into a major account; I'd like you to do the campaign personally."

Dave shrugged and deliberately kept his voice reasonable. "I'd sooner not, Trevor."

"You'd sooner not?"

"I can oversee Gary – keep a close eye on what he's at – but it's not a campaign I want to handle personally."

"Really?" Lawrence made little effort to mask his impatience. "And may we know why?"

"I've no empathy with the burger chains . . . I . . ."

"You what?"

"I was given a protest leaflet outside a ReadyBurger outlet last week. I don't know. . . it seemed to crystallise all my . . . unfocused objections."

"Your objections to what?"

"To their whole philosophy."

"Meaning what?"

"Low wages, casual labour, no unions, dodgy environmentally . . ."

"Anything else?"

"Just, generally down-market and visually . . . tacky . . ."

Lawrence leaned forward. "Jesus Christ! Downmarket and tacky? Have you any idea what their turnover is? I'll tell you. It's telephone numbers, megabucks!"

"I know."

"Then what's all this objections crap? I can't believe what I'm hearing. Some save-the-whale, brown-rice-and-sandals asshole gives you a crank leaflet, and you let it influence your work!"

"Trevor, times are changing. People are more environmentally aware; the throwaway society will become unacceptable."

"What?!"

"I'm not sure this account would be good for United Advertising long-term."

Holding the cigar between thumb and middle finger, Lawrence pointed at Dave. "Let me decide what's good for us; that's *my* job. And ReadyBurger will be very good for us. Your job is to devise the ads."

"And to do that well you need some feel for the product – some handle."

"You don't have to be an alcoholic to write an ad for gin."

"No, but you won't produce good work if you've some kind of block about the product. That's why, if we *must* handle ReadyBurger . . ."

"We must," interjected Lawrence.

"Then I suggest we give it to Gary." Dave tried for a smile. "Gary won't have any reservations; he practically lives on junk food."

Lawrence didn't smile back. "That's not the point. As General Manager I'd like you to do it."

"And as Creative Director I'm explaining why that won't work."

There was a pause as Lawrence flicked ash from his cigar towards the waste bin, then he spoke slowly and deliberately. "I don't think I like your attitude . . ."

Dave looked at where the cigar ash had fallen on his carpet and felt his irritation mounting. "I'm sorry you feel that way," he said, "but on matters artistic, the final decision rests with the Creative Director. That was the basis on which I took this job."

"A Creative Director not getting on with the General Manager can be replaced."

"That would be a matter for the Board," answered Dave evenly, "but as long as I *am* here I'll do what I think is right. Both for myself and United Advertising."

There was a long silence while Lawrence stared at him, but Dave held the other man's gaze, refusing to be intimidated.

"Right," said Lawrence, rising suddenly, "get Miller working on it immediately – and it better be good! As Creative Director you'll be responsible."

"Fine."

Lawrence moved towards the door, then stopped and turned. "Oh yes, I knew there was something else," he said brightly. "Have the police questioned you yet?"

Dave felt his stomach lurch. "The police?"

"Yes. After your exploits up the Dales . . ."

Dave's mouth felt suddenly dry and it was an effort to keep his voice normal. "What are you talking about?"

Lawrence gave a small insincere smile. "For a man who writes radio ads you ought to listen more to the radio."

"I'm not with you."

"They've been broadcasting appeals for witnesses. Something happened up the Dales yesterday afternoon and they want to talk to anyone who was in the Browsdale region. That, I presume, includes you."

Dave's mind raced as he considered his position. He had heard the appeals and had planned to ignore them, but now the only way he could do so would be to confess that he had been lying about visiting his aunt. And that would surely be suspicious – why should he confess to lying to his manager, unless he had good reason to avoid talking to the police?

"You were in the Dales yesterday afternoon, weren't you?" persisted Lawrence.

He reckons I lied to avoid him, thought Dave. This is his way of making things awkward for me. "Yes, yes, I was up there . . ."

"They'll want your co-operation then," said Lawrence.

"And I'm sure as a conscientious citizen you'll be glad to help."

"Yes . . . I must ring them."

"Better not waste any more time – I'll tell June to ring the special number for you." Lawrence looked him in the eye, and knowing he had no option, Dave nodded.

"Fine . . ." he said.

Lawrence moved to the door. "And keep me posted on ReadyBurger, if that's not too much of an infringement on your artistic freedom." Turning on his heel, he left the room.

Dave breathed out deeply, his heart pounding. Damn Lawrence, he thought. Damn him and the whole stupid fabrication he had caused! This was the first thing to go wrong in his planning but there was no time to dwell on it – in a moment he would be put through to the police. He sat at the desk, nerves tingling, as he waited anxiously for the phone to ring.

8

The atmosphere in the incident room cooled immediately when Chief Superintendent Carrow entered. Standing at the filing cabinets, Penny watched with interest as the staff carried on working without any of their previous banter. It reminded her of school when the Head would enter the class.

Carrow crossed the room, briefly returning the respectful greetings of the staff. Penny wasn't surprised when he failed to approach her, even though he knew she was acting as Thompson's assistant.

"DCI Thompson about?" Carrow asked one of the male officers.

"Yes, sir. He's in the end office."

Carrow went in without knocking, and Penny had returned to her desk when Thompson emerged.

"Penny?"

"Sir?"

"The file on the radio appeals, please."

She quickly gathered the paperwork, then entered

the small office. Carrow was sitting at the desk and nodded curtly to her.

"Good morning, sir," she forced herself to say politely.

"I've been apprising Mr Carrow of the radio responses," said Thompson. "You've the latest two there?"

"Yes, Chief. A Mr David Walker here in Leeds, and a Mr Belal Hussief in Bramhope."

"Have you got people on these?" asked Carrow.

"No," replied Thompson, "they've just come in these last few minutes. DC Hart and I were about to check them out ourselves."

"No joy yet on any of the others?"

"None of the computer runs showed anything on the ones we've done, but the rest of my team are still out questioning."

"In that case I'll lend a hand, do one of these new ones," said Carrow.

There was a short pause as Thompson glanced at him. "If you wish . . ."

"Belal Hussief sounds like an Arab. Probably be my line of country – I'll give him the once-over." Carrow rose and held out his hand. "You've got his phone statement there?"

"Yes, sir," said Penny, passing it over.

"Right, we'll talk when we get back." He nodded, then left the office.

Thompson rose also and took the other file, then catching Penny's eye he stopped and smiled wryly. "I know what you're thinking . . ."

"Yes?"

"I should have kept him at arm's length, let him know this is still a CID investigation."

"I never . . ."

"You never said that – I know. But I can see it in your eyes. This is a tricky case, Penny. The security angle's such that we can't keep the cloak-and-dagger boys out. That's why it's better to give a bit on things that don't matter too much, and keep our principled stands for the important issues. Understand?"

"Sure, Chief. Sure."

Thompson smiled. "You really don't like him, do you?"

"Well . . . no, I don't really. I . . ."

"What?"

"Well . . . his approach seems a bit racist. Mr Hussief sounds like an Arab – so that makes it Special Branch's line of country? It just smacks of 'all Arabs are terrorists, all Jews are moneylenders, all Americans . . . love hot-dogs'."

"You're probably right," said Thompson. "When I worked with him years ago he was a bundle of prejudices – probably still is, only slower now to show it in public . . ."

"Besides, someone with a Middle Eastern background is hardly likely to contact us unless they're clean."

"True," answered Thompson with a grin. "We'll probably find our villain is a solid Anglo-Saxon citizen."

Penny held up the file and smiled. "Well, David Walker sounds solidly Anglo-Saxon."

"Let's go see Mr Walker then," said Thompson.

Feeling slightly dizzy, Penny looked down at the figures hurrying along Station Square in the May sunshine. From the United Advertising reception area on the top floor of a modern office block she could see the citizens of Leeds going about their business, and she felt a sense of satisfaction in being on the city's police force.

Working with Thompson on the radio appeal responses had been an education and she was looking forward to her boss's questioning of the advertising executive – especially as Thompson had told her to feel free to pose any questions of her own – when the receptionist put her phone down and approached them.

"Mr Walker will see you now. If you'd follow me, please."

"Thank you," said Thompson, then they both rose and followed the woman along an expensively carpeted corridor.

She opened a door marked DAVID WALKER, CREATIVE DIRECTOR, and ushered them in.

A tall, fit-looking man in his mid-thirties came from behind the desk, hand extended. "I'm David Walker."

"Chief Inspector Thompson. This is DC Hart."

"How do you do, Inspector, Constable?"

He had a pleasant smile and firm handshake, Penny noted, and as he led them to a couple of leather chairs she took in the expensive but understated decor of the office.

There were two photographs mounted on his desk,

one of an attractive blonde woman displaying an intricate stained-glass window, and another of Walker and the blonde woman on a mountain peak. The walls were lined with framed shots of advertising campaigns, and Penny pointed to one. "You did the chocolate chip ad?"

"Yes."

"I loved that 'chip off the old choc' routine."

"Thank you," Walker answered modestly.

Penny looked at him. "Did you do it personally?"

"Yes, actually."

"It was excellent. Really inventive . . ."

"Thank you."

There was a pause, then Thompson spoke. "We'd like to thank you for coming forward, Mr Walker."

"Not at all."

"May I ask what it was you were doing in the Dales?"

"I was coming back from a company conference in Carlisle."

"Do you live here in Leeds?"

"No, Harrogate."

"So you cut across the Dales?"

"That's right."

"What parts exactly?"

"In from Kirby Stephen, then by Hawes, Langstrothdale Chase, Grassington, Pately Bridge . . ."

"And what time was this?"

Walker considered. "Could have been half-three, four, near Langstrothdale, perhaps half five or six reaching Harrogate."

"Did you see anything unusual?"

Walker shrugged. "No, can't say I did."

"Any parked cars or vans that you remember seeing?"

"No . . . no, I can't recall any – there wasn't much traffic."

"And you saw absolutely nothing that struck a wrong note, nothing anyway untoward?"

"No, I'm afraid not. What should I have seen, as a matter of interest?"

"There was . . . an incident," answered Thompson carefully. "It's security related, so I'm sure you'll understand if I don't go into detail."

"No problem; but I'm afraid I saw nothing remotely untoward."

"I notice from your photo that you do some hiking, Mr Walker?" said Penny.

"Yes, I do."

"Often?"

"Yes, a fair bit," he answered.

"Did you go back to do any walking in the Dales, after you'd returned home last night?"

"No. I was tired having driven from Carlisle – after a bit of a stroll I stayed home."

"I see. Is that when you heard the radio appeal?"

"No, I heard that early this morning."

"Oh. How come you didn't ring us till . . ." Penny glanced at her notebook, "ten-thirty?"

"I didn't think there was any urgency, having seen nothing, but I thought I ought to ring you all the same."

"Fair enough," said Thompson. "See any people on foot during your drive?"

"Not that I noticed, except in the villages."

"Does the name Nigel Gatenby mean anything to you?" queried Thompson.

Penny watched carefully, but no flicker of recognition showed on Walker's face as he shook his head.

"I'm afraid not."

"Would you recognise this man?" Thompson passed over a photograph of Gatenby.

Walker looked at it impassively, then shook his head again. "No, sorry," he said, returning the picture.

"OK. Thank you very much for your time, Mr Walker."

"My pleasure, Inspector. I'm only sorry I couldn't be of more help."

"Well?" said Thompson as they descended in the lift.

"I think he was a trifle nervous," answered Penny.

"You noticed?"

"Well, his manner seemed confident but he didn't expand when I praised his inventive ad – a relaxed person normally would."

"Very perceptive," said Thompson.

"Thank you. Having said that, Chief, a lot of people feel uneasy with the police."

"True. On the other hand he did pass through the crucial area."

"But would he have admitted that if he'd anything to hide?"

"Possibly; if he were devious he might reckon that if he denied it and then the car was reported as seen in Grassington or somewhere, he'd be in the soup. Might think it safer to say he was in the general area and saw nothing."

"No reaction to Gatenby's name," said Penny.

"No," answered Thompson, then as the lift came to the ground floor he turned to her. "So, gut feeling, Constable?"

"Probably quite innocent," she answered as they stepped out into the foyer. "He seems genuinely pleasant."

"I'm inclined to agree," said Thompson. "But then lots of villains seem pleasant – so we'll just keep an eye on Mr Walker."

9

This couldn't be happening, Mary had told herself, not to us, not on a beautiful May morning like this; yet the telephone call to the studio had been all too real.

Last night it had felt as though someone had taken her world and turned it upside down, casually and uncaringly spilling out all her plans, all her dreams. Then this morning the nightmare continued, with the phone call from Dave explaining about Lawrence involving the police.

Despite the shock he must have had, Dave's voice had been surprisingly controlled, and she had realised from the careful way he had phrased things that he was being ultra cautious in case the telephone line wasn't secure. He had explained how he had told the police that he had seen nothing remotely suspicious, and had suggested to Mary that they should meet for lunch.

She had agreed, her hands trembling at the idea of the police already being aware of Dave – albeit through the chance circumstance of Lawrence venting his spleen.

That had been an hour ago, and now, as she walked down Woodhouse Lane in the bright sunshine her mind was made up. In spite of her conviction that Dave should have gone to the police immediately and told the truth, the die was now cast. For better or worse Dave had responded to the radio appeal, had been formally questioned, and had given a totally misleading statement. The priority now, for both of them, would have to be ensuring that every detail of his story was as convincing as possible.

She turned right off Woodhouse Lane, making towards the Civic Centre, then turned into a side street and crossed the road towards the Mezza Luna, an Italian restaurant where she and Dave sometimes had lunch. She paused a moment at the entrance, suddenly unnerved, then, gathering herself, she took a deep breath and stepped in.

Her feelings towards her husband had been in turmoil since the previous night. She had run the gamut from shock at what he had done, to concern at his obvious distress, to anger at his insistence that his course of action was the correct one. And illogical as it may have been, this morning she also experienced guilt, knowing he felt betrayed by her refusal to support his claim. The guilt had quickly switched again to anger when they had argued in the car about the police radio appeals, yet now as she entered the restaurant and saw Dave sitting alone at a corner table, she suddenly felt a rush of love for him.

Perhaps it was his worried-looking expression as he sat there, nervously fingering a bottle of sparkling water. Or perhaps it was a surfeit of pregnancy-induced hormones, she thought wryly. Whatever the reason, her anger evaporated as he looked up, saw her and smiled tentatively.

She smiled in return, then crossed to the table, kissed him briefly and sat. The restaurant was busy with lunchtime diners and in the hustle and bustle their conversation was clearly not going to be easily overheard, yet Dave seemed unable to speak. Mary looked at him, then gently squeezed his hand.

"Mary . . . I'm so sorry," he said contritely. "I really am . . ."

"I know, love, I know . . ." she answered softly.

"Do you – really?"

"I think I do now."

"I'd give anything not to have landed this on you."

"I know, Dave. But the die is cast now, isn't it?"

He breathed out, then nodded. "I'm afraid so."

She squeezed his hand again. "Then seeing as we're committed, we'll be committed together."

"Mary . . . you've no idea how much that means to me . . ."

Just then the waiter arrived, greeting them profusely and producing the menus with a flourish. Mary forced herself to smile as the man fussed around the table, then he bowingly made his exit and she turned back to Dave, her manner business-like. "We'll have to plan this out meticulously," she said softly. "We ought to behave as though everything we do now will be examined later with a fine-tooth comb – just in case it actually is."

"Right," agreed Dave. "Except I'm going to have to

take time out to post back the microfilm. I was thinking of sending it from Manchester."

"London would be better."

"London?"

"Eight million inhabitants, other end of the country – it'll put them off our trail."

"Jesus," he exclaimed softly, "what have I got us into?"

Mary reached out and took his hand. "We're in it together, Dave. My grandfather was a wise old Mayoman and he always said you must play the hand life dealt you, and not waste energy thinking about the hand you might have had. It's not bad advice . . ."

He looked at her a moment. "God, Mary . . . I don't know what I'd do without you . . ."

"It doesn't arise, Dave. I wish to God this had never happened, but now it has, we're in it together. OK?"

"Absolutely."

"OK, then." Mary reached for the sparkling water, wishing she felt as sure as she sounded. She poured for both of them, recognising that Dave was more shaken than she had at first realised. It would be important that she stay strong for him and she would; yet deep inside she felt a faint gnawing sensation, a sensation that she knew was fear . . .

10

Dave could feel the sweat moistening the palms of his hands as he locked the toilet door behind him. It had been nerve-wracking trying to time his visit so that no one saw him enter the cubicle – especially with the rush-hour crowds now starting to fill the city-centre railway station – but he had managed to slip in during a lull.

Once inside the cubicle he quickly divested himself of his business suit, tie and polished shoes. From a holdall he took a sweater, cords, and a pair of loafers. He donned the more casual garb, stowed the clothes he had worn to the office, then took out a tube of hair gel. He rubbed it well into his scalp before combing his thick brown hair straight back. Finally he took a pair of glasses from the holdall and put them on. In spite of his nervousness, he felt a sudden dart of ridiculousness, as though at thirty-five years of age he were dressing up for Halloween.

Forget about that, he told himself. For the journey to

London to post the microfiche back he couldn't be Dave Walker. If anyone forced him into conversation, he had decided to be Phil Evans, a Welsh train enthusiast returning from an excursion on the famous Settle to Carlisle line.

He opened the door, stepped out of the cubicle, and crossed to the mirror. The transformation was striking, the hair gel in particular altering his appearance significantly. The plain-lens glasses, a souvenir of his amateur acting days, looked rather old-fashioned, but somehow seemed right for the train-spotting Welshman. He would have to stay in character from now on but the effect of his disguise encouraged him to believe that he would be able to behave like the fictional Phil Evans.

Feeling more confident, he gathered his holdall and left the toilet, emerging into the bustle of the main hall. Being a Friday evening all the booking windows were manned, with queues at each one. Dave moved towards the nearest one where a red-haired woman with a Scottish accent was finishing her transaction. He waited a moment, appearing to study a timetable, then he moved towards the end of the booking hall.

Through the crowd he saw the red-haired woman, and catching his eye briefly she gave him a tiny smile, then turned and made for the exit. It was amazing, he thought, how the red wig had altered Mary's appearance. Together with the large-frame spectacles and the Scottish accent it made her seem a different person.

He walked towards the baggage storage area,

crossed to a closed section of counter and casually picked up a brown envelope she had just left there. He strolled out of the station, opened the envelope to remove his ticket, then walked past the waiting cabs and into the station again, this time by the main entrance.

It had been Mary who had insisted on what had seemed to him a very involved masquerade for acquiring his Leeds-London ticket. She had argued that having been short-listed as one of the people in the area where Gatenby had disappeared, the authorities might try to determine if he had posted the package from London, to put them off the trail. In which case the ticket-sellers might well be shown his photo.

It had all seemed a bit far-fetched and yet he knew she was right. The only safe approach was to act as if everything would be thoroughly checked later on. That way even the most diligent enquiries wouldn't identify Dave as a ticket-purchaser – and very likely not as a passenger either. They had planned it in detail and he knew he must adhere to the plan.

Crossing the main concourse, he made for the platforms. There was a small queue at the ticket-checker's booth, and he waited, ticket in hand. The queue moved quickly, and he reached its head, passing over his ticket for inspection. The ticket-checker glanced at him and Dave immediately averted his eyes. It struck him that perhaps he was being paranoid – which in itself might serve to draw attention – and he knew that the line between ultra-caution and paranoia was a thin one, yet he felt that on balance it was better to risk paranoiac caution until the whole affair was over.

The ticket checker casually returned the ticket, and mumbling thanks, Dave took it and headed for the train. Most people were boarding at the doors nearest the barrier, but Dave deliberately went to the furthest carriage. To his disappointment there were already several people in the carriage, but they were seated near the door, and he moved to the far end and found it empty.

He placed his bag on the seat and slumped down gratefully beside it. He heard the sound of approaching footsteps and quickly unzipped his bag and produced a newspaper. Shielding his face, he leaned back on the seat and tried to read.

The footsteps came ever closer, then a voice asked heartily: "Anybody sitting here, then?"

Not unless they're invisible, Dave thought, but instead he lowered the paper slightly. "No, it's free," he said, in what he felt was quite a good Welsh accent.

"Cheers," said the man, who had the sort of roly-poly face Dave associated with department store Santa Clauses.

Dave knew immediately that the man was going to be friendly and that was the last thing he wanted.

"Always go for the last carriage, never quite so crowded," said Santa conspiratorially. "I expect you've copped that little trick too, eh?"

This would have to be stopped at once, Dave realised, or he would find himself embroiled in discussions on train travel, the shortcomings of British

Rail, and finally reflections on life in general. He nodded curtly. "Yes, quite," he replied as formally as he could, and immediately raised his paper again.

The other passenger must have got the message for he fell silent then and Dave felt a pang of guilt. He had obviously hurt the feelings of someone who was only being friendly, yet what could he do?

What he could do – what he must do, he told himself, was to keep things in perspective. This was a matter of life and death; he couldn't afford the luxury of petty politeness.

A matter of life and death . . . the phrase ran through his head. Perhaps if he kept reminding himself of it, he could do the journey without making any mistakes . . .

Mary spotted a litter bin and brought the car to a halt outside the shopping centre. She got out of the car, her blonde hair shining in the bright May sunshine, and crossed to the bin.

In her hand she carried a plastic bag full of rubbish which she placed in the bin. She turned away immediately, but a pang of regret hit her as she made for the car. She felt an attachment to the red wig she had just dumped – she had worn it when playing the title role in *The Prime of Miss Jean Brodie*, and it held fond memories.

Except that now it had become a potential piece of evidence, just like the glasses she had dumped separately. You don't treat evidence with sentiment, she told herself. You treat it with caution – great caution.

Which was why in disposing of both articles she had chosen well-used litter bins that would be emptied regularly.

She got back into the car, suddenly depressed by the thought of all the subterfuge that had become part of their lives. She knew she must steel herself against self-pity however, and so she started the engine and drove off, comforted at least by the knowledge that the Scottish woman who had bought the rail tickets had now vanished forever.

Dave felt the train slowing as it approached Euston Station. He had kept a low profile for the whole trip and had avoided conversation with the passengers who had eventually occupied most of the seats in his carriage. When he had finished with the newspaper he had immediately donned his Walkman, indicating clearly – and successfully – his desire to be alone.

He was listening to Beethoven's *Emperor Concerto* as the train pulled up to the platform, but despite it being one of his favourite pieces he had been unable to concentrate on the music and he was happy to switch off the tape as the train came to a halt.

He took the holdall and made for the door, getting there just ahead of the hearty Leeds man he had christened Santa. Dave kept his face averted, then, leaving the man behind, walked speedily down the platform.

The ticket collector never gave him a second glance among the crowd at the barrier and he made for the station exit. Knowing there were only twenty minutes until the last evening train from London back to Leeds, he continued walking quickly, yet not so fast as to be conspicuous. He had decided against posting the film from the station in case mail collected from the rail system might be marked in some special way. He had no idea if this was actually the case but there seemed little point in travelling all the way south to London if the postmark indicated mailing from the principal rail destination from the North.

He emerged from the station onto Euston Road, clamorous with Friday evening traffic, waited for a break in the flow, and crossed over. He headed for the side streets in the University of London area, planning to find a letter box in the general direction of Gower Street.

He had already had the parcel weighed that afternoon in Leeds, and had chosen the busy General Post office in Station Square where the volume of business was such that it was most unlikely the assistant would remember him. He had placed his package inside an envelope addressed to a fictitious printing company and had purchased the necessary stamps. Later in his office he had affixed the stamps to the parcel in his holdall, which he then addressed to the Ministry of Defence.

As he moved now through the side streets he was becoming anxious at not seeing a pillar box. His search was taking him deeper into Bloomsbury and further from the station. Under no circumstances did he want to have to check into a hotel overnight, so it was essential that he make it back in time for the return train.

With each passing moment his nerves tautened. Where the hell did people post things around here? He increased his pace, and then, turning a corner, saw a red pillar box at an intersection. Unzipping his holdall, he approached the post box and tipped the envelope into the slot. He looked carefully around, but none of the passers-by appeared to be paying him any attention and he zipped the holdall closed and turned away.

A quick glance at his watch showed that he had twelve minutes to get back to the train. Time enough to make it without having to run, he decided. He hoisted his bag, then set off purposefully towards the station.

11

In spite of everything Bob Reinholdt was enjoying himself. He was jet-lagged after his return flight from Washington to London, he was missing the family Saturday night barbecue, he had incurred Janet's wrath by arriving home from the States and going out again within a couple of hours, and yet he felt an exhilaration.

He hadn't realised how much he missed fieldwork – even if it were only shaking off a potential tail on the way to meet a source.

He was fairly sure that no one was following him to begin with, nevertheless he had parked his car and set out on foot, quickly slipping into a taxi at a rank past which he was strolling. He had taken the taxi to the Doric Hotel, passed swiftly through the bar and out a rear door to another taxi that he had booked to be waiting, its engine running. Before anyone following could have even reached the bar, he had entered the taxi and lain low in the back as the driver pulled away.

He had dismissed the cabby in Shaftsbury Avenue

and now he walked towards the car park in nearby Brewer Street.

Stepping in through the pedestrian entrance, he made for the stairs. He was a little early and so he took his time ascending, thinking of how he would handle Visser.

Although he had recommended the South African to Krucowski, he had disliked Visser from their first meeting. Despite a synthetic charm there had been an unsettling mixture of styles about the man. His brutal efficiency somehow seemed at odds with an air of fastidiousness and a suggestion of vanity regarding his appearance.

Reinholdt was careful with his own appearance, yet somehow he was irritated by Visser's fussiness – a fussiness epitomised by the neatly trimmed beard fashioned in a style that needed daily shaving.

Forget all that, he told himself, this is business. Finding out about SMORTAR was what mattered, and if he succeeded in that it would give a considerable boost to his standing in the Company.

Reaching the top floor, Reinholdt stepped forward and transferred his newspaper from one hand to another. He scanned the parked cars in the gloom but none flashed its headlights. At the far end of a line of cars a woman entered a blue Renault, then started her engine and pulled away. Reinholdt waited until she was well gone, checked that there was no one else around, then stepped further forward and transferred the paper again.

Immediately he was rewarded by a flash of headlights

from the furthest wall. He approached the car and saw Visser behind the wheel.

The South African's smile was broad but without warmth, and Reinholdt was struck again by the coldness of Visser's watery blue eyes. *Cruel eyes*, he had thought on first seeing them. They always suggested an air of detachment. He looked at the agent, deciding that he had aged little in seven years. Perhaps the thinning sandy hair was a little thinner, and the face ever so slightly more debauched, otherwise there was no discernible difference.

He nodded in greeting to Visser, then got in beside him as the South African turned up the volume on the car tape deck, filling the vehicle with loud classical music. Reinholdt raised an eyebrow, but Visser smiled again.

"Can't be too careful in a high-tech world," he said in his clipped Afrikaner accent.

"That's true," answered Reinholdt.

"Well . . . I don't suppose you got me from Bangkok to enthuse about Johann Sebastian," said Visser.

"Sorry?"

"Bach," explained Visser, indicating the tape deck.

There was a hint of condescension in the South African's tone but Reinholdt suppressed his irritation. "No," he answered, "I've a job for you. I'd better tell you from the start . . ." He gave the background information on Gatenby and the stolen film, as Visser listened attentively and without interruption.

When he had finished Visser looked at him enquiringly. "What do you wish me to do?"

117

"Find out what happened. Who took the data. Where it is now. Who it's for. What they plan to do with it – and when."

"That's a tall order."

"Let me make it taller. We want this information as quickly as possible, but you'll also have to be very discreet."

"Meaning what?"

"Meaning this isn't Nicaragua. The police here take civil rights seriously."

"Maybe you should let them handle it then."

Reinholdt felt his temper rising but he controlled it. "We are letting them handle it. Officially, this is a purely British matter. Our enquiry would be *strictly* unofficial."

"Or to put it another way, if anything backfires the Agency doesn't know me. I'd be the one hung out to dry?"

Reinholdt looked at him unblinkingly. "You could put it that way."

Visser smiled briefly. "Once we know where we stand."

"Exactly. And I meant what I said about discretion."

"Let's not confuse discretion with hypocrisy," said Visser evenly.

Reinholdt looked at him quizzically. "Say more . . ."

"You want information, so you come to me. You want it really quickly and you know I may be able to arrange that. But you also know . . . my style. You can't have your cake and eat it."

Reinholdt looked at him, unable to keep at bay a sense of loathing. He knew that if he gave this man the go-ahead dreadful things could happen. And yet if he didn't, if SMORTAR got into the wrong hands, dreadful things would also happen. To say nothing of his career. Or his marriage, if he lost his London posting.

"All right," he said quietly. "Do what's necessary. But as discreetly as humanly possible – an absolutely minimum force approach."

"Right," said Visser. "What's the position with the British? Have they notified you formally about this?"

"No, not yet."

"How do you know so much then?"

Reinholdt paused, then decided he would have to tell. "We've got our own source in M15."

Visser raised an eyebrow.

"That's absolutely confidential."

"Of course." Visser thought a moment. "That could be very important; how good a source?"

"*Very* good – let's leave it at that.."

"OK. Have the British any leads your source has passed on?"

"Not yet. We've been doing some work of our own however." Reinholdt took a sheet of paper from his inside pocket. "We fed into our computer everything we know about Gatenby; his previous career, postings, contacts, friends and acquaintances, and everything we had on the SMORTAR secondment. Then we made another list of all known terror groups and their suspected contacts. When we removed groups like the Red Army Faction . . ."

"Why remove them?"

"High-profile terrorists but without the technical

backup to build from scratch a highly complex guidance system."

Visser nodded. "OK."

"So, we narrowed the second list down to groups with backing from sympathetic governments. Quite a few, as you can see. We fed this into the computer and told it to cross-reference both lists for any contacts in common."

"And?"

"We get the name of Ali qi Aksor. A diplomat at the Iranian Embassy suspected of contacts with Fundamentalist groups."

"What's the connection with Gatenby?"

"We're not sure there is one. But Gatenby attended a reception at the Turkish Embassy some months ago. We had people spotting who talked to whom. One of our people noticed that Gatenby – we knew he was M15 – was talking to Ali qi Aksor, a diplomat with a shady pedigree, so a note was filed on it."

"Interesting . . ."

"Not very at the time. Gatenby spoke to other people, and others spoke to Aksor. It was a routine notice, filed with countless others."

"Did they talk for long?"

"No, though our report says they seemed familiar with each other."

"It's starting to sound a bit tenuous . . ."

"Maybe, but it's all we've got for now."

"OK, I'll explore it." He thought for a moment then turned to the American. "Do the British know of this link with Aksor?"

"No. We haven't been officially informed of the SMORTAR leak, so we can't offer leads on it."

Visser nodded in satisfaction. "Good, that gives me a clear field. I'll get moving straight away." He smiled at Reinholdt. "Once we've agreed the money . . ."

"What's your proposed fee?"

"How does four hundred thousand dollars sound?"

"Too damn much!" He looked sharply at Visser. "That's a hell of a lot more than you got in Marseilles."

"This is a hell of a lot more difficult – and important. Plus Marseilles was seven years ago."

"I could offer you two hundred thousand plus expenses," said Reinholdt.

Visser seemed to consider. "Bearing in mind our past association I can make some adjustment. Say . . . three hundred and fifty thousand?"

"You've become greedy."

"You've become tight."

"OK, let's say two hundred and fifty thousand – that's a quarter of a million dollars, cash, plus expenses."

"Mr Reinholdt, if you want a cut-price job, there are lots of people who'll do it. If you want a professional job, I provide that – but only if I'm paid the proper fee."

"Three hundred and fifty thousand is too much."

"All right then, three hundred, and I can start straight away. But . . ." Visser raised a hand in warning, "don't offer me any less. If you do I simply drive out of here."

Reinholdt looked at him. His instincts told him the South African was bluffing. It would be nice to see him climb down after having his bluff called, yet he knew he couldn't risk it. Visser had already been approved by Krucowski, and he was efficient and ready to begin immediately. To start seeking a replacement in order to save fifty thousand dollars would be madness. He mustn't let his personal distaste get in the way of his judgement.

He paused a little longer. *Let the bastard sweat a bit before he gets his way.*

"Well?" asked Visser.

"All right, three hundred thousand then."

"Plus expenses."

Reinholdt looked hard at the South African. "It better be worth it."

"It will be. Where can I contact you?"

The American handed him a piece of paper with a phone number on it. "Please destroy this immediately you've memorised the number."

"Naturally." Visser took from his pocket another piece of paper. "And please destroy this when you've finished. It's my bank and account number. Shall we say an advance of fifty thousand dollars?"

"Very well," said Reinholdt. "Where can I contact you?"

"You can't," said Visser simply.

"We're paying you three hundred thousand bucks and we can't contact you?"

"It's not the way I work."

"You ever hear the phrase 'He who pays the piper'?"

"Yes, lots of dead agents believed it. I'll be in contact daily. More often if there's anything to report."

Reinholdt looked at him and sensed that there was no point in pushing the other man on this. "OK then. But the minute there's anything. This really is crucial." He opened the car door, then turned and looked at Visser. "Good luck."

"Thank you. Have a nice day."

Reinholdt closed the car door and walked away. He sensed that the South African had been mocking him, aware as he was that other nationalities found the American admonition to have a nice day somewhat amusing.

To hell with it, he thought. It doesn't matter if I like Visser or he likes me. The important thing was to find out what had happened with SMORTAR. And if there was one person who could unearth that information, he had no doubt it would be Jan Visser.

12

Just in case she had missed anything, Penny went through the data again. It was ten thirty on Saturday night and she was tired, but she had taken to heart Thompson's dictum that cases were broken by vigilant officers latching on to some tiny slip.

Since the radio appeals of the previous day a number of people who had been in the area at the time in question had come forward. They had been questioned by Thompson and Carrow, and it was the transcripts of these interviews that Penny was painstakingly reviewing. She knew that the statements were all the more important since the car had been located in the lock-up garage. The significance of the abandoned van had increased now that it appeared that Gatenby's own car hadn't figured in his escape or possible abduction.

Despite being questioned in detail, none of those who had come forward so far had seen anything untoward, and their own behaviour – on the surface at any rate – seemed entirely lacking in suspicion.

124

"Worked out who the villain is?"

Penny looked up to see Thompson standing by her desk. She had been so engrossed that she hadn't heard him approach, but she smiled and shook her head ruefully. "Waiting for that blinding flash of inspiration – but it hasn't come."

"Here, try this; keep you awake, anyroads," said Thompson, handing her a mug of coffee.

"Thanks." She took the mug gratefully and sipped the hot drink. It struck her that it was typical of Thompson not to think himself too grand to bring coffee to a junior. In fact, she had been impressed throughout the investigation by his ability to get things done quickly and efficiently, yet though there was never any doubt who was in charge, he managed to operate with the minimum of fuss, largely due to his excellent rapport with his staff.

The only thing that made Penny uneasy in her relationship with him was the recognition of her own wish to impress Thompson with her professionalism. She knew she had been extremely lucky to be seconded to work with him, but she had nevertheless been angry at herself for wanting too much to win his approval.

At first she had feared it was because she wished to prove herself as good as, if not better than, her mostly male colleagues – something she had always felt should be unnecessary for women officers – but then she had realised that Thompson was the sort of natural leader who inspired everyone who worked for him, and she told herself she would probably have wanted to impress him just as much were she a man.

Now in the late-night quiet of the Incident Room

Thompson sat back easily and yawned. "Been a long day."

"I'll drink to that," answered Penny, raising her mug.

Thompson glanced at his watch. "Twenty-five to eleven. Most of the others are gone, Penny. If you want to head off . . ."

"No thanks, Chief. I said I'd wait till you get the call from Mr Carrow. There might be something."

"Shouldn't be too much longer; I suppose this has mucked up your Saturday night anyway."

Penny thought of the cancelled night out with the members of her tennis team but didn't mention it. "There'll be other Saturday nights," she said philosophically.

Thompson smiled. "How many times have I said that to the wife . . ."

"Does she mind?" Penny asked.

"Pretends not to for my sake. No problem tonight though, she's in Manchester – RSPCA conference. I can burn the midnight oil with a clear conscience. So . . . how are you finding detective work?"

"Fascinating, I'm really hooked."

"The first few days on a big crime are all activity – expect a bit of a let-down when we go through the hard slog part."

"OK."

"Getting on all right with the others?"

"Fine. I half-expected there might be a bit of resentment . . ."

"Really?"

"You know – young-whipper-snapper-working-with-the-boss sort of thing – but they've been great."

126

"Aye. They're a good team; they'd be too professional for that kind of nonsense. Oh, and talking about nonsense – you don't have to take it from Carrow, but be careful. He's a Chief Superintendent and he can be vindictive."

"You knew I was going to respond yesterday, when he said about blabbering to a boyfriend."

"That's why I cut in," Thompson smiled. "There's no love lost between Len Carrow and me. But for your own sake, watch your step with him."

"OK. Thanks, Chief."

"What do you make of our other friend?" asked Thompson.

"Mr Mathieson?"

"Aye, the James Bond of the North Country."

Penny laughed. "I don't know about that – he didn't get that accent in Yorkshire."

"Oh no, our Mr Mathieson would be strictly Home Counties."

"He does seem quite urbane," said Penny.

"Good-looking bugger too – if I'm allowed say that . . ."

Penny smiled. "Only if you like that type. "

"You don't?"

"Not really, not that that's of any consequence."

"Right."

"The thing is, although he seems very laid-back, I sense . . . I don't know. Despite being pleasant, I could imagine him being devious, ruthless even."

Thompson looked at her directly. "You're good at reading people," he said seriously. "Very important in a detective."

Penny felt flattered and was about to make some

kind of joking response, but when Thompson continued he was still serious.

"You're quite right not to be fobbed off by the *Boy's Own* air. He's no starry-eyed subaltern – if indeed he was ever starry-eyed."

"You reckon he's ex-army?"

Thompson nodded. "Tell them a mile off. Saw enough of them in my time."

"You were in the army?"

Thompson sipped his coffee, then replied. "National Service. Chasing bloody EOKA terrorists in Cyprus."

Penny was intrigued and decided to probe a little while her boss was in reflective mood. "What was it like?" she asked.

"National Service or chasing terrorists?"

"Either."

Thompson paused, then smiled. "They were both bloody awful."

"My dad was called up too, just before conscription ended."

"How did he find it?"

"Not to his liking. He was sent to Aden and hated every minute of it!"

"Best thing they ever did, scrapping conscription – bloody daft idea."

"You didn't fancy army life?"

Thompson put the mug down and shook his head. "Too much bowing and scraping wanted. Not in my nature."

"Did they give you a hard time?"

"They gave everyone a hard time, but I made the

mistake of getting on the wrong side of our officer."
Thompson looked up suddenly at Penny. "But all this
was before your time. I mustn't bore you . . ."

"No," she said, "I'm really interested. Honestly.
What happened with the officer?"

Thompson stared into space a moment, then spoke
more softly. "He was beating an EOKA suspect with
a stick. And, believe me, I'd no love for EOKA. They
could be right . . ." He paused, then smiled wryly.
"Oh, I can say it in front of you, can't I? Well, they
could be right bastards – I suppose like terrorists
everywhere. This bloke was only a suspect though; and
our lieutenant was beating him senseless while his
hands were tied behind his back. I didn't want to take
on the system, but . . . well, I couldn't just stand
watching . . ."

"What did you do?"

Thompson smiled ruefully. "I was only nineteen, so
it probably sounded a bit self-righteous . . . but I told him
the British Army wasn't in Cyprus to torture the locals."

"And what happened?"

"I managed to stop the beating but I was a marked
man. Every dirty job, every dangerous patrol – JF
Thompson was chosen."

"That's so unfair."

"That was the Army. I wasn't their type and after a
while I stopped trying to be. The leopard can't change
his spots . . ." Suddenly Thompson smiled. "If he could
I might be Chief Constable by now instead of a Chief
Inspector."

"You wouldn't really want that though, would you?"

129

"No, I leave jockeying for position to the Carrows of this world."

Penny was dying to hear more but was afraid to push too much. Keeping her voice reasonably neutral she said, "You don't like Mr Carrow very much . . ."

"I don't like his style of policing."

"He does have a – a combative approach. Especially on the terrorist angle."

"His brother was killed in Northern Ireland," said Thompson, "serving with the Parachute Regiment."

"Oh, well, I suppose that would explain it."

"Only in part. Long before that he was always . . . heavy-handed, shall we say. He's from Yorkshire originally, and years ago when we were young constables together, I remember -"

Just then the phone rang, and Penny felt a stab of frustration at having an insight into the Special Branch man cut short.

"Thompson speaking . . ."

Sitting close by, Penny could hear both sides of the conversation.

"Carrow here, I said I'd get back."

"Thank you. Any luck?"

"No. We've run the computer check on those who came forward from the radio appeal. Nothing on any of them."

"And the names and numbers in Gatenby's address book?"

"No joy there either," answered Carrow. "What about your end – nothing from the local search, I suppose?"

"Afraid not. We combed the area adjoining the van and we'll extend to neighbouring areas at first light."

"Waste of bloody manpower if you ask me."

Penny noticed Thompson drawing in his breath, but he kept his tone reasonable.

"It won't be a waste of time if we turn up something."

"You haven't and you won't, not plodding the fields. This Gatenby bastard's covered his tracks."

"Well, perhaps we plodders can uncover them . . ."

"Right. Keep me posted. Goodnight."

"Goodnight." Thompson put the phone down and turned around. "When you're Chief Constable someday, Penny, don't become like that."

"I'll try not to," she replied with a grin.

Thompson rose. "Come on, let's call it a night."

She got up and they made for the door.

"It'd be nice to see Mr Carrow's eye wiped by mere plodders," said Thompson, "so get a good night's sleep. We've a murderer to catch – and we're going to get there first."

"Amen to that," said Penny as they walked out the door.

13

Jan Visser savoured his sense of anticipation. The first contact with a quarry always generated a thrill, and as he reached now for the phone he felt in control, yet excited.

He had chosen a medium-sized hotel that had two phone booths in a corridor outside the lounge, and as he had expected there were few people around the side corridor at 10.00 a.m. on a Monday morning. He dialled the number and was promptly answered.

"Good morning, Iranian Embassy."

"Good morning, I'd like to speak to Mr Ali qi Aksor please."

"Whom shall I say is calling?"

"Bruce Kenny."

"Of?"

"The Melbourne Post."

"One moment please."

"Thank you." Visser waited, pleased at how authentic his Australian accent sounded. There was a click on the line and he heard a man's voice.

"Aksor speaking, may I help you?" The tone was confident, the English easy and assured.

"Good morning, Mr Aksor. My name is Bruce Kenny. I'm a journalist with *The Melbourne Post*."

"What can I do for you, Mr Kenny?"

"It's more what I can do for you. I've just got in from the Middle East and I was asked to give you a message . . ."

"I see . . . may I ring you back in a few minutes?"

Visser smiled to himself. He had reckoned the Iranian would be afraid his phone was bugged. "How many minutes?"

"Say . . . five."

Visser smiled again. *The public phone booth around the corner from the embassy.* "OK. Five minutes then."

He gave the number of the payphone, then hung up. Reaching into his jacket pocket, he took out a small card with OUT OF ORDER written on it, glanced around to ensure no one was watching, and stuck it to the telephone with Blu-tack. He moved to the adjacent booth and took out the directory, pretending to look through it as he waited for the return call.

Nobody came near however, and when the phone rang he answered it immediately, removing the card and the Blu-tack at the same time.

"Mr Kenny?"

"Yes."

"I can talk a little more freely here. May I ask who the message is from?"

"You may, but I'm hardly going to give names over the phone. I think we should meet."

133

"Forgive me, but this isn't some . . . journalistic ploy?"

"It's nothing to do with journalism. I've just returned from Beirut, where I believe you have contacts. I've information for you regarding . . . let's say a recently disappeared associate . . ."

There was a long pause. "I see . . ." said Aksor.

"Suffice it to say it will be very much in your interest to have this information . . ." Visser waited, then after a further pause Aksor spoke.

"Very well, Mr Kenny. Where are you now?"

He was taking the bait. Play a little hard to get now, thought Visser, just to hook him. "Where I am now is of no consequence. I'll meet you tonight."

"If it's that important I'd like to have the information sooner."

"It'll keep till this evening. I'll meet you at nine o'clock in the lounge of the Cherry Tree pub. It's just off the Mile End Road near Stepney. Got that?"

"Yes, all right. How will I know you?"

"I'll be sitting beside the lounge door, reading a copy of *The Daily Telegraph*."

"OK."

"Oh and Mr Aksor – come alone. What I have to tell you is *strictly* for your ears."

"Understood."

"See you tonight then."

"All right."

Visser hung up, checked that no one was looking, quickly wiped his prints from both telephones and walked out of the hotel.

It had gone well, and now he had the rest of the day to make the necessary arrangements. He would inform Reinholdt that a meeting was set up but he wouldn't tell the American the details of what he had in mind. For by midnight tonight he expected Mr Aksor would be doing a lot of talking. Talking after first screaming for mercy. It was going to be an enjoyable mission, he just knew it . . .

14

Mary sat in the Green Room, pretending to study her script. The studio schedule on the wall indicated Monday 11.00 a.m. for the recording of her next scene, but although it was only half an hour away, she couldn't keep her thoughts on her role – a problem she had had since Dave's arrival home the previous Thursday.

Glancing across the room, she saw Arnold Beazley, soundlessly yet ostentatiously mouthing his lines, and she thought how ironic it was that their flare-up had actually been timely. She knew that the other actors would now attribute any tension on her part over the last few days to the strained atmosphere that prevailed after the row with Beazley.

Despite her initial opposition to Dave's plan of lying low, she had subsequently immersed herself in the cover-up, and they had deliberately had a busy weekend, providing themselves with alibis for as much of it as possible. On Sunday afternoon she had had a telephone call from her brother Tom in Ireland, during which she had striven hard to sound normal. Tom was completely trustworthy, but this wasn't a problem she wanted to burden him with, and she hoped the strain hadn't shown in her voice as they had chatted.

Now as she looked back on their weekend activities, her thoughts returned to Dave's car. He had used the car to move Gatenby's body from the woods to the edge of the tarn, and Mary's big fear had been forensics. She had watched enough television to know what the police could do with fibres of clothes or minute samples of blood or tissue. Dave had wanted to drive to Manchester to have the car valeted there, but she had vetoed the proposal. If for some reason the police ever came to suspect them it was just the kind of thing they might check. Far better, she had argued, to avoid being on anyone's records.

And so they had washed the car and scrubbed the interior themselves, finally scuffing the boot lightly to disguise the fact that it had been so thoroughly and recently cleaned. Surely they had taken every reasonable precaution, she reasoned, and yet her mind kept running over their actions, kept seeking the tiny fatal error they might have made. Dave had told her that he had collected the gun from the forest floor and placed it in Gatenby's jacket before weighing the body down, so that was another potential loose end taken care of. Had anything else been overlooked? she wondered.

Her thoughts were interrupted by the ringing of the wall telephone, which Beazley rose and answered.

"Greenroom," be intoned theatrically. "Yes, she is. A moment, if you would . . ."

Why did he always have to sound like a character in a fifties play, Mary thought.

Beazley turned to her. "Telephone call for Ms Adams," he said, with just a hint of mockery on the 'Ms.'

"Thank you," said Mary as she rose heavily and crossed to the phone.

"Hello, Mary Adams here."

"Putting you through to Dave, Mary. One moment please . . ."

There was a click, then she heard Dave's voice.

"Mary?"

"Hi."

"Hi. I was just thinking about my chat on Friday – with Mr Thompson . . ."

Mary realised he was talking carefully in case his line wasn't secure. "Oh yes?" she said, keeping her tone casual.

"It occurred to me he might want to double-check the times – with *you*, this time. It *was* around half five or six when I got home, wasn't it?"

"Yes, that's right."

"Once we're both sure about that, in case he wishes to confirm it . . ."

Mary turned and realised that Beazley was listening surreptitiously. She smiled into the phone. "Yes, I can see how he might want to do that," she answered brightly.

Dave immediately picked up on the change of tone. "Turkish Delight available for tea break there?"

"Yes, indeed."

"Well, I just thought I'd check the time."

"Fine, I'll be able to confirm that – if asked. Everything else OK?"

"Yes. Talk to you tonight. Better run now."

"All right. Bye, love."

"Bye."

Mary hung up and glanced over at Beazley. He was casually fingering his cravat with one hand while holding his script in the other.

She crossed to her armchair, aware that he had listened to her end of the conversation. It shouldn't matter, she had kept her utterances entirely non-incriminating, but she wished yet again that the involvement with the police hadn't been forced on them. However well Dave felt the interview with Thompson had gone, it still meant that he was now known to the authorities. The thought scared her, even when she told herself that once they stuck to their story they could brazen it out. She leaned back in the armchair, script in hand, but her thoughts had never been further from Oscar Wilde . . .

15

Chief Superintendent Carrow had a bad feeling about the case. Everyone else in Leeds seemed to have been cheered up by the settled spell of glorious weather, but Carrow couldn't shake off the unease he had felt from the beginning.

He had been doing particularly well at a clay-pigeon shoot near his home in Surrey when Special Branch HQ in London had paged him and despatched him to Yorkshire, and although he didn't believe in omens, nonetheless he had sensed that it would be a difficult case. Just the sort that could affect his career if handled badly, yet which if pursued successfully would mean lots of damage limitation – a situation not conducive to rewarding good police work.

He had only been forty-seven when promoted to Chief Superintendent, four years previously, and with his ambition far from sated he knew his handling of this case was crucial.

The previous Friday's interviews with David Walker

and Belal Hussief had yielded nothing worthwhile, the only point of interest being that Walker and Hussief had driven through the area involved. Carrow was mulling over a large-scale map of the Dales, tracing Walker's route, when his phone rang. "Carrow?"

"I have a Mr Mathieson for you, sir," said the operator.

"Right, put him through." *Mathieson.* He wasn't quite sure what to make of the intelligence officer, but he had sensed an air of ruthlessness in him, despite the suave exterior and upper-class drawl. No harm in staying on the right side of this one, he thought, as the call came through. "Good morning, Mr Mathieson. Carrow speaking . . ."

"Morning, Mr Carrow. Any progress from your end?"

"Nothing dramatic. Going through Gatenby's house with a fine-tooth comb and following up the radio responses. Anything at your end?"

"Yes, actually," answered Mathieson. "My associates in London have just received some interesting mail."

"Really?"

"Appears that the – the goods misplaced last Thursday have been returned."

"Returned?!"

"Yes, posted to the Ministry . . ."

"Good Lord!"

"Quite. Plain brown envelope, posted in London. Definitely the originals and entirely intact."

"That's – that's an interesting development, to put it mildly . . ."

"Indeed. I have to confer with my associates in London later this afternoon, but I thought we should get together with Chief Inspector Thompson – then I can brief my superiors on the latest state of play."

"Of course," answered Carrow. "I'll see Thompson and set up a meeting if you like. It's just eleven thirty now; how about twelve thirty at the incident room?"

"Fine. Should I speak to Thompson personally perhaps?"

"No need really. I have to talk to him anyway," Carrow lied easily.

"Right, twelve thirty it is. Talk to you then."

"Cheers." Carrow lowered the phone, his mind racing. Perhaps the case might go well after all; getting the film back certainly achieved an important goal. And ringing Thompson to pass on the news would give him an edge over the CID man. Thompson was an effective detective, but far too independent for Carrow's liking. No harm at all to break the news to him, let him feel that Special Branch was higher in the pecking order than Thompson's investigation team.

Feeling better now, Carrow leaned back in his chair, lifted the phone, and dialled Thompson's extension.

The warm noonday sunshine streamed into the office off the incident room, but Carrow was unconscious of it in his eagerness to get down to business. Mathieson sat opposite him, the sunbeams backlighting his thick dark hair as he leaned back in his chair, exuding an air of unflappability that Carrow found vaguely irritating.

Thompson entered, followed as usual by his assistant, Penny Hart. Although he did not like her manner, Carrow had to admit that with her fine features, jet-black hair, and sallow complexion, she was quite striking-looking, and he wondered if there was something going on there with Thompson.

"Sorry to keep you, gentlemen," said Thompson, as they sat.

Sorry my eye, thought Carrow. He's making the point that this investigation is being run by CID – well, nominally, at any rate.

"So," said Thompson, "the film has been mysteriously returned."

Mathieson nodded. "Arrived at the MOD this morning."

"And the postmark?" asked Thompson.

"Friday. Sent in the London area."

"Any note or message?"

Mathieson shook his head. "Just the film, undamaged and intact."

The Inspector smiled briefly. "That must have been a relief."

"Indeed," answered Mathieson

"So who goes to the trouble of acquiring the film and then returning it?" asked Carrow.

"Well, getting it from Gatenby for cash sounds like an intelligence operation; getting it by force more like a terrorist one," said Thompson.

Mathieson shrugged. "Except that neither would be likely to send it back."

"Supposing Gatenby sent it back himself?" suggested

Thompson. "Supposing he never gave it to anyone, had second thoughts?"

"Or perhaps copied the film and sent back the original," put in Carrow, "hoping to take the heat off?"

"That's possible," said Mathieson. "In either case, the key is locating Gatenby."

Thompson nodded in agreement. "Absolutely. There's a major check being run at all points of exit. I'm convinced we'll nab him if he tries a runner. Meanwhile we're pulling out all the stops to locate him if he's still here."

"My gut instinct says it's not Gatenby alone," said Carrow. "The whole thing smacks of subversives."

"Any idea whom, from the modus operandi?" asked Mathieson.

"Could be Red Army Faction, IRA, Fundamentalists . . ."

Except they all know how the police work," said Thompson, "and they'd realise that we wouldn't give up just because we got the film back; so it doesn't seem very rational to copy and return it."

"Maybe it wasn't rational," said Penny.

Carrow looked at her in surprise. He had regarded her protégée role with Thompson as dubious to begin with; now it seemed she wanted to contribute as an equal. Before he had a chance to show his displeasure, Mathieson had turned to her.

"How do you mean, not rational?" he asked.

"Well, all our theories presume that what happened was rational, planned for," she answered. "But suppose it wasn't?"

"Go on," the intelligence officer encouraged.

"Well, it's just occurred to me now, so I haven't

really thought it through, but supposing Gatenby's van did break down, and what happened to him then was a spur of the moment thing?"

"You don't normally abduct someone on the spur of the moment," said Carrow.

"Perhaps he wasn't abducted – perhaps he was assaulted."

"By whom?"

"I don't know, sir," she answered. "But if some – psychopath say, attacked and killed him, it would explain why he hasn't shown up, and possibly the return of the film."

"The psychopath, being a patriot, posts back the film?" asked Carrow sarcastically.

"Stranger things have happened," said Thompson. "Such people's minds work in odd ways."

"It's a possibility we shouldn't rule out," said Mathieson, "but I'm not sure what steps we could take to follow it up."

"Well, I assume the film and envelope are being checked for prints?" said Thompson.

Mathieson nodded. "As we speak."

Carrow shook his head dismissively. "There won't be any prints. This wasn't the work of some raving lunatic bumping into Gatenby."

"We'll see," said Thompson. "Actually there's another possibility if we follow the 'unplanned' line of thinking."

"What's that?" asked Mathieson.

"A hit-and-run driver. Killed him by accident, or through drunkenness . . ."

"And took away the body as a souvenir?" interjected Carrow sarcastically.

"Might possibly have hidden the body," mused Mathieson. "Though somehow I don't see it . . ."

"I don't think it's particularly likely myself," said Thompson. "However, the ground searchers will work their way through every ditch, wood and stream for miles around."

"Fair enough," said Mathieson. "To go back to those who answered the radio appeal – I don't suppose any of them has a criminal record, dubious associations?"

"I'm afraid not," the inspector answered. "What we really need is for someone to describe a walker or a driver who *hasn't* come forward."

"Quite," replied Mathieson. "Meanwhile, what's your next move?"

"Go back painstakingly over the statements of those who have come forward. Try to piece together a picture of what might have happened."

"How many non-locals have responded to the radio appeals so far?" asked Carrow.

"Six who were in the general area. Here's the list," replied Thompson, passing each of them a photocopied sheet of paper. "Jenny Wallace and her seventy-six-year-old mother, out for a drive. Came down from Newbiggin, through Buckden, on to Grassington. Ben Murray, a pensioner out painting near Kettlewell. Ralph Taylor, a civil servant on holidays from Kent. Hiking near Hubberholme."

"Civil servant? What sort?" asked Mathieson.

"Nothing sensitive, works in the VAT section of the

Inland Revenue. Then there's Anne-Marie Fabien," continued Thompson.

"Belgian au pair who was taking photographs near Arncliffe. Belal Hussief, a social worker, bringing a child to Appleby. And finally David Walker, advertising executive, on his way to Harrogate from Carlisle." Thompson looked up and shrugged. "It's not much to go on, but pending a lead from some other source, these people are the best we have."

"In that case let's get working on them," said Mathieson. "Agreed?"

"Agreed," answered the others.

16

Jan Visser awaited his man. Parked down the road from the Cherry Tree public house, he had a clear view of the front entrance, and he could feel his excitement mounting as he waited for the Iranian diplomat.

The rented van in which Visser sat had been booked in the name of Richard Jeffries, using a false Canadian driver's licence, and the South African now wore the same baseball hat and dark glasses that he had worn when collecting the van as Jeffries. The chance of anyone noting the appearance of a man sitting in a parked van were slim, but nevertheless he had retained the disguise.

He had been waiting about twenty-five minutes when he saw a taxi pull to a halt opposite the pub. A dark-skinned well-dressed man of about thirty got out, crossed the road, and entered the pub. Confident that he had spotted his man, Visser checked his watch and smiled. 8.55 – Aksor was obviously eager for the meeting.

Starting his ignition, Visser pulled out onto the road

and drove around the block. He turned left twice, then pulled into the Cherry Tree's large rear car park. He drove to the furthest corner and parked in an area partly secluded by mature cherry trees in riotous blossom. There were quite a few other parked cars, but the area was devoid of customers. Visser picked up his mobile phone and dialled the pub's number. A cockney voice answered on the third ring.

"Hello, Cherry Tree."

"I'd like to speak to a Mr Aksor, please," said Visser in his assumed Australian accent.

"Aksor, he ain't a regular. You sure he's here?"

"Yeah. Arab bloke in a blue suit."

"Hang on then."

Visser waited, then recognised the Iranian's voice as he came on the line.

"Hello?"

"Hello,Mr Aksor. Bruce Kenny here."

"Mr Kenny, I thought we were to meet in person."

"Still are, mate, still are. Head out the back door and walk to the far end of the car park. There's a row of cherry trees along the boundary wall. I'll be waiting at the last one."

"Why not meet here in the pub? There are plenty of quiet corners."

Visser detected a note of caution in the Iranian's voice. "Plenty of quiet corners but plenty of people too; I'd rather be discreet."

"Then why choose a pub in the first place?"

"To make sure you arrived alone, before contacting you."

"Then you'll know I did come alone. That makes me wary of meeting a stranger in a secluded car park."

Visser injected an impatient edge into his voice. "I told you I was on your side, but if you're not interested in what I've to say, there are others who certainly will be."

There was a pause and Visser stayed silent, allowing the other man to reach his decision.

"All right," the Iranian responded, "the last cherry tree. I'm on my way."

"Fine." Visser put the phone down, then got out of the van. Just as he did a car pulled into the car park. Visser quickly moved behind the overhanging cherry tree and went to the rear of the van, unlocked the back and waited there, out of sight. He watched as a man in black slacks and a white shirt got out of the parked car and entered the pub without glancing again at the parked van.

A moment later Aksor emerged, looked about, then moved along the boundary wall. Visser watched unseen as his quarry approached gingerly, dabbing perspiration from his forehead in the lingering warmth of the summer evening.

Visser felt his pulses racing, aware that his plan depended on the car park remaining deserted. He stepped suddenly from behind the van as the Iranian approached. "Mr Aksor, we meet at last." He smiled and extended his hand.

The man, obviously on guard, nevertheless took his hand and shook it firmly. "I'm eager to hear your information, Mr Kenny."

"I don't think you'll be disappointed," answered Visser with a grin. A quick glance past the overhanging cherry tree told him that the car park was still deserted and he immediately looked again towards the Iranian.

"In fact, the people in Beirut who asked me . . ." Visser trailed off and looked worriedly back towards the pub.

Aksor turned to follow his gaze, and in the moment that he turned Visser pulled a truncheon from the waistband of his trousers and landed a stunning blow on the other man's head. The Iranian slumped, and Visser immediately landed a second blow with the heavy rubber truncheon.

Another glance assured him that the car park was still empty. He quickly dragged his unconscious victim to the back of the van, opened the rear door, and bundled him in. Jumping in himself, he immediately closed over the door and took two open sets of handcuffs from the floor. With the first set he secured the Iranian's hands behind his back, then he secured his ankles with the second pair, looping the connecting chain through a floor bracket. He forced a length of strong cotton cloth into the unconscious man's mouth as a gag, then bound it on firmly with pre-cut strips of masking tape.

Moving rapidly, Visser opened a small first-aid box. He withdrew a syringe, administered an injection into Aksor's wrist, then covered the body with a blanket.

He got out the back, closed the rear door, climbed into the driver's seat and started the engine. He drove through the car park, the baseball cap low over his face, but no one came out of the pub, and he felt a wave of exhilaration as he drove towards the main road heading for the docks.

He was looking forward to going to work on Aksor when he got him to the derelict warehouse he had rented. Looking forward to it very much. Yes, he thought, it was good to be back in business.

The blaring radio had reverberated through the basement for hours, making the sudden silence all the more shocking when the machine was finally switched off. Despite the late-night chill Visser was soaked in sweat from his exertions, yet there was a spring in his step as he crossed back from the radio to the table.

Aksor lay spread-eagled on the table, his naked body a ghastly mass of charred flesh. Visser turned off the blowtorch, then looked with satisfaction at the dead Iranian. He had been a worthy opponent and had taken a long time to break – just the kind of challenge Visser liked.

Despite working in the basement of an isolated dockland warehouse, the blaring radio had been needed to drown the man's screams of pain and defiance, but in the end he had talked, as Visser knew he eventually would.

Glancing at his watch, he saw that it was three minutes to one. Plenty of time to dispose of the body in a marsh he knew in the North Downs and still get a few hours' sleep before briefing Reinholdt.

It had seemed to Visser that for a senior CIA man

Bob Reinholdt was something of a bleeding heart, and not the type to shrug off the news that Aksor had died under interrogation – until he heard what had been extracted from him. Yes, thought Visser, then he would know that he had chosen the right man for this case. It would be enjoyable to watch the American's face when he heard what Visser had to tell him. Meanwhile he had to clean up and dispose of Aksor. Turning away from the table, he went to collect the body bag from the van, fulfilled and still stimulated by his night's work.

17

Penny felt her excitement mounting as she drove. The sunlit Yorkshire countryside slipped past in a green blur as she navigated automatically, her mind on what would happen when she got to Harrogate. She was both delighted and apprehensive about Thompson allowing her to call alone on Mary Adams. It had been the Chief's idea to call unannounced on David Walker's wife, allegedly to clarify the time of her husband's arrival home the previous Thursday, in reality to probe for any differences in their stories.

Penny had tentatively suggested that a solo visit from another woman might result in the subject being less on guard. Thompson had considered it for only a moment before agreeing, then altered his own plans with a view to further questioning Anne-Marie Fabien, the Belgian au pair who had been taking photographs near Arncliffe.

Penny's initial pleasure at the compliment inherent

in Thompson's trusting her was now giving way to concern. She mustn't let the Chief down; she mustn't miss any detail during her conversation with Mary Adams.

Reaching the outskirts of Harrogate, she pulled in to the side of the road. She consulted her map of the town, then sat in the car and breathed slowly and deeply for several moments. She must suppress her excitement, she told herself, and forget that this was her first solo enquiry in her first murder investigation.

She continued the deep breathing a little longer, then, satisfied that this was as calm as she was going to get, she started the engine and drove into Harrogate.

Mary was startled by the knocking as she sat in her workshop cleaning a sheet of stained glass. Placing the glass carefully down on her bench, she moved to the door, curious and alarmed as to who could be calling to the house at ten o'clock on a Tuesday morning. She closed the workshop door behind her, crossed the neatly trimmed lawn, and went around the side of the bungalow, reaching the front garden in time to see a young woman knocking loudly again. "Can I help you?" she asked.

The woman turned around quickly, her black hair shining in the sunlight.

"Sorry if I startled you," said Mary. "I was round the back."

"Forgive me for knocking so loudly," the other woman said, "but when I saw the car I reckoned you were probably about somewhere."

155

She smiled pleasantly, and Mary found herself smiling back. "That's OK. I wouldn't have heard you otherwise."

"Ms Adams, is it?"

"Yes."

"I'm Detective Constable Hart. Penny Hart."

Mary felt her hair rise on end but she kept her smile in place as they shook hands.

"We were very grateful to your husband for answering our radio appeal."

"He was glad to help," replied Mary.

"I was wondering if perhaps you could help us a little, Ms Adams?"

"Me?"

"We'd just like to talk a bit more about times last Thursday."

"Surely Dave is the one to talk to?"

"I couldn't get through to United Advertising on the phone this morning. And I had to drive out to Ripon anyway, so I thought I'd drop in on spec. I hope you don't mind."

"Not at all," answered Mary easily. "The house keys are in my workshop . . ."

"We can chat in the workshop if that's handier," suggested Penny.

"All right. It's round the back," said Mary. She had managed to keep her manner casual but her heart was pounding madly. She figured that this had to be a test by the police to see how well co-ordinated their alibis were – for she knew that there was nothing wrong with United Advertising's telephones, having herself phoned Dave twenty minutes previously. She was going to have to give a very careful performance here, she realised.

As they crossed the lawn she spoke to the policewoman, pleased at how normal her voice sounded. "You were lucky to catch me on a day off. I'm working all tomorrow and Thursday."

"Really? I was fortunate then . . ."

I doubt it, thought Mary. Probably rang the BBC and checked my schedule. "Now, in here," she said, ushering the detective into her workshop. She saw the younger woman taking in the neat rows of cut glass, stains and enamels.

"Stained glass – it's my hobby." She pulled out a couple of stools and passed one to the policewoman before sitting herself.

"This is really good," said Penny, indicating a three-quarters-finished piece.

"Thank you. It's a commission for the shopping centre in town."

"I'm impressed."

"Keeps me out of mischief when I'm not acting," said Mary. "Pays better too . . ."

Penny turned from the glasswork, sat on the stool, and looked at Mary directly. "Talking of acting, I'm sure I've seen you in something. "

"I did some stuff on TV a few years ago . . ."

"No, I think this was more recently . . . I . . . wait now, I have it! Weren't you in *Time and the Conways*?"

"Yorkshire Playhouse, January fourth to February second," Mary said, smiling. "Guilty as charged."

"It was wonderful – and so were you."

"Thank you very much."

"But your hair . . ."

"Ah – a black wig. The rest of the family were dark-haired, so . . ." Mary indicated her blonde hair and smiled ruefully.

"I see. Any other parts coming up?"

"Yes, *Separate Tables*. I'm in a radio version about to be broadcast. Obviously I'll only be doing radio work till after this production," she said, indicating the bump in her maternity smock.

"When's the baby due?"

"June the 29th."

The policewoman smiled. "Getting close."

"Don't remind me."

"Your first?"

"Yes."

"Congratulations."

"Thank you."

"Well, to business, I suppose," said Penny as she settled on her stool and took out a notepad. "We're just trying to get a better picture of timescales for those who were in the Dales last Thursday."

"When this incident – whatever it was – occurred?"

"Yes."

"I take it my husband's not the only one involved?"

"No, there were several others in the general area."

Thank God for that, thought Mary. "The thing is though, as I wasn't actually with Dave, I can't be precise about the times."

"But you were here when he got in?"

"Yes."

"What time would that have been?"

Mary gave the impression of casting her mind back. "About half five, six."

"Would it have been nearer to half five or six, would you think?"

Mary shrugged. "I'm sorry but I really can't remember."

"Were you working yourself last Thursday?"

"Yes, in BBC Leeds."

"And what time did you leave there?"

"I think about half three."

"Off-peak it's about a thirty-minute drive to Harrogate, so you'd have been in around four?"

"Something like that," said Mary.

"How long do you feel you'd been in when your husband arrived?"

"I'd been home a while. Maybe . . . an hour and a half, two hours – I wasn't watching the clock."

"No, of course not." The policewoman put down her notepad, then looked again at Mary. "Does your husband have a car phone?"

"Yes."

"Did he ring you on Thursday afternoon?"

"No, no, he didn't ring on Thursday at all."

"Even though he'd been away for two days?"

"He'd rung the previous night, and I was going to see him on Thursday evening . . ."

Penny looked at her searchingly, but Mary held her gaze.

"Fair enough," said the policewoman. She smiled and rose from her stool. "Well, I won't keep you from the work any longer. Thank you very much for your time."

"You're welcome," said Mary, hoping the relief didn't show in her voice as she moved to open the workshop door.

"It's OK," said Penny, moving ahead of her, "I'll see myself out." She stepped out of the workshop, then turned back to Mary. "Oh, one last thing."

"Yes?"

"What day is *Separate Tables* being broadcast – I'd love to hear it?"

"Next Friday. Eight in the evening."

"I'll try to catch it. Bye, Ms Adams."

"Bye."

Mary watched the young woman cross the lawn, then she stepped back into her workshop and closed the door. She stood with her back to the wall, trying to steady her nerves.

Maybe they were doing this to everyone who had come forward, she reasoned. Maybe it was just her own guilt that made innocuous questions seem ominous. And yet there had been the moment when she had locked eyes with the policewoman. She had sensed then that they both knew there was more going on than simple clarification of times. Still, she had said nothing incriminating, nothing at odds with Dave's story. All they had to do was keep their nerve.

She moved back to the stained-glass window and began working again, but somehow it was mechanical now and unsatisfying, and she knew the young policewoman had taken the good out of her day.

Penny sat in the car, marshalling her thoughts. Everything Mary Adams had said sounded reasonable and in keeping with her husband's statement. And yet something didn't quite ring true.

Penny went through the interview again in her head, then suddenly realised what it was. Vagueness. The woman had shrugged vaguely and spoken of perhaps getting home at four, perhaps seeing her husband at half five or six. Yet nothing else about her was vague. The lines of different-coloured glass were meticulously separated; her stains and enamels were neatly stored on marked shelves; she had not said she had been in *Time and the Conways* several months ago, but from January the fourth to February the second.

Was it significant that she seemed vague only about the time of her and her husband's arrival home? Or was it all perfectly normal? Maybe I'm making a mountain of a molehill, thought Penny. Maybe I'm too eager to have something to report back to Thompson. And after all it could have been a normal nervousness of police questioning that created a suggestion of cautiousness behind the woman's pleasant manner.

Penny reflected a few moments more, then decided that she would mention a slight – but only very slight – unease when she reported back to Thompson. Starting the car, she drove off, still undecided as to whether her first murder enquiry had yielded anything or not.

18

"It's absolute bullshit!" said Dave. The setting sun cast an amber glow over the kitchen as he and Mary sat at the table, cradling cups of coffee. "Dropping in here on spec because United Advertising's phones are on the blink? What do the police think we are – idiots?"

"Maybe it was deliberately obvious," suggested Mary, "to try and scare us."

"Yeah, that occurred to me too. Having said that, she admitted others were on their list. Maybe they're getting the third degree as well."

"I hope so," said Mary. "That policewoman is smart. No matter how watertight we keep our story, I'd hate to be getting their sole attention."

Dave shrugged. "Even if it comes to that, there's nothing we can do except sit tight."

"I'm not so sure."

Dave looked at his wife quizzically. "How do you mean?"

"I was thinking about it this afternoon, and it struck

me – maybe as a fall-back we should have an escape plan. Just in case the worst came to the worst."

"What, prepare to run for it?"

"Only as a last resort."

"God . . . I don't know, Mary. I mean I only acted in self-defence . . . running away would confirm my guilt."

Mary squeezed his arm. "I know you're innocent, love, but it'd be poor consolation if you were locked in prison."

"Jesus, I'd go mad!"

"I'm sure it won't come to that," said Mary reassuringly, "but just in case things go wrong we should have a contingency plan."

Dave looked up and smiled wryly. "Which you've already worked out, yeah?"

Mary smiled back and held out her mug to be refilled. "If – God forbid – but if things went wrong, and we had to make a run for it, I think we should go to Ireland."

"Ireland?" Dave stopped midway through pouring the coffee.

"It's not the dark side of the moon."

"No, it's – it's fine," answered Dave, filling the mugs. "It's just a bit . . . nearby . . ."

"It's a separate, sovereign state though – which means we couldn't be extradited without a fuss. Always assuming they knew we'd gone there, and that they could find us – which they wouldn't."

"How can you be so sure?"

"Had you ever heard of Ballyard, County Kerry, before we visited it?"

"Well, no . . ."

163

"Neither will they have."

"You're not suggesting we'd live with your brother?"

"No," answered Mary, "but Tom and Jenny would hide us till the heat died down."

Dave shook his head. "We'd be tracked down."

"I don't think so. I've been gone from Ireland since 1978. Tom emigrated to Canada the following year."

"Even still . . ."

"Think about it, Dave. Years later, when Daddy dies, the family farm is sold – in *Mayo*."

"So?"

"The link is severed. When Tom gives up fishing in Nova Scotia he buys his own trawler in Ireland. But where does he settle? Down in *Kerry*. The trail is dead – stone cold."

Dave shook his head. "They'd still find us. Two blow-ins from England, Mary – we'd stick out a mile."

"Less than you think. Lots of foreigners have settled in West Cork and Kerry, and besides, no one would even see us at first. Tom would hide us well."

"For how long could he do that?"

"Till the heat was off."

"Who says the heat will *go* off?"

"It always does. Some other story grabs the attention, then another. Pretty soon a couple missing from England is yesterday's news. Especially in Ireland."

"It wouldn't be that simple. I mean, would we assume false names? And if we did, how would we open a bank account, get a driving licence – any of that stuff?"

164

"Ways can be found round all of that."

"How?"

"Tom and Jenny live there. They have contacts. Things can be arranged."

"We'd be asking them to break the law."

"Tom's my brother – and Jenny's dead sound. In a crisis he'd do anything that was necessary. I'd do it for them if the boot was on the other foot."

Dave looked at her, still unconvinced.

Mary leaned forward, speaking with conviction. "Look, it's messy and it would take some arranging, but believe me, if we had to, we could disappear on the Beara Peninsula."

"Supposing we did, what would we do there? I mean, you couldn't act . . ."

"No. But I could go into the stained glass full-time."

"And what would I do?"

"Farming. You've often talked about getting out of the rat-race, working on the land."

"Well, yeah, but . . ."

"We could buy a farm through Tom."

"How could we finance it?"

"With our savings and the proceeds of selling the house here."

"Hang on, Mary, hang on. Just supposing the worst came to the worst, and we opted for something like this – how could we sell the house unnoticed? It's not something that could be done overnight."

Mary nodded. "Yes; I was thinking about that."

"And?"

"If things started to look really worrying we could

165

sell the house to an estate agent. Drop the price a bit to ensure the sale. The police need never know."

"They'd know if we moved out."

"We wouldn't move out. We'd tell the estate agent we were building a house in Wales or somewhere – and arrange to lease this one back while it was being built. Meanwhile we'd have a fat cheque from the house sale in case we had to make a break for it."

Dave breathed out and looked in admiration at his wife. "You have it all worked out, haven't you?"

"No," answered Mary, "not at all. It's just a rough plan, but . . ." She paused, a catch in her voice.

Dave rose and held her. "What's wrong, love, what is it?"

"Oh, Dave. I . . . I just couldn't bear if anything were to happen to us. Not now, not with the baby due and everything before us."

He saw the tears welling in her eyes and felt a lump in his own throat. He softly cradled her face on his shoulder and spoke reassuringly. "It won't, honey. We'll come through this thing together. And we'll look at your plan, just in case. We'll think it all through." He took her face in his hands and kissed her gently. "I promise you, no matter what, our future is together. Together with our baby – and free. OK?"

She looked at him and smiled wanly. "Yeah . . . OK . . ."

19

Bob Reinholdt wondered how many CIA officers ended up in the divorce courts as a result of the hours they worked. It wouldn't be on record, of course, despite the Company's encyclopaedic data banks, but it was an interesting thought nonetheless. He had just had a row with his wife about having to cancel their planned visit to the movies, and he knew he faced another anti-Company diatribe from Janet when he arrived home that night.

Moving briskly along the crowded London pavements, he tried to put it from his mind as he made his way towards Brewer Street car park, a hive of activity as it disgorged its vehicles into the evening rush-hour traffic.

Reinholdt had had an unsettling day due to a cryptic phone call from Visser at ten o'clock that morning. There had been a scheduled security review at the embassy, which had ended up taking all of the day, and so he had been unable to meet the South African until now.

Entering the car park, he quickly climbed the stairs to reach the top storey. He reached the head of the stairwell, then moved along the rows of parked vehicles, but he could see no sign of Visser's car. Suddenly there was a flash of headlights from a white van parked in the furthest corner. Reinholdt approached and saw the South African sitting in the cab.

The passenger door was pushed open and Visser gave his cold-eyed smile. As soon as Reinholdt seated himself and closed the door Visser turned up the volume on the car tape deck as before, filling the vehicle with loud classical music.

The American was also struck by the smell of expensive aftershave and had to suppress what he knew was an irrational sense of irritation at the other man's vanity. "You said you'd made progress?"

"Indeed. I've spoken to our friend, Mr Aksor . . ."

"And?"

"An interesting man. Lots of contacts in dubious places . . ."

"Can we get to the point?" said Reinholdt, struggling to control his impatience.

"This is to the point," answered Visser. "Aksor was central to the SMORTAR plans being stolen. In fact he persuaded Gatenby to take them."

"You're certain of that?"

"Positive."

"Whom was he acting for?"

"An Islamic fundamentalist group called 'Sons of the Dawn'."

Reinholdt nodded. "Lebanese, aren't they?"

"Based in Lebanon. Members are drawn from various parts of the Gulf and Middle East," replied

Visser. "Religious fanatics, rabidly anti-Israeli, equally anti-American. A weapon like SMORTAR is the stuff of their dreams; so Gatenby was offered a lot of money."

"Provided by whom?"

"Sons of the Dawn themselves – seems they're not above a little bank robbery in pursuing their ideals."

"But they wouldn't have the technology to build a SMORTAR system – they'd need a sympathetic government."

"True."

"So who is the government?" asked Reinholdt impatiently.

"Aksor couldn't say."

"Godamn it, he told you all the rest. Couldn't you persuade him on that?"

"I persuaded him all right. Terminally, in fact."

Reinholdt looked at the South African in disbelief.

"What?"

"You heard me."

"Jesus Christ, are you out of your mind?! You're telling me you killed a diplomat?"

"A terrorist."

"For Christ's sake, I said minimum force! I emphasised that."

"You also emphasised the importance of getting this information – and quickly."

"Not this way."

"What way then? Did you think Aksor would give me the information over a friendly drink?"

"This could create serious problems."

"It won't create any problems at all," said Visser evenly. "The body is already disposed of and will never be found. I've left no traces linking myself to Aksor. And it's got absolutely nothing to do with the CIA if a dodgy Iranian diplomat goes missing."

"What did you do to him that he died?" asked Reinholdt.

"What difference does it make? I got you vital information."

"I don't like your methods, Visser."

"Really? Maybe you'd prefer Aksor's methods. Maybe you'll like it when a SMORTAR's put into an American Embassy somewhere – wiping out half the occupants. I can stop working on the case if that's what you'd prefer . . ."

Reinholdt looked hard at him, then turned and stared out the windscreen. He knew he had no choice. The SMORTAR plans couldn't be left in the wrong hands. Countless American lives were at stake, to say nothing of his own career as CIA Chief of Station in London. "Tell me the rest," he said resignedly.

"Aksor genuinely didn't know what government had been lined up to give Sons of the Dawn the technical support." The South African smiled briefly. "I think I can definitely vouch for that. However, he knew all about the plan with Gatenby, and here's the crucial thing – the terrorists never got the SMORTAR drawings."

"What?"

"Gatenby was supposed to fly from Manchester to Dublin with the drawings. He was to give a portion of them to Aksor in a hotel there, and the Arabs were to check that they were bona fide. Then when Gatenby got a call from his bank in Zurich that the funds had been lodged, he was to hand over the rest of the drawings. Gatenby never arrived in Dublin. Never left Manchester, it seems."

"What happened?"

"Nobody knows. The terrorists are totally in the dark about what went wrong."

"They wouldn't have intercepted him in the Dales, stolen the stuff to save paying him?"

"Extremely unlikely. Aksor insisted they were all set to pay him, money wasn't a problem. It makes no sense for them to risk everything in the hope of guessing the route he'd take, counting on being there at the right time, and committing a successful kidnap in broad daylight." Visser shook his head. "No way . . ."

"So where does that leave us?" asked Reinholdt.

"It removes Sons of the Dawn from the equation. Though I believe you'll find this of interest," said Visser, passing an envelope to the American.

Reinholdt took it and looked quizzically at the other man.

"A breakdown on everything Aksor knew about Sons of the Dawn. Contacts, objectives, command structure. I think you'll find it very interesting."

"Thank you."

"You're welcome," said the South African smilingly. "I like to provide good value. However we're still left with the elusive Mr Gatenby."

Reinholdt thought a moment, then shrugged. "Well, it's one of two things. Either he's gone to ground and left the van in the Dales as a red herring, or else he encountered a person or persons unknown and was abducted."

"Or he could have encountered someone who knocked him down. Say a drunken driver who dumped the body to save his own hide."

"The police are combing woods, dragging rivers – all the usual stuff."

"You said the police appealed to anyone in the area to come forward?" said Visser.

"Yes."

"Can you get me a list of those names?"

"I don't see how," answered Reinholdt.

"I thought you had a source."

"In M15 – and even then he's not privy to everything that happens. Particularly when the investigation is being handled by the Yorkshire Police."

"He'll have to find some way of getting access to the list. Until something else breaks it's the only lead we have."

Reinholdt thought a moment, then turned to the South African. "If I get this information, there must be no repetition of what happened to Aksor."

Visser went to speak but the American quickly raised his hand to silence him.

"No! I know what's at stake, I know we're under pressure, but the people on this list are British citizens who came forward to help the authorities. You can talk to them, tail them, tap their phones, make enquiries – but no abductions, absolutely no violence. Understood?"

"OK," said Visser. "OK."

"It may take a few days to get this list, but I'll get onto it."

"The sooner you do, the sooner I can get going," pressed Visser.

"Why don't I ring you at your hotel the moment I have it?" suggested Reinholdt.

Visser smiled. "I'd rather stay . . . anonymous . . ."

"Now look . . ."

"No, here's what to do. Buy a rubber plant. As soon as you have the list, place the plant in the window of the third office to the right of the embassy's front entrance – as viewed from the street. I'll check several times every day, and as soon as I see it, we'll meet."

Reinholdt looked at him, then nodded and opened the van door.

"Don't forget," said Visser. "As soon as possible."

The American nodded again, then shut the door and walked away. He glanced at his watch. It was only six thirty. Still time to get home in time for the movies if he rushed. But there would be no movies tonight. With a murdered diplomat, and Gatenby still missing, he had too much on his mind. Lost in thought he descended the stairs and entered the rush-hour crowd, unconscious of the city's bustle as he pondered his next move.

20

Chief Superintendent Carrow put the phone down and returned to his files. He had just confirmed his place at a weekend clay-pigeon shoot, and unless there was some kind of break in the Gatenby case he could look forward to being out with his shotgun this time tomorrow.

Now that the case was making little headway, he was glad that Thompson was formally heading the investigation. He had never liked Jack Thompson; too much a maverick, never had the cop-on to know how to make the right noises. But now the detective would provide a convenient fall-guy if no breakthrough was made, while if there was a successful conclusion Carrow would make sure that the crucial role of Special Branch – and his running of it – would be well recognised.

Leaning back in his swivel chair, Carrow looked once more at Gatenby's personal file, obtained from MI5 by Mathieson. Going through it again, Carrow found it hard to understand what had made a man with a background like Gatenby's turn traitor. His father had served as a naval officer during the war, his mother had been in the Wrens. They had impeccable war records; both were members of the Tory party; their families were very comfortable financially. Model establishment figures – and yet Gatenby had gone wrong. Had it all too easy, thought Carrow. If Gatenby had had to work his way from mill-worker's son to Chief Superintendent, as Carrow had, he might have had more loyalty to the system in which he had risen.

Pushing aside the file disdainfully, the policeman took up another file marked Browsdale Radio Appeals. There had been no reported sightings in response to the Missing Person's message, and although several more people had come forward who had been in the Browsdale area, none of them had been in the vicinity during the crucial timescale. Carrow looked at the original list again. Ralph Taylor, the Inland Revenue man from Kent, had been hill-walking in the Dales every summer for the past thirty years, and it had been patently evident at his interview that the timid bachelor would have been incapable of any subversive activity.

Likewise Ben Murray, the pensioner from Settle who had been out with his watercolours. His questioning had revealed a simple man with little interest in politics, yet one who was fervently patriotic, a fact endorsed by his exemplary army record.

After five minutes' questioning Carrow had mentally dismissed Jenny Wallace, the seventy-six-year-old woman from Darlington, and her daughter, an unmarried midwife with whom the older woman lived.

Belal Hussief was a middle-aged social worker from Bradford who had been bringing a child to a foster family in Appleby. His background had checked out after a thorough investigation, and Carrow believed his story of deciding to take the child by the scenic route over the Pennines.

Which left Anne-Marie Fabien, the Belgian au pair living in Manchester, and David Walker, the advertising executive from Harrogate. He took out their typed-up statements and was about to go through them again when the phone rang. "Carrow . . ."

"Call from Special Branch in London, sir. Chief Superintendent Wilson."

"Put him through."

There was a click, then the other policeman came on the line.

"Good afternoon, Len, how are you?"

"Fine, Jim, fine."

"Good to be back in Yorkshire?"

"Not too bad. Got something for me?"

"Possibly. It's the Missing Persons report on the Iranian. We asked for a list of all telephone contacts for this Aksor chap in the last ten days . . ."

"Go on," said Carrow.

"Bit of a long shot, but with a possible link between the Browsdale business and a shady diplomat vanishing, we were painstaking."

"So what turned up?"

"Dozens of names, mostly mundane stuff. One was interesting though, and we chased it up. On Monday –

the last day Aksor was seen – he took a call from a Bruce Kenny. A reporter with *The Melbourne Post*."

"And?"

"We rang *The Melbourne Post*, and they've no one of that name."

Carrow leaned forward, experiencing a stirring of excitement. "He wouldn't have been a stringer – a freelance?"

"We asked that. They checked their records and no Bruce Kenny has ever written for them. They'd never even heard of him."

"Did you check with the NUJ?"

Wilson laughed. "Still ahead of you, Len. We've been onto them."

"Don't tell me. They've no such journalist on their files?"

"Got it in one."

"Interesting . . ."

"Might be nothing. Might be some novice freelance who thought he'd a better chance of an interview if he pretended to be from a proper paper."

"On the other hand they spoke last Monday, and Aksor hasn't been seen since . . ."

"Quite. We're putting out Aksor's picture on TV tonight," said Wilson, "and we're also running all the normal checks against the name Bruce Kenny – Immigration, Social Services, and so on. I'll keep you posted."

"The moment there's anything. Anything at all, Jim, we're drawing a lot of blanks on this one."

"OK, the moment there's anything."

"Thanks, Jim. Cheers."

"Cheers."

Carrow put the phone down and gazed out the office window. On face value the likelihood of a connection to the Browsdale incident seemed slim, yet several times in the past Carrow had found it very profitable not to accept things at face value. Fingers crossed, he thought, fingers crossed . . .

21

"Silly sod!" said Chief Inspector Thompson. "He wants a good kick in the backside!"

Penny suppressed a smile and nodded sympathetically. "Why do you think he's holding back on us, Chief?"

"Because he's Len-bloody-Carrow! Always out for glory, always trying to make himself look good. I don't say he's not effective, mind, but he's bloody awful to work with. A real self-serving – " Thompson stopped in mid-sentence.

Penny looked round her boss's office with theatrical exaggeration as if to ensure she wasn't being overheard, then volunteered "Bugger?"

Thompson laughed, his irritation suddenly defused. "I was going to say bastard, actually . . ."

"I'm scandalised," answered Penny with a grin.

"So you should be, Miss. I'm setting a bad example talking of a senior officer that way."

"I'll try my best not to be led astray."

"Some hope," said Thompson humorously as he sat

on the edge of his desk. "No," he said, his tone becoming serious again, "Carrow is playing his usual Special Branch games. He should have informed us immediately about the Iranian. This business of not wanting to waste our time till he'd checked it out is rubbish. Remember, Penny, in all successful cases you get some kind of break. It's obvious sometimes, other times it's not – but you still have to check the ones that aren't obvious. The fact that the possible link to Aksor is pretty tenuous doesn't matter. He should have told us immediately."

"He clearly resents the investigation being headed by the Yorkshire Constabulary," said Penny.

"Pity about him. We're the ones giving up our Saturday to work on it. He's probably out somewhere doing his country squire routine. And I'll tell you another thing," he started, just as his phone rang.

"Thompson speaking," he said, picking up the receiver. "What? When was this?"

Penny listened closely, picking up immediately on the excitement in his voice.

"You're sure about the identity?" asked Thompson. "Right, we're on our way." He put the phone down and rose from the desk as Penny looked quizzically at him. "That, Constable," he said with relish, "is a perfect example of an obvious break."

"Yes?"

"They've just found and identified the body of Nigel Gatenby. Fished out of a tarn a couple of miles from where he abandoned the van."

"Wow."

"Wow is right. Get your stuff. We're on our way to the Dales."

"Sweet Jesus!" said Mary in horror. "Dave! Dave, quickly – in here!" She stood immobile as her husband rushed into the sitting-room.

"What's wrong?!"

Mary indicated the flickering images from the television in the corner. "They've found the body," she said softly.

"What?!" But even as he spoke Dave saw footage of divers surfacing, and a corpse being winched from the water. He watched in shock for a moment, then looked at Mary.

"They gave the location – it's Gatenby," she answered, turning down the sound as another news item came on-screen.

"Oh Christ!" said Dave.

"I know. Just when I thought it was going to be OK."

"They'll see the head-wound," said Dave. "They'll realise he was killed and then dumped in the water."

Mary nodded ruefully in agreement.

"Damn! Damn! Damn!" cried Dave. "They'll start narrowing the time of death now . . ."

Mary stared unseeingly out across the lawn, then turned to her husband. "There's nothing we can do about it, Dave. This was always a possibility."

"I know. But I underestimated them."

"We've been diligent too. We've done everything possible."

181

"I hope it's enough."

"We'll just have to brazen it out," said Mary. "We'll probably come under more intense scrutiny now, but we'll simply stick to our alibis. "

"Christ, I wish I'd never set eyes on that bastard!"

Mary moved to him and took him in her arms. "It wasn't your fault, Dave. It just happened." She stepped back a little, then squeezed his arm reassuringly. "We'll stick to our story and sweat it out, right?"

"Yeah. Yeah, right."

"Look on the bright side. In a couple of months you'll be a proud father, and this should all be history then."

Dave looked at her upturned face and gently touched her cheek. "I hope so, love," he answered earnestly. "I really hope so . . ."

Penny felt her flesh creep as she watched the pathologist working. Initially she had been sorry to miss Sunday lunch with her family – a tradition that meant more to her since she had moved into her own flat – but now the thought of lunch seemed revolting. Even the breakfast she had shared with Thompson was adding to her queasiness.

She forced herself to watch however, as Dr Kershaw, the pathologist, cut the flesh around Gatenby's skull. He was giving a brisk running commentary to Thompson, who seemed unaffected by the grisly nature of the work in hand. Penny suspected that her efforts to look normal were not entirely successful, and she was glad that Carrow and Mathieson were absent in London, following a lead in the Iranian diplomat development.

"There's your cause of death," said Kershaw in a strong Scots accent. "Penetration of cranium, death practically instantaneous."

"How long do you reckon he'd been in the water?" asked Thompson.

"Impossible to say precisely . . ."

"An educated guess?" prompted Thompson.

Kershaw thought a moment. "Maybe a week, though it could be anything from two or three days upwards."

"Any idea how long he'd been dead before going into the water?"

Kershaw shrugged. "Guessing again, but with the heat we've had, and the rate of decomposition . . . probably not much more than a day or so."

"Thanks, Doctor. Anything else you can tell us?"

"Yes," answered the Scot. "Bruising on the cheekbone, abrasion on the knuckle of the right hand – clear suggestions of a fight or struggle."

"But the killing blow wouldn't have been delivered with a fist?" asked Penny.

"No. No, pointed stick, sharp metal bar – something like that for this sort of penetration," he answered, indicating the shattered skull.

Penny made herself glance at the dead man's head and nodded.

"Lot of force required for this, probably done by somebody fairly strong," mused the pathologist.

"Anything else?" asked Thompson.

"I may be able to say more about the murder weapon when I've done a full autopsy. I'll try to narrow down the time of death too."

Thompson passed the pathologist his card. "Can you give me a buzz, please, the moment you have anything?"

"Certainly. Heading back to the station now?"

"Yes," answered the detective. "And thank you again for your help."

"All part of the job," answered Kershaw cheerily. "Drive carefully now."

"Good morning, Doctor," said Penny, making for the door.

"Good morning, Constable," the Scot answered, before returning with interest to the remains.

Once outside the mortuary, Thompson stopped and turned to Penny. "Well?"

"Two possibilities, I'd say," she answered. "A: Whoever it was killed Gatenby on Thursday near where the van broke down, and dumped the body in the lake."

"There and then?"

"Probably . . . though not necessarily."

"And B?" prompted Thompson.

"Or B: He was abducted, perhaps interrogated, then killed within a day or so and the body brought back, probably under cover of darkness, to be dumped a few miles from where his van broke down."

"Why would the villains go back to an area being combed by the police?"

"It wasn't being combed during darkness."

"OK, but why go back at all?"

"Perhaps to give the impression of a hit and run accident – drunken driver who panicked, dumped the body in a local tarn, and posted back the film to take the heat off?"

"Pretty convoluted," said Thompson thoughtfully, "but possible. So – next move by a bright young constable?"

Penny smiled. "We go back to the office, take out the statements of how our volunteers spent last weekend, and go through them again?"

"Line by line. Let's go."

22

Despite the Monday morning traffic, Jan Visser was in good spirits as he drove along the North Circular Road. He had decided to enjoy his time in London after Reinholdt had made it clear that it could take several days to get the list of names through his contact, and although the English brothels lacked the eastern sophistication that Visser favoured, he had found several that catered for his tastes. He had also attended first-class concerts in the Albert Hall and the Royal Festival Hall, so that the time had passed pleasantly until Saturday, when he had met the American.

Having delayed his departure for another couple of days due to the discovery of Gatenby's body, Visser now figured that it had been worth waiting to find out that the defecting intelligence officer had died of a shattered skull, and had probably been dumped in the water about ten days previously.

Of course it was entirely possible that killing Gatenby had been a hit done by someone who hadn't been seen, before or after the killing, and who had dumped the body at night.

On the other hand to carry out a hit would require transport, and as a car or van might be spotted in a remote area, it was well worth talking to those who had come forward. A really devious hit-man might, through contacts, have lined up a driver with a clean record, who would go forward with an innocent explanation of why he had been driving through the region. Or it simply could have been a drunken driver who had tried to hide the evidence of his or her misdeed. Whatever the truth, the Belgian au pair and the ad-man from Leeds sounded the most interesting on the list; he would try them first.

Negotiating into the correct lane for the motorway, he followed the signs and turned onto the MI, then cruising along the middle lane, his mind went back to the case.

The Belgian woman might be entertaining, he thought. Perhaps he could mix business with pleasure – it was a while since he had used that sort of charm to progress a case. And if he drew a blank in Manchester he would push on to Harrogate. The file on David Walker included an interview with his wife, an actress apparently.

Might be interesting to work on her, he thought, a tingle of anticipation running through him. Yes, it might be very interesting. He glanced left and right at the traffic pouring out of the city, then eased back in the seat and accelerated, keen suddenly to head north and get down to business.

Chief Superintendent Carrow fought his way through

the congested city streets, irritated that the drive from the airport to Leeds had taken twice as long as expected due to a combination of roadworks and the Monday morning rush-hour traffic. By contrast Mathieson sat easily in the passenger seat, apparently unperturbed by the fact that they were running late.

It was typical of the intelligence officer, Carrow thought. There was an unfussable air about him, a sense of languidness that the policeman found increasingly irritating – the more so because it would have been unwise to express it.

Carrow's discreet inquiries had established that Mathieson, despite his relatively youthful appearance, was a long-serving and highly regarded figure in M15. It was also said that the languid manner was a cultivated exaggeration, designed to deceive, and that as a young army officer Mathieson had been decorated after active service in Borneo, Aden and Oman. All of which, taken with Mathieson's good family connections, made Carrow very cautious in his dealings with him.

He couldn't quite shake off his impatience with him however, for it was as if Mathieson wore his laid-back air like a badge, as if he felt he would succeed anyhow, and that it was not quite the thing to be seen trying too hard. I'll bet he's really successful with women, thought Carrow. He could remember the type from courtship days, the sort who effortlessly turned your girlfriend's head.

"Home sweet home," said Mathieson wryly, breaking the other man's reverie as they pulled into the yard of the police station.

"About bloody time," said Carrow.

"Not to worry. Hardly start without us, eh?"

"No," answered Carrow, getting out of the car. He couldn't tell the intelligence officer but he had planned to arrive early, to keep Thompson off balance. Now the CID man would have the edge.

As they entered the general office, Carrow saw by the wall clock that they were ten minutes late. "We're looking for Mr Thompson," he said to a uniformed officer.

"Interview Room Two, sir."

"Thank you," responded Mathieson pleasantly, before following the Special Branch man down the corridor.

Carrow knocked perfunctorily, then entered the room immediately. It was medium-sized with no windows, a large glass panel along one wall, and a long table. Thompson was already seated, going through some paperwork with his acolyte, Penny Hart.

Carrow nodded briskly to them in response to their good mornings. "Got the autopsy report?" he asked.

"Yes," answered Thompson easily. "Good morning, Mr Mathieson. Won't you take a seat?"

"Thank you." He smiled at Penny. "Good morning."

"Good morning, Mr Mathieson."

"Can we get straight to business?" said Carrow.

"Certainly; we don't want to waste any further time," said Thompson with a quick glance at the clock. Before Carrow could respond the detective said: "Perhaps, Mr Mathieson, you'd be good enough to update us on any developments from your people?"

"Not much to report, I'm afraid. Been watching selected groups for any flurry of activity, increased telecommunications, that sort of thing – nothing out of the ordinary though."

"No rumours, intelligence community gossip?"

"Nothing whatsoever. Sorry, but we've rather drawn a blank."

"And the Aksor connection, Mr Carrow?"

Not wishing to appear unreasonable before the intelligence officer, Carrow kept the annoyance from his voice despite his irritation at the way Thompson was underlining his role as Investigating Officer. "There's been no sign of Aksor at any of his known haunts," he replied. "At my request, my Special Branch colleagues in London put his picture out on TV. It was a good move – we had an immediate response. As Mr Mathieson here was already in London consulting his superiors, we spent the weekend following it up. A barman in the Cherry Tree pub positively identified Aksor."

"Where's the Cherry Tree?" asked Thompson.

"Stepney. Off the Mile End Road."

"Stepney?" Thompson raised an eyebrow. "I wouldn't see a foreign diplomat as a regular there."

"No, the barman had never seen him before."

"Yet he remembered him?"

"There was a phone call for him," answered Carrow, "a few minutes after he came in. Immediately after the call he went out the back door to the car park, and that's the last anyone saw of him."

"And the person who rang?" asked Thompson.

"Australian accent again."

"The elusive Bruce Kenny . . ."

"Who doesn't exist," answered Carrow. "That's a dead end, I'm sure of it."

"So where's the lead then?" asked Thompson.

"We questioned all the bar staff and Mr Mathieson here struck gold."

Mathieson smiled and took up the story. "Seems a few minutes earlier a second barman arrived for work. As he pulled into the car park he noticed someone getting out of a white van. Just from the corner of his eye, paid no attention to it. A few minutes later he went back to the car park – wanted a pack of cigarettes left in his glove compartment – and the van was gone."

"You think Aksor may have been in it?" said Thompson.

Mathieson shrugged. "A possibility. Not a bad modus operandi if one had to abduct someone from a public place."

"True," said Thompson, "but were the events simultaneous? Aksor leaving just after the second barman arrived?"

"Yes," answered Carrow. "The first barman specifically remembers it was nine o'clock. In fact, the second chap was coming to relieve him. The last thing barman number one did was take the phone call and page Aksor."

"Interesting," said Thompson.

"Spot of luck with the second barman," said Mathieson. "He's convinced of the van's make, a Toyota Hiace."

"Even though he just glimpsed it?"

"Seems the chap's brother runs a scrapyard," answered Mathieson. "Got an eye for a motor. He's quite convinced of the make."

"Any Hiace vans reported stolen to the Met in the previous few days?" asked Thompson.

"First thing we checked," said Carrow. "There weren't any. We're running checks right now on every rental company in the London area. We'll follow up on any white Hiace rentals."

"Of course Aksor could have walked out the back door and driven to some other rendezvous," said Mathieson, "but the rentals are well worth checking."

"We ought to give priority to checking foreigners whose mother tongue is English," said Thompson.

"What, the Bruce Kenny thing?" queried Carrow.

"Well, if our caller was English, why not speak in an English accent, why draw attention by becoming Australian?"

"Could be a ruse," answered Mathieson. "And if he's actually Australian he'd hardly advertise the fact."

"Agreed," answered Thompson. "So if our man isn't English, then rather than assume an English accent – which might well be seen through in England – he opts for an Australian one. Which suggests to me that he might be an American, Canadian, South African, Irish . . ."

"The data's being collected as we speak, I'll keep you posted," said Carrow.

"If you would," said Thompson, "*immediately* you have it, if you don't mind."

Carrow stared hard at Thompson, who held his gaze

briefly before reaching for his papers and giving a file to each of the other men.

"A copy of the autopsy report, gentlemen," Thompson said briskly.

"Anything of interest?" asked Mathieson.

"Estimated time of death – last Thursday week, late afternoon. Estimated time of immersion in the water, probably within twenty-four hours, unlikely to be much more than forty-eight. Particles of pine wood found in the head-wound."

"Is that significant?" queried the intelligence officer.

"I think so," said Thompson. "Originally we thought the skull had been shattered by a blow from a stick or rod."

"And now?"

"Now the options are wider. It was DC Hart here who pointed out that she'd seen pine trees in the area."

Carrow looked quizzically at the young woman.

"It occurred to me that Mr Gatenby may have been killed by a branch or stump, sir," she said.

"How does that widen our options?"

"Well, sir, not every woman would have the strength to shatter a man's skull, but lots could trip a man, make him fall backwards onto . . . say a sharp branch or stump?"

"You're thinking in terms of Mademoiselle Fabien?" suggested Mathieson.

"It's a possibility," answered Penny.

"If the corpse went into the water between Thursday and Saturday, then the weekend activity of our radio appeal volunteers becomes important," said Thompson.

"*If* any of them had anything to do with it, I'd choose David Walker or Anne-Marie Fabien."

"How did Walker spend his weekend?" asked Mathieson.

"You can ask him yourself," said Thompson with a smile. "He's here now."

"Here?" said Carrow.

"Yes, I thought it might be good to question him again, on our turf this time. If he's hiding anything he'll be more nervous here."

"Sounds good," said Mathieson.

"Show him in, would you, Penny?" said Thompson.

"Yes, sir," she answered, then left the room.

"Anne-Marie Fabien's coming in too. Scheduled for ten-thirty."

"Good," said Mathieson. "The envelope with the film was posted on Friday. Bit of a drive to London and back for either of them."

"All the more reason for doing it," said Carrow, "if they were trying to put us off the scent. And they needn't have driven – could have flown or taken the train."

"We'll question them about their movements that Friday night," said Thompson, "then show their pictures to British Rail staff on ticket and guard duty. Bus company and airline staff too."

"Have we got pictures of them?" asked Carrow.

Thompson smiled and pointed at the one-way glass panel behind them. "Will have shortly, I've lined up one of our photo boys, and Penny's already got a photo of Walker's wife – in case he sent her in his place."

"Where did she get a photo of the wife?" asked Carrow.

"She remembered that the woman's an actress and got a copy of *Spotlight*. It's a listing book of actors – photos included."

"Good thinking," said Mathieson.

"Aye, she's bright," answered Thompson.

Just then there was a knock, and the returning policewoman ushered Dave Walker into the room. Carrow looked at the advertising executive. He was slim, handsome, mid-thirties. He looked smart in a well-cut suit, and his manner failed to suggest someone overawed by being called in for police questioning. Cool-looking bastard, thought Carrow. Well, we'll see how cool he'll be when the interrogation is over . . .

Determined not to appear cowed, Dave looked easily around the room and took in the three seated men. He immediately recognised Thompson again.

"Good morning, Mr Walker," said the detective. "Thank you for coming. Won't you have a seat?"

"Thank you," answered Dave.

"This is Mr Mathieson, and Chief Superintendent Carrow . . ."

They exchanged good mornings, then Dave sat in the vacant chair with the three men opposite him, and Penny Hart to his right at the end of the table.

Although he had suspected as soon as the body was discovered that further questioning lay ahead, it had still been a shock to get the phone call in work, and he had experienced a sinking feeling when Thompson had asked him to come down to the station. A ten o'clock appointment on a Monday morning – did that mean he was the first for questioning, top of their list?

He had told his secretary that he had a toothache and was going to the dentist – there was enough hassle with Trevor Lawrence over the ReadyBurger account without him knowing of this – and had left immediately, planning his approach en route.

He reckoned that an innocent man would be a bit affronted at this stage; he would try for a don't-mind-helping-the-police-but-enough-is-enough sort of tone.

"We've had some developments regarding the Dales incident, as I mentioned over the phone," said Thompson. "We'd like to go over your movements again, if you wouldn't mind."

"Actually, Inspector, I *am* beginning to mind," said Dave. "I've answered all your questions. My wife has even answered questions. What more can I tell you?"

"You've already given us some information on your movements the following weekend. We'd like you to elaborate on that."

"What?" Dave stared at them with what he hoped was the look of a man surprisedly affronted. "Look, I came forward in case I could help police enquiries – what's my personal life at the weekend got to do with it?"

"It's not just you, Mr Walker," answered Thompson. "Others in the area that Thursday will be questioned also."

"About their movements the following weekend?"

"Yes."

"What, we're all . . . *suspects* now? That's the reward for being a good citizen and coming forward?"

"You weren't particularly fast about coming forward," said Carrow.

Dave looked at the big policeman with the ginger hair. Presumably his role was going to be Bad Cop in the Good Cop/Bad Cop game. Dave wasn't sure about the other one, Mathieson. No rank given, probably some kind of spook. He was up against professionals here. He'd have to handle himself carefully.

"I came forward at ten thirty on Friday morning," he answered, "and frankly I'm beginning to regret my desire to assist."

"You must understand, Mr Walker, that we've a job to do," said Thompson pleasantly. "It's our duty to look at all possibilities, then we can eliminate anything that's not involved."

"You mean *anyone* who's not involved . . ."

There was a pause, then Thompson nodded. "Yes, that too."

Dave shook his head. "This is ridiculous but, if we must, let's get it over with."

"If we could start with the Friday in question," said Carrow.

"I was in work all day," answered Dave. "Plenty of witnesses," he added sarcastically.

"And Friday night?"

He forced himself not to think about the train trip to London.

"Friday night . . . I was home with my wife."

"All night?"

197

"Yes, let's see . . . I was reading; Mary was studying a script."

"Anyone call on you?"

"Eh . . . no, I don't think so. Well, we'd a phone call, from Linda Browne, Secretary of the Tennis Club."

"What time would that have been?"

"I'm not sure. Maybe eight, nine . . ."

"Did she speak to you?"

"Eh, I may have answered the phone – no, no I didn't, now I think of it."

"You can remember who answered the phone?" said Carrow.

"Yes, my wife was sitting nearer to it, but learning lines. She wanted me to get it, but I said no, it'll be for you – and it was."

"No other calls?"

"No, I don't think so. After that we both read, listened to some music, then went to bed.

"About what time?"

"Probably around eleven."

"I see," said Carrow. "Saturday then?"

"Got up about ten. We did some work on the front garden – our neighbour can confirm that, before you ask. In the afternoon my wife went to the hairdresser, I played tennis. That night we went to a barbecue in the Tennis Club at about eight."

"Till what time?"

"About half one in my case. Mary left around eleven."

Carrow raised an eyebrow. "Eleven?"

"She's almost eight months pregnant. She felt tired and went home."

"But you stayed on till half one?"

"Yes, she insisted."

"Can you remember the people you were with till one thirty?" asked Thompson.

"Linda Browne, Norman and Sue Forrestal – they're all in the phone book if you need to . . . cross-check."

"We may well do," said Carrow.

"Do then."

"And Sunday, Mr Walker?" interjected Thompson.

Dave shrugged. "I went for the papers about eleven, my wife got half-eleven Mass. After lunch we went for a stroll."

"Whereabouts?" asked Carrow.

"Around Harrogate."

"Where specifically around Harrogate?" persisted Carrow.

"*Specifically* from our house to the Valley Gardens; then from the Tea Pavilion to the far end of the park and back."

"Talk to any one in the Tea Pavilion?"

"We didn't enter it. But we'd coffee in the Crown Hotel on the way home. I daresay you could find our fingerprints there if you put your mind to it."

"And that evening, Mr. Walker?" asked Thompson.

"Dinner at home, I did some work, watched TV."

"Can you confirm that?" queried Carrow.

"Yes, my wife got a phone call from Sue Forrestal. I spoke to my secretary on the phone."

"Did you ring her or did she ring you?" asked Thompson.

"Both. I rang her about some work I knew she was

doing over the weekend, and she rang me back when she'd tracked down what I wanted."

Thompson nodded. "And what time would this have been?"

"Perhaps . . . half eight, nine, something like that."

"And the rest of the evening?"

"We relaxed, then went to bed about half ten."

"Are you a member of any political party?" asked Carrow.

Dave looked sharply at him, not needing to assume irritation this time. "What concern of yours is that?"

Carrow held his gaze. "It's a simple straightforward question."

"Then I'll give you a simple straightforward answer. Mind your own business."

"Perhaps it is our business to know your allegiances," answered Carrow unperturbedly.

"Oh yes," replied Dave sarcastically. "Yes, I could be a member of The Party, couldn't I? Bit behind the times, but who knows?" He turned to the other man. "I suspect, Mr Mathieson, that might be your area?"

The flicker of a smile crossed Mathieson's face before he replied. "Hardly likely to elaborate on that, am I, sir? But you could save us a lot of time, Mr Walker . . ."

"How's that?"

"If you remain as helpful and forthcoming as you've been to date."

Dave paused, not wanting to push the offended innocence too far. "All right then," he replied. "I'm not in any party, not a Communist or a neo-Communist or

a member of Greenpeace or CND or Animal Rights –
I'm not even a vegetarian. Happy now?"

"Fine, answered Mathieson. "Not that any of those
groups is illegal."

"Oh good," said Dave, "then I can risk saying I'm
against blood sports without going into your computer
as a subversive?"

"Do you travel abroad in your work?" asked
Carrow, ignoring the sarcasm.

"Yes, occasionally."

"What countries?"

"France mostly, sometimes Holland, Germany,
Switzerland."

"Kindly notify us if you're planning to leave the
jurisdiction," said Carrow.

"The *jurisdiction*?!"

"Yes."

"Jesus, I'm being spoken to like a criminal here!"

"If we thought you were, Mr Walker, you'd hardly
be free to travel," said Thompson.

"Well, if not a criminal, a – a suspect of some kind . . ."

"You *were* in the area where the incident occurred,"
said Carrow.

"So what?! I mean – "

"Just notify us if you're planning to leave the
country."

"I've no immediate plans," answered Dave tightly.
"Things are very slack in Moscow these day. Is there
anything else?"

Thompson glanced at the other two men who
indicated no. "That'll be all for now, Mr Walker," he

said. "Thank you again for your co-operation. DC Hart
will see you out."

"That's OK," said Dave rising. "I'll see myself out.
Good morning." He left the room, closed the door hard
behind him and walked quickly down the corridor and
out of the police station.

He paused on the busy street and tried to collect his
thoughts. Had he been too sarcastic, overdone the
innocent man offended? It was difficult to know exactly
how he would have reacted had he genuinely been
innocent, but he felt he had been right to appear angry.
Apart from everything else, it meant that any trembling
of his hand or voice could reasonably be interpreted as
indignation. Provided, that is, that they bought the
outraged innocence. Of course they would have wanted
to give him the impression of being suspicious – why else
call someone in for questioning like that if not to rattle
him, to try to panic the person who was guilty? Probably
trying the same tack with everyone else too, if what
Thompson said about others being questioned were true.

The more he thought about it though, the more he
was glad that Mary had insisted they behave as though
everything would be checked later. He started along the
street towards his office, trying hard, but in vain, to get
his mind back to the world of advertising.

"What do you think?" said Thompson, after the door of
the Interview Room had slammed shut.

Carrow shook his head. "I don't like the cut of that
one's jib."

"Not a crime in itself," observed Thompson wryly.

"Perhaps you could save the repartee for elsewhere," snapped Carrow.

"Gentlemen, gentlemen, let's stick to the business in hand, shall we?" interjected Mathieson. He stroked his chin thoughtfully as he continued. "Seems to me our friend Walker's weekend is interesting in several ways – not least the detail in which he can remember it."

"Some people genuinely have excellent memories," said Thompson.

"True," conceded Mathieson. "However he has absolutely no alibi for Friday night. Could easily have caught a train to London, plain brown envelope in hand."

"Let's get some uniforms down to the train stations with his picture," said Carrow. "We'll do Leeds and Harrogate. Fax the photos to the Met – they can do the British Rail staff in Euston. Likewise the bus stations and airports."

"I'll organise it when we're finished here," said Thompson. "Bit of a long shot ten days later, but worth chasing."

"The problem, though, is timing," said Mathieson. "Walker was in the area on Thursday, so it's possible he could have killed Gatenby and disposed of the body there and then. But if the body was brought to the tarn on Friday or Saturday, then I doubt if it was via Mr Walker."

"You said yourself he has no alibi for Friday night," said Carrow.

"But his wife has. So if he were posting the film from

London, he'd presumably have had to do it himself."

"That still leaves Saturday night, after the barbecue," suggested Carrow.

"Possibly," said Thompson, "but if I were dumping a body I'd definitely want to do it in darkness. By the time he'd have driven to the tarn from Harrogate, dawn would have been breaking."

"My thoughts precisely," said Mathieson.

"Are we ruling out Sunday night?" asked Carrow.

"Well, the pathologist reckoned probably no more than two days before immersion," answered Mathieson.

"It's not the most exact of sciences . . ."

"True, but bearing in mind the very hot weather, I don't see the corpse being kept all weekend. I think we're talking no later than Saturday night if the body was brought back for dumping."

"May I make a suggestion?" asked Penny.

"Of course," the intelligence officer answered encouragingly.

"I don't think we should rule out the wife."

Mathieson looked at Penny quizzically. "Assuming her Friday night phone call checks out, I don't see how she could have got to London to post the film. She was in the BBC during the day."

"I wasn't thinking of the film. She left the barbecue at around eleven on Saturday; that would leave her time to drive to the Dales, dump the body and drive back in darkness."

"Dump the body, a woman almost eight months pregnant?" said Carrow.

"It's only a thought, but I play tennis with a girl who

won a doubles match three days before giving birth," answered Penny.

"But carrying a dead weight – Gatenby was over eleven stone," said Mathieson.

"She could have used a wheelchair. I know eleven stone is a lot to manoeuvre, but disposing of a body is a life-and-death, adrenaline-pumping situation – it's amazing what people can do when it comes to the crunch."

"There is that," conceded Mathieson.

"I'm not saying she actually did it; probably not," replied Penny. "But just supposing her husband *was* involved in this, and for whatever reason he killed Gatenby and panicked and took the body away – might they not gamble on our reaction being just what it has been, that a pregnant woman wouldn't shift a corpse? I've seen a photo of her in mountaineering gear and I've met her, and she's a strong, fit-looking woman."

"But why not dump the body elsewhere?" asked Carrow. "Why go back to the area of the crime?"

"Maybe to suggest a hit-and-run if the body were ever found," offered Thompson. "To suggest it was disposed of at the time of the killing rather than days later, to make the disposal point a fair distance from where the killer lives? Who knows?"

"Hmm, interesting point," said Mathieson. "Worth bearing in mind."

"Just on the subject of pregnancy, if I might make another comment?" said Penny.

Thompson nodded. "Feel free."

"It's a very small thing, but it immediately struck a

wrong note with me when Walker described that phone call on Friday night. He claimed his wife asked him to answer it, but he said no, he reckoned it was probably for her."

"What's odd about that?" asked Carrow.

"Well, I've met both of them," continued Penny, "and they seem to have a good relationship. And yet when his heavily-pregnant wife was sitting down, he wouldn't get up to answer the phone. I don't know, it just rang a bit hollow to me . . ."

"I hadn't thought of it that way." said Thompson.

"Hang on, hang on," said Carrow, turning to Penny. "A moment ago you had the woman shifting an eleven-stone man – now her husband has to answer the phone for her? Not a very consistent line of argument, is it?"

"Perhaps not, sir . . ."

"Not entirely mutually exclusive as attitudes though," said Mathieson.

"I think we might keep an open mind on the subject," said Thompson. "The biggest problem for me is the alibi. Just supposing Walker *was* involved in Gatenby's killing, he'd have to have gotten the film to London, and possibly the corpse to the Dales that weekend. But there's no way he could have constructed a watertight alibi for the whole weekend, there'd have to have been gaps . . ."

"As there are in Walker's case," said Carrow.

"Exactly," answered Thompson. "Which leads me to the fundamental question; why come forward to the police then?"

"Hadn't we postulated the brazen approach?" said

Mathieson. "Might be seen driving through villages – therefore less suspicious to come forward than perhaps be tracked down?"

"I don't know," said Thompson. "It's just not all that convincing . . ."

The intelligence officer shrugged. "Could be some other reason we simply don't know about."

"Like what?" asked Carrow.

"Can't say, I'm afraid. Just shooting in the dark."

"Well, as long as we're shooting in the dark," said Carrow, "I've a feeling about this Walker man. Despite his cocksure air I sense something not quite kosher about him."

"Not a native of these parts, is he?" asked Mathieson.

"Shouldn't think so," replied Thompson. "I couldn't pin down the accent but I'd say he's from somewhere a lot further south."

"Talking of accents, his wife's is a little unusual," said Penny.

Mathieson looked interested. "In what way?"

"Well, as you know, she's an actress. I heard her on a radio play doing a perfectly convincing Yorkshire accent, but when I spoke to her, her own accent wasn't northern. It was . . . I don't know . . . quite a pleasant middle-class sort of tone, but with a hint of something underneath."

"She's not a foreigner?" said Mathieson.

"No. There could have been a suggestion of – of Welsh – Irish perhaps . . ."

"Irish?" said Carrow.

"Just – a possibility. The most I'd suggest was that maybe she didn't always speak as she does now."

"Pity you didn't report this at the time," said Carrow.

"It seemed of no consequence then. It's still a pretty nebulous observation."

"Quite," agreed Mathieson. "But even the slightest hint of a possible IRA background should be explored. You have photos of her?"

"Yes, sir," replied Penny.

"Let me have them, would you. I'll run them past our Irish Section people."

"What about the husband – from a similar perspective?" asked Carrow.

"Already done against all our subversives' lists," answered the intelligence officer. "Absolutely nothing on file."

"Time is marching on, gentlemen," said Thompson. "We need to prepare for Ms Fabien. Let's follow up as agreed with the photos and the bus, train, and airline enquiries. We'll also check Ms Adams' picture against SB, Intelligence and police records. And I'd suggest we keep an eye on Mr Walker and his wife."

"Agreed," said Mathieson.

"Definitely," said Carrow. "Definitely . . ."

23

Mary picked up the phone in the empty greenroom, aware that it wasn't an ideal place from which to make her call. She was scheduled to be in studio all morning however, and this might be her only chance. She felt her mouth become dry as she dialled the number. Worse than an opening night, she thought, as she waited, half-hoping not to get a reply.

After a moment a sing-song voice came on the line. "Good morning, Brompton and Company."

"Good morning, may I speak to Mr Brompton, please?"

"He's on another call. Will you hold please?"

"Yes, OK."

"May I say who's calling?"

"Mary Adams."

"One moment, please."

Mary waited uneasily, her pulses racing. The call from Dave after he had been questioned by the police had settled it. No matter how well he may have handled himself she felt that the net was slowly tightening on them, and despite Dave's protests that they shouldn't act rashly she had finally convinced him about contacting the estate agent.

"Good morning, Ms Adams, Terence Brompton here. How may I help you?" The fruity voice of the estate agent sounded down the phone, breaking her reverie.

"Good morning, Mr Brompton. My husband and I are interested in selling our house. We've a bungalow in Harrogate, off Bighton Lane."

"Excellent location," said Brompton smoothly.

"Yes. I know you do a lot of rentals as well as sales and I wanted to put a proposition to you."

"Please – proposition away." Brompton chuckled artificially.

Mary ignored the attempted badinage and kept her tone businesslike. It was just like a performance, she found, and now that she was embarked on it her nervousness had been replaced by an adrenaline surge. "What I'd like to suggest is the possibility of selling to you, and then taking it back out a short lease."

"Leasing back your own house?"

"Yes. You see we're moving to Wales, building a new house there, and there's been a budget overrun. So we need the capital from the house sale, but the new one won't be ready for a few months, so we also need accommodation."

"Yes, I can quite see the logic. I'd have to say though the market's very depressed at the moment. Prices being as they are, we wouldn't be in a position to offer what might normally be expected . . ."

Excellent, thought Mary, once he starts adopting a poor-mouth approach it means he's interested and starting to bargain. "I'm aware of the market conditions, Mr Brompton, but we could be somewhat flexible on the price."

"Well, in that case . . ."

"There is one condition I must stress though. Were we to agree a three-month lease, we'd want absolutely no advertising of the fact that the house would be coming on the market . . ."

"Oh?"

"We've had enough trauma with the builders in Wales. The last thing we want is signs in the garden, and prospective buyers trooping through the house each weekend." *Not to mention the police knowing.*

"I see . . ."

"Perhaps at the end of the three months it could be advertised." *When we'll have either bought it back ourselves or had to flee the country.*

"Yes . . . however, I'd have to say that were we to purchase, our resale prospects would be lessened – with obvious financial loss – by failing to advertise during the lease period."

"I daresay we could make some adjustment to the purchase price, but it's an essential condition for us, OK?"

"All things being equal, Ms Adams, I'm sure we won't let it become a problem," answered Brompton in an oily tone. "Now may I just jot down a few particulars?"

"Certainly, Mr Brompton," said Mary. Then she

looked around as Arnold Beazley entered the greenroom.

"Could you tell me the size of the site?" asked Brompton.

"Three quarters of an acre," answered Mary softly. She watched uneasily as Beazley placed his script and a bag of Turkish Delights on the table, then lowered his bulk into an armchair and began an ostentatious performance of his breathing exercises.

"And the number of bedrooms?" asked the estate agent.

"Four." Mary knew that despite Beazley's voice preparation, he would probably try to listen in, and she resolved to keep her end of the conversation as cryptic as possible.

"And would the rear garden be north or south-facing?" asked Brompton.

"South-facing," she answered quietly.

"Single or double garage?"

"Double. Perhaps I could give you the details when we meet?"

"As you wish, my dear, as you wish. When would you care to consult?"

"As soon as possible, really."

"Let's see now . . ." said Brompton. "I *could* give you an appointment this afternoon."

"No, I'm afraid I'm working . . ."

"Well, if it would facilitate you I could call over this evening?"

He's eager to make a killing, thought Mary. "Yes, that would be fine. Say about eight?"

"Eight it shall be. And the address?"

"Primrose Cottage, Bighton Lane.

"Ah yes, lovely area, know it well. Till this evening then. I look forward to meeting you in the flesh – as it were!" Brompton chuckled at his daring.

"Yes, see you then," replied Mary, then she hung up.

Beazley turned to her and smiled insincerely. "Hope my vocals didn't disturb your tête-à-tête . . ."

"Hardly a tête-à-tête."

"Oh good. Looked sort of intimate, crouched over the phone like that. I was almost going to leave."

"Really?"

"Yes. Then I thought, the greenroom is for all the actors – not Mary Adams' private suite – so I stayed . . ."

"Congratulations! I hope you'll be very happy here," retorted Mary. She turned before Beazley could reply and was halfway along the corridor when she was struck by the enormity of what she was setting in motion.

Despite the consoling knowledge that they could buy back the house if everything settled down, she felt uneasy. If Brompton made them a reasonable offer tonight she knew they would take it, and somehow she sensed that in doing so things would never be the same again.

Disturbed by the thought, she walked on slowly towards the studio.

Carrow's mind wandered as he drove through the city. He was unsure what to make of Anne-Marie Fabien, the Belgian au pair. Her heavily accented English and mousy appearance had provoked an instinctively unsympathetic response from him, yet his normally reliable gut feeling told him that the woman was not the type for any kind of lawbreaking.

Unless, of course, she was well-trained and giving a first-class performance. They had drawn a blank however in finding anything on her, either in the files of Special Branch or Military Intelligence. Probably just another Continental come here to gain some badly needed improvement in her English, he reckoned, but still not to be ruled out of the picture completely.

His musings were suddenly halted by the ringing of his mobile phone. He switched it on, keeping one hand on the wheel. "Carrow . . ."

"Jones here, sir. We've got some information on the white Hiace."

"Just a minute, Jones. I'll pull in." Carrow crossed into the left-hand lane, then turned into a side street to avoid the noise of the traffic heading through the centre of Leeds. "OK, let's have it," he said.

"We've had the details faxed from SB in London, sir. Three white Hiace vans were rented to English-speaking foreigners in the period."

"Yes?"

"We can probably dismiss two of them, sir. One was an order of American nuns, moving bunks into a children's refuge, the other was a New Zealand amateur dramatics group, transporting scenery and props to a drama festival in Reading."

"And the third?"

"More interesting, sir. A Canadian, male, in his forties, hired a van the day Aksor disappeared."

"What's his name?"

"Jeffries, sir, Richard Jeffries. We have a copy of his rental application from."

"Have we an address?"

"Yes, sir, the Russell Hotel in Bloomsbury."

"Right!" said Carrow. "I'm on my way in."

24

Visser reckoned it was a promising start. He had pulled into the car park of the Manchester Excelsior Hotel and was wondering if he would find a parking space, when another driver vacated a berth directly ahead. Visser accelerated to secure the space, then pulled in, applying the handbrake and cutting the engine in one easy movement. If only the rest of his mission would go as smoothly, he thought.

Sitting back in the driver's seat, he savoured the familiar thrill of the chase. It was curious to think that his quarry, Anne-Marie Fabien, was – despite his plans for her – unaware of his very existence. Well, he would soon change that. It would be good to seduce her; in fact if he could bed the Belgian au pair he would have come full circle. He thought back to his first woman, a Belgian prostitute who had fled the Congo in the early sixties for the safety of South Africa. She had left Katanga penniless, and had propositioned Visser at a price that even a working-class teenager could afford. It had been a memorable night for him, and he recollected it fondly now as he took his suitcase, locked the driver's door and crossed towards the hotel lobby. Who knows, he thought smilingly, perhaps Anne-Marie Fabien would turn out to be memorable too.

He climbed the hotel entrance steps, feeling deliciously alive and eager to progress his mission. And in spite of Reinholdt's fussing he was confident that he had nothing to fear regarding Aksor's disappearance. He had been extremely careful, and Aksor's body would not be found, much less traced to him.

He crossed to reception, laid down his case and nodded pleasantly to the young woman behind the desk.

"Good afternoon, sir."

"Afternoon. I've booked a room . . ."

"And the name, sir?"

"Franklin. Thomas P Franklin."

"That's fine, Mr Franklin. If you wouldn't mind registering," she said, handing him a pen.

"Of course." Funny how easy it was to adopt a new identity, he thought, once you were well-prepared. He had switched to his American alias of Franklin from his Canadian persona of Richard Jeffries. He had also returned the white Hiace van, and hired his present car from a separate rental company. Good field practice, he thought. Never leave any kind of trail.

"Here we are, Mr Franklin," said the receptionist, handing him a key as he finished registering. "I'll get you a porter."

"That won't be necessary, I'm travelling light."

"As you wish, sir. Have a pleasant stay then."

"Thank you," said Visser, practising his smile. "I'm sure I will."

"I can't believe it's really happening," said Dave, closing the hall door.

"I know. It's weird," answered Mary, as they returned from the hall to the sitting-room.

Dave stood at the window looking across the sunlit lawn as Terence Brompton drove away.

"Not a bad price in the end," said Mary.

"It's less then the house is worth."

"Well, we knew that would happen. He'd never have gone for it otherwise."

"I know . . . I know . . ."

"I'm less sure about Brompton himself," said Mary. "He is rather gushing."

"Noel Coward gone wrong," said Dave wryly. *"Quite delightful interior – entirely sympathetique!"* he enthused, mimicking the estate agent.

Mary laughed at the accuracy of the fruity tone.

"Quite delightful chance to pick up a house on the cheap, more like," said Dave.

"You don't think he'll blabber that the house has been sold?"

"He'll keep quiet. Didn't you see his eyes light up when I said a colleague would be returning from Bahrain in a few months and looking to buy a house?"

"Yes," answered Mary.

"Don't let the Cricket Club blazer fool you. He's a

right little money-grabber. Can't wait to get a contract signed before we change our minds. He won't rock the boat. He'll stay quiet."

"You're probably right," acknowledged Mary. "And even allowing for dropping the price, it's still a hell of a lump sum. If the worst came to the worst, it would buy a nice farm in Ireland."

"Yeah . . ." He shook his head pensively. "Jesus – I – I just hope we're not overreacting."

Mary reached out and squeezed his arm. "Dave . . . we've had all this already. If the worst comes to the worst we're not going to have any choice in the matter. We'll *have* to run for it."

"I know . . . I know. We'll take his offer. It's just . . . if we end up having to run for it, it makes me look like a criminal."

"Not really being a criminal would be scant consolation if you were convicted of manslaughter, murder even."

"I know. Just at a gut level I can't help but feel they've won somehow if they make us flee."

"No. If that happens we're still the winners. We'll have escaped an injustice, we'll be together as a family, and we'll start a new life. That's the way we must think of it."

Dave looked at her, her determined expression softly lit by the setting sun, and he felt a sudden welling up of affection.

"What is it?" asked Mary.

"You." He looked at her tenderly. "What would I do without you?"

"What would *I* do without *you*?" she said.

Dave enclosed her in his arms, and they embraced, then after a moment he gently released her.

Mary indicated the garden, its lawns, trees and shrubs resplendent in the evening sunlight. "I'd really miss this."

"I know. It might be pretty strange for you if we'd to live in Ireland again after all this time."

Mary nodded thoughtfully. "It might." It was, she knew, less than twenty years since her father had broken up her first real love affair because the family of the boy involved didn't have land. She wanted to believe that such primitive rural attitudes had changed for the better, as her brother Tom claimed, but it wasn't the kind of thing for which guarantees existed. "It might be a bit strange," she said "but there are good and bad points about living anywhere."

"Right . . ."

"And I'd have Tom and Jenny and the kids nearby, and more time to do my stained glass work."

"Either way, before we know where we are, Brompton's going to have a contract and cheque," said Dave. "We need to sort out a Swiss account."

"How do you do that?"

"I'm not sure," he answered. "But we'd better find out – and fast."

25

Visser felt his pulses start to race when the phone was answered on the second ring. He had tried repeatedly to contact Anne-Marie Fabien the previous night, eventually driving to the suburban address he had for her only to find the luxurious villa in total darkness. He was relieved as well as excited now to hear a woman's voice on the other end of the phone.

"Hello."

"Hello, I wonder if I might have a word with Miss Fabien?" He kept his voice deep and pleasant-sounding.

"I'm afraid she's not here, right now."

Visser rated the clipped accent as upper middle-class. "Perhaps you could tell me when I might catch her?"

"Who is this, please?"

The woman's tone had shifted from brusque to antagonistic.

Arrogant bitch, thought Visser, but he kept his voice

pleasant. "My name is Franklin, Thomas Franklin . . ."

"What is it you want with Miss Fabien?"

None of your fucking business, thought Visser. "I'm a feature writer," he answered reasonably. "I was hoping to have a word with Anne-Marie for a piece I'm doing for *Cosmopolitan.*" It occurred to him that the police had possibly been on the phone to these people a good deal – perhaps that would account for the woman's attitude. "May I take it that it's Mrs Cadwell to whom I'm speaking?"

There was a pause, then the woman spoke frostily. "This number is unlisted – where did you get my name?"

Jesus, but he'd like to be strapping a few electrodes onto this irritating cow. "I hope you'll forgive me, Mrs Cadwell, if I've taken a liberty," he said obsequiously, "but I'm writing a piece on the au-pairing profession – the upper end of the market, specifically. I went to a top agency and asked for the name of a foreign au pair who had been placed with a good family. I wanted to show how well these girls can do. Nice house, pleasant working conditions, that sort of thing . . ."

"I see . . ."

"The agency spoke very highly of your good self, and I persuaded them to give me your number. If in doing so any impropriety has occurred, I must take the blame entirely."

"Well . . . I daresay no harm was meant. It's simply that one wouldn't wish one's number given to all and sundry."

"Of course. I appreciate perfectly how undesirable that would be for a lady such as yourself."

"This piece, you say it's for *Cosmopolitan*?"

"That's right." He could sense her interest now, she could already envisage impressing her friends. Better move before she saw herself at the centre of the article. "It would be written from the point of view of the au pair – the opportunities, the duties, the rewards and so on. That's why I'd like a word with Anne-Marie, with your permission, of course."

"Yes, that would be acceptable. I can arrange it when she returns."

"She's away?"

"On a day's leave."

"Ah . . . well, I'm not surprised; I expected your terms and conditions would be generous."

"Yes, well, we like to look after our staff. She won't be back until late this evening, but I can tell her about the article."

"Excellent, I'd be most grateful. In fact if I could trespass further on your good nature, Mrs Cadwell, I wonder if we could arrange for me to meet Anne-Marie when she returns? Truth to tell, I'm rather behind schedule."

"You could come out here tomorrow if you wish. My husband and I have to go to London in the morning, but I could instruct Anne-Marie to show you around."

"That would be wonderful." Especially being able to meet her without anyone else seeing him, thought Visser. "I'm really most grateful."

"When is the article being published?"

"The edition after next. We've a fairly short advance schedule."

"I see. Will you be bringing a photographer?"

"Eh, no . . ."

"Surely you'll require shots of the house?"

Vain Cow. "Yes, yes, of course. What I was going to say is that I'm actually a photo-journalist, I prefer to do my own shots. That way I can be sure that justice is done to beautiful surroundings – as I'm sure your own are, Mrs Cadwell."

"Quite. Well, I'm sorry I shall miss you, but we're socially committed to spending several days in London."

"Too bad. However, you will of course receive proofs of the article and photographs prior to publication."

"Good."

"So shall I ring Anne-Marie, to arrange a time?"

"No need. I'll tell her to have the place prepared and to expect you – let's say about two-thirty. The boys will be at their riding lesson then, so she'll be free."

"I'm most grateful."

"Not at all. Good morning."

"Good morning, Mrs Cadwell."

Visser smiled as he hung up, gratified that he hadn't lost his touch. Now all he had to do was work on Anne-Marie Fabien and that, he suspected, might be quite rewarding.

26

"This bastard is a pro!" said Carrow.

Despite the sweltering summer atmosphere in the interview room the Special Branch officer wore his tweed suit, and Penny wondered if it was a power-dressing gesture, to give him an edge over Thompson and Mathieson, who were in their shirt sleeves.

"We're still not absolutely sure the white van is linked to Aksor's disappearance," said Thompson mildly.

"Not sure?" Carrow looked at the other policeman witheringly. "There's no Richard Jeffries in the Russell Hotel, our man pays cash for the van hire, wears dark glasses and a hat when picking it up. Likewise when returning it. To say nothing of the Canadian driver's licence"

"What's the significance of that?" said Thompson.

Carrow threw his eyes to heaven and Mathieson answered in his place. "No ID picture on Canadian licences. Rather useful in avoiding having one's features compared to a photograph."

"The whole thing screams suspicion," said Carrow.

"I agree," said Thompson, "but it's just possible the van was hired for some other dubious purpose. I'm simply saying we shouldn't automatically assume it was used to abduct Aksor. At any rate, as our mystery man has vanished – "

"For the moment," interjected Carrow.

"For the moment," conceded Thompson. "Let's continue with the other areas. Penny?"

Penny opened a file on the table before her. "Mr Walker's alibi for Saturday night checks out. We've spoken to Linda Browne, the Tennis Club secretary, and Norman and Sue Forrestal who confirm that Walker was in the club till 1.30 a.m."

"What about Walker and his wife's movements during the day?"

Penny nodded. "We've confirmed all the other details about him playing tennis, her visiting the hairdresser and so on."

"What about Anne-Marie Fabien?" asked Carrow.

"Her story stands up. Minding the Cadwell children on Friday and Saturday, at a Belgian Society function on Saturday night till two-fifteen, plenty of witnesses." She shrugged. "Every detail matches both their statements."

"Which still wouldn't rule out a late night/early dawn trip to the Dales for either of them," said Thompson.

"Quite," agreed Mathieson. He turned to Penny. "No alibi for Walker's wife after she left the barbecue at eleven?"

"No, sir."

"Hmm. Means that – in theory at any rate – she could have been to the Dales and back under cover of darkness."

"In theory," said Carrow. "Let's stick to realities, though. Any progress from Forensics on Walker's fingerprints?"

"Yes," said Thompson, "they got a clear set from the table here after we questioned him, and compared them with the three remaining unidentified sets from Gatenby's house." He shook his head. "No dice."

"What's the state of play on the unidentified prints?" asked Carrow.

"Being pursued," answered Thompson, "but it's a hell of a job. They could be anybody's – a casual pick-up, tradesman working in the house, whatever . . . I doubt if it will yield anything significant."

"So what else are your people doing?" asked Carrow.

"Checking every car-valeting outfit within fifty miles," said Thompson.

"Car-valeting?"

"Yes. We reckon our murderer may have transported Gatenby's body to the tarn. Almost certainly that would have been done in a van or the boot of a car. If you'd had a body in your vehicle wouldn't you consider a thorough cleaning as soon as possible?"

"They could do that themselves," suggested Mathieson.

"They could," answered Thompson, "but lots of people nowadays are aware of what Forensics can do with a tiny sample. They might want their car thoroughly worked over by professional cleaners."

"Fair point," said Mathieson.

"It's a long shot," admitted Thompson, "but it would be worth the effort if it threw up a name off our list."

"What about the bus, train and airline staff?" asked Carrow.

"We're working our way through them. We've good quality pictures of Fabien, Walker and Walker's wife, but we have to cover staff in Manchester, Leeds, Harrogate and London. So far no joy, but we'll stick at it till we've tracked down everyone on duty that Friday night."

"I still reckon our best chance of a lead is with this Richard Jeffries," said Carrow.

"He has rather vanished," said Mathieson.

"For the moment," agreed Carrow, "but I think he'll resurface."

"Why so?" asked Thompson.

"Because if he abducted Aksor, and if there's a link from Aksor to Gatenby, then presumably this Jeffries is privy to that knowledge by now – why else abduct Aksor? And if he is privy to that knowledge, he's likely to act on it."

"Depending on who he is, and who he might be working for . . ." said Thompson.

Mathieson turned around, his languid air temporarily gone. "If you're suggesting, Chief Inspector, that he's one of our chaps, I can assure you otherwise."

"Fair enough," answered Thompson. "No chance of . . . SIS involvement?"

Mathieson smiled wryly. "Don't read too much into the stories of competition between M15 and SIS. Home territory is our turf. Our colleagues aren't players in this one."

"Seeing as we're discussing undesirable possibilities," said Carrow, "no chance CIA might be involved?"

"No," replied Mathieson. "We only informed them of Gatenby's disappearance last Wednesday. Aksor had already been abducted by then, assuming of course that he *has* been abducted. Besides, there'd be hell to pay if the Agency went behind our backs and mounted that sort of operation on British soil."

"Who could our mystery man be then?" asked Thompson.

"Who knows?" said Carrow. "My people in London have given his description to every vehicle-hire company in the metropolitan area. Any foreigner resembling that description and going to hire a vehicle will be reported to us. And remember, hiring the van in the first place suggests a solo operator, someone acting without back-up teams and transport. Which means that if he wants to pursue his mission he'll need a car. I reckon that's our best chance of a break."

"Anything else, gentlemen?" asked Mathieson.

"No," replied Thompson, "I'm afraid it's the wait-and-see period. We're doing all the checking. We have to hope that it turns up something, or that our killer makes a mistake."

"Quite." Mathieson sat back in his chair, then turned to Thompson. "There is one possibility. I know it's a tremendous drain on manpower, but we could go for twenty-four-hour surveillance on Fabien, Walker and Walker's wife."

Thompson stroked his chin. "Three separate individuals for twenty-four-hour surveillance – that's a hell of a commitment of resources when we haven't a shred of evidence against them."

"We could agitate for more staff if necessary." said Carrow. "This case is a top priority."

"I'm not sure I want to ask the Commissioner for surveillance teams to pursue people who actually approached us."

Carrow smiled humourlessly. "Covering your back, Inspector?"

"No, more like using our resources as productively as possible."

"No surveillance then?" persisted Carrow.

Thompson considered. "I don't think so for the moment. If any of our other enquiries point towards them in any way, then immediate round-the-clock surveillance." He looked at Mathieson. "OK?"

"Sounds reasonable."

"Mr Carrow?"

"All right."

"Well, if there's nothing else, gentlemen?" Thompson looked around.

"Back to the grind," said Mathieson, rising.

"Right," said Carrow, pushing back his chair and following the intelligence officer to the door.

Penny rose also, waited until Mathieson and Carrow had left the room, then turned to Thompson. "Could I have a word, Chief?"

"Of course."

Penny closed the door and turned to him.

"My word, this looks ominous. Haven't called you "lass" in an unguarded moment, I hope?"

Penny smiled. "Nothing like that, Chief."

"That's a relief. Don't want to cross swords with you as well. Carrow's enough to be going on with."

"Yes, he is rather . . . well . . ." She smiled again. "I'd better not badmouth a senior officer or you'll be reaching for the 'cheeky bugger' label again."

"No need – had you labelled that way since day one!" He grinned, then he regained his seat and gestured for Penny to sit also. "So, what's on your mind?"

"You remember, Chief, the meeting last week when I said that killing Gatenby might have been a spur-of-the-moment thing?"

"Aye."

"I suggested that perhaps some psychopath might have been responsible . . ."

"We checked up on escaped prisoners, mental patients. There was nothing."

"I know. But the actual psychopath thing was just a top-of-the-head suggestion. I reckon now that the element of chance was what I was really getting at."

"Go on."

"I was thinking about it last night, but bearing in mind Mr Carrow's reaction last time, I didn't think he'd want to hear my efforts at lateral thinking."

"But you've figured something out?"

"I think so."

"Let's have it."

"OK, if our starting point is that the killing had nothing to do with SMORTAR, it explains why the killer sent back the microfilm. No interest to him or her, and only likely to produce a lot of heat – so it's posted back."

"OK."

"OK, so why kill Gatenby? Let's rule out a hit-and-run and my imaginary psychopath, and what are we left with? Two things. One, Gatenby bumps into a stranger and has a row for some reason, a row that gets out of hand. Conceivable, but as it ends with Gatenby having his skull shattered, rather unlikely."

"I agree," said Thompson.

"So that leaves just one other explanation that seems plausible."

"Which is?"

"Gatenby bumped into someone he *already knew*. Someone with whom there was bad blood, and somehow it ended in violence."

Thompson looked into space, then turned to her. "It hangs together better but think of the odds, Penny. It's damned sparsely populated where this happened. What are the chances of Gatenby bumping into someone he knew and disliked up in the wilds?"

"The odds are against it, Chief. But last year I went to Turkey on holidays; we'd hired a car, and one day I drove up into the mountains above Usak, stopped at a tiny roadside cafe – and met a girl from my class in school. Has nothing like that ever happened to you?"

Thompson thought, then nodded. "Years ago on a

golf course in Portugal, I met my old company sergeant. Once in a lifetime thing, though . . ."

"Maybe that day was Gatenby's once in a lifetime meeting."

"So where's this leading us?"

"To our list of people who were in the Dales. We've more or less written off Ralph Taylor, Mrs Wallace and her daughter, Belal Hussief, and the pensioner, Bill Murray. So let's look at Anne-Marie Fabien and David Walker."

"OK."

"Starting with the au pair. Woman meets man in remote spot, ends in sudden death – why?"

Thompson shrugged. "Hardly attempted rape . . ."

"I thought of that, but as Gatenby had a case full of stolen film, raping someone – even if he were the type – would probably be the last thing on his mind."

"Precisely, so what then?"

"If it's to do with either Fabien or Walker I reckon it's a grudge thing. Say Gatenby met her on holidays once, had an affair, jilted her, maybe even got her pregnant. They meet by chance years later, old wounds are opened . . ."

"Possibly . . . and Walker?"

"Maybe they'd met sometime . . . clashed over something."

"Very different social circles. No work convergence. Gatenby's been in the service since leaving college."

"In childhood then, in the Boy Scouts, at summer camp, whatever. Gatenby was four years older than Walker, maybe . . . maybe he baby-sat as a teenager, sexually abused younger boys. Suppose we compare backgrounds in real detail. Everything from their births to the present, looking for a link. Were any two ever on holiday at the same resort at the same time – anything like that."

"It's an interesting line of reasoning, Penny. Gatenby's no problem, we have official records and I'm sure we can get more detail. Fabien and Walker are private individuals though, the former a Belgian national. Getting the kind of personal information you want isn't so simple."

"I'm sure the au pair agency would have a very detailed CV on anyone wanting to mind children," said Penny. "And Walker's employers would probably have his job application on file, with a detailed CV."

Thompson quickly raised a hand. "Tread carefully, Penny, tread carefully. Civil liberties, data protection . . . these are sensitive issues."

"I thought in a murder investigation, with national security implications . . ."

"Yes?"

"Well, I thought there might be some . . . leeway?"

Thompson looked at her appraisingly, then smiled wryly. "You're growing up fast. And, don't tell me, I think I know who you have in mind to pull the necessary strings . . ."

It was Penny's turn to smile. "I daresay with all your years of successful police work you're owed a few favours here and there."

"Hmm . . ."

"If it comes to nothing, Chief, we can quickly

dispose of the information, and no harm done. And if anything does come to light – well, maybe the top brass will forgive a slight bending of the rules."

"Assuming they ever need know," said Thompson. Then he shook his head. "What am I saying? I'm supposed to be teaching you procedure."

Penny looked him in the eye, and despite his protestation, thought she detected a touch of irony.

"Let me think about it, Penny," he said.

"Thanks, Chief."

"I didn't say yes. I said let me think about it."

"Of course, sir."

"And not a word of this to Carrow or Mathieson – not for now anyway," said Thompson, rising.

"OK, Chief." Penny rose also, returned the inspector's nod of dismissal, and went out.

She headed back towards her desk, pleased at how seriously Thompson had taken her, and trying hard not to get her hopes up too high.

27

Bob Reinholdt sat staring into space. As CIA Chief of Station in London he had a large office, but he sat immobile, unconscious of his luxurious surroundings. He reflected on the call he had just received from Visser, and wondered again if choosing the South African had been a mistake.

He didn't know which worried him more, the agent's unsettling independence and the unpredictability that went with it, or the man's lack of any moral values, any basic decency. In rising to his present rank, Reinholdt had seen and done things he would like to forget, and operations in Vietnam, Iran and El Salvador had not been for the faint of heart, yet he was uncomfortable with what he could only think of as an innate depravity, a zest for cruelty, in Visser.

His reflections were disturbed by his secretary on the intercom. "Call from Langley, sir."

"Who is it?"

"Mr Johnson, European Desk.

Reinholdt paused a moment. "OK, put him through." A call from 'Mr Johnson' meant that Krucowski wanted another update on the SMORTAR affair. And in using the Johnson alias, wanted no link to himself if things went badly . . .

"Good afternoon."

Reinholdt recognised the voice, but despite the secure scrambled line he would mention no names and keep the conversation oblique.

"Good afternoon," he answered.

"What's the latest?"

"Our friend up north visited his first relation . . ."

"Well received?"

"Apparently. Seems she's very poor though. Couldn't contribute at all to his cause."

"That's disappointing, very disappointing."

Reinholdt fought back his irritation at how Krucowski made it sound like his fault. "He's moving on to the next one, hoping for better fortune there."

"I see. When will he be in touch?"

"Tomorrow. The moment there's anything."

"I'm very anxious that he has good news, very anxious indeed."

Time to change tack here, thought Reinholdt. "Yes, we're all anxious for good news; I hope his first offering has been well received . . ." Even a bastard like Krucowski couldn't deny the value of Visser's data on the Sons of the Dawn.

"First-class product," answered the Deputy Director. "The appropriate people are licking their lips."

"Glad to help," said Reinholdt, thinking that he might as well store up some credit.

"First-class product, but a side issue now," continued Krucowski. "We need progress on the main story. What about your friend on the inside?"

"He's keeping me posted. Nothing much new – some inter-service rivalry, still being formally headed by the locals, no-stone-unturned approach. Seems the guy in charge is a bit of a maverick . . ."

"That's a word sends chills down my spine," said Krucowski.

"Not that kind of a maverick. Sound politically. Just a tad unorthodox – but with a good reputation for results. The feeling is that if anyone can break it, he will."

"Jesus, we need more than feelings!"

"I know, but – "

"We need results. This could be vitally important."

"Yes, sir."

"Stay tight on this, I'd like to see some progress."

"The moment there's anything, I'll make contact."

"Discreetly. But make it soon, make it very soon. Good day."

"Good day, sir." Reinholdt hung up, then banged his desk-top in frustration. "Asshole!" What the hell did Krucowski want of him, what more could he do? It was well known that the Deputy Director was a twenty-four-hours-a-day man; ever since he had left a new bride for a tour in Vietnam and returned to find her demanding a divorce, his whole life had been devoted to the company. Unfortunately he expected the same obsessive dedication from everyone else. Reinholdt knew that even that wouldn't be enough however; Krucowski demanded results as well. But there was nothing further that could be done; all of that was now in the hands of Jan Visser.

He thought of the South African, presently on his way to Harrogate, thought again about Krucowski's impatient tone, and hoped against hope that they would get a break.

Penny felt disappointed, in spite of her resolution not to get her hopes up too high. There was no sign of Thompson returning to the office, despite her having suspected strongly that he was following her suggestion and unofficially getting the background information on Anne-Marie Fabien and David Walker. Why else, she had reasoned, would he suddenly have had to attend a series of meetings without her? She had felt certain that he was calling in some favours, and meanwhile she had joined Inspector Powell in the laborious and unfruitful task of tracking down and questioning the British Rail staff who had been on duty the night the microfilm had been posted back from London. But now her shift was finished, and the other members of the team were drifting towards the locker-room.

Normally she would have been happy to work late, but she felt that if she waited back until Thompson returned it might appear that she was pressurising him for a response – or even worse, that she was presuming he had acted on her suggestion and that she was waiting for him to deliver the data. Better to finish up and go home, she thought.

She rose from her desk, left the office, and walked down the corridor, her movement scattering dust that danced in the strong rays of the late afternoon sunlight.

"Penny!"

The voice came from behind her and she turned to see Thompson at the door to the offices with several folders under his arm.

"In my office for a minute, please," he said.

She walked back swiftly to where Thompson held the door open for her and preceded him into his office.

"Sorry to drag you back. Were you going home?"

"Yes but it's OK."

"It's just that I've got something for you." He smiled and tapped the folders.

"The stuff on Fabien and Walker?"

Thompson nodded and handed them over.

"Great." She glanced at the contents.

"It's all there. Birth certs, marriage certs, CVs, credit ratings, loan applications, passport and driver's licence applications – you name it."

Penny smiled. "Thanks, Chief, you've obviously got a lot of contacts."

Thompson raised a hand. "Don't ask . . . let's just say this is irregular and leave it at that."

"'Nuff said, Chief. I'm looking forward to ploughing through this – I'll start straight away."

"It can wait until the morning."

"I don't mind staying back."

"Your dedication does you proud, Penny, but you've been working like a Trojan since this case started. Take a night off – have a few drinks with your friends."

"Honestly, Chief, I don't mind working on."

"I mind."

Penny looked at him in surprise.

"I've gone out on a limb to get this stuff," explained Thompson. "I don't want you sifting through it when you're tired. Take a night off and come to it in the morning with a fresh mind. No arguments, Penny," he said as she prepared to respond. "That's an order."

Penny smiled resignedly. "OK."

"Right . . . So I'll see you bright and early in the morning?"

"Absolutely."

The golden evening light illuminated the Yorkshire countryside, and Mary watched from the window of the train as the fields glided by. The landscape seemed to be bathed in lazy summer warmth and it complemented her own mood of quiet satisfaction. Her back was beginning to ache now, as it had sometimes done in the recent stages of her pregnancy, but otherwise she felt well, especially considering how busy the day had been.

It had started with the nine-thirty appointment to sign the contracts with Brompton, the estate agent, who had moved with amazing speed to close the deal. Their initial assessment of Brompton as eager to make a quick killing had been accurate, and the estate agent's solicitors had clearly been instructed to move at top speed through the mechanics of house conveyancing.

The result had been that the deeds had changed hands, contracts had been signed for both the sale and a short-term lease, and they had received a banker's order for one hundred and eighty thousand pounds. Nothing like a bit of greed to get things moving, as her old Uncle Pat used to say, and it was true; Brompton's desire to get the house at a bargain price – and before they might change their minds – was the obvious explanation of why he had closed the deal so rapidly.

Mary had emerged from the estate agent's office in the main street of Harrogate and seen in Dave's eyes a look that reflected perfectly her own mixture of awe at the step they had just taken, and satisfaction in knowing that they would have the benefit of their chief asset if their worst fears came true and they had to flee the country.

She took a lift into Leeds with Dave and then cautiously made her way towards the train station. She knew that it would be disastrous were the police to tumble to their house-sale plan and just in case they might be under police surveillance she took a circuitous route, as she had done earlier in the day on her way to Brompton's office, stopping and looking in shop windows to check if anyone did likewise. Once again she felt rather self-conscious, but by the time she entered the railway station she was satisfied that she was not being watched.

She bought a return ticket to London, dined on the southbound express, and then took a taxi to

Threadneedle Street and the offices of the Commercial Bank of Switzerland. Following their earlier telephone instructions she had brought her passport and a letter from Dave confirming joint authority of the account, and she deposited the one hundred and eighty thousand, plus the bulk of their savings, withdrawn from the Nat West in Harrogate, and requested that the deposit be immediately transferred to their new, numbered Swiss account. Forty-five minutes later she was on the train back to Yorkshire.

A good day's work, she thought, and now, as the engine slowed on approaching Arthington viaduct, she shifted her aching back and told herself that they had taken every precaution they could. She still hoped fervently that the police enquiries would fizzle out, and that they could buy back the bungalow in a couple of months. Maybe then they could forget all of this and start their new life with the baby. Maybe, she thought, yet however hard she tried to stay positive she couldn't quite shake off a niggling undercurrent of fear.

28

Penny stopped dead. Her skin came out in goosebumps as she sat looking at the file on her desk, then she quickly sought another folder from the desk top. She tried to keep her excitement in check as she opened it and scanned its contents. "Christ!" she said softly. She compared the two sheets of paper for a moment, and made a quick written note before scooping up the files and crossing the room to Thompson's office.

She knocked and entered immediately. The Chief Inspector was at his filing cabinet, and she realised from his expression that in spite of her efforts to stay cool, her excitement must be showing.

"You've found something?" he asked, not making any attempt to hide the eagerness in his tone.

"Yes."

Thompson reached over and closed the office door, then turned to her. "Let's have it."

Penny laid the two files on his desk and pointed at them in turn. "Nigel Gatenby, boarder at St George's

College, Sussex, from 1962 to 1973. David Walker, day pupil, then boarder, St George's College, 1966 to 1977. Seven years in the same school . . ."

"Jesus!" Thompson shook his head in awe. "Seven bloody years!" He looked at her. "That's damn good police work, Penny. Well done."

"Thanks, Chief. Do we pick Walker up then?"

Thompson thought a moment. "Yes, but not right now – he's not going anywhere. He's a cool customer, that one, brazening it out."

"Absolutely."

"I'll speak to the school. Before we pick him up I'd like all the facts; be nice if we knew that the pair of them had some history, some grudge maybe."

"And to think he never batted an eyelid that day we showed him Gatenby's picture," said Penny.

"He'll be batting a few today, I can tell you. Pity about Carrow and Mathieson, though, isn't it?"

"How's that, Chief?"

"Well, Mathieson went to London last night, seems the cloak-and-dagger gang wanted a personal briefing. Carrow's down there too, leaning on the Met to speed up the car rental enquiries. One in the eye for both of them if the case were broken in their absence by mere provincial plodders, eh?"

Penny smiled. "I could live with that."

"Right, what time is it? Six minutes past nine. I reckon that St George's College should be open for business. Got the number?"

"No, sir, not on the CV's. I'll get it from Directory Enquiries."

"Use my phone," said Thompson, indicating his desk, "and then get me the school Principal, please. We're going to have a little chat about Mr Walker's schooldays . . ."

Standing naked before the mirror, Jan Visser regarded himself appraisingly. Despite the heat of the summer morning he felt fresh, the tiled floor of his bathroom in the Harrogate Moat House Hotel cool beneath his feet. He reached out and tilted the mirror to consider himself from another angle. Pretty good for a man of forty-nine, he thought. His stomach was flat, and his hairless chest taut and muscular from his gymnasium workouts. He had a good all-over tan, only slightly marred by a light ridge of scar tissue along his left ribs, where a ZANLA suspect had slashed him years ago during the guerrilla warfare in Rhodesia. He remembered with grim satisfaction how the man had taken hours to die, his screams echoing through the bush as Visser patiently exacted his vengeance. Pity about Rhodesia, he thought, run by *kaffirs* now – they'd even made the whites go native and refer to the place as Zimbabwe. Still, no use crying over spilt milk, he reckoned, especially when there were fresh pastures at hand.

Visser reached out and splashed on a liberal dose of aftershave. He softly hummed Bach's *Suite in D major* as he crossed to the bedroom where his slacks and a tight-fitting silk shirt were laid out on the bed.

He wanted to look his best for his meeting with Mary Adams. She had sounded attractive over the phone, and he was looking forward to meeting her in person. It hadn't been easy setting up the meeting; on ringing yesterday he had been told at the BBC that she wasn't recording that week, then there had been no answer to his calls to her home all during the day, and when he had finally contacted her later in the evening she had been reluctant to agree to an interview.

He had been persistent however, simultaneously laying on a practised good-natured charm and explaining how important it was to highlight the strength of the dramatic arts in the regions as well as in London, and she had relented and agreed to his calling at eleven the next morning.

He glanced at his watch now as he donned his clothes. Ten forty – just the right amount of time to stroll through Harrogate to her bungalow in Bighton Lane. He had already checked out the area the previous night and found it pleasantly secluded. It probably would have been possible to park unseen by neighbours, but better still to go on foot and leave no trail at all, he thought.

He slipped on his shoes, checked his hair in the corner mirror, then took up a small attaché-case before leaving the room. He travelled down in the lift, crossed the hotel foyer, and emerged into the bright sunlight. He turned right into King's Road and walked past the Conference Centre towards the Royal Hall.

The hot May sunshine seemed to add to the holiday mood of the visitors arriving in coaches to view the historic buildings of the town, but Visser walked past the Royal Baths and Assembly Rooms, oblivious of the elegant architecture as he thought about the job ahead.

Mary Adams and her husband were the only leads he had left – Fabien, the Belgian woman, had been a waste of time. Notwithstanding the disappointment of her extremely plain looks, he had invited her to dinner after the mock *Cosmopolitan* interview, but despite plying her with drink to loosen her tongue his questioning had yielded nothing even remotely suspicious, and he had been quite convinced that she was incapable of anything subversive.

Which meant that a lot rode on this coming meeting. Still, he had his implements in the attaché case, and if Adams and Walker were the ones involved, he would soon have her talking. Excited by the thought, he walked on through the town, impatient to meet her and see how things might develop.

"Damned smart girl," drawled Mathieson.

"Yes, I daresay," answered Carrow.

The Sussex countryside looked glorious as they drove towards East Grinstead, but Carrow's mood was not as buoyant as Mathieson's, the Special branch man being unable to shake off his frustration that the break in the case had come via Penny Hart. He was still smarting from the evident satisfaction in Thompson's voice when the other man had rung earlier from Leeds with the news about Walker. Carrow was glad to see Walker implicated – he would enjoy giving the cocky bastard a good grilling – it was just irritating that Thompson and Hart would claim the credit for the breakthrough.

Still it was good fortune that the school that Walker and Gatenby had attended was in the countryside between Crawley and East Grinstead. Being so close to London it meant that Carrow and Mathieson were the obvious ones to take charge of things at that end.

Thompson had explained that the Principal and most of the present staff had not been employed in the school between 1966 and 1973, but according to their records a retired teacher called Julian Brotherton had been a form master for both Walker and Gatenby at different times. Brotherton still lived in the area and though he didn't have a phone at his small country cottage he could almost always be found working in his garden.

Thompson had been eager to have the full facts before arresting Walker, and Carrow and Mathieson had agreed to ring Leeds immediately after speaking to the former teacher. Carrow reckoned that had he been in Yorkshire he would have collared Walker first and asked questions later, but at least Thompson's approach afforded him a role in breaking the case – a role he planned to enhance in retrospect to the credit of Special Branch.

"Can't beat England on a morning like this," said Mathieson, indicating the fresh greenery of the summer pastures.

"No, it's beautiful," answered Carrow.

"Grew up in the Chilterns myself," continued Mathieson. "Great backdrop for one's childhood."

"Yes, very nice."

"Country chap yourself?"

God, thought Carrow, the break in the case had

obviously gone down well in intelligence circles. "Yes,
have a place out Dorking way . . ." No need to mention
the grim terraced houses of his childhood in Barnsley,
he thought – Mathieson's attitude showed enough
unconscious superiority already. "Left here," Carrow
called, pointing to a road sign.

Mathieson changed gear, swinging the car around
the bend.

"Slow down, please," said Carrow. "I think the pub
up ahead may be our landmark."

The Sheaf of Wheat," said Mathieson, peering
through the windscreen. "Yes, that's the one." He drove
on, then pulled into the pub's car park, almost empty in
the hot stillness of the morning. Both men got out and
looked around.

"That must be it," said Mathieson, pointing to a
small cottage at the end of a grassy lane.

"Yes. Good directions, makes for a pleasant change,"
said Carrow, starting briskly towards the cottage.

As they approached they saw that although the
house itself was small, there was a large carefully
landscaped garden to the side and rear. On reaching the
front door they spied an elderly man working at the
end of an apple orchard.

"Good morning," called Mathieson.

The man looked up in surprise. "Good morning," he
called back, then approached them across manicured
lawns. He was a thin man in his seventies, with wispy
white hair protruding from beneath his gardening hat,
and he had watery light-blue eyes. "Not very often one
receives visitors out here," he said.

"Sorry to disturb you," said Mathieson.

"Not at all, dear boy, not at all."

"You're Mr Brotherton?" asked Carrow.

"Oh yes – one immutable in a changing world, eh?"

"Eh, yes," answered Carrow. "I wonder if we could ask you some questions, sir. I'm Chief Superintendent Carrow. This is Mr Mathieson." He showed the older man his ID.

Brotherton raised an eyebrow slightly. "Is something the matter?" he asked mildly.

"Nothing regarding you, sir," said Mathieson pleasantly. "Just need to know something about a couple of past pupils from St George's. We were told that you'd be our best bet."

"Quite. Never forget a boy. Faces implanted up here." He tapped the side of his head. "Hundreds of boys, all in here . . ." He tapped his head again.

Jesus, thought Carrow, spare us the Mr Chips routine. "That's very good, sir," he said. "If we could get down to specifics though?"

"Not out here, dear boy," said Brotherton. "Much too hot for specifics in the sunshine. Door's on the latch," he said, crossing towards it. "Cooler inside . . ."

Carrow looked impatiently at Mathieson who indicated not to protest, then they followed the retired teacher into the cottage.

The front parlour was dark and cool, its walls festooned with photo after photo of school groups. "Take a seat, gentlemen, won't you?" said Brotherton.

"Thank you," replied Mathieson as he sat, followed by Carrow.

"Shall I make a pot of tea?" asked Brotherton. "Got some splendid Earl Grey . . ."

"No, thanks, we *are* pushed for time, sir," said Carrow, his impatience at the older man exacerbated by the sight of a new mobile phone in the hallway, and the realisation that they could have rung this idiot and saved themselves a journey.

"Well, then," said Brotherton, sitting opposite them, "how may I help you?"

"We'd like to ask you about two of your past pupils," said Mathieson. "Do you remember a Nigel Gatenby?"

"Nigel Gatenby . . . yes, remember him well . . ."

"You do?"

"Oh, yes. He's not in trouble, is he?"

"No, no, he has no troubles," answered Carrow. "What about a David Walker? Remember him?"

"Oh, yes." The older man smiled. "A fine boy. I remember David very well." Brotherton's face clouded. "He's not . . . ?"

"No, no, he's fine," said Mathieson.

"Oh . . . good," said Brotherton. He sat forward in his chair, then looked at the two men earnestly. "So, gentlemen, what exactly is it that you want to know?"

Penny watched from her desk as Thompson took the call in his glass-panelled office. She was unable to adopt even a pretence of attending to her paperwork but instead waited expectantly.

Suddenly Thompson put the phone down and

entered the general office excitedly. "Right, let's go! DI Powell and Ron will take one car, Penny will travel with me!"

"It's been confirmed, Chief?" she asked.

Thompson turned to address all of the assembled team. "Mr Carrow has been on from Sussex. Nigel Gatenby and David Walker definitely knew each other. In fact Gatenby was at one stage Walker's dormitory prefect. Gatenby also had a reputation as something of a bully – and it's suspected that Walker may have been bullied on first becoming a boarder. Which leaves Mr Walker with a lot of explaining to do. Right, let's move it!"

There was a cheer from the assembled officers, then Thompson was on his way to the door. Penny rose, excited at the prospect of helping to arrest her first murder suspect, and thrilled that it was her thinking that had led them to Walker. Moving swiftly, she followed Thompson, eager to join him on the short journey to the offices of United Advertising.

Dave wondered if he was being too scrupulous, as he sat at his desk looking at the mock-ups of the ReadyBurger advertisement. As he had expected, Gary Miller had come up with some clever and cheerful copy, but the more Dave thought about it the more he felt he wasn't being swayed by personal prejudice in rejecting it. It was one thing to present the ReadyBurger as a cheap, convenient food, served in strictly hygienic surroundings – but the line had to be drawn at Gary's suggestion that it was healthy. Tasty, perhaps, but healthy? Something containing fat, salt and phosphate preservative? *"Chemoburger – taste the additives!"* No, he thought with a wry smile.

He jotted a note for Gary and clipped it to the mock-ups.

It was fortunate, he knew, that Trevor Lawrence was at an advertising symposium in Paris – he'd probably have wanted to run with the copy as it stood. Dave was due to meet him in Paris that evening for an advertising awards ceremony, but he resolved simply to tell Lawrence that the copywriting on the ReadyBurger account was still being refined.

Just then the phone on Dave's desk rang, and he placed the mock-ups and attached memo in his out tray, then picked up the phone. "Hello?"

"A Mr Brotherton for you, Dave. Says it's personal. Shall I put him through?"

Brotherton, his old form master? Surely he wasn't going to put the squeeze on United Advertising for another prize for the Past Pupils' Union? "OK, June, put him through."

"Hello, David?"

"Good morning, Mr Brotherton. How are you?"

"Splendid, dear boy, splendid. And you?"

"Fine thanks, fine – though something tells me the PPU is about to loom on the horizon!"

"No, David, nothing like that." The older man's voice was devoid of banter.

"Oh . . . nothing the matter, is there?"

"I hope not. Just had a rather strange visit. Thought I ought to let you know."

"Yes?"

"Yes, two policemen called. Chap named Carrow and a Matthews . . . Matthewson – something like that."

Oh Jesus, no! thought Dave.

"Asking a lot of question about your good self. Nigel Gatenby also – you remember Nigel?"

Dave struggled to control his voice. "Yes . . ."

"Seems he's, I don't know, in a bind of some sort. They were awfully vague . . ."

"Really?"

"Not in some kind of trouble yourself, David, are you?"

"No, sir. What . . . what did they want to know about me?"

"Did you know Gatenby well, what was he like, what were you like, was there any bad blood between you. They wouldn't say where Nigel is now, quite evasive really . . ."

That would figure, thought Dave, the name of the person recovered from the tarn hadn't yet been released by the police. "So what did you tell them about me?"

"Well, I mentioned that when you started as a boarder you were a bit unsettled but that you wouldn't confirm if you were being bullied."

Oh Christ! "And about Gatenby?"

"That he was clever and a good leader but inclined to treat the younger boys a bit harshly – the truth, really. I . . . I hope I haven't caused you any problems . . ."

"No."

"David, you may confide in me . . . are you in some sort of trouble?"

Still coping with the shock, Dave struggled to answer.

"No, I'm . . . well, yes. Yes, I am – but not due to any wrong-doing on my part. Tell me, when did the policemen leave?"

"Just a couple of moments ago."

"I'm going to have to go now. Thank you for alerting me."

"Don't do anything rash, David . . ."

"I won't. Thanks again for warning me. Good morning, sir."

"Good morning . . ."

Dave put the phone down and rose immediately from the chair. If the police had clear confirmation of the St George's connection it was probably being relayed to Leeds right now, which meant that they would be on their way for him. Jesus, but he'd have to move fast! No, no don't panic, he told himself. Even if they were on their way it would take a few minutes. Despite his pounding heart he was surprised at how clearly he was thinking. He realised that if he were to escape, the priority must be to buy time by putting them off the trail. He quickly picked up his phone and buzzed his secretary. "June, there's a problem with McQueen's account, I'm going to have to go out there for a meeting. Should be back about two, two-thirty."

"OK, Dave. You haven't forgotten your flight's at four forty-five?"

"No. I'll definitely be back in time to go through next week's appointments. Oh and don't divert any calls to Mc Queen's – I'll return calls when I get back here. See you later."

"OK."

He put the phone down, thought of ringing Mary, then dismissed it. It was him they would come looking for first. He would have to get away immediately, then he could ring Mary to implement their contingency plans. Moving quickly, he opened his desk drawer and removed his passport, French banknotes, airline tickets and cellular phone. From the rear of the drawer he took a sealed envelope containing his contingency funds in foreign currencies. Pocketing it all, he moved out of the line of sight of anyone in the open-plan copywriting office and went to the wardrobe in the corner. He took out his already packed holdall and moved to the far end of the office, gingerly opening the rear door.

He could feel the sweat breaking out on his brow. Please God, don't let the police arrive now, he thought. Then he stepped out into the corridor. To his relief there was no one about, and pulses throbbing, he moved swiftly along the corridor to the doorway leading to the stairwell. He opened the door, went through and quietly closed it behind him. Gripping the holdall in one hand, he held the banister with the other, then started descending three steps at a time, grimly aware that is spite of all his efforts, the chase was now on.

29

Mary stood back, admiring the fresh white paintwork of the workshop walls. At first she had questioned the effort of painting a place that was technically no longer hers, but on reflection she had changed her mind, regarding the input of her labour as a symbolic investment – a vote of confidence in a future in which they would buy back the bungalow.

She admired the walls again, then wiped the excess paint from her roller, using newspaper that she threw into the dustbin. She poured a liberal measure of turpentine into a spare painting tray and was starting to soak the roller when she heard a knock on the door. Crossing to the transistor radio, she switched it off, then opened the workshop door.

A middle-aged man with a neatly trimmed beard stood before her and smiled. "Good morning."

"Good morning," she said, "you must be Mr Franklin."

"At your service," he said smiling again.

"Mary Adams. Forgive my not shaking hands," said Mary, indicating her paint-stained rubber gloves.

"Not at all," he answered, then held up a piece of paper. "Found your note on the hall door and followed directions . . ."

"Fine, won't you step in?"

"Thank you," he replied politely, following her into the workshop.

"I hope you don't mind if I quickly tidy up here. I just wanted to get the painting finished."

"No rush at all," said the man, his soft American accent striking Mary as somehow slightly smug.

"Beautiful garden you've got here," he observed.

"Thank you."

"Wonderfully . . . secluded . . ."

Mary felt a twinge of unease. She had, after all, made no enquiries to check Franklin's bona fides following his call the previous night. Don't get paranoid, Mary, she told herself. Yet there was something about him, from his expensive aftershave to his tight-fitting silk shirt that suggested – what? *Coming on*, was the expression that came to mind. Which seemed ridiculous when she was eight months pregnant, and he was a total stranger.

"Nice to have no neighbours breathing down your neck – lovely and all as *your* neck may be," he added smilingly.

Mary cringed inwardly and knew that she should have stuck to her original response and not granted an interview. "I'll just get this out of the way," she said, ignoring his personal comment and lifting the tray of turpentine onto a workbench.

"No rush, I've all the time in the world . . ."

The mobile phone rang and Mary quickly peeled off her rubber gloves, then moved across the workshop to answer it.

"Hello?"

"Mary, thank God I got you!"

She felt a stab of anxiety. "Dave, what . . . what's wrong?"

"They're onto us!"

"What?"

"The link with Gatenby's been discovered."

"Oh God, no! Listen, hold on a second, Dave, I'm with the interviewer." She turned to the journalist, to find him sitting on a stool. "Will you excuse me a moment, Mr Franklin – it's rather a personal call?"

"Of course."

Mary nodded, then moved down the workshop and into a small storeroom, closing the door after her.

"Sorry, Dave, now I can talk."

"There isn't much time for talking, love."

"How do you know they've linked you to Gatenby?"

"The police contacted Brotherton, my old form master. They didn't know we'd stayed in contact, and that he'd warn me they called. I'd say I just got out of the office with minutes to spare."

"Oh Jesus, no . . ." Mary felt her voice cracking, then she determined to pull herself together. "Where are you now?" she asked.

"On the motorway. When I reach the airport I'll bring my flight forward. We have to put the contingency plan into action."

"They'll contact the airports surely?"

"Not yet, I hope. To buy time, I told June I was going to visit a client. That's where they should go looking for me. But, Mary, you've got to get out of there – when they don't find me at the client's they might come checking the house."

"OK. OK, Dave."

"I'm sorry it's come to this, love . . ."

"Don't worry about that. The main thing is to get away safely."

"OK, let's follow the plan exactly. So . . . I'll see you in a couple of days."

"Right. And, Dave, I . . . I really love you . . . make sure you get there safely."

"I love you too. Always . . . and don't worry about me. I'll make it. You just mind yourself and the baby."

"Yes, we'll be fine."

"Let's do it then. Bye, honey – love you."

"Love you too. Bye . . ."

She switched off the phone and breathed deeply, trying to gather her thoughts. The first thing was to get rid of Franklin. She opened the storeroom door to step back into the workshop, only to find him standing right in front of her.

"Oh, you gave me a start!" she said.

"Dear me," he answered, his previously smug tone now sounding sardonic.

"I'm afraid a family crisis has arisen, Mr Franklin. I'll have to ask you – "

"Cut the crap!"

"I beg your pardon?"

"Thin wooden partition," he said pointing to the storeroom wall. "I listened to it all."

"What?"

"'How do you know they've linked you to Gatenby?' Wasn't that what you said? I'm interested to know – and you're going to tell me. You're going to tell me everything. Who your husband is working for, why the SMORTAR plans were sent back, the how, why and where of it all."

Mary felt herself breaking out in a cold sweat. "Who the hell are you?" she asked, her voice quivering.

"I'm nobody. Nobody saw me coming here. Nobody will find me when I've gone. It's nice and secluded here, good thick walls in your workshop, but just so that no sound carries . . ." He reached over and flicked on the radio, turned up the volume, then quickly closed the two open windows.

Fighting down her sense of panic, Mary suddenly made for the door. She had almost reached it when he caught her from behind. He spun her around, smacked her hard in the face and clamped a hand over her mouth.

"Don't scream, you hear me, don't scream. You'll never be heard anyway and you'll only make me angry. And believe me, you don't want to make me angry. Got that?"

Mary nodded in terror, and he slowly took his hand from her mouth.

"If you tell me everything about Gatenby and your husband, you won't be hurt. If you fail to co-operate in the slightest degree you'll know agony such as you wouldn't believe." He reached out, opened his attaché case, and smiled. "Let me, show you my equipment. I think you'll find it interesting . . ."

"Good morning, we'd like a word with Mr Walker please," said Thompson.

Penny noticed the look of surprise on the secretary's face at the sudden arrival of the four detectives in United Advertising's Copywriting Department.

"Good morning – Chief Inspector Thompson, isn't it?" the woman said.

"That's right."

"I'm sorry, Inspector. Mr Walkers's not in the office at the moment."

"Where is he, please?"

"He had to attend a client conference."

"Whereabouts?"

The secretary hesitated. "Unless it's very urgent, sir, he did ask me to hold all calls until he gets back."

"When will that be?"

"About two, half two."

"It's more urgent than that. I have to know where this meeting's taking place."

"Very well, sir. It's in the McQueen plant."

"Is that here in Leeds?"

"No, Inspector. It's past York, near Sheriff Hutton."

"Would Mr Walker be there now?"

"Oh no, Inspector. You just missed him. He's not long gone."

"I see," said Thompson.

"If . . . if it's that urgent, sir, I could contact him on his car phone."

"Eh, no, no thank you . . ." said Thompson.

Penny watched, fascinated to see how the Chief would explain his not wanting to alert their quarry.

"Too sensitive for discussion over the airwaves," said Thompson. "I'll get someone to meet him at Sheriff Hutton. May I use Mr Walker's office to make some calls, please?"

"Eh, yes, yes, of course."

"Oh, and I'd appreciate it if you'd say nothing about this to the other staff members." Despite the polite phrasing there was a clear note of instruction in Thompson's tone.

The woman looked at him a moment, then nodded. "As you wish, sir."

"DS Annesley will stay with you here – in case Mr Walker returns unexpectedly."

Or in case you try to ring Walker, thought Penny.

"Thank you again for your help," said Thompson. He entered Walker's office through the secretary's side door, and Penny and Inspector Powell followed him, closing the door behind them.

"Right, Frank,!" said Thompson, "get on the blower. I want an unmarked car sent immediately from CID in York to the McQueen plant near Sheriff Hutton. To await arrival of – what's Walker's car, Penny?"

She took out her notebook. "Metallic blue Rover K 841 DCY."

"Got it," said Powell, jotting down the details.

"If he hasn't already been picked up en route,

they're to detain Walker for questioning, and notify me immediately."

"Right, Jack," said Powell, starting to dial on the office phone.

"Penny, you contact Control. I want an alert out for Walker. Same instructions, detain for questioning, and notify me immediately."

"OK, Chief. Should I specify the A64 to York?"

"No. No, the entire Yorkshire region, in case he changes his plans. I want Mr Walker – and this time I'm going to have him!"

30

Mary's stomach knotted in terror. As a child she had once been so frightened of a local bully that she used to feel physically sick on seeing him. Her brother Tom had solved the problem, immediately confronting her abuser on learning that Mary was being bullied simply for not belonging to a larger family. The terror she felt now was similarly sickening, but much worse, and this time she had no big brother to fight her corner. She could feel the baby kicking and she knew her own agitation was being communicated to the child, but she was powerless to control her fear. She had never before sensed such a frightening air of evil as from this soft-spoken man who called himself Franklin.

She watched in horror as he opened the attaché-case and removed a pair of handcuffs and a leather strap with buckles attached.

"Gag and cuffs," he said conversationally. "And this is a small battery-driven drill." He quickly assembled several compact metal components. "Last year, in

Paraguay, I drilled a series of holes into a prisoner's skull with one of these. Must have been excruciating. He was begging me to stop. To *let* him tell me what I wanted to know. Mind you, with women I normally do the cheekbones." He smiled. "More disfiguring, especially for an actress like yourself – unless of course you plan to specialise in horror roles . . ."

Mary felt herself gagging, but she forced herself not to be sick as he reached again into the case.

"And here's another good one," he said, withdrawing a small clamp-like device. "Clips onto your finger, then when I turn the ratchet the metal probe burrows under your fingernail. You wouldn't believe the pain . . ." He placed it on the worktop, then turned to Mary. "I think from your expression you've probably got the message. Now the thing is, we haven't as much time as I'd like – sooner or later the police will want to talk to you. And I want to be well gone when they arrive, so we'll dispense with the cuffs, the gag, and, if you're lucky, with these," he said, indicating the items he had removed from the case.

He took a pack of cigarettes and a lighter from his shirt pocket, lit up, placed the lighter and packet on the workbench, then pulled over a stool and sat. "Now, we're going to have a quick chat, and if I'm certain that you've answered every question quickly, fully and truthfully, I won't use my equipment. Understand?"

Mary nodded, her mouth dry with fear.

"So, first question. Who was your husband working for?"

"No one, it was a mistake and – Jesus!" She

screamed in pain as Franklin brought the burning cigarette down on her hand.

"Don't waste my time with lies! You know who killed Gatenby, don't you?"

Despite her fear, Mary hesitated, not knowing who this man was, and what the result of implicating Dave might be.

Franklin reached out his free hand and raised the drill. "If I have to use this, I'll drill *three* holes before asking you again. Now, you know who killed Gatenby, yes?"

"Yes," answered Mary weakly. "Dave did – but killing him was an accident."

"But, of course," said Franklin sarcastically. "And then your husband took the microfilm?"

"Yes."

"And sent it to the Ministry of Defence?"

"Yes. "

"Why?"

"To get them off our backs."

"Why did he come forward to the police?"

"He had to. The boss in United Advertising knew he'd been in the Dales, and Dave was forced to contact the police."

"And his other boss – his *real* boss?"

"I don't understand."

Franklin shook his head sadly. "You don't really want to lose your baby, do you?"

"What!"

He quickly brought down the cigarette onto Mary's hand, again causing her to cry out in pain. "I ask the questions – you answer them. That way you and your brat might live. Think about that. Now, who is your husband working for?"

"Just United Advertising – this was all a mix-up. I swear it!"

"Stop!" He rose, and Mary felt sick when she saw him place a small drill into the battery-operated machine.

"No! No, look . . ."

"Silence!" he roared, then after a moment he continued conversationally. "Take my advice and do this the easy way. Pregnant women always talk once I've started on the foetus."

"Jesus, no!"

Franklin smiled and patted the drill. "Works every time. Now, last chance. Who was your husband working for?"

"Look . . . look, I'll tell you everything you want to know. But you must believe me. He just encountered Gatenby by chance. They'd never met since schooldays – that's what Dave rang me about just now – the police have made the connection to the school."

"Your husband bumped into an old school chum, and then killed him and took top secret microfilm?"

"They weren't chums. They'd hated each other. That's what happened. They had a fight."

"Because of a schoolboy tiff your husband beat a man to death? An armed man?" He shook his head. "I think that insults my intelligence."

"No, that's what . . ."

"Say nothing! Not another word! Now I'm doing

you a favour. I'm going to give you a final chance to tell me the truth."

"I swear I will. I swear on my dead mother's grave to tell the truth! Dave killed him and posted the film back from London. He dumped the body in a tarn. But the meeting with Gatenby – it was a chance meeting that just went horribly wrong. My husband had no idea he was an intelligence officer!"

Franklin picked up the drill and slowly approached Mary.

"I wonder would your baby have been a boy or a girl?" he said.

"No!" she screamed, backing away. "For God's sake, no. I'm telling the truth!"

"I don't think so," he said as he moved towards her.

Mary backed away in terror. "Don't harm my baby, please! I swear I'll tell you anything I can, anything, but please, please don't harm my baby . . ."

Franklin raised the drill and smiled. "Obstetrics time . . ."

Terrified, Mary stumbled backwards against the workbench, her left hand splashing into the tray of turpentine – then before she knew what she was doing she gripped the tray, swung round and flung its contents into the face of her tormentor.

Franklin drew back in shock, dropping the drill as his hands clutched his eyes. He stumbled blindly, and Mary instantly started for the door. Despite his temporary incapacity, Franklin lunged wildly for her as she went to pass.

Mary felt his hand grasp her shoulder, his fingers

digging into her flesh, but fuelled by terror she drove forward, barging past her disoriented assailant. She reached the workshop door, her fingers trembling as she tried to undo the catch of the lock. Behind her she could hear Franklin gathering himself, and with a mounting panic she realised that if she didn't get the door open quickly he would be upon her again. She fumbled again with the catch, her fingers slippery from the turpentine and trembling with fright. Then suddenly it opened. She swung the door inwards, forcing herself not to waste precious time by looking behind her, despite an intense urge to see where Franklin was.

She stepped towards the open door, then Franklin lunged wildly at her. His flailing hand caught the sleeve of her smock, and she felt a surge of terror as he stumbled, hauling on the garment. She twisted about frantically as her assailant fell against the door frame, then the sleeve ripped from her smock, and she pulled free. Immediately she slammed the heavy door shut behind her, locked Franklin into the workshop, and stood a moment, trembling uncontrollably. She heard Franklin beginning to pound on the door, and panting from fear, she drew back, then turned and ran panic-stricken towards the bungalow.

If it were a Sherlock Holmes story Walker's office would yield a wealth of information about him, thought Penny, as they waited for word from either the patrol cars or the CID at Sheriff Hutton.

What could she guess from the surroundings? she

wondered. That Walker was very successful at his job, for one thing. She knew that companies tend to have a pecking order regarding office size and fittings, and this room was spacious and luxuriously furnished, which suggested a high-achieving, gung-ho side to Walker's nature. It also indicated financial security, a theory borne out by the secluded bungalow in Harrogate.

What else did the surroundings suggest? That Walker was witty and a creative thinker, if the framed advertisements on the walls were his own work. That he was health-conscious and physically fit – from the large no-smoking sign and the photograph of himself decked out in hiking gear atop a high mountain peak. Probably had a good marriage too – his wife was standing smilingly beside him in the mountain-top picture, and he had another photograph of her on the other side of his desk. In addition to which she had probably been covering up for him on the whole business about Gatenby. Nice to have someone who loved you that much, thought Penny, then her drifting thoughts were arrested by Thompson suddenly thumping the desktop.

"We should have heard something by now!"

"Don't worry, Jack. We'll get him," said Inspector Powell.

"It's twenty-five to twelve, Frank. He should have been picked up en route."

Powell shrugged. "Maybe he made good time, got off the main roads before our units spotted him. If he has then we'll still lift him at McQueen's."

"If he'd made such good time, he'd already be at McQueen's," said Thompson. "So why isn't he?"

"Car trouble perhaps?" suggested Penny.

"Hardly," Thompson replied. "That Rover's a brand-new car. Unless . . . wait a minute, wait a bloody minute." He rose suddenly. "Frank, you stay here, man the phone. Penny, come on!"

"What is it . . . ?" asked the bewildered Powell.

"Talk to you in two minutes," said Thompson, already heading out the door.

Penny ran after him, catching up as he reached the lift. Just as she did, the lift door opened and Thompson stepped in. She joined him, but with another man and two women already occupying the lift she couldn't question him as they descended.

The other people stepped out on reaching the ground floor, and Thompson pressed the button for the basement.

"What is it, Chief?" Penny asked.

"Just a notion. Here we go," he said, stepping out of the lift into the underground car park.

Over to the right there was a large United Advertising sign, and Penny hurried after the Chief as he made for it. Suddenly he stopped. "I knew it. I bloody knew it!" he cried, pointing to Walker's parked car.

Penny thought for a moment. "Could he have taken the train, Chief?"

Thompson shook his head. "Doesn't go to Sheriff Hutton."

"Taken a lift with someone?"

"No, the secretary offered to ring him on his car phone. The bastard's given us the slip!"

"But he can't have known we were coming for him, Chief. Well, unless . . ."

"Unless his old teacher tipped him off." Thompson frowned. "But then again, the school said that Brotherton had no phone, and he'd have had to get to one pretty fast to warn Walker."

"And also, would the teacher have known where to contact him, eighteen years after he left school?"

"I don't know," said Thompson. "But he's not here, and he's not in Sheriff Hutton, so where is he?"

"Well, if he *is* doing a runner, Chief, mightn't he be joining his wife?"

Thompson looked at her thoughtfully for a moment, then nodded. "Aye. Let's get out to Harrogate – fast."

Visser's reddened eyes still stung from the turpentine, but he no longer noticed, such was his fury. To think he had had Adams trapped, at his mercy in this very room, only for her to outwit him. She'd pay for this, the bloated cow. She'd scream for mercy when he caught up with her. He would wring every last ounce of information from her and then he would continue anyway for the pleasure of watching her suffer. When she was begging to die he would douse the bitch in turpentine – seeing as she was so fond of it – then set her alight.

Stop fantasising! he told himself. First he had to get out of here. After Adams had escaped he had stumbled to the workshop sink and bathed his eyes with cold water, then surveyed his surroundings. The windows

274

of the workshop were too small to climb through, and the entrance door was too sturdy to kick down. He had tried using his fine drill to burrow between the lock mounting and the door frame but had only succeeded in snapping the drill in two. Picking the lock was the only answer, he knew, but so far all his efforts to do so had been in vain.

It was some time now since he had heard Adams revving up her car and accelerating down the drive, and he was aware that with her husband having taken flight the police might arrive at any moment. He had to get out as quickly as possible but he paused for a moment, wiped the perspiration from his brow, then removed the blade of his penknife from the door lock and forced himself to breathe deeply and calmly. Panicking would get him nowhere, and his anger at Adams was consuming precious energy. After a moment he felt the tension that had gripped him lessening somewhat and, compartmentalising his fury with Adams and his fear of the police arriving, he began working again on the lock, this time with total concentration.

The taxi pulled to a halt, and Dave checked his watch as he got out the passenger door. Eleven-fifty – the driver had certainly met his request to make good time to Manchester airport.

"Thanks, Guv," said the taximan, pocketing the fare and tip.

Dave nodded, took up his holdall and made for the

terminal. He could feel his pulses beginning to race. This was the risky part, he knew, for if his secretary had informed the police of his trip to Paris they might be waiting for him here. He told himself again that there was no reason why June should mention the trip to France; the destination she would give them would surely be the McQueen plant. But how long would the police wait before realising he wasn't going to Sheriff Hutton?

Long enough, with any luck, and even then there would probably be such a flap that he would be out of the country by the time the police discovered that United Advertising had booked him on the four forty-five Manchester/Paris flight. That was the theory at any rate, and under the circumstances it had been the best plan he had been able to devise.

He entered the busy terminal, forcing himself to slow down as he moved towards the British Airways counter. No point rushing into the arms of the police if they were there, he thought. He scanned the ticket clerks and the customers but there was no one who seemed to be loitering, nobody who looked particularly like a police officer. Or would they wait out of sight, to be summoned by the ticket clerk pushing a panic button?

He hesitated, then went ahead, confidently approaching the Business Class counter. There was no queue, and the waiting clerk looked up expectantly.

"Good morning, sir."

"Good morning. I have a seat booked on the four forty-five to Paris, but I've got to take an earlier flight."

The woman smiled politely. "No problem, sir. And the name?"

Despite his nervousness he kept his voice under control.

"Walker, David Walker." He watched carefully to see if her expression gave anything away, but she didn't react at all to the name. Look to see if she presses anything, he thought, but she simply took his ticket and keyed some details onto her console.

"Hand luggage only, sir?"

"Yes."

"There's a flight leaving at twelve fifteen. Boarding right now at Gate 10 if you hurry, sir."

"That would be excellent."

She stamped the ticket and handed him a boarding pass. "Just made it in time," she said. "Have a nice trip, Mr Walker."

"Thank you," he answered, alert for any air of irony in her tone, but there appeared to be none. He nodded and walked away without being intercepted, whereupon he relaxed slightly.

Maybe the gods were smiling on him after all, he thought, as he made for the departure area. Grateful for his own good fortune so far, his mind turned to Mary, and he wished he could be with her, despite accepting the wisdom of separate escape plans. If only he knew that she had got away safely, he reflected. Well, at least he had no other family. There was only Mary and the baby to worry about. His father's family had been killed in the Blitz, and his mother's surviving relations were living in New Zealand, so there wouldn't be embarrassment and hassle for relatives if he and Mary succeeded in their plan.

Turning a corner, he found himself approaching the entrance to the departure area. His mouth started to go dry. Perhaps *this* was where they'd intercept him. Probably always be armed police on stand-by at the metal-detectors and security checks. Too late to turn back now, he thought. Instead he breathed evenly, forced a slightly jaunty air into his stride, and walked briskly towards the entrance.

Visser juggled the blade of his penknife in the lock, ignoring the rivulets of perspiration that trickled down the side of his face. The air was heavy with the smell of turpentine, and the hot May weather, allied to the tension that he felt, was making him sweat profusely.

Try as he might to concentrate on the job in hand he couldn't escape the nightmare vision of the police arriving and finding him locked in the workshop of a fugitive. He who prided himself on evading the attention of the authorities could suddenly find himself on the receiving end of extremely awkward questioning.

He was trying vainly to concoct some kind of plausible reason for being there when he heard a click from the lock. Fearful of having his hopes raised only to be dashed, he steeled himself, then tried the handle. To his immense relief the lock disengaged. He breathed out deeply, then opened the door a fraction and looked out.

The end of the driveway was clear. He stepped quickly out the door, glad to breathe in fresh air after the turpentine-tainted atmosphere of the workshop. Travelling at speed, he crossed to the bungalow, then he peered cautiously around the side of the house to survey the rest of the driveway.

His luck was in again; nothing was amiss. And unless the police arrived just as he was walking down the drive he knew that he was going to get away. Moving swiftly, he rounded the corner of the bungalow and started down the drive.

"Bloody idiot!" said Thompson, switching off his mobile phone. "Can't answer a simple question without giving a Command Performance!"

Penny smiled but kept her eyes on the road as she drove through Harrogate as fast as the traffic would allow. "Well, I suppose if you ring the BBC you *will* get actors in the Drama Department," she said.

"'Arnold Beazley at your service'," mimicked Thompson in an exaggerated deep-throated drawl. "Why can't the bugger speak like a normal human being?"

"At least we know Adams isn't working there this week."

"Aye. Pity I had to suffer that daft bugger sucking sweets and doing his silly voice to find out."

"This is it coming up, Chief." Penny turned onto a narrow tree-fringed thoroughfare marked Bighton Lane and after about thirty yards swung left at a pillar bearing the name Primrose Cottage. She drove up the driveway, then stopped and switched off the engine.

"No car," said Thompson, disappointedly looking at the empty carport.

"She might still be here. Maybe the husband borrowed it."

"Maybe. Park over at the side, Penny. No point advertising our presence."

Thompson got out and made for the halldoor as Penny drove over to the carport. She parked, then crossed to the front door.

"No answer to the bell," Thompson said. "Where's her workshop?"

"Round the back."

"Let's have a look."

They rounded the corner of the house, the garden echoing with birdsong in the summer sunshine, then crossed to the workshop, its freshly painted door ajar. They looked inside, but the room was empty.

Thompson indicated the paintwork. "This isn't long done."

Penny gingerly touched a wall with the tip of her little finger and held it up to show a white spot. "Very recent. Hardly what you do if you're about to do a runner."

"It's possible that Walker hasn't been able to contact her. She may not know we're on to them."

"Could be. So, what do we do, Chief?"

"In a situation like this you follow your instincts. And my gut feeling is that she knows we're onto them. Let's go!"

Moving quickly to keep up with him, Penny followed Thompson back across the lawn. "Where to now, Chief?"

"We'll base ourselves here, in case she does return," he answered, striding towards the driveway, "but I reckon they've made a break for it. Call in from the car and tell Control to put out an alert. All airlines and ferry companies to be contacted immediately and passenger lists checked. And a watch put on all points of exit – nationwide – for Walker and Adams, travelling under either name, separately or together. Got that?"

"Got it, Chief!"

Carrow walked quickly through the terminal at Manchester airport, eager to cover the remaining distance to Leeds and to make his presence felt at the interrogation of Walker.

On leaving the retired schoolteacher's house near Crawley he had driven with Mathieson to nearby Gatwick airport and had booked them onto a flight departing for Manchester. To hell with budgets, he had decided. He wasn't going to spend hours on the train while CID Yorkshire revelled in the limelight of the arrest, and Mathieson, although irritatingly lacking a similar sense of urgency, had agreed to fly with him.

Carrow's impatience during the short flight hadn't been helped by the intelligence officer's preoccupation with how the mysterious driver of the white van fitted into the picture now. Carrow had suggested that in the light of Walker's likely guilt perhaps the Iranian abduction was unconnected with the SMORTAR affair. At any rate all such matters could be sorted out shortly when they had David Walker in the interrogation room.

Pleased by that prospect, Carrow was leading the way past the baggage claim when his mobile phone rang.

"Carrow," he snapped into the mouthpiece, without breaking stride.

"Hello, Mr Carrow, DC Hart speaking."

"You've picked Walker up?"

"No, sir, I'm afraid not."

"What!" Carrow came to an abrupt standstill, ignoring Mathieson, who looked at him quizzically.

"Mr Walker had just left when we reached United Advertising, sir. We're trying to find him."

"Christ! Hold on." Carrow moved over to an alcove to avoid being overheard by passing passengers.

"What is it?" asked Mathieson, following him.

"They haven't got Walker."

"Why not?"

"What the hell happened?" said Carrow into the phone.

"We think he may have been tipped off, sir."

"Tipped off!" Carrow turned to Mathieson. "That bastard Brotherton! In spite of what we said!" He returned to the phone. "So you've bloody lost him?"

"Not entirely, sir. Have you left Manchester airport yet?"

"That's where we are right now – what's that got to do with Walker?"

"DI Powell discovered Walker was booked onto a

four forty-five flight to Paris. We'd requested passenger list checks, and the airline's just informed us that Walker changed his ticket to the twelve fifteen Manchester/Paris flight. Inspector Thompson wants you to take the next flight to Paris, if you would."

Carrow felt his initial anger at Walker's escape growing at the prospect of taking instructions, however politely phrased, via this irritating woman. "Put Thompson on!" he snapped.

"I can't, sir. He's trying to raise the French authorities – the flight will be landing soon, and he doesn't want Walker to slip through the net."

"Just a second." Carrow turned to Mathieson. "Walker's on a flight to Paris, landing soon. Thompson's trying to get the French to pick him up; they want us to follow immediately."

Mathieson looked pensive. "I see . . ."

"The French might botch it, and if they do, I want to be at Walker's heels."

"Quite. Although overseas intelligence is normally M16's area . . ."

"And international police work is normally Interpol's, but time's of the essence – we can sort out the paperwork later."

Mathieson thought for a moment. "All right then."

Carrow spoke again into the phone. "Right, we'll be on the next flight . . ."

"One other thing, sir. Mr Thompson doesn't want the French making a formal arrest. Because of the security consideration he's requesting a low-profile approach."

"I don't need a bloody lecture on how sensitive a security breach is!"

"No, sir. If you could check with the Airport Police on landing, they'll have been notified of your ETA."

"I'll handle all that when I get there," said Carrow. "Is Walker travelling alone or has the wife gone with him?"

"We think alone, sir – we're trying to track her whereabouts too."

"Right, you see if you can't catch a pregnant woman without botching it, and leave Walker to us." He hung up and turned to the intelligence officer. "Right, let's nail this fucker once and for all!"

"Quite," answered Mathieson wryly, but the Special Branch man was already making for the ticket desk.

Mary lifted the phone and dialled the number, nervously drumming her fingers as she awaited a reply.

"Good afternoon. British Airways, may I help you?"

"Yes, please," answered Mary, relieved at not having to waste precious time on hold. "I'd like to book a seat to Amsterdam this afternoon. Can you tell me what time the next flight leaves?"

"Well . . . the one-fifteen is actually boarding now, the next one is the three o'clock, or after that there's one at five-fifty."

"OK, I'd like a seat on the three o'clock, please."

"Certainly, madam. Single or return?"

"Single, please."

"Smoking or non-smoking?"

"Non-smoking."

"And the name, please?"

"Adams, Mary Adams."

"Very good, Ms Adams."

Was there a hint of recognition, a tiny shift in the clerk's tone, or was that imagination? Before Mary had time to consider it, the desk clerk asked how she wished to pay, and Mary gave her credit-card details.

"That's fine," said the clerk. "The ticket will be ready for collection at the British Airways desk. Check-in time is two o'clock."

"It might be nearer half two when I get there," said Mary.

"Well, once it's not too much later – boarding will begin about two forty."

"OK, thank you very much."

"You're welcome. Thank you for flying British Airways."

Her hands trembling, Mary hung up, stuffed the credit-cards into her bag, and rose to go.

Penny peered in through the back windows of Primrose Cottage, seeking any signs of sudden flight. Seeing nothing untoward, she tried the handle of the French doors, only to find them locked. She was starting towards the bedroom window when she heard Thompson shouting her name.

Sprinting round the side garden, she found him already in the car, gunning the engine to life.

"What is it, Chief?" she asked, jumping into the front seat and strapping herself in.

"British Airways rang," answered Thompson, reversing at speed out of the carport. "They've just booked a flight for a Mary Adams."

"To where?" asked Penny, as Thompson accelerated down the drive and pulled out into Bighton Lane.

"Amsterdam!"

"From Leeds?"

"No, Manchester."

Penny smiled. "Which is where we're headed?"

Thompson nodded with satisfaction. "Which is exactly where we're headed."

31

Dave glanced anxiously at his watch as he walked down the tunnel-like corridor at de Gaulle airport with the other arrivals. One twenty-five. The police in Leeds would know by now that he wasn't going to arrive at the McQueen plant, but would June have told them of his four forty-five flight to Paris? Quite possibly, he reckoned, and if so would they have checked in case he had brought the flight forward?

He was counting on the fact that it would all take time, with further time needed if they had to notify Interpol, but in case the police had uncovered his tracks and forwarded a description he had felt he should take some precautions.

Although there was little scope for disguise, he surmised that any description or photograph faxed ahead would have the French authorities on the lookout for a businessman. And so he had removed his tie, folded his suit jacket into his holdall, and rolled up his shirtsleeves. Prior to landing he had entered the aeroplane toilet and wet his hair, combing it straight back off his forehead, and this, combined with wearing his reading glasses, would, he hoped, alter his appearance enough to lessen considerably the likelihood of detection. Mostly though, he hoped to be through the exit channel before the French police could be alerted.

Coming towards the end of the long terminal corridor, he began to feel nervous. Under the new European Community Free Movement policy there were supposed to be no systematic passport checks for EC citizens, but it would still be necessary to go through passport control, and he felt his mouth go dry at the prospect. If the French *had* been alerted, would they check every individual passport, he wondered, or would they concentrate instead on passengers matching Dave's description? He had no way of knowing.

He decided to approach the passport barrier chatting with other passengers as though part of a group, but most of the passengers were sharply dressed businessmen. Better to approach with others informally dressed, he had figured, if he were to pass as a travelling companion.

He fell into step with two casually dressed men in their twenties whose conversation betrayed their Yorkshire origins.

"Bit lacking in the legendary French flair, isn't it?" said Dave smilingly, indicating the long featureless corridor.

"Aye, gives a whole new meaning to tunnel vision," said the first Yorkshireman.

Dave grinned, and the second Yorkshireman made a

gesture towards the claustrophobic corridor. "Even Yeadon airport has the edge on this," he said dryly.

"Yeah," said Dave with a smile. "Probably don't even serve jam butties in the restaurant here!"

The Yorkshiremen laughed. "Frogs' bloody legs more like," said the first one and they laughed again.

Despite the tightness in his throat, Dave joined in their laughter, avoiding eye contact with the waiting officers as, passport in hand, he approached passport control with his new-found companions. To his immense relief, every individual passport wasn't being checked. Overcoming his nerves, he kept to a relaxed stride as, waving his EC passport, he went through the barrier. The Yorkshiremen followed him and they headed towards the escalator leading to the baggage area.

"*Monsieur!*"

Dave felt his blood run cold, but continued walking.

"*Monsieur!*"

The two Yorkshiremen stopped, and Dave reluctantly did likewise. "I think Marcel wants a word," said one of the Englishmen as the first of two French officials approached.

Even in avoiding direct eye contact, Dave could see that they looked like policemen and he had to fight back a desire to run.

"What's the problem, mate?" asked one of the Yorkshiremen.

"*Passeport, s'il vous plaît,*" said the older of the Frenchmen, looking intently at Dave.

The second, younger man was also staring at him as Dave handed over the document.

"So much for all being Europeans now, eh?" said the other Yorkshireman.

The younger Frenchman looked inside Dave's passport, then turned excitedly to his partner. "*C'est lui!*"

It's him! Christ, no! thought Dave, his heart sinking.

The other French officer turned to the Yorkshiremen. "Merci, monsieurs . . ."

The Englishmen looked quizzically at Dave, who didn't return their gaze, then the Frenchman indicated with an imperious hand gesture for them to go. "*Allez! Allez!*"

The Englishmen paused uncertainly as the policeman turned to Dave and pointed down a corridor. "*S'il vous plaît, monsieur.*"

"Is there some problem?" Dave asked, straining to keep his voice sounding normal.

"Yes, I think there is," said the younger policeman in accented English.

"I'm sure there's some mistake . . ."

The French officer smiled bleakly. "Yes, there's been a mistake, monsieur. And you, I think, have made it. This way . . ."

Carrow felt a bump when the plane touched down, then he leaned back as the jet hurtled along the runway. His mood had lifted during the flight and the more he thought about it the less Walker's elusion of the Yorkshire CID seemed a disaster. In fact it meant that along with Mathieson he had now become the central figure in the pursuit – with every prospect of being the one to bring Walker in if the French authorities had detained him at the airport. And even if they hadn't, he would be the British policeman on the spot if an Interpol manhunt were launched, so that one way or another the odds were good that he would wipe Thompson's eye by bringing Walker to boot.

As the plane slowed down and began to taxi towards the terminal, Carrow looked up to see a blonde-haired Air France steward approach and smile at Mathieson.

"*Trois minutes,*" she said.

"*C'est bien,*" the intelligence office answered. "*Merci beaucoup, mademoiselle.*"

"*De rien, monsieur,*" she said with a flirtatious mock bow.

Carrow looked at his companion, envious in spite of himself. Typical of Mathieson's privileged background that he should speak flawless French, he thought. Earlier in the flight the M15 man had suggested that they discreetly inform the airline captain that they were on police business and request to be allowed off the plane first. "Speak the language all right, do you?" Mathieson had asked.

"No, never really took it up," Carrow had replied, making it sound like a definite choice he had made. Hadn't been much call for French among the potential mill-workers when he was a lad in Barnsley, he had thought ruefully.

Mathieson of course had spoken like a native, to the obvious pleasure of the blonde-haired steward who had taken him to the Captain. Notwithstanding his irritation, Carrow recognised that it meant precious time would now be saved, and despite the seat-belt warning light still being on he began to undo his seat straps as the plane slowed down.

"Think they'll have nabbed him?" he said to Mathieson.

"Well, the French can be quite effective. We'll soon know," he added, then he smiled as the blonde steward approached again.

"*Quand vous êtes prêts, messieurs*," she said, her gaze entirely directed at Mathieson.

"*Merci, mademoiselle*," he answered easily.

I'll bet he's a big hit with the women in his badminton club, thought Carrow irritably as they rose from the seats. Then the plane slowed to a halt and he put aside all thoughts of Mathieson's urbanity. Instead he felt his excitement start to mount and he moved forward quickly, anxious to disembark.

Any minute now, thought Penny, glancing at the car clock as Thompson drove at speed towards Manchester airport. According to her calculations, Carrow and Mathieson should just be arriving at de Gaulle airport. The French police had sent word that Walker had been detained, and the two Englishmen would question him before charges were brought.

Although delighted at such a successful conclusion, Penny couldn't help but wish it were her own boss, Jack Thompson, making the actual arrest. Still, they were planning to intercept Walker's wife, who had obviously been an accessory, and assuming they picked her up shortly, it would make for an excellent day's work.

"She should be checking in by now," said Thompson. "Raise the Airport Police, Penny, would you, and get an update?"

"Sure, Chief," she answered, reaching for the car's radio set. "Hello, Victor Two to Tango One. Over."

"Come in Victor Two. Over."

"DC Hart for Inspector Hendricks, please. Over."

"Just a second. Over."

Penny waited, then a lilting Welsh voice came on.

"Hendricks here. Over."

"DC Hart, sir. Mr Thompson asked me to get an update, please. Over."

"The suspect hasn't appeared at the ticket counter. No sign of her anywhere about the concourse as yet . . ."

"I don't like the sound of it," said Thompson quietly. "This pair are devious."

"We're on full alert," continued Hendricks. "The moment there's any . . . sorry – sorry, just a second please, over."

Taking his eye briefly off the road, Thompson glanced at Penny, raising his eyebrows questioningly. She raised her hand, her fingers crossed, then Hendricks' voice came back on air.

"Hello, Victor One to Tango Two. Over."

"Reading you, sir. Over."

"Promising development at this end, I'm pleased to say. I'm just in receipt of a report from one of my team . . ."

Thompson reached out impatiently and without taking his eyes off the road, took the radio in his left hand. "Have you got her? Over."

"Well no, not yet," answered Hendricks, "but we

now know that she's here. Her car's just been located in the airport car park. Green Citroen Diane, registration F 321 NYX. Over."

"Good," said Thompson. "She may be waiting till the last minute to check in. I want you to search the place from top to bottom. Every shop, every phone-booth, every nook and cranny. Send female officers into the ladies' toilets, including the toilets in all bars, coffee shops, and restaurants. We'll be with you in about ten minutes. And remember, this woman is eight months pregnant. She shouldn't be that hard to find – so you turn the place over till you do. Understood? Over."

"Understood, sir. Over and out."

Gripping her seat tightly, Mary felt her stomach heave. She wasn't sure if it was the baby kicking or the sudden descent of the Piper Cub, but either way she felt a distinct unease, and she tried to relax her tension-wracked muscles as the pilot throttled back on his approach over the sunlit fields of Anglesey.

She had chartered the small plane back at Manchester airport, quickly agreeing to what she reckoned had probably been an exorbitant price for the hundred-mile journey to North Wales. While the pilot had made the necessary preparations for the short internal flight, she had gained permission to use the phone in his small office, ringing British Airways and booking her seat on the flight to Amsterdam.

With any luck she felt that the attention of the police

would now be focussed on the false trail while she left the country by a more circuitous route.

First though she had to reach the town of Holyhead, and as the Piper Cub touched down bumpily onto the runway of the Anglesey Flying Club, she was pleased to get a glimpse of the waiting taxi that she had asked the pilot to book over the radio.

She knew the pilot was curious about her motives, having sensed his scepticism when she had claimed a need to get to north Wales urgently on family business. However, his curiosity and the likelihood of his discussing the flight would, she hoped, soon be of academic interest. For once the taxi took her to the car ferry in Holyhead she would be only seventy miles from Ireland, and the safety of a separate jurisdiction where she could go to ground.

As the Piper taxied towards the hangars she glanced anxiously at her watch yet again, uneasily aware that there wasn't much time to spare in getting to the port. Despite her precautions she still feared the possibility of the police awaiting her arrival at the airfield, but when the plane came to a halt there was no sign of anyone waiting for her other than the taxi-driver, and as the pilot cut the engines she immediately undid her seat belt, eager to be out of the plane and heading for the ferry.

There was no prospect of escape, the windowless storeroom being locked from the outside, and so Dave sat unmovingly, staring despondently at the wall.

The meal his French captors had brought lay pushed

aside on the table. He had tried to eat, telling himself that
he needed to keep up his strength, but he had no appetite
for the bland airport food, tasteless despite liberal
applications from the supplied salt and pepper canisters.

He had known from the start that being intercepted
was a possibility, yet now that it had happened he felt
devastated. There was the same sense of numbed
unreality that he had felt when his parents and sister
had been killed in a car crash back in the summer of
1972. He had never forgotten any detail of that awful
evening; he could still remember watching *Top of the
Pops*, and the DJ introducing Don Mc Lean's number
one hit, "Vincent", when the policeman had come to the
door. He still felt a stab of pain whenever he heard that
song, but he hadn't expected to experience ever again
that same awful mixture of incredulity and desolation –
and now he had. Only this time the feelings seemed
even more intense, particularly the thought of being
imprisoned and not seeing his baby being born, and of
being in captivity while the child grew up.

He knew he mustn't dwell on that or he would
break down in despair. He had tried to convince himself
that he had been too harsh on the judicial system, that he
could trust the basic soundness of British justice, yet he
couldn't bring himself to feel genuinely convinced. And
so he had decided instead that he would have to brazen it
out. He could still claim to be in Paris simply on business,
and that the authorities had no proof he had killed
Gatenby. He could claim that his pretence of not knowing
the dead man stemmed from an irrational fear of getting
involved with the police. Even though they probably

wouldn't believe him, it might buy time and at least allow Mary to escape.

His thoughts were disturbed by the sound of the door being unlocked, and looking up, he saw the younger French police officer opening the door. Instead of locking the door after him however he held it open and smiled. Dave's heart began to pound and he looked up expectantly. He was half-rising from his chair when the Frenchman said: *"Voila!"* and pointed at him, then the two men he knew as Carrow and Mathieson stepped into the room.

Visser sat in the back of the taxi lost in thought as the car sped southwards from Harrogate. The driver was making good time, and Visser knew they would easily reach their destination on schedule, but he also knew that speed was not the overriding factor now. Brainpower would be his most potent weapon in seeking Adams, brainpower allied to experience and his finely honed instincts.

He had got back safely to his hotel after picking the lock on the workshop door, his relief at not being intercepted by the police replaced by another wave of fury at Mary Adams and the problems she had caused him. Once back in his room he had divested himself of the turpentine-stained clothes and quickly showered; then, notwithstanding his anger, he had sat down and tried calmly to analyse the situation.

As was his normal practice when tracking someone he attempted to put himself in his quarry's shoes. He doubted whether she had ever been involved in anything like this before, so what would she be thinking now? Well, certainly she would be feeling frightened, which might make her panicky and illogical. Even so she knew now that the game was up regarding her husband and Gatenby, but from what he had overheard in the workshop it was obvious that the couple were not going to give themselves up to the police. In which case they clearly had some strategy. Which probably meant that despite his presumption of fear on Adams' part her behaviour would *not* be panicky and illogical. Not if they had a fall-back plan that she was now following.

In the event of Walker having got involved in this affair on a one-off basis – which seemed likely to Visser – then it was quite possible that whoever had hired him might hang him out to dry now that the heat was on. In that case Walker and Adams would be depending on their own planning – but what might it be? He had heard her say, "Make sure you get there safely", which suggested a rendezvous for later. He had also heard her say "They'll contact the airports, surely?" – after which Walker has said something to which she had replied, "OK." That suggested that the rendezvous was outside the country. So assuming they both got out of Britain before a clampdown was in place, where would they join up later? Again he tried to put himself in Adams' shoes. Where do you go when you're pregnant and terrified? Someplace you can hide, somewhere you can feel safe. Somewhere like . . . somewhere like *home*. Home, where you'd have friends, relations, protectors.

He remembered the background information he had read about Adams in preparation for the phoney interview and the reference to her Irish roots.

Perfect, he thought. That's where I'd go if I were pregnant and on the run. Somewhere not too far away, yet a separate jurisdiction. A place where she would know the terrain and could hole up. And for good measure there was free movement between Ireland and the UK – she wouldn't even need her passport.

He thought again about her reference to airports "They'll contact the airports, surely?" – which of course the authorities would. And then it struck him. *There was another way to Ireland.* It was an *island* after all – she could go by ship. Much easier to step on board a ferry than a plane, he thought, what with cars, vans, and foot passengers all embarking simultaneously. Far more scope also for hiding yourself away during the journey.

There wasn't a shred of concrete evidence linking Adams to such a plan, of course, but Visser's instincts told him it was a real possibility. And in the absence of anything else, his gut feeling of how his quarry might behave was all he had to go on.

The nearest ferry was the Holyhead/Dun Laoghaire one and he had checked the ferry times, then booked a flight to Dublin that would get him to Ireland a couple of hours ahead of the ship. He had then quickly checked out of the Moat House Hotel and returned his hired car to the Harrogate branch of the rental company. He knew that Reinholdt would be awaiting anxiously his call regarding the meeting with Adams, but he couldn't ring the American and explain what had happened – it would involve too much loss of face. Instead he would concentrate on tracking down Adams, after which he could ring Reinholdt with the information the American wanted.

In the meantime the CIA man would be frantic, perhaps even actively seeking him, which was another reason, over and above Visser's normal observance of fieldcraft, for leaving no trail that could be followed. Instead after he had returned the rented car he had hailed a taxi to take him to Leeds airport, from where he would travel under one of his other aliases. Being kept in the dark would make the Americans angry, he knew, the more so if he caught Adams and gave her the kind of treatment he had in mind – but to hell with American bleeding-heart liberals, he thought. They would be assuagable – as they had been with the Iranian diplomat – by the sheer quality of the intelligence he could extract from Adams. And with that intelligence Walker could then be picked up at the rendezvous point.

First though, he had to find the fleeing Irishwoman, and as the taxi turned onto the airport approach road, Visser sat forward expectantly. He knew this was a shot in the dark, he knew that someone like Reinholdt would regard it as travelling in hope, but his instincts were all he had to go on.

The taxi pulled to a halt at the terminal, and Visser paid the driver, then exited quickly, keen to be on his way.

It was moments like this that made it all worthwhile, Carrow thought. He looked into Walker's eyes and relished the look of despair. Not so cocky now, he thought, not so suave away from his plush office, his tailor-made suits, his fancy car. Carrow had met smart-Alec prats like this before and he always enjoyed watching them crack.

The French officer indicated Walker. "Yes, monsieur?"

"Yes," answered Carrow, "very definitely yes."

"We leave you then," said the Frenchman. He pointed to a wall-mounted telephone. "You call us at 310 when you finish?"

"Yes, thank you."

"*Merci beaucoup, monsieur,*" added Mathieson smilingly as the Frenchman nodded acknowledgement and left.

Carrow stared down at the prisoner, who was sitting at the table, a half-eaten meal before him. "You've been playing silly buggers, Mr Walker. Weren't as smart as you thought though, were you? Did you really believe you'd get away with murder?"

"I didn't commit murder."

"No? Well, we'll see." Carrow pulled out a chair as did Mathieson. Then both men sat opposite Walker.

"Maybe you'd like to tell us what you did commit," said Mathieson.

"I didn't commit anything."

"Then why flee the country?"

"I wasn't fleeing the country – I was coming to Paris on business."

So the bastard was still brazening it out. Carrow realised he was almost pleased that Walker wasn't coming clean. It would make breaking him all the more satisfying. "On business," he replied sarcastically, "dressed like that?"

"It was hot. I took off my jacket and tie."

"Your flight was for four forty-five, but you switched to twelve fifteen."

"I changed my plans."

"And left the country without telling your secretary."

"I'd have rung her from here."

"Care to say why you left the jurisdiction without notifying the police?" said Mathieson.

Walker shrugged. "It seemed pointless. I was only going to Paris for one night."

"So, let me get this right," said Carrow, as though seeking clarification. "You weren't doing a runner. This had nothing to do with being tipped off by Mr Brotherton?"

He watched Walker carefully, but the man's face was impassive.

"I told you I was just coming here on business."

"You do *remember* Mr Brotherton?" said Carrow.

"He used to teach me."

"In St George's College?"

"Yes."

"Where Nigel Gatenby was a fellow pupil for seven years?"

Walker nodded. "Yes."

"Not what you said previously," said Mathieson mildly. "You claimed you'd never seen him before."

"I know."

"Why was that?"

"I . . . I know I shouldn't have . . . but . . ."

"But what?"

"But I didn't want to get involved with the police. I was afraid a wrong conclusion might be drawn."

"Such as?" said Mathieson.

"I don't know. I knew something serious had happened. I knew Gatenby must have been involved. I didn't want to be linked to it."

"But you did meet him that day in the Dales?" asked Carrow.

"No."

"Cut the bullshit, Walker! We know you met him – we know you killed him."

"No!"

"Yes! You're lying through your teeth, Walker. You've misled police officers conducting a murder inquiry, you've ignored instructions not to leave the jurisdiction, and the very day we link you to the murder victim, you flee the country."

"I didn't murder him!"

"Tell it to the jury, son. We'll bring in your Mr Brotherton. He won't be long admitting he tipped you off. Not when he's up for perverting the course of justice." Carrow pointed across the table. "You're going down, son – twenty years, minimum!" He watched with satisfaction as the other man's jaw tightened, but he said nothing further. Let the bastard ponder that, he thought.

After a moment Mathieson leaned across the table. "You're in serious trouble, Mr Walker. There'll be a sufficient case here to try you for murder. If there are extenuating circumstances, it's really in your interest to

303

reveal them. Far better to tell us the whole truth, right now."

There was a long pause while Walker seemed to come to a decision. "I . . . I can't prove my story."

"No need to prove it," said Mathieson encouragingly. "Just tell it to us."

He's done a lot of this kind of thing, thought Carrow approvingly, as he allowed the intelligence officer to take the lead.

"Please," said Mathieson, "we'll listen with an open mind. OK?"

After a moment Walker nodded slowly. "All right then. I . . . I was driving through the Dales, and Gatenby thumbed a lift. Said his car had broken down. He looked familiar, and after a few minutes in the car I recognised him from schooldays. We . . . we hadn't got on back then . . ."

"In what way?" asked Mathieson.

Walker grimaced. "He was a bully. Not just with me, other younger boys too. Anyway, as we drove along I told him who I was, made him feel uncomfortable. I pulled in, planning to let him walk to Grassington, then . . ."

"Yes?" said Mathieson softly.

"Then he produced a gun. Made me drive up a forest track. He said he needed the car and . . . well . . . I was scared – terrified in fact."

"That's only natural," said Mathieson.

"I told him to take the keys, but he said he couldn't leave a trail. He screwed a silencer onto the gun, and I knew he was going to kill me. He made me walk into the trees, and I managed to catch him with a tree branch. There was a struggle, and I – I didn't plan to kill him, but I was fighting for my life . . ."

"Sure," said Mathieson.

"We rolled down a hill, and he struck his head against a sharp tree stump – and that was it."

"Why didn't you report it to the police?"

"Because when I went back to his car I found the microfilm marked top secret. I realised then he was something to do with . . . I don't know, Military Intelligence, SIS, something really sensitive. I thought what the hell was he doing carrying stuff like that? I really felt out of my depth, terrified I'd be implicated. I mean I had no proof I was only acting in self-defence, and there'd been bad blood between us. I thought I might be stitched up. So . . ." He shrugged.

"So you decided to hide the body?" said Mathieson.

David nodded. "It was an impulsive reaction. At the time it seemed the lesser of two evils. Jesus, little did I know!"

"So you sent back the film and disposed of the body?"

"Yes."

"Why did you approach the police after the radio appeal?"

"I had to. I'd told our general manager I was visiting an aunt up in the Dales, on the way back from Carlisle."

"An aunt?"

"I made it up. I didn't want to have to travel with him. He suspected a lie, and to spite me he insisted I give the police details of my trip through the Dales."

"So you lied to him and then you lied to us," said Carrow.

"I had to."

"How do we know you're not lying now as well?"

"Because I've no reason to lie now."

Carrow raised an eyebrow. "Haven't you? How do we know you didn't deliberately kill Gatenby? How do we know you didn't copy the film?"

"Who the hell would I copy the film for?"

"You tell us."

"There's no one – this is crazy!"

"There are terrorists who'd pay a lot for that film."

"I don't need money! Look, I never set eyes on Gatenby since I left school."

"You're certain?" said Mathieson.

"Positive. I swear it. I've no links with any subversives. This was just a chance meeting that went wrong." Walker looked appealingly to Mathieson. "Look, you said it was in my interests to come clean. Well I've done that. I've admitted what I did. I should have notified the police. I was wrong there. But that's the only wrong thing I've done. Killing Gatenby was purely in self-defence. All right?"

Mathieson shrugged. "That remains to be seen, Mr Walker."

"Where's your wife now?" demanded Carrow.

"I don't know."

"You don't know?" Carrow snorted. "She's doing a runner, just like you were trying – isn't she?"

"She's completely innocent. She'd nothing to do with any of this."

"She covered up for you," persisted Carrow.

"She knew I'd done nothing wrong, so she backed up my story."

"So where is she now?" asked Carrow.

"I don't know."

"You know damned well! Where is she?"

"Look, she's an innocent woman, eight months pregnant. None of this is good for her or the baby. She just wanted to go somewhere quiet. I told her not to tell me where, in case I was caught."

Carrow leaned across the table and looked him in the eye. "I don't believe you, no more than I believe your cock-and-bull hitch-hiking story."

"I swear, every word of that story is true. I never planned to meet or kill Gatenby. It happened exactly as I told you."

Mathieson took up the questioning again. "Where were you planning to go after Paris?"

"I don't know. I just . . . I had a company flight to here – I simply used it to get out of the country."

"Who were you planning to meet here?"

"No-one! Look, I told you. I'm not working for anybody. I'm just a copywriter."

"And your wife?"

"Her only involvement is being married to me."

"If she's that innocent there's no reason for her to hide," said Carrow.

"I told you. I don't know . . ."

"Walker!" Carrow raised his hand in irritation. "Don't give me that rubbish about not knowing where she is."

"I can't tell you what I don't know!"

"Bullshit! We'll pick her up anyway. You're just making your sentence longer."

"No – "

"Yes!" Carrow watched with satisfaction, aware of the other man's dismay at the thought of imprisonment. "Not so cocky now, Mr Walker? Don't fancy the prospect of – what, say a twenty-year lagging?"

Walker looked appealingly to Mathieson. "You said if I told the truth, explained the extenuating circumstances . . ."

"But you haven't told us all the circumstances – like your wife's whereabouts," said Mathieson evenly.

Walker bit his lip but said nothing.

"You won't be seeing much of her in the future, mind," said Carrow. "Not even on visiting day if she's serving a term herself – as she may well do if you keep her a fugitive."

"You're being foolish, Mr Walker," said Mathieson.

"We'd have to put the child into care, of course," said Carrow.

"No!"

Carrow smiled bleakly, savouring Walker's anguished expression. "Yes, actually. If both parents are in jail . . ."

"No . . . no . . ." said Walker softly.

Carrow leaned forward. "Yes, pal. Count on it."

Walker looked down dejectedly, like something had snapped in him. Then he shook his head as he toyed distractedly with one of the canisters on the table. "No," he said again softly, but, with conviction, "no . . ."

Carrow felt that now was the time to heighten the pressure, but as he went to lean nearer his quarry Walker suddenly sprang forward, taking him by surprise.

Walker threw the pepper from the opened canister into Mathieson's eyes, then swung round from the blinded intelligence officer and overturned the table.

Shocked and enraged, Carrow rose quickly from his chair, but Walker was upon him before he had gained his balance properly. Walker got in the first blow, a vicious thump to the stomach, and Carrow doubled up in agony, falling heavily to the floor as Walker swiftly tripped him. He lay there, badly winded and with his eyes watering, and saw Walker deliver a similar blow to the disoriented Mathieson. Gasping for breath, Carrow lay on the floor, then he levered himself against the table leg and turned around to see Mathieson clutching his stomach, the phone ripped off the wall, and Walker heading out the door.

His heart thumping madly, Dave slammed the storeroom door shut behind him and found himself in the corridor. He immediately turned left, in the opposite direction to that from which the French officers had brought him. Charged by adrenaline, his movements were almost automatic, and his overriding instinct was to lose himself in the airport throng.

He reached a doorway at the corridor end and opened it to discover a staircase. Just then he heard Mathieson shouting for help from the storeroom, and he swiftly closed the door behind him and began ascending the stairs three steps at a time. Reaching the top of the stairwell, he came to a door and gingerly tried the handle. Locked. Damn! he thought, then he turned about, grabbed the banister with his right hand and swiftly climbed to the next floor.

There was another door in a similar location to the floor below and he carefully tried it. To his immense relief the door was unlocked. He peered through the opening and realised that he was on the periphery of the baggage claim area. Without pausing he opened the door and stepped through.

The area about the baggage carousels was thronged with passengers concentrating on withdrawing their luggage from the moving belts. Any minute now he expected to hear an alarm siren sounding, followed by a flurry of police activity – or would they be more subtle than that? Perhaps the airport police, alerted by Mathieson and Carrow, would simply contact their personnel by walkie-talkie. Maybe they would unobtrusively seal all exits and pick him up that way.

Speed was his only hope. He had to get out of the terminal before it could be cordoned off. Moving briskly, but not so fast as to be noticed, he passed the baggage carousels and approached customs.

He wished there were more passengers passing through, but the majority of those from the flight just landed were still awaiting their baggage, and so he had to run the customs gauntlet almost alone. Walk at a normal speed, he told himself, don't lock eyes with the customs officials but don't stare shiftily at the ground either.

He was aware of a sheen of perspiration on his brow

but he resisted the urge to wipe it off in sight of the customs officers. He kept going, and after what seemed an eternity he reached the exit door without being halted, then it opened automatically, and he passed through and into the arrivals hall.

Picking up pace, he made his way through the crowds towards the exit. How long had elapsed since his escape, he wondered. One minute, two, three? Say three minutes; could they have the place sealed off that quickly? *Of course they could, probably had a security procedure expressly designed for sealing the building.*

He came towards the exit, slowing slightly to scan those around the door. There were no uniformed police officers, nor was there anyone who looked particularly like a waiting security agent, but then if they were professional, perhaps they wouldn't look obvious . . .

Suddenly he was at the door. He half-expected a hand on his shoulder as he passed through, but he continued unchallenged and emerged into the open air.

He felt a surge of joy at having got out but immediately repressed it. He was still sixteen miles from Paris. And he was still in the airport precinct. He looked across at an Air France bus that was parked directly opposite the exit. From past experience he knew that they left every twelve minutes for Porte Maillot but to his dismay the one parked before him was only filling up. He couldn't risk waiting about for eight or nine minutes. Turning to his left, he quickly followed the curve of the building to the taxi rank, only to find a queue there. Damn, he thought, then retraced his steps past the Air France bus. There was no sign of the Roissy coach, so he continued around the circular building seeking the airport bus that connected to the RER station.

To his relief he saw one, almost full, at the kerbside. Just as he reached the door he stopped dead. What the hell was he thinking of? Once the authorities realised that he had escaped from the terminal they would extend the net. And the first thing they would think of would be the buses. They could radio ahead to ensure that every bus that had just left the airport would be met. Maybe even radio the drivers and instruct them not to allow any passengers off en route. Christ, but he'd nearly delivered himself into their hands!

He turned away from the bus, a sense of desperation beginning to overtake him. Despite the coming and going of passengers, he was starting to feel obvious. He knew he had to do something quickly and after a moment's reflection he realised what his only option was. He turned and made his way back towards the taxi rank, taking in at a glance those near the head of the queue.

Second in line was a family made up of a man and woman accompanied by a teenage girl and a younger boy. The boy wore a Toronto Blue Jays tee-shirt, and the girl had a maple leaf sown onto her rucksack.

"Excuse me," said Dave, his tone urgent, but, he hoped, non-threatening, "I wonder if you could help a fellow Canadian?"

"Yes?" The father looked at him quizzically.

Dave had assumed an American accent, despite knowing that it differed somewhat from the more modulated Canadian tones, but it was the best he could do. "I'm in desperate need of a taxi," he said. "I've got to get to the hospital – I wonder if you'd please let me have yours?"

The Canadian looked at him appraisingly. "You don't look ill."

"I'm not. It's my sister. She's had a coronary. I've just flown in and I've got to reach her urgently. *Please.*"

The Canadian exchanged glances with his wife, and Dave felt his heart lift when he saw her nodding assent.

The man turned back around. "We've been queuing for some time," he said measuredly, "kinda wearing, especially with youngsters in tow . . ."

"Dad . . ." said the teenage girl appealingly.

"Well, it's true, honey . . ."

Jesus! thought Dave, glancing back at the terminal. The gendarmes could be at the door at any second.

A taxi pulled in and began to load up, placing the Canadian family at the head of the queue.

"Maybe we could drop you off on our way into Paris," said the father.

Dave looked at the mounds of luggage the family had at their feet, then back at the terminal exit door. He couldn't hang about out here while they laboriously stowed every piece. "Look, the hospital is in the other direction to Paris," he said. "And it's – well, it's touch and go with my sister. You'd only have to wait another few minutes for the next taxi. *Please*?"

"Chris . . ." said the mother.

Just then a taxi pulled in. Dave bit his lip, then the Canadian turned back to him. "OK, it's yours."

"Thank you. Thank you so much." Dave swiftly entered the back of the vehicle as the Canadian family tried to explain the situation to an angry businessman in line behind them. *"Monsieur?"* asked the taxi driver.

Dave closed the door so he wouldn't be heard from outside, and leaned forward. *"Gare du Nord, s'il vous plaît."*

"Gare du Nord," repeated the taxi man, then he let off the handbrake and drove speedily away from the airport.

Penny looked disappointedly at the British Airways ticket desk again, then glanced anxiously around the rest of the busy terminal.

This was like being stood up on a date. She remembered when she was sixteen having a crush on an older boy in school and the awful sinking feeling when he hadn't shown up for a date. She had stood outside the cinema, glancing at her watch, looking surreptitiously in every direction, and wondering if there could have been some mistake, yet knowing at heart that there wasn't.

It felt the same now. Her watch read three forty, and there was still no sign of Mary Adams. She caught a movement from the corner of her eye and turned around. Heading in her direction was Thompson, his frustration clearly evident. He reached her and breathed out in exasperation, "I think we've been had."

"What's her game, Chief?"

"I don't know. She booked the flight at ten past one – at which time her husband was still in the air, en route for Paris. She couldn't have known he was going to be apprehended, so booking the flight made sense if she wanted to join him on the Continent."

"Yes, unless . . . what if – what if *he* were to make his way to *her*, someplace totally different?"

Thompson nodded slowly. "Then this whole episode would make sense – a red herring to distract us."

"Except for her driving here in her car . . ."

"For all we know she could have parked it here last night."

"True," said Penny. "There's no way she could be hiding somewhere in the airport, to take a later flight when we're not expecting it?"

Thompson shook his head. "Everywhere's been searched, top to bottom; I'm certain she's not here."

"OK," said Penny, "why don't I check with Inspector Hendricks whether there's any way of knowing when her car was parked?"

"Yes, check it out," agreed Thompson, "but if she's at what I think she's at, she'll be making her break someplace else while the spotlight is on Manchester."

"So what do we do, Chief?"

"We wait. After the French got Walker I lifted the alert on all points of exit; for him – but not for her."

"Even though we thought she was here in Manchester?"

Thompson smiled wanly. "Can't be too careful. So they're still watching out for her, and if everyone does their job – we'll still get to meet Miss Adams."

Bob Reinholdt felt something was wrong. In his twenty-six years with the CIA he had learned to respect his instincts, and despite his attempts to rationalise to the contrary, his instincts told him something wasn't right.

He threw his pen down onto his desk, rose from his leather swivel chair and crossed restlessly to the office window.

It was three forty-five now, and still Visser hadn't phoned. He had said his appointment with Mary Adams was for eleven, so what the hell was keeping him? Even allowing for the South African's independence of approach, not to have heard anything over four and a half hours later was definitely worrying, especially when Visser had promised to report the outcome after leaving the woman's house.

Reinholdt pondered on how things might somehow have gone wrong. He had impressed upon Visser that there was a veto on adopting the tactics he had used with the Iranian, yet a niggling doubt hovered at the back of the American's mind.

Ultimately there was no telling what a man like Visser would do when operating in the field – a point he should have been aware of when recommending him to Krucowski. Things were starting to shape up into a no-win situation. If he didn't have progress to report to the Deputy Director it would reflect badly on him, as London Chief of Station. Yet if Visser had fouled up in pressing for that very progress, it would also be his ass – as the one who had recommended using the South African.

Reinholdt stood at the window staring into space as he pondered, almost with detachment, how his career hung in the balance. He consoled himself that in the past he had been at his best under this kind of pressure. He had come through before in crises in Tehran, Beirut,

El Salvador. Damn it all, he thought, he hadn't risen to CIA Chief of Station without taking some gambles, and now he'd simply have to gamble further to hold on to what he had.

He turned from the window and returned to his desk, his mind made up. It was time to stop being passive, time to take some positive action. He sat in his chair, lifted the telephone and buzzed his secretary. "Glenda, I want to see Marty Schulman, please."

"At what time, sir?"

"Right now. Tell him to drop whatever he's doing."

"Very good, sir."

He put the phone down, strangely relieved now that he was taking the initiative. Of course, there would be hell to pay if Pete Krucowski ever found out that Company personnel were being drawn into the case, but it was a risk Reinholdt had decided he must take.

Something had happened in Harrogate, and he wanted to know what it was. It would take Marty Schulman and his team a couple of hours to fly up to Yorkshire, during which time Visser might ring in, allowing Reinholdt to call off his men. But deep down he doubted if that would happen – in which case he was determined to find out exactly what was going on . . .

32

Another five minutes or so and Mary reckoned the car ferry would be outside British territorial waters. She sat in a sheltered suntrap on the upper deck, out of the strong sea breeze and away from most of the other passengers. Her hopes were beginning to rise, but she forced herself not to relax prematurely. There was, after all, the ship's radio, and it wasn't beyond the bounds of possibility that the ship could be summoned back if the police felt she was on board. On the other hand the police couldn't know for sure that she was on the ship, and with every passing minute the vessel came closer to international waters, if in fact it hadn't already entered them.

No, the chief risk now would be if the British authorities had tumbled to the flight to Holyhead and requested their Irish counterparts to intercept her on arrival. Well she would worry about that when she reached Dun Laoghaire. Besides, even if they were looking for her they would be going on the description that had misled the police at the ferry. For they had been seeking a pregnant white woman; the last thing they would be expecting would be an overweight black woman, which was how she was travelling now.

She had dismissed the idea as impractical, ridiculous even, when Dave had suggested it during their contingency planning the previous week. She had pointed out that the photographs he had seen of her as a teenager, blacked-up in the chorus of an amateur production of *Showboat*, were just that – amateurish and unconvincing.

Dave had argued however that with brown contact lenses, a good Afro wig, and a costume that covered most of her limbs, she would only have to deal with her hands and face. He had had a fascination with stage make-up from his own acting days, and with his old instruction book in hand he had gone to Mary's make-up kit and taken out sticks number ten and seven, using a mixture of them to produce the skin tone of a medium-complexioned black woman.

He had broadened the nose with highlights, shaded the declivity underneath it, and created the appearance of enlarged nostrils using a stick of black, then he had darkened the eyes under the brow to give the appearance of shortening them. Finally he had extended and thickened the lips with shadows and highlights.

The effect had been startling, and when embellished with a coloured headscarf, dangling earrings and the dark contact lenses and wig, Mary had realised the potential of the disguise. She had assiduously practised

319

both the make-up technique and the most effective way to pad herself with sponge foam under a large floral dress, so that when the taxi driver had delivered her to the Grand Hotel in Holyhead an hour and a half ago she had been able to transform herself in a cubicle in the ladies' toilet in less than fifteen minutes.

When boarding the ferry she had chatted to fellow passengers in a West Indian accent, timing her approach for about three twenty, to coincide with the last-minute rush of foot passengers, and also with the time when police attention should have been focussed on her expected presence at Manchester airport for the three forty-five flight.

She had resisted the temptation to try to identify potential plain-clothes police officers in the crowd about the gangway, concentrating instead on staying in character and boarding in a low-key fashion.

She thought now how pleased Dave would have been that their ruse had worked, then found herself worrying as she did whenever she thought of him. She knew it was pointless – they each had to follow their agreed itineraries alone, before being reunited – yet the thought of her husband being apprehended haunted her. The idea of Dave being jailed, of his first contact with their baby being in a prison, was just unbearable. Even a short sentence for either of them would mean missing out on the baby's formative years.

She didn't really believe in an interventionist God, yet she found herself praying that everything would work out OK for them. Leave it at that, she cautioned herself. She would need her energy for whatever was to come. And despite her reassurance to her husband that life together in Ireland would be fine, she was still worried about the future.

After all she had left Ireland as an eighteen-year-old and lived in England ever since. Would she really be able to slot back in? Would much of Ireland still be a conservative rural society at heart? She had seen numerous encouraging changes on her visits home; there was a greater openness now, less of the narrow-mindedness she had found suffocating, yet visiting and living there were two different things. She had been much encouraged by the liberalisation of attitudes on things like contraception, and there was now a greater tolerance, epitomised, she felt, by the election of a progressive like Mary Robinson as the country's first woman President.

What, she wondered, would her father have thought of that? Ever since her teens she had argued with her father, whose opposition to her growing belief in feminism – 'aul ramesh and nonsense' as he called it – had been a major factor in her emigrating.

Things had come to a head one day in the summer of 1977 when she had gone turf-cutting with Dad and her brother Tom. Her father had ordered her to leave what she was doing to make tea for the three of them and there had been a blazing row. All the ill-feeling and resentment on both sides had surfaced; Mary had lashed him for his chauvinism, for deriding her aspirations to act, for his attitude to her mother, and he had called her a spoiled, brazen hussy.

To please her mother, Mary had eventually agreed to

a reconciliation of sorts with her father during her final weeks at home, but at the end of that summer she had left for London, determined to live where her aspirations and values might be more sympathetically received.

And now, sixteen years later, she was coming home. No, not home, she thought, her home now was with Dave. And with both her parents dead, Ireland wouldn't be the childhood home it once was. Still, she knew she would be well received by her brother Tom and his wife Jenny, who lived in an old rambling house at Ballyard, from where Jenny managed the farm while Tom ran the trawler.

Listening now to the seagulls reminded Mary of happy childhood days in Mayo and leaning back in her chair, she let the sun shine on her face and determined to relax.

It would all be OK once they got safely to Kerry – she would make it work somehow. Meanwhile she had three hours before running the final gauntlet at Dun Laoghaire. Right now her stomach ached, her back and shoulders felt sore, and her legs were leaden with tiredness, and so she raised her feet and sat back further, anxious to conserve her strength for whatever lay ahead.

Chief Superintendent Carrow strove to keep his temper in check. Sitting in the police offices in de Gaulle airport, his solar plexus still hurt, almost an hour and a half after Walker had punched him, and he felt a cold fury towards the advertising executive. If he got his hands on that devious bastard again there would be no escaping, he would see to that. The trouble was that they were no nearer to getting their hands on him.

The airport had been discreetly sealed off and thoroughly searched, the connecting buses to the RER station had yielded nothing, the Air France coaches to Porte Maillot and the Roissy and Orly connections had been intercepted without Walker being among the passengers, and eventually Carrow had had to ring Leeds and report the escape of the prisoner.

He had made the call in private and had been careful to draw attention to the fact that Walker had been in French custody, and he had further intimated that the escape and the failure to recapture Walker had been largely French matters. Nevertheless it was infuriating, for no matter how skilfully he tried to cover himself, it was going to look bad if Walker wasn't picked up quickly.

Carrow was also annoyed at Mathieson, whose continuing sangfroid seemed wholly inappropriate. Admittedly the intelligence officer was presently on the phone to the BBC, trying to find from Mary Adams' colleagues if she had any family or friends in France, but still Carrow wished the man weren't so damned unflappable.

Carrow had tracked down Trevor Lawrence, the general manager in United Advertising, and spoken to him on the phone from the conference Walker was supposed to have attended. Despite the man's horror at the thought of adverse publicity for United

Advertising, Carrow had sensed an antipathy in the way Lawrence spoke of his colleague. Yet in spite of Lawrence's apparent willingness to help, he hadn't been of much assistance. The only contacts he had known Walker to have in France were people in the advertising industry. He wasn't aware of any special friendships, and the people Walker would have known were all present at the conference.

Carrow looked round the airport police office with its illuminated maps, computer screens and touch-button data-processing. Very high-tech, he thought sourly, but if the bastards had confiscated Walker's passport, money and credit cards instead of just taking his holdall, he would now be in a much weaker position.

As it was the holdall had been thoroughly searched, its walls and base sliced open with a blade lest there be any secret compartments. All that the bag had contained however was several changes of clothes, some toiletries, a map of Paris and a paperback novel. The French officers had squeezed out all of the toothpaste and shaving cream from their respective tubes, but nothing had been hidden within.

They desperately needed a lead, thought Carrow, and seeing Mathieson putting the phone down, he crossed the office and looked at him quizzically. "Well?"

"No one at the BBC knows of anything connecting her to France."

"Damn! And Adams – as a person?"

"Punctual, good worker, popular with her colleagues, excepting that last chap I spoke to."

Carrow looked interested. "Oh? What did he say?"

"Claimed she was unreasonable, highly-strung."

"Nothing more specific?"

"One thing," answered Mathieson. "I asked if she had behaved oddly – anything even remotely suspicious – in the last few weeks."

"And?"

"Seems one day a while back this last chap – Arnold Beazley's his name – well, seems he walked in on her when she was using the phone in the greenroom . . ."

"The what?"

"Greenroom – where the actors relax. Anyway he thought she was a bit on edge at his presence . . ."

"What was she talking about?"

"He thinks from the trend of the conversation that she may have been trying to sell her house."

"Well, now . . ." Carrow stroked his chin thoughtfully. "That would figure if they were planning to flee the country."

"Exactly. She'd also be likely to want to sell rather rapidly, which brings us to Mr Brompton."

"Who?"

"Name of the person she spoke to. This Arnold Beazley chap remembers the name, said he recalls it from once starring in a play by J W Brompton."

Carrow thought a moment. "If money changed hands we should try to find out where it's lodged. They only found out this morning we were onto them – she may be tempted to go to where she lodged it."

"Maybe," said Mathieson. "Or if not her, perhaps Walker."

"Let's get on to Leeds, see if there are any estate agents or auctioneers with the name Brompton in the Yorkshire region. Failing that, they can list all Bromptons in the Harrogate and Leeds areas and work through them."

"Bit of a long-shot, really . . ."said Mathieson.

"Better than sitting on our arses!" snapped Carrow, losing patience with the other man's languid air.

"Well, yes, quite . . ."

"Anyway," said Carrow, calming down, "we've nothing else to go on. I don't fancy just hoping the Frogs pick Walker up, so let's get after this Brompton character."

"As you wish then," said Mathieson agreeably. "As you wish . . ."

In her excitement Penny ran up the stairs three steps at a time. She turned down a corridor, then briefly knocked on a door before entering one of the offices of the Manchester airport police.

Thompson was alone in the room, the telephone in his hand, and she knew immediately from his face that something was wrong. Curbing her excitement, she looked quizzically at him, but he barely nodded in reply. She knew then that the problem was serious; one of the things she liked about Thompson was the fact that he rarely vented his frustrations on his junior officers.

"OK, keep me posted the moment's there's anything," he said into the phone, then hung up.

Penny said nothing, and after a moment he turned

to face her. "They've bloody lost their prisoner!" he said venomously.

"Walker?"

"Who else?"

"Oh no!"

"I should have gone to France myself instead of trusting that pair of fucking idiots! I . . . I'm sorry, Penny, I don't mean to . . ."

"No, it's OK, Chief," she said softly. "It's OK."

Thompson shook his head. "After all our efforts . . ."

"What happened?"

"The exact details are hazy – that's probably Carrow covering himself as usual – but there was some sort of struggle and Walker escaped into the airport crowd."

"No! And he hasn't been sighted since?"

"No; and I wouldn't assume he will be either."

"Have the French police been openly alerted to find him."

"They have now, though of course the background isn't being made public."

"Must be a fairly good chance then of still getting him, Chief."

"Normally perhaps. But this Walker chap is smart – he's already shown himself to be very resourceful. There's no two ways about it. This is really bad news."

"It won't quite make up for that, but I have some good news."

Thompson perked up. "They haven't picked up the wife?"

"No," said Penny, "but I think I've found out where she's headed."

"Go on."

"When you told us to check all the airlines in case she'd booked any other flight, it set me thinking. Supposing she took a flight – but not with any of the airlines?"

"I'm not with you," interjected Thompson.

"We got nowhere with the airlines, as I'm sure Inspector Hendricks told you, but it struck me that there are several small aircraft based at the hangars here. While you were liaising with Leeds, I nipped over and asked a few questions." Penny paused briefly, unable to resist savouring her moment. "A woman fitting Mary Adams' description left in one of those planes at about one thirty."

"Good God!"

"She hired a pilot to fly her to Anglesey."

"Anglesey?"

"The Aero Club there is just a few miles from Holyhead."

"From where the ferries run to Ireland!"

"There are two that leave each afternoon, Chief. I checked with Tourist Information. She would have been in time to catch the second one."

"What time did it leave?"

"Three forty-five. Arriving in Dun Laoghaire at seven fifteen."

Thompson looked at his watch. "It's just ten past four. By the time we could do anything she'd be out of British waters. Right, we'll get her at the other end! The flight to Dublin is less than an hour. Book us onto one immediately. While you do, I'll clear everything with Leeds."

"Great."

"And, Penny?"

"Chief?"

"Bloody good work!"

"Thank you."

"Now get us onto a plane – and fast."

"On my way!"

The man in the jeans and the lumberjack shirt rose from the barber's chair, looked appraisingly in the mirror at his closely-cropped hair and paid the elderly barber.

"*Merci, monsieur,*" said the older man gravely as he accepted the tip.

"*De rien. Bonjour, monsieur,*" said Dave in farewell, then he took up his new Lacoste holdall, opened the door, and stepped into the noisy Parisian street.

The barbers had been just the right kind of establishment, busy enough that he hadn't stood out as too much of an oddity, yet not so packed as to entail a long wait. Dave glanced at his watch as he headed towards the nearby shopping centre. Four o'clock; he had fifteen minutes before making his crucial telephone call.

Moving briskly, he entered the shopping centre, its atmosphere heavy with the smell of freshly roasted coffee. He slowed down slightly and made for the toilets that he had located earlier. The centre was full of shoppers, with a steady flow of customers entering the toilets. Dave waited until several others were going in, then he also dropped a coin onto the plate of the toilet attendant, entered a cubicle and locked the door. Opening his holdall, he removed a shaving mirror that he propped above the cistern, then he took out a box of tissues and packed several around the collar of his shirt. Finally he produced a can of black hair mousse, and using disposable gloves, began to apply it carefully to his severely trimmed hair.

In the taxi from the airport he had decided that changing his appearance was an urgent priority, and he had stopped the taxi driver before reaching the Gare du Nord. Instead he had walked back to the bustling suburban shopping centre and bought several pairs of jeans and slacks, shirts and underwear, and a pair of tennis shoes. He had changed into his present casual outfit in this same toilet, used the phone in the shopping centre's main arcade, then visited two separate chemists. He had bought Roux "Black Rage" hair mousse and toiletries in one, and then a blond highlighting-cum-bleaching kit, disposable gloves, and the small shaving mirror in the other.

Now, as he finished blackening his hair, he carefully removed all traces of the mousse from his skin and observed himself critically in the mirror. The French police would be looking for a man with longish thick brown hair, dressed in a white shirt and the trousers of a business suit, and Dave's present image with short black hair, jeans, casual shirt and tennis shoes was as markedly different as he could make it.

He placed the mousse, the mirror, and the folded up disposable gloves back in his new bag and looked again at his watch. Five minutes to go, he thought nervously, then he flushed the mousse-stained tissues down the toilet, left the cubicle and washed his hands. On the off-chance that his altered appearance might be noticed by the toilet attendant, Dave timed his leaving with another customer getting change from the attendant, then he headed for the telephones in the main arcade.

So much depended on the outcome of this phone call, and he wondered, yet again, if he was being foolhardy in persisting with his plan. When making contingency plans with Mary the previous week they had agreed that if they fled Harrogate she would take the Holyhead ferry alone, while Dave would travel to Zurich to withdraw from the bank the proceeds of their house sale.

Dave had argued that the money could simply be transferred from their Swiss Account to a bank account in Ireland, without any need to travel in person to Zurich, but Mary had been adamant in her opposition. The whole point of going to Ireland was to disappear on the Beara Peninsula – instead of which there would inevitably be speculation if a large sum from a numbered Swiss Account arrived in the local bank. Even were they to open an account in Dublin, they would need to produce identification, and an address for statements, and there would be official involvement through government tax on deposit account interest. Far safer, Mary had reasoned, to withdraw the money in cash, then eventually when the heat died down they could lodge it locally in smaller amounts. The other advantage was that if the authorities were on the lookout for them, they wouldn't expect Dave to enter Ireland alone – particularly from continental Europe.

Now, however, things had changed. He wasn't just fleeing Carrow and Mathieson; for all he knew the entire might of the French security services could be seeking him. Still, there was no reason why they should suspect an escape route eastwards – they had no knowledge of his Swiss account. And, he reminded himself, the money was critically important. Channelled via Tom, it would buy them a farm in Ireland.

Reaching an empty phone booth he paused, then picked up the instrument. He consulted the slip of paper on which he had earlier written the bank's phone number, took a deep breath, then inserted his phone card and dialled. The call was answered on the second ring. "Hello, Commercial Bank of Switzerland."

"Good afternoon," answered Dave in fluent German, thankful as never before for the colloquial ease he had acquired as a student, working in a Munich factory. "I'd like to speak to Herr Masthaus, please."

"Who's calling, please?"

"David Walker."

"One moment, please."

There was a click, then a man's voice came on the line. "Otto Bloch speaking."

"Hello, David Walker here. I was on earlier. You said to ring back at four fifteen for Herr Masthaus."

"Yes, but I'm sorry. A message was left from Herr Masthaus a few moments ago. He won't be coming back to the bank this afternoon. His meeting has been extended."

Damn! thought Dave. Then he made his tone as pleasant as possible. "There must surely be someone else who could authorise a withdrawal tomorrow."

"I'm sorry, sir, but our normal banking hours are Monday to Friday. A Saturday transaction could be authorised only by Herr Masthaus himself."

I can't hang about for three days, thought Dave. *I must convince him.* "It's an extremely urgent, situation," he said. "I'm sure Herr Masthaus would be sympathetic. Can I contact him myself, by phone?"

"I'm sorry, but he's consulting with a client and can't be disturbed."

"This evening then, if I were to call him at home."

The man hesitated. "I'm afraid we don't disclose staff telephone numbers, sir."

"Of course not, but I must emphasise that this isn't a normal case." Despite the desperate need to convince him, Dave kept his voice calm. "You see a great deal of future banking hinges on this transaction. I don't think Herr Masthaus would be pleased if such an opportunity were lost through over-protectiveness on your part – however well intentioned."

He could sense the man wavering and he spoke again quickly and in a friendly tone. "Why don't I just give him a buzz? If he can facilitate me – and I'm confident he'll want to – then fine. If not, then a thirty-second conversation settles the matter. OK?"

There was a long pause. "Very good, sir. The number is 211 1256."

Dave quickly wrote down the number. "Thank you very much. Any idea when he may get home?"

"He expects to be with his client until around six. Perhaps if you rang about seven."

"Fine. Thank you again. Good afternoon."

"Good afternoon, sir."

He hung up slowly, then moved off deep in thought, but hopeful that his plan might still be on course.

Mary leaned on the rail as the ship steamed towards Dun Laoghaire. In spite of her apprehension, her heart had lifted at the familiar backdrop of the Dublin/Wicklow mountains, their purple outlines bathed in the warm evening sunshine. Other passengers were now lining the rails, picking out landmarks as the ship sailed into Dublin bay in the still of the evening.

Mary looked wistfully at the heather-clad mountains, their outlines seemingly growing larger as the boat approached the coast. She could imagine being among similar mountains in Kerry, the air sweet with gorse and hawthorn, but first she had to land safely in Dun Laoghaire.

Was it really only this morning, she thought, when she had worked at her stained glass – then taken the call from Dave and had the terrifying encounter with Franklin? But she mustn't dwell on that now. The whole nightmarish episode must be put in abeyance if she were to concentrate on getting safely to Ballyard.

She had made herself eat and drink during the three-and-a-half hour ferry crossing, determined to restore her energy, yet her mind kept flitting back to what had happened, and ahead to what might happen in Dun Laoghaire. Would the Yorkshire police have tumbled to her ruse of flying to Anglesey? And if so, would they have flown ahead to meet her? Or asked the Irish Police to pick her up? And if they were awaiting her, would she get away again with her disguise?

She checked her watch as the boat neared the harbour. Seven o'clock. Fifteen minutes to disembarkation, at which time, she thought ruefully, her questions would be answered.

"God damn it!" said Thompson as the gates came down on the level crossing. He viciously applied the handbrake, cut the engine, and banged the steering wheel in frustration.

Penny sat in the passenger seat, a road map of Dublin spread on her knees. "Merrion Gates, Chief. We're only about two miles from the ferry."

"I've been before, Penny. I know where we are!" snapped Thompson.

"Sorry, Chief . . ."

"No . . . no, look I'm sorry. It's just . . . to come this far and maybe miss her by a minute of two."

"It's only seven o'clock, Chief. It'll take a few minutes for the boat to tie up, gangplanks to be attached. Even if she's first off, she'll hardly be away before twenty past."

"Yes, you're right. It's just we can't afford any more cock-ups." He looked at the level crossing. "No sign of the bloody train. Still, no use fussing. It'll come when it comes."

"Right," said Penny, trying not to let her tension show as she folded up the map and sat back. She had known time might be tight in catching the five o'clock flight from Manchester to Dublin and then having to cross the city from the airport to Dun Laoghaire, the ferry port at the far side of Dublin Bay. Thompson had rung ahead to have a hired car waiting for them on landing, but to Penny's surprise he hadn't asked the Irish police to intercept Mary Adams.

Better if they discreetly followed her themselves, he had said, for with Walker still at large his wife could then act as unwitting bait. What a one in the eye for Carrow, Penny thought, if they should be the ones to catch both fugitives. She would give a week's pay to see the Special Branch man's face if he were told that they had caught the prisoner he had allowed to escape. Her fantasy was abruptly interrupted by the blast of a train's horn, and looking out the car window she saw the approaching green coaches of an electrified DART train.

Before the carriages had passed, Thompson started the car and was leaning over the wheel. "Time, Penny?"

"Three minutes past seven."

"By God, we'll get her yet!"

Just then the level crossing gates lifted automatically, and the car in front moved off. Penny smiled excitedly at Thompson. Then he let off the handbrake, drove bumpily across the tracks and turned at speed onto the main road to Dun Laoghaire.

Everything hinged on the habits of the Swiss banker, and if the man wasn't at home now Dave knew his plans would go seriously astray. After his earlier phone call to the bank Dave had taken the metro to the Gare de l'Est, the station from which trains for Switzerland departed. He had checked train times, eaten a meal in a nearby bistro, and generally fretted as the time had passed with agonising slowness.

He knew that Mary should be safely on board the ferry by now if her end of things had gone to plan, yet his mind conjured up all sorts of possible snags she might have encountered. And if she *were* caught by the police, what was he to do then? Would they go easier on Mary, would it perhaps prevent her having to deliver the baby in detention, if he were to give himself up? No! No, he told himself firmly. He mustn't imagine either of them being caught, otherwise it would undermine his conviction – and he might well need all his conviction to persuade Masthaus to agree to his request.

He had strolled the Parisian streets to pass the time, but for once he was immune to the city's charm and at six thirty he had found himself unable to resist any longer and had rung the banker's house. He had hoped the man might be in early, or failing that that the phone might be answered by a wife or family member who could confirm when Masthaus was expected home. Instead the phone had rung six times before switching to a message on an answering machine. Dave had hung up without speaking, then waited in a café, trying to read a newspaper. At a minute to seven he had made again for the phone booth at the Gare de l'Est, and now his hand trembled as he lifted the handset, inserted his phone card and dialled.

If the banker were a bachelor living alone then who could say where he might go after work on a Friday night? Hearing the first of the ringing tones, Dave swallowed hard. The phone rang several times, then a man answered.

"Hello?"

"Hello, Herr Masthaus?"

"Yes, this is Masthaus."

Thank God! thought Dave. He noted that the man's German had little trace of the Schweizerdeutsch accent and his tone was neither friendly nor forbidding.

"I'm sorry to disturb you at home," said Dave, "but it's rather urgent . . ."

"Who is this, please?"

"My name is Walker, David Walker. My wife and I recently opened an account with your bank, Herr Masthaus."

"And there is some problem?"

"I'm afraid so. I tried to contact you at the office several times, but they told me you were tied up with a client."

"That is so. The office gave you my number?"

"Yes, I impressed upon them the urgency of the situation. Normally I'd leave it until opening time on Monday, but my company is about to land a very lucrative contract in the Middle East. It's going to be worth millions of pounds to us, much of which we hope to bank with the Commercial Bank. However there's been a last-minute hitch regarding – how shall I phrase it? Let's say a consultancy fee must be paid in cash, this weekend, to ensure we land the contract."

"I see."

"This was originally to be paid on the day the contract is signed but – competition has stiffened, and to guarantee matters, now we must pay the fee immediately. I'm afraid it's – well, it's the way commerce works in some quarters."

"I am aware of such practices," said Masthaus evenly.

No hint of disapproval, Dave noted with hope. "The sum involved is one hundred and seventy-five thousand pounds, which isn't out of proportion to the size of the contract. It would be in all our interests, Herr Masthaus, to close this deal, so I'm hoping you could facilitate me with a withdrawal. I can arrive in Zurich early tomorrow."

"I see," said the banker in the same infuriatingly neutral tone he had used throughout the call.

I've got to hook the bastard, thought Dave. "I should say, Herr Masthaus, that our client has very sizeable holdings in Zurich, so a great deal of the banking on this and future contacts will be done there. I think you'd find it lucrative to act as our local banker . . ."

Dave held his breath, then the other man responded. "Yes, it sounds like a promising situation. Perhaps you could furnish me with your account number?"

"545-06JF-700."

"One moment please. I'll access your account file from my study."

Jesus, he's buying it! thought Dave.

After a moment Masthaus came back on the line. "Now, Herr Walker, I have the figures. Yes, 191,300 pounds in your account. In what currency do you wish the 175,000?"

"Dollars, for preference."

"Very well. You know our main branch in the Banhofstrasse?"

"Yes." *He'd find it.*

"I'll arrange with our security people to allow you in. Not at the main entrance, but if you would ring the bell on the small side door. Shall we say ten a.m. tomorrow?"

"That would be excellent."

"Very good. Until tomorrow then."

"Until tomorrow – and thank you, Herr Masthaus."

"You're welcome."

Dave hung up, whooping inwardly for joy. Walker: one, Gnome: nil! he thought giddily, then he turned and walked swiftly towards the ticket office, keen to take his place on the seven-twenty train to Switzerland.

Visser felt his pulses beginning to race as the ship came to a halt at the ferry terminal. If his reasoning and instincts were wrong and Adams wasn't travelling by ferry it was going to be really difficult to track her down. A lot rode on what would happen in the next few minutes, but he was as prepared as it was possible to be.

On arrival in Dublin he had hired a van – specifically one with no rear windows – and driven straight to Dun Laoghaire to be sure of a parking place close to the ferry terminal. He was now parked on the road that ran above the exit point for the ferry passengers, and to a casual observer he reckoned he would appear entirely innocuous, a middle-aged van driver looking out over the harbour on a fine summer evening as the Holyhead ferry pulled in.

In reality he was in a state of high alert, well positioned to cover the exit point for both car travellers and foot passengers, and with the van pointed towards Dublin, the direction most travellers would be likely to take.

He still hadn't rung Reinholdt, and the blow to his professional pride of not being able to report back as scheduled irked him, yet the fury he had felt at Adams was now mixed with another emotion as the moment of truth drew near. In spite of his anxiety that it might all be a wild-goose chase, in spite of the shame of being seen to fail by Reinholdt were that to happen, he recognised a certain buzz – the adrenaline charge that always accompanied contact with a quarry.

He smiled wryly. Even after all these years it still happened every time. Yes, he thought, in a world of jaded pleasures, there were few things as exciting as the thrill of the chase.

Mary felt a contraction just as the ferry docked. She had had an uncomfortable feeling about thirty minutes previously, but had dismissed it as tension induced by the sight of the Irish coastline. Now, however, the discomfort was stronger, her stomach knotting. Please God, she thought, not labour. She couldn't face that, not here, not now.

Maybe it was just a muscular spasm, she rationalised. Nervousness at having to run the gauntlet, allied to the trauma of her encounter in the workshop with Franklin. Or could that actually have brought on her labour prematurely? Be positive, she thought, breathing deeply and evenly, and hoping that it was just nervousness.

She watched the foot-passengers mill about the doorway leading to the gangplank, then they began to exit as the doors were opened. No harm to let the first lot of passengers disembark, she reasoned. A few more minutes either way shouldn't make much difference to her, and the more people milling about when she reached the quayside the better.

She continued her breathing exercises for a few moments, then cautiously stopped, aware that her discomfort had eased. She rose tentatively, and not encountering any further pangs, reached for her travelling bag and started for the gangway. There were still lots of passengers leaving the ship, and Mary joined them, moving with the stately walk of the heavy black woman she purported to be.

She reached the quayside and looked as casually as possible towards the exit gates, lined by people awaiting the boat passengers. She moved forward at a moderate pace, aware of the curious glances of some of the others about her. Only to be expected, she told herself. There weren't many black people living in Ireland's largely Caucasian society.

She neither avoided nor deliberately caught anyone's eye, then when she was about twenty yards from the exit gate she spotted the policemen. There were two of them scanning the arrivals in an apparently casual fashion. They're not looking for me, she told herself. They're watching out for known subversives, drug dealers, logging the comings and goings of criminals. And even if they were looking for her, it would be as a pregnant blonde, not a rotund black woman. *Keep your nerve, Mary. You're nearly there.*

She drew level with the policemen, aware from the corner of her eye that one of them was looking over at her. She kept going, resisting the temptation to glance back and see if he was consulting with his colleague. Reaching the exit gate, she braced herself, dreading the thought of a hand on her shoulder or a cry from one of the policemen. She held her breath and passed through the gate, skirting returning emigrants who were dropping their cases and embracing relatives, then she moved through the crowd and started for the steps leading up to the roadside.

Visser waited unobtrusively to the right of the throng outside the ferry terminal exit gate. He had left the van to take up this vantage-point from where he could more closely observe the foot passengers streaming along the quayside, and also watch the occupants of the cars now beginning to drive out of the ferry. Knowing that he couldn't give his full attention to both at once he concentrated more on the foot passengers, reasoning that Adams would be more likely to opt for the anonymity of being part of a crowd rather than being a readily identifiable car driver or passenger.

So far there had been no sign of Adams, and

although Visser had spotted two pregnant women neither had been remotely like her – even allowing for possible attempts at disguise. Visser's heart thumped from a mixture of excitement and fear that he might draw a blank, or, even worse, that Adams might disembark without him spotting her.

She *won't*, he thought, scanning the passengers coming through the exit, not if she's a foot passenger.

He noticed a fat black woman waddling towards the steps that led up to the road where the van was parked, and he shook his head ruefully. Fucking *kaffirs* moving in everywhere! he thought, even in as white a country as Ireland.

He turned back towards the ferry and looked again at the cars disembarking, then he returned his gaze to the quayside, scanning the crowd and hoping for a glimpse of Mary Adams.

Mary reached the stairway and began to climb. Halfway up the steps she cautiously glanced back at the quayside and the two uniformed policemen. They were still scanning the passengers, still looking in the direction of those leaving the boat.

Her spirits suddenly soared. She had made it! She was home! Tremendously relieved, she started up the steps again, moving quicker now despite her fatigue. She arrived at the busy road, a hive of activity as boat passengers and those meeting them loaded bags and cases into the boots of cars. Mary paused a moment to catch her breath. Across the road she saw the gate to a small park, behind which rose the imposing mass of the Royal Marine Hotel. She had decided on the boat that the Royal Marine would facilitate her entering as an overweight black woman, visiting the ladies' toilet, and leaving the hotel – preferably by another door – as a pregnant white woman.

She moved along the kerb, flanking a number of parked cars, then seeing a break in the traffic, she crossed the road and approached the gate to the park. Still thrilled at the success of her unhindered arrival, she went through the gate, returning the greeting of a middle-aged man who entered behind her, then moved through the neatly manicured park. The small park was a pleasant oasis of quiet, and she made her way up the path towards the main entrance to the hotel.

She was only about ten yards from the driveway when she stopped abruptly. She leaned against a stone urn and turned her face away from several people coming from the hotel into the park. The middle-aged man who had followed her through the gate came up behind her.

"Are you all right?" he asked.

"Yes. Yes, thanks."

"Sure?"

"Yes, fine." She nodded several times before he smiled and continued on his way. But she wasn't fine. Far from it. She fought back a grimace as she felt the sharp pain of a contraction. This time there was no doubt, and she realised with despair that she was going into labour.

"Devious bastards!" said Carrow venomously as he put down the phone. The late evening sunshine flooded through the window of the airport police office, touching the furniture with a golden hue, but Carrow had no eyes for the setting sun.

Mathieson raised an eyebrow as the Special Branch man turned from the phone. "I take it Brompton bought their house?"

Carrow nodded. "At their request paid with a bank draft rather than a cheque."

"So it can't be stopped."

"No."

"Still traceable though. The money has to be transferred to an account."

"Yes," said Carrow irritably, "but now the banks are closed for the weekend. That means having to locate the branch manager, having to gain access, time spent trying to find where the money was transferred. Possibly to find that Walker or Adams has already withdrawn it and scarpered."

"In a worst possible scenario," agreed Mathieson. "It's quite possible though that Inspector Thompson might intercept the Adams woman."

"Giving us the rigmarole of extradition proceedings . . ."

"Not necessarily. It's really Walker we're interested in; handled properly the wife might disclose his whereabouts."

"Maybe," said Carrow without conviction.

"And we mustn't write off the French. They may well find Walker yet."

"The French? I'd like to believe it," snorted Carrow.

"Let's be fair, old man. The French did pick him up; it was we who let him escape."

"It wasn't us who failed to hold him in a secure environment, who left him his passport, credit cards, money . . ."

"The French didn't arrest him. They acceded to our request for a low-profile detention."

"Detention – in a bloody storeroom!"

"We shan't get anywhere dwelling on all that now," said Mathieson equably. Then the telephone beside him rang. "Excuse me," he said, reaching for the phone. "Hello? Yes, this is Mathieson . . . yes, I'll wait. Thank you." He covered the mouthpiece with his hand. "They're putting Simpson through," he informed Carrow, then he swivelled round at the desk and sat, pen and paper at the ready.

Carrow looked at the intelligence officer, his hair backlit against the sunset, and felt a stab of irritation. Like a bloody model, he thought, all lustrous hair, firm jaw-line and effortless poise. Damn all to be poised about, thought Carrow, for Mathieson's enquiries with the BBC's personnel people had proved fruitless. No home address in Ireland for Mary Adams, never any BBC film work in France – lest Walker be heading to a French location known to both of them – no useful information from any of the theatre companies with whom she had performed, and now they had finally tracked down one Wally Simpson, her theatrical agent.

Carrow moved Walker's possessions across the desk on which they had been spread, then sat on the corner of it as Mathieson spoke to the agent. He listened to Mathieson's end of the conversation, then after a few moments the intelligence officer put the phone down and shook his head.

"No known links to anyone or anything in France, and nobody seems to know where in Ireland she hails from."

"Obviously didn't advertise her Irishness," said Carrow.

"Odd though that no one should know her original background."

"Is it? Not something I'd bloody boast about," said Carrow. "Anyhow, the uniforms in Leeds are still questioning neighbours, tennis-club acquaintances and so on, though somehow I doubt if any of them will know where exactly she's from."

"Still, one never . . . hang on." Mathieson stopped and looked intently at the desk.

"What?" said Carrow, regarding at the other man with puzzlement.

"The book, Walker's novel." Mathieson picked up the paperback.

"Been through it, nothing inside, nothing written on the pages."

Mathieson had risen and was holding the book at an angle to the window. "Nothing written on the pages, but something written on this," he said, indicating the back cover.

"What? I can't see a thing."

"The way the sunlight caught it there showed an indentation. Look, someone leaned on it to write."

Carrow came closer and turned the book so the light caught the shiny back cover. "It's . . . it's like figures . . ."

"Lay it down here," said Mathieson, "facing up." He tore a thin sheet of paper from a scribbling pad, then produced a lead pencil from a nearby desk. Holding the piece of paper flush with the cover of the novel, he gently rubbed the lead of the pencil back and forth over the indented area until one by one the figures emerged in faint outline.

"1941 . . . 32 . . . is it a two? Yes, 320 . . . 2251" said Carrow.

"Phone number?"

"Let's find out."

Mathieson lifted the phone on the desk and dialled the number, then stood immobile, listening intently.

Carrow watched impatiently, then the other man replaced the phone and turned round. "Well?"

"Recorded message, regarding opening hours . . ."

"From?"

"Would you believe a bank?" answered Mathieson. "A *Swiss* bank?"

"Christ!" said Carrow excitedly. "He's cashing in his chips! That's where the money's been transferred. You can bet on it!" He consulted his watch. "Seven twenty-three now, he couldn't have got to Zurich – I presume it is Zurich?"

"Yes."

"Then he couldn't have got there before close of business today."

"No. Probably en route right now," said Mathieson.

"Perfect! And the best part is he won't know that we know his destination."

"Quite."

"Right. Let's have Inspector Clouseau and his merry men in here," said Carrow. "They can alert their people to pick up Walker at the border."

"Provided he's travelling by road or rail. If he's gone by air he may have left France already."

"That's a possibility," conceded Carrow, "though I doubt if he'd want to use airports. Too much security, ID checks . . ."

"There is that," said Mathieson.

"On the other hand he might have gambled on a quick bolt for Switzerland – in which case we simply wait for him at the bank."

"Why don't we see if the French pick him up first?"

"No!" said Carrow emphatically. "This bastard is smart. He might get past the French. I want us outside that bank first thing in the morning. He's not slipping though our fingers a second time."

"Bit of a wasted journey if he's picked up at the border – why don't we wait a couple of hours?"

"Because by then the last flight to Zurich may be gone."

"We don't necessarily have to fly there tonight," said Mathieson. "The banks don't re-open until Monday morning."

"Officially. But this is Swiss banking. Who knows what sort of irregular arrangement he might make?"

Mathieson shrugged. "Well . . ."

Carrow breathed out impatiently. "Look, are you interested in getting him or not?"

"Yes. Though I'm inclined to believe his story that the whole thing was non-subversive. "

"You're inclined to believe it? Don't you want to know for certain?"

"Of course. Look, I *do* wish to apprehend him . . ."

"Then let's leave nothing to chance," interjected Carrow. "Let's alert the French, then get the next flight to Zurich. Walker took us by surprise earlier – this time we do the surprising. Right?"

Mathieson paused briefly, then nodded. "Right."

Visser felt a growing sense of despair as the flow of foot passengers from the ferry thinned out. He was still watching the occupants of the cars that emerged from the bows of the ship, but his hunch had been that Adams would travel as a foot passenger. Of course it was possible that she might wait until the very end to disembark, but if he were in her shoes Visser would have exited when the crowd was at its thickest.

He watched as another pocket of foot passengers drew near the exit gate, his interest having been aroused by a heavily pregnant woman with shoulder-length auburn hair. She looked nothing like Adams however, the man accompanying her definitely wasn't Walker, and in addition they had two young children with them. His gaze lingered on the woman nonetheless as she made toward the exit. There was something about her stride. Something about the way the pregnant woman walked . . . waddled almost. *Waddled* . . . His mind flashed back to the heavy black woman he had seen earlier. She had waddled also . . . Jesus, could it be possible?! He hadn't bothered to study

351

her face, dismissing her as just another overweight *kaffir* such as he had seen thousands of times in South Africa. But what better way for a pregnant white woman to disguise herself? And Adams was an actress; she would know about make-up and wigs.

He could be letting his imagination run away with him, he knew, and if he left now to try to catch the slow-moving black woman he might miss Adams were she still on board as a foot passenger or about to leave by car. He paused, weighing up his options, then he decided to heed the sixth sense that had served him well in the past. He turned his back on the ferry and moved swiftly across to the steps that the black woman had climbed, then he sprinted towards the roadway two steps at a time.

Driving as fast as the speed limit would allow, Thompson negotiated the Dun Laoghaire streets while Penny looked searchingly out the car window at the passing pedestrians. They drove by the entrance to the Royal Marine Hotel, then turned right onto the road above the ferry terminal. Cars were driving out of the opened bow of the ship, but Penny noted with dismay that only the occasional passenger was still emerging onto the quayside.

"I think we may be too late, Chief. They're mostly off."

"Mostly isn't everyone," said Thompson, concentrating on guiding the car into a vacant kerbside parking space.

Penny said nothing, but despite her boss's refusal to

accept defeat, her earlier optimism had evaporated. They had lost twenty precious minutes due to an accident on the Blackrock bypass, where a juggernaut and three cars had been in a pile-up.

Penny glanced at her watch as she got out of the car. It was seven thirty-five, and as she watched the last of the foot passengers walking up the quay she sensed that their quarry had eluded them again. Keeping her reservations to herself, she joined Thompson who leaned on the rail overlooking the quayside.

They looked intently, but none of the approaching figures was pregnant, and after a few minutes the trickle of foot passengers dried up. Finally, after nobody else had appeared in several minutes, Thompson turned his back on the quayside. "Well, that's bloody that. We've lost her."

"So it would seem."

"Seem?" queried Thompson.

"Is it possible, Chief, that the ferry could be another red herring?"

Thompson considered a moment, then shook his head. "I doubt it. Red herrings are usually planted so they'll be discovered. If you hadn't been inspired to check the private hangars, we'd never have known about her trip to Holyhead."

"I suppose so," conceded Penny, "but how could she have got onto the ferry without being spotted."

"I don't know. Changed her appearance somehow – though disguising being eight months pregnant is a bit of a trick."

"But you think she made the boat?"

Thompson shrugged. "Nothing more rational than instinct, but I reckon so."

Which means we've just missed her by minutes."

"Aye. Bloody frustrating, but there you are." He turned to look at her directly. "So, what would a bright young police officer do next?"

Penny thought a moment. "Can we ask the Irish police to help?"

Thompson grimaced. "They'd need a strong case to arrest one of their own citizens for extradition – makes things a bit messy. Having said that, I've some good personal contacts. If need be I could call in a few favours unofficially. Also, in an important case we can call on the resources of the embassy here."

"Then I'd suggest an immediate watch on train and bus stations," said Penny.

"OK, what else?"

"Roadblocks in case she travels by car. But that would require formal involvement of the Gardai."

"Which rules it out. You think she's headed somewhere tonight?"

"Don't you?"

"No," said Thompson, shaking his head. "Remember she's been on the go since this morning. She's had to flee her home, drive to Manchester, fly to north Wales, catch the ferry, and cross the Irish Sea – all of this while eight months pregnant. I'd say she'd be exhausted and want to rest up in Dublin tonight."

"Fair point, Chief," said Penny. "Supposing though that Dublin isn't a stopover? Supposing it's her final destination?"

"Then we have a problem. If she seeks a place to stay overnight though, that's another matter. A pregnant woman stands out – no pun intended – and if we do enough checking we might unearth her."

"So where do we start?"

"We head for the embassy," said Thompson, starting towards the car, "where I make some calls."

Penny quickly followed him, then he opened the driver's door, turned and looked at her before climbing in. "It's not over yet, Penny," he said softly. "It's not over yet . . ."

Visser pulled to a halt in the car park of the Royal Marine Hotel, got out of the van and made for the entrance. He had driven along the main road to Dublin looking out for a heavy black woman, then after about a mile or so had turned and driven equally fruitlessly in the opposite direction. Finally he had combed the side streets of central Dun Laoghaire, but to no avail.

The large hotel – the nearest to the ferry terminal – was his last hope. He quickly ascended the steps to the entrance, automatically going into persuasive mode as he crossed to the receptionist, a friendly-looking woman in her late twenties.

"Good evening," she said. "Can I help you?"

"I hope so," said Visser, forcing himself to smile. "I'm looking for a Prudence N'Kromo," he improvised, "black woman, heavily built."

"Is she a guest, sir?"

"Probably not but I think she might have come in recently."

"No . . ." said the receptionist, looking at the register. "No one of that name I'm afraid."

"And you haven't seen a black woman come in during the last few minutes?"

"No, sorry. Were you to meet here?"

"Yes," answered Visser.

"She might have entered by the side door and gone to the bar," suggested the receptionist. "Through the lounge and down the corridor," she said, indicating the way.

"Ah . . . thank you. Thank you very much," said Visser, then he followed her instructions, moving briskly but not so fast as to draw attention.

Visser turned into the hotel lounge and looked about, but there was no sign of a black woman. He checked each corner, then the adjoining corridors, and finally the bar, all to no avail. Then it occurred to him that Adams might have used the ladies' toilet if she wanted to divest herself of the *kaffir* disguise. Always assuming that the black woman *had* actually been Adams, he reminded himself. He was struck by a thought, and he turned on his heel and made for reception again.

"No luck?" said the woman behind the desk.

"No, but I wonder if you saw a heavily pregnant white woman recently?"

The receptionist looked at him bemusedly and despite Visser's impatience for a response, he could see that she was beginning to regard him as strange – first looking for a heavy black woman and now interested in a pregnant white woman. To hell with it, he thought, there wasn't time to try and think up a plausible explanation. "About five feet five, blonde, maybe eight months pregnant," he persisted.

The receptionist looked at him a trifle warily, then nodded. "Yes."

"Yes?"

She nodded again. "She left a few minutes ago."

"Thank you," said Visser. "My sister-in-law," he added hurriedly. "I've a message for her. Thank you again."

He turned and made for the exit, momentarily elated at having his instincts vindicated. The reality of course was that although he had missed her only by minutes, she had got away, but as he reached the van he found his excitement rising. She may have eluded him for now, but he had guessed right and he was on her trail; and when he caught her she would pay – and pay dearly – for every moment's trouble she had caused . . .

The pains were getting worse as Mary sped towards town, and she struggled not to grimace in sight of the taxi driver. She hadn't given him the name of the maternity hospital when he had asked her destination, fearing that if the pursuing police discovered her escape via the ferry they might be thorough enough to question Dun Laoghaire-based taxi drivers. And so instead of Holles Street hospital she had asked to be driven to Jury's, a large hotel about three quarters of a mile from Holles Street.

"Ye brought the good weather with ye, what?" said the taximan, blithely unaware of her discomfort.

"Yes," answered Mary, struggling to keep the pain from her voice.

"Brilliant for May, we won't know ourselves if this keeps up."

"Yes, it's lovely . . ."

"Sure what would ye be goin' to Spain or Majorca for? When we get the weather here, ye can't beat Ireland."

"That's . . . that's true," she answered, then gritted her teeth as another contraction hit her. She turned her head to the side as though looking out the window. He mustn't see that she was in pain, mustn't guess that she was in labour, lest he be questioned later. She prayed that she hadn't reached the point where the waters would break – how on earth could that be explained away? No, she thought, recalling her reading on the matter, that's usually later on in labour. *Usually* . . .

"Let's just hope we're not havin' our summer in May, what?"

"Yes . . ."

The driver glanced in the rear-view mirror and smiled conspiratorially. "So when's the new arrival due?"

In about two hours. "Oh, not for another few weeks," she answered, pleased at how casual she made it sound.

"First one?"

"Yes."

He laughed ruefully. "Ye have it all in front of ye!"

"That's for sure . . ."

"Ah, sure one is nothin'. I have four."

"Really?" said Mary trying for a smile.

"Oh, don't be talkin'. I come to work for a rest! Now, here we are – Jury's."

He pulled in at the entrance, then Mary opened the door with relief and handed him the fare and a tip.

"Thanks very much – and good luck with the nipper."

"Thank you," said Mary. She watched as he turned and pulled out onto Merrion Road. She waited until he was out of sight, then she turned away from the hotel entrance and went round the corner to the taxi rank in Landsdowne Road. The first driver in line was a grey-haired man who was reading a tabloid newspaper as he leaned against his car.

"Where to?" he said, lowering the paper.

"Merrion Square, please," answered Mary. It was around the corner from the hospital, no point leaving a trail for the sake of thirty yards.

"Right," the driver said gruffly. He opened the door for Mary, got in and started the engine.

He was probably unenthusiastic at the prospect of such a short trip, Mary thought, as they drove along Northumberland Road, but at least she wouldn't have to make conversation. Instead she would use the time to think out how she would handle her admission. She couldn't register under her own name, in case the Irish police had been alerted, and she couldn't quote her medical insurance number in the UK, which the hospital would surely ask for. Likewise she couldn't give the name of her GP in Harrogate if they wanted medical details. She would have to be from somewhere outside the European Union, somewhere with a different medical and insurance system. America, she thought.

Supposing she were an Irish woman living in America who had gone into premature labour while home on a visit? She could then pay cash for the services of the hospital and say she would claim it on her medical insurance back in the States. But what to call herself? Something common, unremarkable. From the depths of her mind she remembered reading somewhere that one of the most common names in Dublin was Byrne. Right, Byrne it would be. Say . . . Anne Byrne. No. No, better keep her own first name, she reasoned. It might arouse suspicion if someone called her Anne and she didn't respond. Mary Byrne then, that's who the new mother would be.

And suddenly, for the first time since the whole nightmare had begun, she found to her horror that she was crying. Something deep within her seemed to proclaim that this wasn't how motherhood should be. The birth of her child shouldn't involve skulking and hiding; it should be joyous, a celebration. She shouldn't be frightened and on her own; she should be sharing it all with Dave. At the thought of her husband she felt the tears roll down her cheeks, and she experienced an aching lost feeling that was worse than the pain of the contractions.

She saw out of the window that they were

approaching Merrion Square and she tried hard to regain control of herself. *Come on*, she thought, another minute and they would be there. She dabbed surreptitiously at her eyes, bit hard on her lip and hoped somehow that she could handle the ordeal to come.

33

The last town before the border was Mulhouse, and Dave felt the train slowing as it approached the brightly lit station. He rose from his seat and reached for his holdall, ready to alight as soon as the train came to a halt.

He had decided that crossing the Swiss border into Basle was out of the question. Although it seemed likely that the British authorities wouldn't want a high-profile manhunt because of the security nature of the case, nevertheless it was French custody from which he had escaped, and although they wouldn't be expecting an escape bid eastwards to Switzerland, the gendarmes would probably have alerted all points of exit.

Besides which, even if the French border police adhered to their normal procedure of not checking the individual passports of exiting EC nationals, there would still have been the problem of Swiss passport control. The last time he had visited Switzerland his passport number had been keyed into a computer. All it would take would be a phone call from Interpol in Paris to the Swiss authorities, and he would be walking into a trap. Far safer to enter Switzerland unofficially, and thus ensure no formal record of his visit.

He felt a slight jolt as the train came to a halt, then he moved to the carriage door and stepped down onto the platform. Quite a number of other passengers alighted also, and he delayed just long enough to be in the middle of the group that made for the station exit. Probably paranoiac to assume the police would be watching for him at every railway station in France, he thought, but still it would be no harm to keep a low profile.

He left the station without seeing any signs of a police presence, and on reaching the street found several taxis awaiting the train's passengers. Moving briskly, he claimed one.

"*Bonsoir, monsieur,*" said the driver.

"*Bonsoir. Lucroix, s'il vous plaît,*" answered Dave, giving the name of a village about eight miles away, near the Swiss border.

"*Bien,*" said the driver.

Dave had deliberately pitched his French at a schoolboy level of pronunciation, and, as he had anticipated, the driver refrained from conversation. They soon left the outskirts of Mulhouse, travelling along dark country roads. Dave noted mentally the signposts they passed, with a view to keeping his bearings, then after about twenty minutes the taximan slowed, and Dave saw a road sign indicating the entrance to Lucroix.

"*Monsieur?*" said the driver.

"Eh . . . straight ahead," answered Dave in his halting French, pointing in the direction of some distant lights on the far side of the village.

The driver accelerated, and after a couple of moments they left the village behind. Dave decided to pass the first couple of farmhouses he saw, then seeing a more isolated one ahead he indicated to the driver. "The next house, please."

The taxi driver slowed and was about to pull into the drive leading to the farmhouse.

"No! No, here will do. This is fine" insisted Dave.

The driver shrugged, then pulled in to the verge.

Make this quick, thought Dave, before some nosy farmer decides to investigate a running engine. He got out of the taxi, quietly closed the door, and paid off the driver, adding a generous tip.

"Merci, monsieur," said the man.

"Merci, monsieur. Adieu." Dave waited as the taxi driver started to reverse the car. The revving of the engine carried in the still summer night and suddenly a loud barking erupted from the side of the farmhouse. Dave smiled and waited as though too friendly to walk away up the drive while the taximan was doing a three-point turn. The barking grew louder, then Dave heard a bolt being undone on the farmhouse door. Come on! he thought, beads of sweat forming on his brow as the taxi-driver reversed carefully to avoid the ditch.

Dave heard another bolt being undone on the farmhouse door, then saw a flood of light as the door opened outward. Just then the driver finished his turn. *For God's sake don't shout a farewell,* thought Dave, seeing a heavy-set farmer silhouetted at the cottage door.

The taximan pulled away, giving a brief wave, then Dave stood stock-still in the dark as a voice carried above the barking of the dog.

"Who's there?"

Dave remained immobile. The farmer had come from a lighted room, and with the departing taxi disappearing round a bend the countryside was plunged into darkness again. Surely the man's night-sight wouldn't enable him to locate someone standing still thirty yards away in the dark, thought Dave. Unless the dog approached. . .

"Who's there?" the farmer called again, and getting no answer he stood a moment in the door, then turned to the dog. "Easy, Rex! Easy!" As suddenly as it had started barking, the dog fell silent at its owner's command. "Good boy," said the man, who looked out one last time, then stepped back into the cottage and closed the door.

Dave breathed a massive sigh of relief and moved up the road to a copse of trees that blocked the farm from sight. He took out a large-scale map and matches that he had bought in the newsagents in the Gare de l'Est, then studied the map in the light of a match. Due east about three miles should take him over the border into Switzerland. The terrain wasn't unduly rugged, certainly not compared to the Yorkshire peaks where he normally hiked, and assuming that he didn't run into any border patrols he would be there in about an hour and a half. Then he would find a barn or stable to sleep in till dawn, after which he planned to walk into Basle, wash and change in the station there and get the early train to Zurich.

But first he had to get out of France, and putting away the map and matches, he took a bearing on the north star, then entered the adjoining field and started walking carefully eastwards.

Mathieson sat at the hotel window, his binoculars trained on the entrance to the bank. The mature leafy trees that lined the Banhofstrasse, Zurich's main thoroughfare, partly blocked the view of the impressive stone building, but by sitting at the very edge of the window Mathieson could keep the entrance in view.

It was almost midnight now, and the building was in total darkness. He lowered the binoculars and turned round on hearing Carrow replacing the wall phone on the far side of the bedroom. "Any joy?" he asked.

"Some," answered Carrow. "Bloody cautious, though, these Swiss."

"Renowned for it, old man . . ."

"Superintendent Vincenz wants to proceed "with discretion", as he puts it."

"Well, I suppose from his point of view all we have is a phone number on the back of a book."

"He'll have more than that when Leeds trace the branch manager and confirm the money was transferred to Zurich. I told him they were working on it as we spoke."

"So, what's his response?"

"He doesn't want to upset the banking bigwigs by

enquiring here if a meeting's been set up with Walker. Customer confidentiality being "a highly sensitive issue" to use his phrase."

"Interesting set of priorities," said Mathieson.

"Isn't it? His attitude is that crime is one thing, banking another. If we want to apprehend a criminal here, fine, he'll assist us, but he wants it to be *before* Walker visits the bank. That way there are no complications for Vincenz about funds found on Walker, and no embarrassment for his banker chums."

"I suppose there's something in that," said Mathieson. "What assistance is he providing?"

"A rotating team of three officers seconded to us, plus top priority on any backup needed. The team to keep the bank under observation from six o'clock tomorrow morning onwards."

"Fine."

"He seems to share your view that a middle-of-the-night transaction is a non-starter," said Carrow.

"Yes, well, it does seem extremely . . ."

"Extremely nothing! I'm taking no risks with this bastard Walker; if you value your sleep that much, I'll watch all night myself."

"All right, old man, I'll do my stint. Let's just hope our quarry shows up after all this."

"He'll show up."

"Could have decided to lie low in France . . ."

"No, he's coming for his money."

Mathieson shrugged. "He wasn't on any flight, hasn't registered through passport control, didn't travel on the train into Basle . . ."

"Ways can be found round all of that."

"Perhaps. There's one other possibility," said Mathieson.

"What's that?"

"He might forget about the money – for now. Leave it in the bank till the heat dies down, then have it transferred."

"He might, but I don't think he will. Remember he has no idea we're onto this. He won't know we got the number of the bank from his paperback; he won't know Arnold Beazley overheard his wife call the estate agent by name. He'll think his little Swiss secret is dead safe."

"Hmm, I hope you're right," said Mathieson. "We've been led rather a merry dance so far."

"The dance ends here," said Carrow emphatically. "The one thing he can't do is get into the bank unobserved, not if we watch it round the clock. So we will – and we'll get him."

Penny leaned against the headrest of the bed, the Golden Pages propped up beside her, and dialled the last telephone number in the alphabetical list of hotels. A woman answered it on the second ring.

"Good evening, Wynn's Hotel."

"Good evening," said Penny. "I wonder if you could help me?"

"If I can," replied the woman pleasantly.

"I'm trying to contact an old friend and it's possible she may be staying in your hotel."

"I see. And what's her name?"

"Well, I know her as Mary Adams," said Penny, "but she may be using her married name now."

"OK," answered the woman, flicking over some pages, "let's see . . . eh, no . . . no, I'm afraid we've no Mary Adams. What would her married name be?"

"I don't know," Penny replied. "You see, we lost contact after school, but I know she arrived in Dublin tonight for a conference, and she's staying in a city-centre hotel. She's expecting a baby shortly – would you have booked in anyone tonight who was about eight months pregnant?"

"No, no, I'm afraid not . . ."

"She couldn't have been dealt with by another member of your staff?"

"No, I've been on all evening. I would have seen her. Sorry . . ."

"OK, thanks for your help."

"Not at all. I hope you find her."

"Yes, so do I. Goodnight."

"Goodnight."

Penny replaced the receiver, disappointed at failing to trace her quarry, but pleased to have finally reached the end of a long list. Her hotel room was comfortable, with a bathroom en suite, and she was looking forward to a long hot bath, yet her tiredness was partly offset by the excitement of her first manhunt.

It had been an education watching Thompson's technique as he had mobilised the resources of the embassy with a finely judged balance of persuasion and authority. He had also proved to have an excellent rapport with several of his counterparts in the Irish police, who, in spite of his not asking officially for assistance, had provided him with the locations of train stations, bus depots and taxi ranks, to which the staff from the embassy had been despatched.

Having established the importance of the case from a security perspective, Thompson has also been able to arrange for other embassy staff to ring every guest-house in the greater Dublin area, while Penny had done the same with all listed hotels.

Now as she crossed her hotel room to report to Thompson in the room next door, Penny couldn't shake off a nagging feeling that they were overlooking something. She paused for a moment, trying to pin down the nature of her unease, but the notion was too nebulous, and so she shrugged and continued on her way.

Reaching Thompson's door, she knocked, then entered on his call.

"Oh, sorry, Chief," she said, seeing him poring over a map of Dublin with Dewsbury, an official from the embassy.

"That's OK," said Thompson.

The diplomat was a corpulent man in his late thirties who spoke with an ostentatious public school accent. "Good evening, Constable Hart," he intoned.

"Good evening," she replied, noticing that his smile didn't extend to his eyes.

"Any luck?" asked Thompson.

"No, 'fraid not."

"Damn!" said the Inspector. "Mr Dewbury's people drew a blank on the guesthouses."

"And the bus depots, taxi ranks?"

"Nothing. We were hoping you might strike it lucky."

"I'm really sorry the news isn't better."

"Not your fault, Penny, not your fault . . ."

"Never the British way to shoot the messenger," added Dewsbury smoothly, "especially one combining beauty *and* ability."

Spare us the smarm, thought Penny, aware that the diplomat was trying for a style of urbane flirtatiousness. "So where does that leave us, Chief?" she asked, ignoring Dewsbury's remark.

"Can't do much more tonight," said Thompson, "unless we hear from one of the stations or taxi companies."

"No, I suppose not."

"You've worked hard, Penny. Better get some rest now." Thompson smiled. "I'll pound on the wall if Ms Adams is sighted."

"Oh?" said Dewsbury. "Staying next door, are we?"

"Yes," answered Penny.

"Hmm . . . handy arrangement, Inspector, eh?" He chuckled suggestively, then winked at Penny.

Before she could retort, Thompson turned to the other man. "Meaning what?" he asked stonily.

"I . . . I merely jest . . . late night humour, no more," answered Dewsbury raising his hands in mock defence.

Despite his attempted insouciance, Penny noted with satisfaction a touch of fluster behind the man's response. Good old Thompson, she thought.

"Right," said the policeman, turning away from him. "Get a good night's sleep, Penny. Busy day ahead"

"OK, night, Chief. Goodnight, Mr Dewsbury."

"Goodnight, Constable."

Turning away, Penny closed the door, went down the corridor, and entered her own room. Despite her tiredness and Thompson's instruction to get some sleep, her mind was still buzzing. What was the thought that eluded her, she wondered. Yet the more she tried to fasten onto it, the more it seemed to dance out of her reach.

She went into the bathroom, turned on the water to fill up the tub, then started to undress. Sometimes she did her clearest thinking in the bath or shower. Maybe tonight she would too. She stepped out of her clothes and lowered herself into the bath, luxuriating in the hot soapy water, then she lay back, rested her head on a towel, and began to review carefully the day's events.

"Push hard, Mary! Come on. Push. Bear down!"

"I'm pushing, for God's sake! I am!"

The midwife grinned and patted her on the leg. "I know. You're doing great."

Mary tried to nod in acknowledgement, but her face was rigid as she gritted her teeth. No one tells you about the pain, she thought, not in the books, not in the ante-natal classes; no one tells you just how much it *hurts*. Maybe if they did, women wouldn't want to go through childbirth, she speculated. Then the thought was driven from her mind by another build-up of pressure.

"OK, Mary?" asked the midwife, her lilting country voice solicitous.

Holding her breath, Mary nodded back. They had

told her earlier that her labour was going to be short, as they had injected her with pethidine to lessen her pain. When had that been, she wondered. She knew she had lost all sense of time; it seemed like she had been in the delivery room forever, yet she recalled the nurse telling her she was lucky because she was having a short labour. Lucky? If this was lucky, what would a long labour be like? Her thoughts went back to her childhood, and she found herself in awe of how couples in Mayo used routinely to have six or seven children. How did the women bear it, she wondered, knowing that such agony lay ahead of them each time?

She was in a lull between contractions when she heard another nurse tell the midwife that Dr Collins was on his way.

"Not much longer, love," she said to Mary with a smile.

Mary tried to smile back, touched, despite her distress, by the unceasing kindness and good humour of the midwives, but she was hit by another wave of pressure.

"OK, Mary," she heard a man's voice saying, "a few more minutes and it'll all be over. Just hang on in there."

She opened her eyes to see a youthful-looking man in a green smock. Dr Collins was written on his nametag.

"Nearly there now," he said with a smile.

What the hell was he smiling about, she thought? Easily known he had never gone through this. No sooner had she thought it than she felt guilty. He was just trying to be nice to her, she knew. All of the staff were. They had probably felt sorry for her when she had told the nurses earlier that her husband couldn't be present because he was still in the States, where they lived. Reverting easily to her Irish accent, she had explained that she had come back to Ireland on a visit and her husband was following her next week after finishing some business in New York. She wished now that Dave really were with her. It would mean so much to be able to squeeze his hand. She had tried not to dwell on what they were missing together, but the thought brought a lump to her throat nonetheless. As though sensing her distress, Dr Collins patted her arm reassuringly. "Well, Mary, we're going to have some surprise for your husband. An extra little Byrne four weeks sooner than expected, eh?"

She nodded weakly. *Byrne.* It seemed like ages ago that she had told the nurse her husband was Connor Byrne. For some reason she had said he was a record engineer, a flight of fancy that had generated endless questions. Had he recorded in Muscle Shoals, worked with Paul Simon, ever met Bruce Springsteen? She had realised that the litany of questions might have been humorous in other circumstances. Now though the pressure of the contractions was increasing again, this time reaching an almost unbearable pitch.

"OK, Mary, on the last lap now," said the midwife. "The baby's ready to come out. Try to push hard with the contractions. Come on. That's it. That's it, keep pushing . . ."

Mary felt as though she were going to burst.

374

"That's it. Here's the head!"

"Oh God!"

"You're doing fine, Mary. You're doing fine," said Collins.

Her body relaxed momentarily and looking down she could see a dark round shape between her legs. Her eyes welled with tears. Then she felt the pressure again.

"OK, Mary," said Collins, "that's great. Gently now. Push again . . ."

"A small push for the shoulder, Mary," said the midwife.

She pushed gently, her eyes screwed tightly and the tears running down her cheeks.

"We're winning, Mary. One shoulder out!" said Collins. "Now another push. That's it."

"That's it," echoed the midwife. "That's it! Good girl yourself!"

Suddenly Mary felt an enormous easing in pressure, and then incredibly, the baby was out and in the arms of Dr Collins. The baby screamed, and seeing the obstetrician swiftly examining the infant, Mary felt a rush of panic. "Is it OK?" she cried.

Dr Collins looked over at her. "More than OK," he answered with a smile. "You've a perfect little daughter."

A daughter. She felt overcome, a mixture of joy, relief, and awe causing the tears to flow down her cheeks. A nurse clipped an ID band onto the baby's wrist, and Mary got an Syntometrine injection as the midwife cut the umbilical cord. The baby was quickly dried, then wrapping her gently, the midwife offered her to Mary.

She reached out eagerly and took the baby. Despite the infant's wrinkled expression and blood-smeared appearance she seemed like the most wonderful thing Mary had ever seen. She cradled her, and felt another wave of emotion as the baby snuggled against her breast. Mary held her tenderly, then after a few minutes the nurse took the baby to weigh her and Mary felt further abdominal pressure and pushed again.

"Just the placenta," said Collins. "That's it . . . grand!"

After the midwife removed the afterbirth Mary turned and took back the baby from the other nurse. Every tiny feature was perfect, and despite her exhaustion Mary felt an overwhelming sense of joy as the baby began to suckle.

"What'll you call her?" asked the midwife.

"Fiona," answered Mary happily as she kissed the baby's head. "Fiona . . ."

"Nice name."

"Yes, my husband always wanted a daughter – now we have Fiona."

"I think she's fallen asleep," said the other nurse after a few minutes. "Why don't I wrap her up a little better?"

"OK," answered Mary, allowing the woman to lift the baby gently from her. "I'm so exhausted I'm nearly falling asleep myself."

"Why don't you?" said Collins. "I think you've really earned it."

"I don't want to miss out with my baby."

"You won't," said the midwife, cradling the child. "She's sleepy and you're sleepy, so why don't you have a doze, and we'll bring Fiona in to your room when you wake. How does that sound?"

"Sounds . . . wonderful."

"Here you give her a kiss, and we'll take her in later."

Mary reached up and softly kissed the baby's forehead, then she sank back onto the bed and closed her eyes.

Dr Collins patted her arm before he left. "Congratulations, Mary."

"Thank you . . ."

"Mission accomplished," he said happily. "All worries over . . ."

She opened her eyes and smiled drowsily, then with a wave he was gone. *All worries over.* Hardly, she thought, but for now she was too happy and too tired to worry about anything, and closing her eyes again, she allowed herself to drift into a deep exhausted sleep.

Bob Reinholdt sat in the conservatory at the rear of his detached Tudor house. In the sky the last deep blue streaks of light were merging into the dark of the summer night. On starry nights like this he sometimes ate here with his wife, Janet, and just now she entered carrying a tray laden with the supper things. She put the tray down and was pouring coffee when the phone rang inside the house.

"Never let's up, does it?" she said.

"Sorry, honey," replied Reinholdt as he rose, "but this case is kinda urgent."

"Aren't they all . . ."

He leaned over and kissed her on the cheek. "Sorry."

Janet indicated his mug. "Take the coffee with you – probably be cold by the time you're finished."

He took the mug, stepped in from the conservatory, and crossed the hallway into his study. He closed the door behind him, went to his desk, then put down the coffee and picked up the phone. "Hello?"

"I said I'd call when there was something."

Reinholdt recognised the voice of Marty Schulman, calling as arranged from Harrogate, but although they knew that the line to Reinholdt's house was as secure as anti-bugging could make any phone, they nevertheless fell into their usual practice of speaking obliquely and without using names. "What's happening?" said Reinholdt, ignoring both his coffee and the comfort of his swivel chair in his eagerness to find out why Visser hadn't rung.

"No sign of our friend," answered Schulman. "We've located his hotel but he checked out at one thirty.

"What the hell is he at?" said Reinholdt.

"Hard to say. We discreetly checked the location of his appointment."

"Yes?"

"Staked out by the local uniforms."

Reinholdt felt a shiver run up his spine. If Visser had gone out of control during his meeting with Mary Adams, as he had with Aksor, there would be hell to pay. Could the South African have gone too far again, despite his direct orders? And if so, could he have been arrested and taken for questioning? "All right, tread very carefully here," he said. "It's absolutely crucial not to be linked to anything damaging."

"Understood," said Schulman.

"OK. Keep a discreet watch – and I really mean discreet. Also on his hotel in case he returns. And notify me, whatever the time, if anything transpires."

"Got it."

"OK, stay tight on this."

"Will do."

"Goodnight."

"Goodnight."

Reinholdt sat down, took up his mug and sipped. It was good coffee, ordered by Janet from Fortnum and Mason, but he hardly registered the taste as he sat, staring into space, and trying to imagine what could possibly have happened to Jan Visser.

The cars sped past on the dual carriageway, a regular flow of traffic that was visible from the hotel car park even at two forty-five in the morning. The balmy evening had given way to a cool night, and Visser shivered slightly having left the warmth of the hotel reception area to cross to his van.

He sat in the driver's seat and closed his eyes briefly. He couldn't afford the luxury of sleep even though his body was weary, but he had to rest his aching eyes for a moment. He had been on the go non-stop since rising at eight thirty that morning back in Harrogate, but the idea of sleeping tonight was out of the question.

Earlier he had driven from the Royal Marine Hotel into the centre of Dublin – the route he assumed Adams would probably take – but there had been no sign of her, either on foot or in any of the taxis he had seen. Knowing that he had to pick up her trail before it went cold, Visser had taken a copy of the Golden Pages from the public phone booth of a café, and looked up the entry for taxis. There were fifteen or sixteen ranks listed and scores of taxi companies.

Visser had quickly made a run of photocopies of the photograph of Adams that he had taken from *Spotlight*, then he had driven to each of the ranks, distributing copies to all the drivers. He had explained that it was a missing person's case involving a very wealthy family, and that the first driver to ring him with a location for the missing woman – no matter what hour it might be – would get one thousand pounds cash.

Visser had then retraced his route to Dun Laoghaire, visiting the reception desks of all hotels along the way, but to no avail. By that time it was approaching midnight, and wanting to leave his mobile free in the hope of a call, he had located a suburban telephone booth that was unlikely to be used at that hour and had begun calling the taxi companies. Again he had given the missing person story and offered the reward for an immediate sighting. When he had eventually rung them all he had been exhausted, but sleeping simply wasn't an option. Time enough to sleep when he had dealt with Mary Adams.

He had finally begun calling to any hotel that looked big enough to have a night porter, but again had drawn a blank every time.

Sitting now in the warmth of the van he caught himself drifting and immediately opened his eyes in irritation. Dozing off through tiredness was for amateurs. He reached forward, opened the glove compartment and took out his toilet bag. He unzipped it, moved his razor and shaving-brush aside, then opened a small side pouch. He reached inside, withdrew one of several round white tablets, and quickly swallowed it.

He had been saving the upper for when he needed it, and he knew that it would soon wire him up and get him through the rest of the night. He closed the pouch, re-zipped the toilet bag, and put it back into the glove compartment.

He paused a moment, motivating himself. He *had* to find Adams. She had eluded him twice, which was a blow to his professional pride, and worse still she had blinded him with the turpentine, an assault that made it personal. No matter what the effort involved, he had to find her. He reached forward with renewed resolve, started the engine and set off for his next destination.

34

Dave looked carefully left and right, then crossed the road in front of Zurich's train station and began walking down the Bahnhofstrasse. Electric trams glided up and down the street, disgorging their cargoes of Saturday-morning shoppers. Dave knew he was early, and so he matched his pace to the leisurely weekend mood of those around him.

At the end of the Bahnhofstrasse he could see the blue of the *Zurichsee*, its clear waters sparkling in the bright sunshine, while on the chic tree-lined thoroughfare itself he noted the imposing offices of the many financial institutions. Cleansville with a capital C, he thought. No wonder James Joyce was supposed to have said that you could eat minestrone soup off the street here – it really would be hard to find anywhere a city as orderly, prosperous and clean.

He had been glad of the Swiss propensity for cleanliness in public facilities earlier in the morning, when he had washed, shaved, and changed into fresh clothes in the Gents' toilet in Basle railway station. He had felt rather grubby having slept in a remote barn after his unchallenged hike across the French/Swiss border. Despite the warm weather it had grown cool during the night, and without a sleeping bag he had resorted to covering himself with hay to stay warm. On awakening at six thirty he had brushed himself off as best he could, but he had still felt somewhat bedraggled when he had hitched a lift into Basle with an elderly Swiss farmer. Having changed, he had then gone to the newsagents and discovered to his relief that there were no photographs of himself in any of the French or Swiss papers. After eating a good breakfast he had taken the early train to Zurich, and now, surprisingly fresh despite having slept in the hay, he felt rather pleased with himself as he went to collect his money.

Of course, there was still the worry of not knowing how Mary was doing, but if all had gone to plan she should have arrived in Dublin last night. Which meant that by now she should be leaving the city and heading for the safety of Ballyard. While trying to sleep in the barn the previous night his mind had battened onto what he should do if the worst came to the worst and Mary were caught. He had wondered again if it would lighten her sentence, perhaps enable her to keep the baby, if he gave himself up, but in the end he had decided that negative thoughts would only sap his energy. They were both going to make it, he had decided, and now, walking in the bright sunshine, he felt increasingly hopeful.

Approaching the main entrance of the CBS, the

Commercial Bank of Switzerland, he paused a moment, his heart beginning to beat a little faster, then he gathered himself and strode confidently towards the bank.

Chief Superintendent Carrow stifled a yawn. He had had less than four hours' sleep, having been woken by Mathieson at 4.00 a.m. for his turn at keeping watch on the CBS building. He shifted now in the passenger seat of their hired car, stretched his long legs and arched his back. They were parked down a side street near the bank, and by looking in the rear-view mirror they could keep the main entrance under observation.

The three Swiss plain-clothes detectives were respectively stationed near the main entrance on the Bahnhofstrasse, and the side door and the service gate on the narrow streets flanking the CBS building.

It was almost ten o'clock now, and although Mathieson was diligently watching the mirror, Carrow suspected a certain lack of conviction in the other man. Despite the intelligence officer's languid air and innate self-assurance, Carrow had warmed to him somewhat during the long hours they had spent together, but although Mathieson had been willing to do a four-hour stint of observation last night Carrow knew that he was still unconvinced that Walker would show.

He could, of course, be right, in which case Carrow knew he would look rather foolish, and yet the Special Branch man had a gut feeling that he had correctly interpreted Walker's plans. He glanced surreptitiously at his watch, not wishing Mathieson to think he was becoming restless. Four minutes to ten, early days yet, he reassured himself. He leaned back in the seat, scanning both sides of the street in which they were parked. There was no sign of Walker, however, only early-morning shoppers strolling past the ornate stone fronts of the insurance corporations and banks that lined the street. He had read once that there was a bank for every fifteen hundred people in Switzerland, giving them more banks that dentists, and he was wondering how they could all make a profit when his musings were cut short by Mathieson.

"Len! Going past the entrance, blue shirt, grey slacks!"

Carrow spun round in the seat and caught a glimpse of a man rounding the corner of the bank. He swiftly raised his binoculars and sought the man's face.

"Short black hair," said Mathieson, "but his build . . ."

"Call in the Swiss!" interjected Carrow, still straining to see the man's features with the binoculars.

"Hello, Angel One, over," cried Mathieson.

"Angel One receiving, over."

Mathieson turned to Carrow. "Is it him?" he asked, covering the mouthpiece of his portable radio.

"He has his back to me!" snapped Carrow. "Wait, he's going towards the side door – intercept him! "

"Intercept approaching subject, blue shirt, grey slacks, short black hair. Over."

"Hello, Angel Two, suspect doesn't match description, may be a bank employee. Over."

"It's him!" roared Carrow, "I've seen his face! Just bloody collar him!"

"Angel One, definite ID. Intercept now please! Over."

"Let's go," said Carrow, then both men were out of the car and sprinting along the pavement towards the Bahnhofstrasse.

"Oh Christ!" said Carrow as a tram travelled down the centre of the street and blocked their view. Ignoring the stares of the Swiss shoppers, they ran towards the rear of the tram, flanking it and crossing the street, then made for the side entrance to the bank.

"Where is he?" called Carrow, reaching the Swiss detective at the closed side door.

"The door opened just as I got your instruction. He's gone inside."

"Didn't you call him?"

"No, the bell was answered immediately – the door closed behind him as I went to intercept."

"Well, can't you knock on the bloody thing now?" said Carrow.

"I think not, sir. Superintendent Vincenz instructed us to be discreet."

"Meaning what?"

"Meaning, sir, that we wouldn't wish to cause the bank unnecessary involvement."

"What the hell are we, policemen or bankers?"

"Sir, the man doesn't know we saw him. We can pick him up when he leaves. He'll still be detained, but without causing a scene."

"I say we pick him up now."

The Swiss policeman's manner was polite but unintimidated. "No, sir, I don't think that would be best . . ."

"Len, a word in your ear," said Mathieson, leading him to one side.

"What?"

"Might be better this way, old man," said the intelligence officer. "We still have the exits covered, so we'll get him anyway, but now we can confiscate whatever he withdraws."

Carrow thought a moment, looked back at the unwavering Swiss detective, then nodded. "OK," he said, returning to the man, "but there better not be any mistakes."

"There won't be," replied the Swiss officer with a faint smile. "It's not our style . . ."

"Now, rashers, sausages, black and white pudding, fried bread, but no eggs, wasn't that it?"

"Yes, thank you," answered Penny as the middle-aged waitress placed the breakfast before her. She had already had juice, cereal and toast but had decided to console herself at the lack of progress in the Adams case with a full Irish breakfast.

"That'll give you the energy to face the day," said the waitress good-humouredly.

Not to mention a month's supply of cholesterol, thought Penny. "Thank you," she said with a smile, "it looks delicious."

"Just give me a shout if you want more tea or toast."

"Thanks very much."

Penny ate with relish, the fried food a sharp contrast to her normal careful diet. She was finishing the guilt-inducing fried bread when she saw Thompson crossing the hotel dining-room towards her. His stride didn't suggest the urgency of a breakthrough, yet she hoped that perhaps he was being discreet. "Any luck?" she asked, as he took the seat opposite her.

"Yes and no. The bad part is that Walker's still at large – Carrow's still staking out the bank."

"And the good part?"

"One of Dewsbury's people spoke to a taxi-driver who picked up a pregnant woman, matching Adams description, in Dun Laoghaire last night."

"What time?" asked Penny excitedly.

"He thinks around half-seven or eight."

"God, we must have just missed her!"

"I know. The man dropped her at Jury's Hotel in Ballsbridge."

"She didn't stay there. I remember asking them about pregnant guests," said Penny.

"So where the hell is she?"

"Bearing in mind how quickly we had lookouts on the stations, the only way I can see her leaving Dublin last night is if someone drove her down the country – and like you said, after the long day she'd had, it's much more likely she rested in the city."

"Let's hope so," said Thompson, "because that brings me to my other bit of good news."

"Yes?"

"I spoke to Superintendent O'Reilly again and there was a major jewellery theft in Dublin last night."

"That's good news?"

"For us it is, because the Gardai have roadblocks on

all the main exits from the city. Tim O'Reilly and I go back a long way, and he's notified his people to keep an eye out for our friend at all roadblocks."

"Brilliant!"

Thompson smiled. "Aye, he's a good lad. And we've already got the stations covered, so if she makes a run for it today we're in business."

"Let's hope she does then. If she's gone permanently to ground in Dublin we might never find her."

"I've been thinking about that too," said Thompson. "Her baby is due shortly, and there can only be, what – three or four maternity hospitals in Dublin? A photo of her and a few bob slipped to someone in each of the Admissions could do the trick. Missing person, please phone the British Embassy if seen . . ."

Penny suddenly hit the top of the table, and Thompson looked at her quizzically. "What?" he said.

She looked back at him thoughtfully. "I'd a nagging feeling last night, Chief, that we were overlooking something."

"Overlooking what?"

"I couldn't pin it down. It seemed to me that a woman over eight months pregnant should be obvious, should stand out – literally."

"Well?"

"Maybe she's no *longer* pregnant . . ."

Thompson stared at her as comprehension dawned. "What . . . had the baby?"

"Women go into early labour all the time, Chief, especially when they've been through the kind of trauma she's had."

Thompson nodded slowly, then pulled back his chair. "I think it's time you and I did a little hospital visitation."

Mary sat looking at the baby, still caught up in the wonder of Dave and her creating a new human being. All parents probably thought their babies were beautiful, she reflected, but curled up in sleep Fiona really did seem perfection in miniature. Probably all parents thought that too, she thought wryly, as she watched the baby gently breathing. She sat staring at her, knowing already that she would love this child all the days of her life. She promised herself that her relationship with Fiona must never be marred by the kind of enmity that had existed between Mary and her own father. The last letter she had ever received from him had concentrated on how disappointed he was in her, and on her refusal to attend Mass while home on a holiday. It had been a poor ending to a poor relationship and Mary had sworn that, should she ever become a parent, differing values and opinions mustn't ever sour her relationship with her children. She had sworn it then and she still felt that way. And now, miraculously, she was a parent.

Right now, however, any problems she might eventually have with Fiona seemed aeons away as she gazed lovingly at her sleeping child. The morning sunlight streamed into her room, and Mary sat back contentedly on the bed, happy simply to spend time alone with her new daughter.

The doze suggested by the midwife the previous night had turned out to be seven hours' deep sleep. The nurses had been more aware of her exhaustion than Mary, and had given Fiona her night feed and wheeled Mary to a private room where she had slept on. She had woken at seven, still feeling a little sore, but considerably refreshed by her sleep. Eager to have another look at her daughter, she had checked Fiona in the nursery. She had delighted again in the baby's features, and what she saw as eyes like Dave's, and soft blonde hair of a shade similar to her own.

After soaking in a warm bath and washing her hair, she had changed into a fresh hospital nightdress, then eaten a breakfast for which she had found herself to be ravenously hungry.

Fiona had been brought in by the nurses then, and between feeding, changing and dressing the baby, the time had passed quickly. It was almost half past nine now, she noted, as she leaned back in the bed, her head and shoulders comfortably supported by an arrangement of pillows. Just then there was a peremptory knock, the door opened, and a nurse entered.

"Good morning, Mary, isn't it?"

"Yes, good morning."

"Everything all right?"

"Fine, thanks."

"And this is the new arrival," the woman said, bending down to the baby.

"Yes . . . Fiona . . ."

"She's a dote. Sturdy too for a premature delivery."

"Six pounds," said Mary.

"And you felt every ounce, didn't you?" said the woman with a laugh. "I did with my first!"

"Well, it did feel . . . I think *excruciating* is the word I'm looking for," said Mary smilingly.

"Better she was a good size though. When they come early every ounce stands to them."

"She shouldn't have any problems, should she – being premature?" asked Mary anxiously.

"Not at all, there's not a bother on her. No problems feeding her?"

"No, that's all worked out fine."

"Good, You've nothing to worry about then, she'll thrive for you. Are you comfortable there? Do you want another pillow?"

"No, thanks, this is great."

"I'll leave you so. The girls will be in later to get the information for the birth cert, you can tell them if you need anything."

"All right. Thank you."

"Not at all. See you later."

Mary watched the woman leave, then sat up in the bed, her mind racing. She hadn't realised that officialdom would swing into action so rapidly. She didn't want to have the birth falsely registered, yet what option had she if they were coming this morning? Well, she could leave, she thought. She hadn't needed an episiotomy so she had had no stitches. And she felt quite strong now, refreshed by the night's sleep and the soothing bath. Nevertheless leaving the hospital so soon was a daunting prospect. She would have no back-up were she to have difficulties breastfeeding, she had no clothes or equipment organised for the baby, nowhere to stay in Dublin. And then there was Fiona's welfare to consider. Would it be all right to move her from the hospital environment? Probably, Mary reasoned. After all millions of non-Western women gave birth without anything to do with hospitals. On the other hand, the baby was several weeks premature, and although she seemed perfectly healthy, perhaps there were tests to be carried out. She would have to check it out, she decided.

Then, her thoughts having been turned to flight, another consideration struck her. Was she safe here herself? The authorities couldn't know that she had gone into labour early, but if the Irish police had been asked to locate her there might be pictures in the newspapers. She couldn't decide if she were being paranoid or not and she sat considering it a moment, then made up her mind. She really didn't want to leave yet so she would ask what tests or examinations Fiona might be due and she would check the newspapers; then assuming there was nothing about her in the papers, she would stay on. Her mind made up, she reached out and pressed the buzzer to summon the nurse.

"You have some identification please?" the security guard stood in the vestibule adjoining the CBS side entrance, his massive frame blocking further entry.

Plenty of Aunt Gwen's Golden Granules on his breakfast table, thought Dave. "Sure," he answered the guard, handing over his credit cards. No point producing a passport, he reckoned, not when he had longish brown hair in his passport photo and short black hair now.

"Thank you," said the security man, handing back the cards, then he keyed some numbers into a console on the wall, unlocking the heavy door between the vestibule and the main section of the bank.

Dave stepped through into a huge ornate room with a fine plasterwork ceiling. Cashiers' booths ringed the walls, and there were numerous counters to deal with the different areas of banking.

The security man closed the door after him, then guided Dave towards a series of offices at the end of the room. He knocked on one, opened it, and indicated for Dave to enter.

Stepping into the office, Dave was greeted by an impeccably groomed middle-aged man who came forward and shook hands.

"Mr Walker, you're very welcome. I'm Ernst Masthaus."

"How do you do, Mr Masthaus."

"That will be all, Hans, thank you," said the banker, dismissing the blond giant who nodded, then left, closing the door behind him. "Take a seat, please," said Masthaus, indicating a plush chair to Dave while regaining his own seat behind a long mahogany desk.

He looked like a caricature of a Swiss banker, thought Dave, with his neatly trimmed grey hair, silver-rimmed glasses, and expensively cut dark grey suit. Dave's own casual dress made him feel uncomfortable, but he could hardly explain that the jacket of his suit was in the custody of the French airport police.

"Good trip?" asked Masthaus.

"Yes, thanks. And thank you for facilitating me at such short notice."

Masthaus gave a little bow.

"You'll have to excuse my informality," said Dave, indicating his clothes, "but I'll shortly be meeting the recipient of this . . . shall we say 'consultancy fee'?"

"Yes, let us call it that . . ." said Masthaus dryly.

"It's meant to look like a casual meeting – a suit would give the impression of actually doing business."

"Ah yes . . ."

"I need hardly add that the rest of our commerce will be more orthodox. As I mentioned yesterday, this client has very sizeable holdings in Zurich. Our deal should pave the way for further lucrative contracts – with banking done by CBS."

"I'm glad to hear it."

Dave smiled. "Yes, well we're both in business to make profits, aren't we?"

"Very much so," agreed Masthaus. "May I ask the name of your company?"

"We'll be trading under Olympic Holdings."

"*Olympic* Holdings? You won't lose your amateur status by making a profit, I presume?"

Jesus, thought Dave, a Swiss joke! "No," he laughed, "profits first, Olympic ideals very much second, I'm afraid."

"But of course." Masthaus smiled. "Well," he said, reverting to his serious banker role, "to business . . ." He reached into the drawer of the desk and pressed a button that was concealed, then he slid the back of the drawer open and withdrew a padded envelope. Opening the envelope, he tipped out six neat bundles of American 100 dollar bills. "Two hundred and eighty-four thousand, four hundred dollars – one hundred and eighty thousand pounds sterling at a rate of one point five eight. If you care to count them . . ."

Dave waved his hand negligently. "No need I'm sure."

"Certain?"

"Absolutely."

"Very good," said Masthaus, replacing the notes in the padded envelope. "If you'd sign here, please," he said, handing over a sheet of paper.

Dave quickly read the document, then signed.

"Thank you. And your receipt," said Masthaus smilingly as he handed over the bottom copy.

The Swiss banker sat back easily in his chair but now that he had the money Dave was anxious to avoid any further conversation, with its attendant need for lying. He packed the envelope into his holdall and stood up. Immediately the Swiss took his cue and pressed a buzzer on the desk.

"Well, it's been a pleasure, Mr Walker."

"Likewise indeed."

"When shall we have the pleasure of doing further business?"

Greedy bugger, aren't you? thought Dave. "Oh I'd say within the next couple of months," he answered easily. *Or whenever it's safe to withdraw the rest of our money.*

"I look forward to it," said Masthaus.

"Me too," answered Dave as the security man entered the office.

"Ah, Hans, would you show Mr Walker out, please?"

"Yes, sir."

"Well, good morning," said Masthaus, shaking hands. "Safe journey."

"Thank you. Good morning." Dave turned away and followed the security guard. He walked behind him across the large banking hall, delighted at how smoothly it had all gone. They came to the heavy vestibule door, and the guard again keyed numbers into a wall console before opening the door. The man followed Dave into the vestibule, closing the door behind them.

Big on security, thought Dave, looking at the heavy door and the massive frame of the blond giant who now opened the side door of the bank.

"Good morning, sir," he said.

Dave smiled happily at him. "Good morning," he answered, then he stepped out into the sunlit Zurich street.

"Good omen, Chief," said Penny, as Thompson found a single parking space directly opposite the entrance to Holles Street Hospital.

"Maybe," he answered as he manoeuvred neatly into the parking bay. Thompson locked the car, then they crossed the road and entered the redbrick hospital building.

There was a porter on the reception desk, and Penny

smiled as they approached him. "Good morning," she said. "I wonder could you help us?"

"Who are you looking for?" he asked brusquely.

"Would a Mary Adams have been admitted since yesterday evening?"

He consulted a list before him. "Eh . . . no. No Adams here. Is that her married or her maiden name?"

"That's her own name. Her husband's name is Walker."

"One of those ones. Causes more bloody confusion with this keeping-their-maiden-names lark," he said bad-temperedly.

"Maybe they don't regard their identity as a lark," said Penny.

The porter looked at her belligerently but she held his gaze, and after a moment he returned to scanning his lists.

"No, no Walker either," he reported with satisfaction. "You've obviously got your facts wrong."

No point requesting this man to look at a picture of Mary Adams, thought Penny. "I wonder if I could have a word with the person in charge of admissions, please?" she asked.

"Look, your friend isn't here. I've checked both names."

"I know you have, but I'd still like a word, please."

"What for?"

Thompson leaned over the sitting porter. "That's a matter we'll discuss privately with the person involved. Now we haven't got all morning, chum, so don't muck about. Just ring whoever it is, all right?"

"All right, all right! Take a seat over there," the man said officiously as he lifted the phone.

Thompson winked at Penny as they crossed and sat on the seats along the wall. They couldn't hear the porter's conversation, but several moments later a stockily built woman in a blue uniform came through the door and looked around. She approached them smilingly when the porter had nodded in their direction.

"Good morning, I'm Sister Roche," she said pleasantly.

"Good morning, Sister," said Thompson rising. "This is Penny Hart and I'm Jack Thompson."

"How do you do?" she said, shaking hands. "Do you want to film this morning, Mr Thompson?"

"Film?"

"You *are* from the BBC?"

"No . . . no, we're not."

"Oh I'm sorry," she said with a laugh. "We're expecting a film crew – they're doing a documentary about Bloomsday – when I heard there were two English people for me in reception I thought you were them."

"No, English all right, but definitely non-BBC," said Thompson with a grin. "What's Bloomsday?"

"Oh it's something to do with *Ulysses* – you know, the book. There's supposed to have been a scene in the Doctors' Common Room and they want to film there."

"I see," said Thompson.

"So, what was it you *did* want to see me about?"

"Well, it's a little delicate," answered Thompson

with a glance in the sullen porter's direction. "Could we have a word in private?"

"Of course," answered the woman. "This way please," she said, leading them into a corridor that smelt of antiseptic and floor polish. They passed a couple of doors, then turned into a vacant office. "Now, what can I do for you?" she asked.

"Well, Sister, we're trying to locate a missing woman; Mary Adams is her name," said Thompson. "She's Irish, but she's been living in England a long time. It's believed she may have gone into labour on a visit to Dublin, and . . . well, there are people very concerned for her."

"Of course. And you think she might be here?"

"Your porter checked his files, but she may not be using her real name. She's been through a stressful time at home. I'm sure you can understand . . ."

"Yes, we get all sorts of – situations."

"We were hoping you might be able to identify her," said Penny, producing a photograph and handing it over.

Sister Roche studied the print a moment, then shook her head. "She's not familiar."

"Would you have seen all admissions since last night?" asked Thompson.

"No. That's why I'd suggest we go up to the nurses' station on each floor and show this to the girls there. They'd know for sure."

"That would be great," said Penny. "Thank you very much."

"Not at all. I'm sure her family must be worried sick."

"Yes," said Thompson, "the family's . . . well, they've been through the mill . . ."

"Come on then," said the sister. "We'll talk to the nurses and settle it one way or the other."

"Len, it's opening!" Mathieson indicated the bank's heavy side door, now slowly swinging inwards. Almost ten minutes had passed since Walker had entered the building, but the impatience Carrow had felt gave way to pleasure now as he saw their quarry emerge into the sunlit side street.

Carrow moved forward immediately, blocking Walker's path. He relished the stunned look on the other man's face. "Surprise, surprise!" said Carrow, savouring the shock his presence had clearly caused.

Walker looked about in panic, but Mathieson stood blocking the footpath on Carrow's right, and one of the Swiss detectives blocked the way to the left.

"I owe you a good thumping, don't I?" said Carrow pleasantly.

Walker stood looking at him, wild-eyed, then suddenly he shouted "Help! I'm being robbed!"

Carrow lunged for him, but Walker spun on his heel and dived back towards the almost closed side door. "Hans! I'm being robbed!" he cried.

Walker had heaved the door open a couple of feet and gone forward when Carrow and Mathieson burst in after him.

"Help! Police!" screamed Walker, as Mathieson caught him from behind. "I'm being robbed!"

"We are police!" shouted the Swiss detective as he sought to gain entry through the partly opened door.

"No, it's a robbery!" shouted Walker, struggling furiously and catching Mathieson in the face with a backwards jab from his elbow. "They're not police! Close the door!"

"Liar!" cried Carrow, punching him viciously in the ribs and causing Walker to drop the holdall he had been clutching.

The big blond security man had been taken by surprise, but seeing a customer assaulted and dropping a bag presumably containing his recent withdrawal, he suddenly launched himself onto Carrow, forcing him back on top of the Swiss detective who was shouting "police" and trying to display his ID card.

"It's a trick!" cried Walker, holding his ribs. "They're thieves!"

"No!" shouted Carrow, but the big blond man had made up his mind who to believe, and the next thing Carrow knew his head was spinning from a punch. He felt his shoulder smack the pavement, having been propelled out the side door, then the Swiss detective, his nose pumping blood, landed on him. Carrow looked up to see Mathieson being manhandled out the door, which then slammed shut.

Despite the ringing in his ears, Carrow scrambled to his feet. "Come on!" he cried to the dazed Swiss officer. "We can't let the bastard get away! Colin, you OK?"

Mathieson was feeling his face where Walker's elbow had caught him but he nodded. "Yes, I'm all right. . ."

"Round to the far side entrance, fast as you can, in case he tries to get out that way."

"Right," said Mathieson, then he ran down the street.

"Raise your men on the radio," snapped Carrow as the shaken Swiss detective picked himself up. "Tell them no one, *no one* goes out any of the entrances. Got that?"

"Yes," answered the man, raising the radio and giving rapid instructions.

"OK, follow me," said Carrow, heading for the side door.

"What now?"

"Now we get into this bank – whatever it takes. This bastard's given us the slip twice. By Christ he's not going to do it again!"

Dave swiftly retrieved the holdall containing the money, his ribs aching from where Carrow had punched him, then he turned to the security guard. "Quick, Hans, get me in to Herr Masthaus."

"Just a minute," the man answered, sliding home the heavy bolt on the inside of the side door. Once secured, he turned to Dave. "Are you all right?"

"Yes, I'm fine, fine. Let's just get away from here."

The big security guard keyed a number into the wall console, then opened the door leading into the banking hall. Dave ran ahead as the man closed the door after them. "Herr Masthaus! Herr Masthaus!" he shouted.

The banker appeared from his office. "What is it? What's wrong?"

"They've tried to rob me!" cried Dave.

"What? Who has?"

"Thieves, for Christ's sake!" screamed Dave. "They're posing as police. They tried to get in after us, but Hans stopped them."

"Hans?" said Masthaus to the approaching guard.

"It's true, sir. They attacked Mr Walker."

Just then there was a pounding from the side door. "Open up, police! This is the police. Open up please!"

"No!" said Dave. "It's a ruse to get in!"

Masthaus paused briefly, then there was more pounding from the side door. He quickly turned around, and Dave watched as the Swiss banker cut in behind a desk and reached for something. "Are all doors fully secured, Hans?" called Masthaus.

"Yes, sir."

"We'll be all right then, Mr Walker," said the banker as he returned. "I've just activated an alarm linked to Police Headquarters. They'll be here within minutes."

"I can't risk that," cried Dave above the pounding of the side door. "I've got to get out!"

"What?"

"I've withdrawn the money. If it's stolen now it's my loss, not yours – I can't afford that."

"Yes, but the police will be on their way . . ."

"Meanwhile this lot might blow in the door! You've got to let me out the back!"

"But that would mean opening the bank. They could get in that way."

"They won't know you're opening another door! Come on, for God's sake. Your vaults will still be locked, and the police are on their way."

"But if we hold tight . . ."

"If we hold tight they might blow their way in and rob me – *they* don't know the police are on their way. Come on, for Christ's sake. We're losing time. Just let me out the back way!"

"Supposing they're waiting for you there?"

"They won't be!"

"Suppose they are?"

"Then that's my loss! For God's sake, Masthaus, I'm not staying here like a sitting duck. Just let me out the back way and I'll take my chances."

There was another bout of fierce knocking, then further cries of "Open up, police!"

"I can't afford to lose this money!" shouted Dave.

"All right! All right!" cried the flustered banker. "Hans, the service door."

"This way," called the big blond man, making for the rear of the banking hall. Dave immediately followed, trailed by the agitated Masthaus.

"Will I deactivate the IR sensors, sir?" asked the guard.

"No, the alarm's been triggered anyway!"

"Right." The man quickly keyed a set of numbers onto a wall console as Masthaus watched, shaking his head.

"This is madness, totally irregular – " said the banker.

"So is being robbed!" said Dave, then Hans swung the rear door open about a foot and looked warily out.

"All clear," he said to Dave. "Round the corner to the right there's a side gate . . ."

"Right, thank you," cried Dave, as he ran out the back without waiting to hear the rest. He found himself in a service alleyway and immediately ran to the right, towards the opposite side of the building to where he had encountered Carrow. Reaching the corner, he turned right again to find his passage to the street blocked by an ornate barred gate set into a stone arch.

Without waiting, he ran towards the gate, his left arm looped through the straps of the holdall. He jumped, clutching the rails high up. Passers-by in the side-street stopped to stare, but he ignored them, quickly wedging his feet between the rails and climbing. Grasping the stonework of the arch, he hauled himself over and was lowering himself onto the other side when he saw a man across the street speaking into a walkie-talkie. Without pausing, Dave dropped from the arch to the ground. The thud on landing sent a painful shock through the soles of his feet, but he ignored it, rolled sideways, and rose in one flowing movement.

"Stop! Police!" called the man, running across to intercept him.

Dave suddenly swung around towards him, surprising the policeman who had obviously been expecting him to run. Caught off guard, the man was unable to retreat in time as Dave joined his hands and swung the holdall as he would a backhand drive, catching the policeman in the stomach.

The winded Swiss detective fell to the ground, but

out of the corner of his eye Dave saw Mathieson running around the corner from the Bahnhofstrasse. Turning on his heel, Dave raced up a side street. His feet ached as he sprinted at full speed, scattering shocked early-morning shoppers. After about fifty yards he glanced behind. Running with equal disregard for the outraged Swiss pedestrians, Mathieson was still in pursuit, and what was worse, he showed no signs of flagging.

Dave sprinted all-out, aware from the brief glance that the man behind seemed as fit as himself and, if anything, was closing the gap. Reaching an intersection, Dave turned right, instinctively making for the more crowded environs of the Bahnhofstrasse. His heart pounding, he raced down the centre of the road, but resisted the time-wasting urge to look behind.

Suddenly he was back in the Bahnhofstrasse, and he swung left and ran up the pedestrian-free centre of the street, ignoring the stares of the strollers on either pavement. Ahead he saw a tram filling up. Calling on his last reserves of energy, he increased his pace to reach it just as the doors were about to close. He jumped on board, and looking behind saw Mathieson closing in on him at speed.

Mathieson was moving at a frightening pace, obviously aware of Dave's ploy, and Dave silently screamed for the driver to close the doors as Mathieson continued towards him. A couple of seconds passed agonisingly before the doors closed and the tram began to move off. Leaning in exhaustion against the rail, Dave looked back at Mathieson, who hadn't stopped running. To Dave's horror he was actually closing the gap. Dave stared at the other man's face, contorted by exertion, then the tram accelerated, leaving Mathieson behind, and the last image Dave had of him was Mathieson coming to a halt and gasping, head between knees, as the tram sped away.

Visser pretended to read a magazine as he leaned back in his seat in Busarus, Dublin's central bus station. He had chosen his spot carefully so that he could watch the entrance and ticket office while appearing like a traveller awaiting his coach, and so far no one had paid him any attention.

He hadn't shaved or showered since the previous day and had been active all night long, so that now he felt grubby and uncomfortable, but he was unwilling to leave his position to wash and shave in the station toilets.

He had watched the dawn coming up as he continued his fruitless round of Dublin's hotels, then he had snatched a quick breakfast in a roadside café and thought out his next moves. He reckoned there was a strong chance that Mary Adams had stayed in Dublin overnight – possibly in one of the bed and breakfast establishments he hadn't been able to check – and if she used a taxi this morning the odds were that he would get to hear of it, bearing in mind the large reward. With that angle covered he figured the stations were where he should concentrate his efforts. He reasoned that if someone were meeting her it would have been at the car ferry, and so he was acting on the assumption that she would make her own way to her final destination.

Of course there was the chance that Dublin itself was her destination, but his hunch was that she would want to go to ground someplace much more remote. Assuming she would shy away from car hire – with its attendant need for identification and a deposit – that left trains and buses. There were three major train stations and one bus depot in the city, and Visser had opted for the bus station on the grounds that buses for all parts of Ireland departed from there, whereas the train stations each ran services to specific regions.

He had parked his van in the nearby Irish Life car park, then settled down in Busarus, surreptitiously checking all the early-morning passengers. It was a tiresome, dispiriting task, but he knew from experience not to lose patience, not to let his concentration slip. At times simply waiting was an important part of the chase, all good hunters knew that, and so he sat there, hoping for a phone call or a quick sighting, but prepared to wait for as long as it took.

Mary felt relieved as she walked along the hospital corridor. Firstly she had been assured by one of the sisters that Fiona was perfectly healthy, and that while there were routine checks to be done, there was nothing to worry about, and secondly, there had been no photographs or mention of Mary in any of the newspapers she had bought, and quickly scanned in the nearest toilet.

She stepped through the door into the old-fashioned open-framed lift, the newspapers under her arm, and pressed the button for her floor. The door was closing when she heard a woman's voice.

"This way, Miss Hart – oops, just missed the lift."

"Not to worry," answered another woman in what Mary recognised as a Yorkshire accent. "I don't suppose the stairs will kill us."

Mary felt her hair stand on end as the lift ascended. There could be no mistaking the tone or the Leeds accent. It was the young detective who had questioned her in the workshop. Hart . . . Penny Hart.

The lift stopped at her floor and Mary stepped out in a panic. She turned into the corridor, her mind racing. Somehow the police had traced her, and they would be halfway up the stairs by now, yet she couldn't run to her room without attracting attention. Instead she walked as briskly as possible, passed the nurses' station without glancing in, then opened the door and stepped into her room.

Fiona was fast asleep in her cot and without breaking stride Mary threw the newspapers into the bin, lifted the baby and looked about frantically. If she stepped out into the corridor now they would probably bump into her, yet if she stayed here they would also find her. *Unless they thought she wasn't in the room.* She quickly crossed to the tall oak wardrobe in the corner and opened the door. Cradling Fiona with one arm, she pushed the clothes hangers aside, then stepped into the wardrobe and swung the door behind her.

Without a handle on the inside of the wardrobe it was impossible to close the door completely, but by holding the inside of the wooden frame she restricted the gap to a small chink. She was attempting to close this further when she heard the door to the corridor being opened.

Mary froze. Someone walked into the room and footsteps came in her direction.

"No, Sister, she's not here," said a woman's voice from a couple of feet away.

Conscious of the nurse standing so close to the partly opened wardrobe, Mary was acutely aware of the pounding of her heart.

"And the baby's gone too," said an older woman's voice.

"The child was here a few minutes ago, Sister."

"Maybe she brought her with her to see some other patient," said the older woman.

"Could be. She's not in the nursery."

Just then Mary felt the baby stir in her sleep. No! she prayed silently. Don't wake now. Don't cry! The baby shifted again, and Mary thought of giving her a breast to suckle, but the nurse was so near that she would be liable to hear any movement or sucking noises.

"I'll tell Mr Thompson she's not in her room," said the older woman, and Mary thought – Thompson – that would be Chief Inspector Thompson, who had questioned Dave.

"Will I check the wards, Sister?"

"Eh . . . yes, and the private rooms."

"OK, Sister."

There was the sound of footsteps, then the door closed. Mary stayed inside the wardrobe as she tried to get her thoughts in order. She gently rocked Fiona, who seemed to have settled again, then she stepped out, her mind made up.

She laid the baby on the bed, quickly took off her slippers and dressinggown, pulled the nightdress over her head, and dressed rapidly in a set of her own clothes, leaving the rest of her stuff in the wardrobe. She hid the discarded items under her pillows, and was about to throw her toiletries and spare clothes into her travel bag but changed her mind, taking instead just her money and credit cards.

She picked up Fiona, still sleeping soundly in her tightly wrapped layette, then moved to the door. If the others saw her in the corridor now it was all over but she had to chance it. Her nerves tingling, she slowly turned the handle and eased the door open. She placed her eye to the crack and looked back down the corridor towards the nurses' station. There was nobody about. She glanced in the other direction, and there was no-one in that part of the corridor either.

Without pausing, she stepped out of the room and headed down the empty corridor in the opposite direction to the nurses' station. A door began to open in one of the rooms, and Mary looked over in alarm, but only a patient emerged, glancing curiously at Mary as she hurried past.

Reaching the door leading to the back stairs, Mary turned out of the corridor, closed the door quietly after her and started down the stairs.

Penny and Thompson looked up expectantly as Sister

Roche rejoined them at the nurses' station. Thompson had declined the sister's offer for him to visit Mary in her room, explaining that he didn't want to distress her, and that he and Penny had been asked simply to confirm for certain the missing woman's whereabouts. Instead he had asked the sister to establish that Mary was definitely there, so he could report back to those concerned about her, which Penny had mentally translated as wanting to be certain that Adams hadn't done another runner.

In reality, Penny knew that in Ireland they had no powers to detain her. Besides which, it was her husband they really wanted. Far better simply to allow her to lead them unwittingly to Walker, with whom she would no doubt rendezvous shortly.

"She's not in her room at the moment," said Sister Roche, "but I've asked one of the nurses to locate her. She might be chatting with someone in another room or in one of the wards."

Penny saw a flicker of apprehension on Thompson's face on hearing that Adams was missing from her room.

"Thank you very much, Sister," he said. "I appreciate all your assistance."

"Glad to help," she answered with a smile.

"Actually, to tell you the truth," continued Thompson, "I feel a little awkward here." He indicated the corridor along which pregnant women and nightdress-clad mothers passed. "As a male, I feel a bit . . . out of place. Why don't I wait down in the hall, and Penny can confirm with your nurse that the woman really is Mary Adams?"

Penny caught his eye, then looked away. What he

really meant was that if Adams were not in her room, he wanted to seal off the hospital entrance.

"No need to feel you're intruding, Mr Thompson," said the sister, "but if you'd feel more comfortable downstairs . . ."

"I would," he interjected.

"OK, then. It certainly appears to be her though."

"Fine," agreed Thompson. "I'll be downstairs."

"OK," answered Sister Roche.

"Right. And thanks again, Sister. I'll wait below – see you there, Penny."

"OK . . ." She nearly said "Chief", but turned it into a cough instead. "OK, see you later," she said as Thompson strode out the door.

Mary paused several steps from the bottom of the stairs. If she sought a rear exit to the hospital she would be less likely to be noticed leaving, but it would take more time to find her way out, and time was precious – they were probably already combing the hospital for her. On the other hand if she brazenly walked out the front door she could be away in seconds – provided Thompson hadn't stationed someone there to intercept her. She bit her lip, knowing she had to decide quickly, then she made her mind up and descended the final steps.

She cautiously opened the door into the main ground-floor corridor, and seeing nobody whom she recognised, stepped into it. It was a busy corridor, with patients, doctors, and nurses travelling in both directions. To the right was the main entrance, and a sign indicated the outpatient department to the left.

Without pausing, Mary walked left, hoping she looked like a mother bringing her baby for a check-up in outpatients. She rounded the corner, her heart racing from the fear of hearing a commotion at any moment from those searching for her, but she reached the busy outpatients waiting-room without incident.

Stopping to get her bearings, she saw people coming into the area from a door in the far wall, and as none of them were hospital staff she reasoned that this must be a side entrance for the public.

She crossed the room towards the doorway, passed through it, and stepped out into a lane. She looked to her left, and there on the far side of an archway was the public thoroughfare of Holles Street.

Holding her sleeping baby, she hurried up the lane. She resisted the urge to look back up at the floor on which her room was situated, but turned instead and walked away down Holles Street.

"No sign of her anywhere, Sister," said the nurse. "I've checked all the wards and rooms on this floor."

"That's odd," said Sister Roche. "What about the bathrooms?"

"Tried them all," said the nurse. "No luck."

"Would she have to bring the baby someplace, for tests or anything?" asked Penny.

"No, not when the baby's just a day old," said the Sister. "Maybe she's slipped down to the shop."

"Hardly bring the baby down too," said the nurse.

Penny felt her unease increasing. "You're sure she has the baby with her?"

"She must have. The baby's not in the room or the nursery."

"I'm beginning to fear the worst," said Penny.

Sister Roche looked at her quizzically. "How do you mean?"

"I think she may have fled the hospital."

"Surely not?"

"We'll see. Could I look at her room?"

Sister Roche paused a moment, then nodded. "Yes, I suppose so. It's just down here," she said, leading Penny and the nurse down the corridor.

They entered the empty room, and Penny looked about in vain for any signs of abrupt flight.

"I'm sure there's some explanation," said Sister Roche.

"Can we check if her clothes are still here?" said Penny.

"Yes, all right. Catherine . . ." The nurse opened the large wardrobe, and Sister Roche shook her head. "No, the clothes are still here," she said.

The nurse stared into the wardrobe then turned to the other two women. "Her shoes aren't . . ."

"Christ, she's gone!" cried Penny. "Thank you, Sister, thank you both very much. I must see Mr Thompson." She turned and raced out the door, then along the corridor and down the stairwell, taking the steps two at a time.

Reaching the bottom, she burst through the doors

into the hall where Thompson sat waiting. Seeing her expression, he rose immediately.

"She's gone!"

"What!"

"I'm sure of it, Chief."

"Christ! She didn't come out this way."

"There must be another entrance."

Thompson moved swiftly to the porter's desk. "What other entrances are there besides this?" he demanded.

The porter drew back slightly. "What?"

"What other entrances are there?"

"Eh . . . there's an entrance through outpatients."

"Where's that?"

"Down the corridor to the left . . ."

Before the man was finished speaking Penny was through the door, Thompson speeding after her. They followed the signs, then turned into the outpatients waiting-room. Penny looked about, but there was no sign of Mary Adams. Thompson crossed the room, then stopped suddenly. He approached a mother feeding a small baby in the outpatients-queue.

"Excuse me, but have you seen this woman around here?" he asked, producing the photo of Mary Adams.

The woman looked at it, then shook her head. "No, sorry . . ."

"I saw her," said a heavily pregnant woman sitting next in line. She looked up at Thompson. "What do you want her for?" she asked, her tone becoming suspicious.

"She left all her photos by mistake on my sister's bed," improvised Penny. "They were in the same ward.

We wanted to catch up with her. Did you notice which way she went?"

"Oh. She went out that door," she said, pointing to a side entrance.

Thompson immediately headed for the door, but Penny paused briefly. "When was this?" she asked.

"Just a few minutes ago."

"Thanks," cried Penny, then she turned and ran to the door.

"Chief Superintendent Carrow?"

"Yes?" Carrow looked round as a swarthy, stocky man in his fifties drew near.

The narrow side street flanking the bank bustled with police activity, but the approaching man appeared unflustered. "I'm Chief Superintendent Peter Vincenz," he, said, shaking hands with Carrow. "And Mr Mathieson, I presume?"

"How do you do?" said the intelligence officer, also shaking hands.

"I've spoken to my men," said Vincenz, "and they've taken a statement from the bank manager."

"Taken a statement?" said Carrow. "Charging him for obstruction might be more like it!"

"I don't think so," replied Vincenz calmly. "Your Mr Walker was a legitimate customer who'd made a withdrawal. The bank manager genuinely thought he'd been set upon by thieves posing as policemen."

"Watching too much bloody television," muttered Carrow.

"So what's the next move, Mr Vincenz?" interjected Mathieson diplomatically.

"Spotting Walker. We've got a good description – tall, slim, short black hair, blue shirt, grey slacks, black shoes . . ."

"Carrying a Lacoste holdall," added Carrow.

"Yes, we've got that too," said Vincenz. "I've put out an alert for him. I don't think he'll get too far."

"Don't bet on it," said Carrow. "This bugger is smart."

"Perhaps. But if he tries to leave the country Passport Control will get him."

"He may go to ground for a while," suggested Mathieson.

Vincenz shrugged. "Not so easy. Every hotel and lodging house in Switzerland has to report passport details of all foreigners to the police."

"He'll know that," said Carrow. "Just like he'll know ID is required to hire a car or buy an airline ticket – so he won't do any of those things. That still leaves trains, buses, taxis, lake steamers . . ."

"Yes, we're aware of that," said Vincenz equably. "Oh and talking of transport, he got away from you on a tram, Mr Mathieson?"

"That's right."

"Did you notice the number?"

"Yes, an eleven."

"Hmm . . ."

"Is that significant?"

"The number eleven passes the train station. Not far from the bus station either. If I were being chased like Mr Walker, I might be tempted to jump off the tram and take the first train or bus out of Zurich. Excuse me a moment." Vincenz leaned in the open window of one of the parked police cars and took up the walkie-talkie. He gave a series of rapid instructions, then returned to Carrow and Mathieson. "I've ordered units to the bus and train stations." He glanced at his watch. "Ten twenty-five, it's only fifteen minutes since he fled the bank. I don't think he'll get out of Zurich."

"Your man didn't think he'd get out of the bank either – when I wanted to go in after him," said Carrow.

Vincenz looked the English policeman in the eye and drew a little closer. "That's true," he said. "but then your eagerness made you intercept too soon, did it not?"

"What?"

"My officer says you confronted Mr Walker before his route back into the bank was cut off. As I'm sure your report will note . . ."

Carrow struggled to keep his anger in check. He needed this man's help; the only way to offset the ignominy of Walker's escaping twice would be to ensure his capture, and for that he needed Swiss co-operation. "Let's not argue about what might or might not go into reports," he said, forcing himself to sound pleasant. "Let's just put all our efforts into getting this man."

Vincenz looked at him, a hint of amusement in his expression. "Good," he said with a nod, then his face became serious again. "Well, now that we're all on the one side, let's get on with our search."

Dave carefully appraised the change in his appearance

as he stood before the mirror. The black mousse had been washed out of his hair, to be replaced by the blond peroxide-and-bleach combination from the kit that he had bought in the chemist's in Paris, and he had also altered the style of his hair, combing it off his forehead. The shirt, slacks and black shoes had now been replaced by a tee-shirt, jeans and tennis shoes.

On alighting from the tram outside the train station he had gone into Shopville, the huge underground shopping complex beneath the station. A couple of quick purchases in a clothes store had provided him with the large plastic carrier bags he wanted, then he had made his way to the station's shower room. He had paid the attendant, collected his towel, and rinsed out the black mousse from his hair. He had then opened his blond highlighting kit, dispensed with the cap and crochet hook used for highlighting, and instead worked the bleach and peroxide combination into all of his hair. He had showered as he waited for the bleach to take effect, and after about thirty minutes his hair had been transformed to light blond.

He examined it now in the mirror to make sure there were no patches that he had missed, but it looked fine, and he nodded in satisfaction. Apart from meeting the vital need to alter his appearance, the shower room had also provided a haven in which he could await the ten fifty-nine train to Rorschach, for which he had booked a ticket on arriving in Zurich earlier that morning.

He glanced at his watch now and saw that it was ten fifty. Time to go. He slipped on the baseball cap he had bought, just in case the shower attendant might notice the change in his hair, then he picked up the two carrier bags in which he had put his clothes and the money withdrawn from the bank.

He walked past the shower attendant, deliberately avoiding eye contact as he wished the man good morning. He stepped out into the station and took an escalator from the underground level up into the station proper, slipped the baseball hat off his head and into one of the bags, and walked across the large concourse to a litter bin. He stood close to the bin, then reached into the other carrier bag, took out the rolled up Lacoste holdall he had been using previously, and dropped it into the bin.

He moved on through the station towards the platforms, his heartbeat accelerating. If the Swiss police were any way efficient they would surely be watching such a crucial departure point, he reasoned. He had toyed with the idea of adding to his altered appearance with dark glasses but had decided it might be too obvious a move for someone in his situation. Instead he now donned his gold-framed reading glasses.

He stopped briefly to buy a newspaper, then moved on towards his platform. Out of the corner of his eye he saw two uniformed policemen patrolling the concourse. He realised he would have to pass them to get to his train, and he felt a shiver go up his spine. He forced himself not to falter but continued on, hoping that the local newspaper and the carrier bags would give him the appearance of a native returning from a little shopping.

Now that he was nearing the trains, he could see

another pair of policemen patrolling near the other end of the platforms. Fighting his nervousness, he strode ahead, aware of the nearest policeman's scrutiny as he walked past. He imagined he could feel the policeman's eyes boring into his back, but he resisted the temptation to accelerate.

Reaching the first open door of the train, he climbed the steps and risked a sideways glance. Both policemen were looking at the passengers approaching from the concourse, and Dave sighed with relief as he ascended the steps into the carriage.

He moved through the train until he found an empty section of a compartment where he stowed his bags and retreated behind his newspaper. The seconds passed with agonising slowness, then on the dot of ten fifty-nine the train eased slowly forward, picking up speed as it pulled out of the station.

For the first time since the chase from the bank Dave relaxed slightly, and as the train moved through the suburbs of Zurich he reflected on what had happened. The police had obviously known he had been going to the CBS branch in the Bahnhofstrasse, but how? Could Masthaus have been suspicious and told the authorities? Yet if that were the case the banker would hardly have allowed him out the rear door. Far more disturbingly, could Mary have been caught? No, no, he couldn't believe that – even if she were detained she would never tell. It was hard to believe though that the police in Harrogate could have checked so soon on the accounts and traced the transfer to Zurich. He wasn't even sure if the police were legally entitled to such information. Not that it mattered, he realised. The important thing was that he had been complacent in thinking he was safe visiting the bank. He had underestimated Carrow and Mathieson, and it had almost cost him his freedom. He sat back, ignoring the Swiss countryside rolling by the window, and firmly resolved not to underestimate his opponents again.

How strange to be a baby and to sleep through all this drama, Mary thought, as she cradled Fiona tenderly and paid the taximan. She had flagged the vehicle down near the hospital and had taken it to the ILAC centre, a shopping complex on the far side of the city.

Standing now outside its Parnell Street entrance, Mary acknowledged the driver's thanks for the tip, then turned and entered the complex. It had made sense to leave her stuff in the hospital room in order not to give notice of her sudden departure, but now she needed to stock up. She had thought it out in the taxi, and apart from toiletries and spare clothes for herself, she would have to get wipes, nappies, Sudocream and Babygros for Fiona. A light collapsible buggy-cum-carrycot would also increase their mobility.

First things first though, she thought, and her most urgent need was for help in getting out of Dublin. Now that the authorities were onto her, she couldn't possibly take a train or bus out of the city. She would have to ring Ballyard and ask her brother Tom for his help. She hated involving him, and had given no warning of her homecoming, being anxious not to cause any trouble for her family if she were apprehended, but now the situation was desperate. Thompson and Hart had come within a hair's-breadth of catching her in the hospital, and the thought of being arrested and separated from Fiona was simply unbearable.

She moved through the busy shopping mall, looking out for public telephones. Reaching the centre of the complex, she saw an unoccupied telephone booth and eagerly crossed to it. Still cradling the sleeping baby, she lifted the phone, wedged it between her shoulder and cheek, and placed her money in the slot. She hesitated a moment, dreading involving her easy-going older brother in her troubles, then she felt Fiona stir. She looked at the tiny face, and the idea of being imprisoned and the baby going into care was just too awful. Tom and Jenny wouldn't want that – she knew that in the circumstances they would want her to ring.

Without further hesitation she dialled the number. Now that she was definitely involving Tom, she prayed that he would be at home. Supposing he were away for the weekend? Or at sea in the trawler? The phone rang and she swallowed hard, willing it to be answered. The ringing seemed to go on interminably, but still there was no answer. Despairingly Mary let it ring, and just as she was about to give up, the phone was lifted, and a woman's voice said "Hello?"

"Hello, Jenny?"

"Yes – is that Mary?"

"Yes. I – I thought you weren't there."

"We were out the back. Are you all right?"

"Yes. Yes, I'm OK. Is Tom there?" *Please, God, please let him not be at sea . . .*

"Yes," answered Jenny, "hold on. Tom," she cried, "Mary's on the phone. He's just coming, Mary."

"Thanks."

"Are you sure you're all right, love?"

"Eh . . . I'll explain it all when I see you, Jenny. OK?"

"OK . . . here's Tom now."

"Mary," he said warmly, "how are you?"

"I'm in trouble, Tom," she answered softly. "I'm in big trouble, and I need your help . . ."

"Realistically, Chief, how would you rate our chances of catching her now?"

Thompson kept his eyes on the Saturday morning traffic as they drove along Merrion Road. "Realistically? Still pretty good if she's from outside Dublin, not so good if she's a native – but I don't think she is."

"Why not?"

"Because she was eight months pregnant, yet no one met her off the ferry. If she'd family and friends here she'd hardly have needed a taxi."

"Unless she didn't want to involve them?"

"Maybe, but having got safely home, if she were from Dublin surely someone from her family would have gone to the hospital with her? "

"True . . ."

"So I reckon she's from the country, and to get there she'll have to take the train, or a bus or car . . ."

"Yes," agreed Penny, "that makes sense. It's just . . ."

"Just what?"

Penny shrugged. "Just that she's a pretty resourceful woman."

"Absolutely. That's why we're heading for the embassy. I want every available body to reinforce those covering the stations."

"I can't see her travelling by train or bus, Chief. She'll guess we're watching them."

"Probably," conceded Thompson, "but we still have to cover them. Meanwhile Superintendent O'Reilly's alert for a pregnant woman has been altered to a woman with a newborn baby. I owe him for this. He's come up trumps."

"Yes, if it's not a contradiction, thank God for the jewellery theft."

"Aye, the roadblocks are a stroke of luck."

"How long will they be manned?"

"All day today, he says, possibly tomorrow as well."

"So we'll be here for the weekend?" asked Penny.

Thompson smiled without taking his eyes off the road. "I told you your social life would suffer in CID."

"I don't mind."

"I bloody do!" said Thompson. "I'm missing a bowls tournament this afternoon and the wife's birthday tomorrow. Supposed to be going out for a meal together."

"Oh no. I'm sure she'll be disappointed."

"She will, but she'll pretend not to be. Sound as a bell, Alice," said Thompson warmly.

"You're lucky, Chief . . ."

"Aye. Many an officer's had to choose between the job and the wife."

"Or the husband, as the case may be . . ."

Thompson glanced at her and grinned. "Don't let me away with much, do you?"

"No, not much," she answered lightly.

"So, what about your weekend?" he asked. "Missing anything special?"

"Not particularly. I'd planned seeing a show in the Playhouse, but . . . constabulary duties to be done . . ."

"That could be quite disappointing for some chap, I dare say . . ."

Penny laughed. "To answer your half-asked question; no, I'm not seeing anyone at the moment."

"Did I ask that?"

"I think so," said Penny, smiling at his innocent expression, "but this is my first murder investigation, Chief, and I don't begrudge a minute spent on it."

"Just as well," said Thompson, slowing as they approached the embassy, "because first time out, you've drawn a worthy opponent . . ."

A sudden movement near the entrance to the bus station caught Visser's attention. Immediately he was alert, despite remaining unmovingly on his seat so as not to bring attention to himself. He looked across the concourse, observing the new arrival. His subject was about thirty, a neatly-groomed man in a grey pin-stripe suit. The way in which the man had arrived in a hurry yet wasn't proceeding to the ticket counter seemed wrong to Visser. That and his attire. For very few of the other passengers travelling on a Saturday morning were dressed in sharp business suits.

The man was moving around the concourse in what he probably thought was a discreet fashion, but to Visser's trained eye it was clear that he was searching for someone. The fact that he hadn't gone through the motions of checking arrival or departure times as a cover suggested a less than fully professional approach, an assessment confirmed for Visser when the man stepped into an alcove and spoke briefly into a walkie-talkie.

Hardly M15, Visser thought, possibly local police, though the man's Saville Row type suit didn't suggest a policeman. Whoever it was, the station was being staked out, but by someone who wasn't very good. There was nothing however to prove that Mary Adams was the subject of the surveillance. They could be after anyone, Visser thought. It could be a coincidence that they were seeking someone at the same time he was seeking Adams. Except he didn't believe in coincidences. He had long subscribed to the adage that in this business there were no coincidences, only enemy actions.

He rose, stretched apparently casually, and strolled to the entrance door. If Adams showed up now he would have to intercept her before Grey Suit saw her, before she entered the building. More difficult, he thought, but not impossible. He stepped out the door, then looked about for a place to wait.

It had been too good to be true, Carrow realised. He had driven with Mathieson and Vincenz from the bank to the train station, where the superintendent had

questioned all the ticket clerks, one of whom had
positively identified Walker, despite his altered hair.
The catch was that although the man had seen Walker
earlier that morning, it was a second clerk at an
adjoining hatch who had sold Walker his ticket. The
second man was now off temporarily, on special leave.

"*Schwingen* accident, his son injured a finger,"
Vincenz had explained.

"*Schwingen?*" said Carrow.

"It's a Swiss sport," explained Mathieson. "Sort of
wrestling match where you grab your opponent's
trousers and upend him."

"Sounds ridiculous," muttered the Special Branch
man.

"So might golf, explained to a Martian," answered
Mathieson with a grin.

But Carrow had been unamused, and now, at noon,
an hour and a half of precious time had elapsed, and
the Swiss police had been unable to locate the ticket
clerk.

Superintendent Vincenz had explained that the man
was a widower who lived alone with the injured
teenage son, but despite despatching a car to their
apartment the police had been unable to locate them.
They had also unsuccessfully tried the accident
departments of all the Zurich hospitals, but that still left
countless general practitioners to whom the man might
have brought the injured boy.

Carrow sat impatiently in the stationmaster's office,
unconvinced by his claims that Zingler, the clerk
involved, was a particularly conscientious worker who

would be sure to return to duty as soon as possible. No progress had been reported from any of the other units seeking Walker, and an air of tension was developing when a knock was heard from the door.

A middle-aged man entered timorously. "You wanted me, sir?"

"Ah, come in, Zingler," said the station master in relief, using English for the benefit of his visitors. "Your son is all right?"

"Yes, thank you, sir."

Vincenz moved forward quickly. "Forgive me, gentlemen, but time is short. I'm Chief Superintendent Vincenz, and I'd like you to look at these pictures, Mr Zingler."

The man studied the proffered photographs.

"You sold this person a ticket this morning?" asked Vincenz.

Zingler nodded. "Yes, his hair is shorter now, but this is the person."

"You're quite sure it's the same man?"

"Yes, he was a foreigner, and I helped him with the timetable."

"Can you remember where he bought a ticket for?"

The clerk thought a moment, stroking his thin moustache.

"Well?"

"So much has happened since then . . . let me see. Eh . . . it was north . . . yes! Yes, I have it. He bought a single ticket, Zurich to Rorschach."

"You're sure?"

"Yes, certain."

"Where's that?" asked Carrow.

"Rorschach's a small town on Lake Constance," replied Vincenz.

"What the hell's he going there for?" said Carrow in puzzlement.

"Lake Constance acts as the border between Switzerland, Germany and Austria," answered Mathieson.

Vincenz turned back to the ticket clerk. "What time train did he book?"

"Eh . . . I think it was about eleven."

"That would have been the ten fifty-nine," said the stationmaster, consulting a timetable.

"Arriving when in Rorschach?"

"Eh . . . twelve twenty."

Carrow looked at his watch. "That's not for another twenty minutes!"

Vincenz took up his personal radio and immediately issued a series of commands, then he spoke to the two rail employees. "Thank you for your help, gentlemen." Quickly turning, he faced Carrow and Mathieson. "I'm having the train met at Rorschach," he explained. "Perhaps you'd like to accompany me there in my car?"

"Very much so," said Carrow, rising. "Very much so."

Dave watched the sunlight reflecting on the sparkling blue waters of Lake Constance as the train slowed down approaching Romanshorn, a lakeside town to the west of Rorschach.

In keeping with his resolution not to underestimate

his opponents again he had been trying to imagine what he would have done in their place. Apart from monitoring all stations, he might well have questioned those selling bus and train tickets out of Zurich that morning, he had decided. The likelihood of the ticket sellers remembering him – and his destination – wouldn't be particularly high, yet it was a possibility.

And so, as the train pulled into Romanshorn, he rose to get off. If they had been quick enough and lucky enough to find out his destination, they would be waiting in Rorschach; however there would not have been time to arrange a reception for him in all of the many stations en route from Zurich. Or so he hoped, as he alighted with the other passengers.

Keeping his stride confident, he walked down the platform towards the exit, surreptitiously scanning the station. No one paid him the slightest heed however, and he stepped out into the street, relieved that his theory had been sound.

His original plan had been to get out of Switzerland on the ferry from Rorschach to Lindau, the German town on the other side of the lake. A couple of years previously he had attended a United Advertising sales seminar in Rorschach, and remembering the frequent criss-crossing of the lake by the ferries, he had determined to evade Swiss passport control by stowing away on one of them.

He would now wait until nightfall, then stow away on the ferry from Romanshorn to Friedrichshaven, seven miles distant on the German side of the lake. He moved briskly through the streets of Romanshorn – still reasonably familiar from a day trip he had taken there during the sales conference – and started towards the outskirts of the town.

He would lie low for the rest of the day in a wood he had seen as the train had approached Romanshorn from Amriswil. Of course, if the police were waiting for him in Rorschach and he didn't show up they might extend their net to the adjoining lakeside towns, but he would worry about that tonight if he had to. Meanwhile it would be important to rest up for what lay ahead, and picking up pace, he headed south towards the cover of the woods.

35

Mary ignored the screeching in the distance and relished instead the warm rays of the late afternoon sun. From where she sat she could observe a flock of flamingos at the lake, and further off she could see a family of monkeys playfully swinging in the branches of a tree. The cries of the animals carried faintly in the breeze, and she thought again what a good choice she had made in spending the day in the wonderfully scenic thirty acres that made up Dublin Zoo.

In one way she felt guilty, subscribing as she did to the modern view that conventional zoos were animal prisons, cooping up large beasts like elephants and giraffes in inadequate enclosures, yet the zoo had provided her with a convenient haven in which to pass the time while awaiting her brother Tom.

She observed a line of small cages, their thick steel bars appearing depressingly symbolic, and she thought involuntarily of her own loss of freedom if the authorities should catch her. They *mustn't* catch her was the only answer. No matter how tired she might become she had to keep her wits about her; she had to keep going.

Fortunately the sunny weather had meant that the zoo was packed with adults and children, among whom she could merge as just another mother wheeling her baby in a buggy. To further throw any searchers off her trail she wore a good-fitting curly red wig that she had bought in the ILAC shopping centre, and she had used a convincing Scottish accent when obliged to speak to others. She had gone directly to the zoo from the shopping centre, and the size of the zoo's grounds was such that she would be able to kill time there without feeling conspicuous.

The zoo had provided gardens in which she had discreetly breastfed Fiona, toilets in which she had changed her, and a restaurant where she had carefully chosen a satisfying and nutritious meal to provide herself with energy.

She still felt sore from the birth but she hadn't expected to feel quite so tired, although after the trauma of labour, blood-loss, and her flight from the hospital, she reasoned that fatigue was hardly surprising. Nevertheless she had to keep her strength up; the coming hours would be crucial to the escape. She had still a lot of time to put in before her rendezvous with Tom, but on a bright summer evening she would be safe and inconspicuous in the adjacent Phoenix Park after the zoo closed at six.

Now however she sat in the sunshine, conserving her energy and lovingly watching the face of her sleeping child. She was fascinated by the baby, intrigued at how her own and Dave's features were mirrored in Fiona. She gazed happily at the baby's tiny features, then, leaning back on the seat, she closed her eyes and savoured the warmth of the sun on her face.

Visser was beginning to lose heart when the phone call finally came through. He had moved from Busarus to the adjacent Connolly railway station, having begun to feel conspicuous after waiting about near the entrance to Busarus. His vigil in Connolly had proved equally unrewarding, but now he felt a surge of excitement as he answered his mobile, knowing that the only people who had the number were those to whom he had offered the reward.

"Hello," he said, stepping towards the wall at the edge of the station concourse and turning his back on the hustle and bustle of the platforms.

"Hello, Mr Jones?" asked a middle-aged voice with a Dublin accent.

"Yes," answered Visser.

"Hibernian Taxi Company . . ."

Visser tried to block out the noise of the station, concentrating on the slightly crackly line.

"You asked us to make contact, in the event of one of our drivers – "

"Have you found her?" interrupted Visser.

"Eh, yes, I think we may have," said the man, sounding a little taken aback at being cut short.

"You *think* you may have?"

"Well, your description was a blonde, heavily-pregnant woman . . ."

"And?"

"And our driver said his passenger had curly red hair – though of course that could be a woman's wig."

"Was she heavily pregnant?"

"No, but . . ."

"No?"

"She had a newborn baby though."

"I see . . ." said Visser, his mind racing.

"The thing is she was very like the woman in your photo – apart of course from the curly red hair."

"Your man got a good look at her?"

"Yeah, he's pretty certain it was her all right."

"Where has he taken her?" asked Visser, consciously keeping his exultation in check.

"From the ILAC Centre to Dublin Zoo."

"Dublin Zoo?"

"Yeah, dropped her right at the entrance and saw her pay in."

"Just now, was it?"

"Eh, no, about a quarter past eleven actually . . ."

"A quarter past eleven?! That was an hour ago!"

"Yeah, well, ye see, I was on an early lunch break," the man explained apologetically, "and then the message didn't get . . ."

"Never mind that now!" snapped Visser.

"Well, about the reward then . . ."

"You'll hear from me. Thank you." *Greedy bastard*, thought Visser, terminating the call and slipping the phone into his jacket as he ran towards the ramp leading from the station down to the street.

So Adams had had her baby in the last twenty-four hours – the one possibility he had never foreseen. Had her baby and gone on the run again, assuming the zoo was some kind of rendezvous. He had to get there as quickly as possible, but the nature of the venue gave him hope. If she were simply being collected by someone she would hardly pay in to the zoo. Whereas if she were *waiting* for someone it might well be a good spot in which to kill time.

Visser reached street level and exited from the station precincts, darting across Amiens Street and making at speed for his parked van.

Even as he ran his mind was in overdrive, reviewing all that had happened. Adams was lucky – some people were, and you couldn't legislate for that – and it had been her good fortune that he hadn't thought of maternity hospitals and going into labour.

She was lucky then, but determined also, going on the run again so soon after giving birth. And the *kaffir* disguise plus the use of the car ferry had been good planning. He wondered had they been her own ideas or whether Walker was the one masterminding it all? Well he would know soon enough if he caught up with her in the zoo. The bitch had led him a merry dance, but she would tell him everything he wanted to know when she realised that he was going to kill her baby. He might kill the brat anyway if Adams caused him any more problems – just to see her anguish. And then it would be turpentine time . . .

But only if he got to the zoo in time, he reminded himself as he sprinted across Gardiner Street and down the incline to the Irish Life car park. He reached the van and quickly unlocked the door, then he jumped in, started the engine, and with a squeal of tyres made for the exit.

"How many of the approach roads has Superintendent O'Reilly covered, Chief?" asked Penny.

"All the major ones," he said.

"Still leaves ways in and out then . . ."

Thompson nodded. "Big city, Penny. Impossible to seal every highway and byway."

"I know, Chief. Sorry – just fretting . . ."

They were observing the crowds at Heuston, the departure point for rail services to the south and west of Ireland, and with the passing hours Penny was finding it increasingly difficult to remain optimistic.

"She has a day-old infant," said Thompson. "Unless she's a very unusual woman she won't want to be parted from the child – and hiding a day-old baby's not easy.

"True."

"We've made all the right moves, Penny," said Thompson. "What we need now is a break."

"Fingers crossed then," replied Penny, trying for a smile. "Fingers crossed . . ."

Visser waited impatiently as a family with young children paid for their entry to the zoo, the children slowing things down by questioning their father regarding the thatched roof on the entrance kiosk. Visser felt like screaming at them but he repressed his anger and waited until they had passed through, then he immediately proffered the exact fee and passed quickly into the zoo.

He wanted desperately for the taxi-driver to have been correct in his identification of Adams, and although the man had said he was certain, there was still the worry that his desire for the reward might have coloured his judgement. Assuming it was Adams, however, it was equally important that she would still be in the zoo, to lose her again by arriving a few minutes late would be unbearable.

Visser knew though that he had responded as swiftly as was possible; and now he was wearing dark glasses and a baseball cap pulled down over his forehead – perfectly natural-looking on a bright summer's day – but difficult to see beyond in describing him should any questions be asked later about Adams going missing.

He saw a stand on his left containing complimentary maps of the zoo and he stopped for a moment and studied one. Better to take minute or two now and be systematic in his search, he reckoned, than to rush about willy-nilly. He realised from the map that the only exit from the zoo was via the thatched kiosk through which he had just passed. Good, he thought, he would work his way methodically through the grounds checking frequently to ensure that Adams didn't flank him and get to the exit. He studied the map for another moment, then set off briskly along the main entrance path.

Mary watched the chimpanzee breastfeeding its baby and she experienced a welling up of emotion, moved by the maternal solicitude of the mother and struck by the degree to which her tender behaviour and sad-eyed appearance were human-like. Aglow with the wonder of motherhood herself, she felt a certain kindred feeling with this gentle creature feeding her young, and with the kindred feeling was a mild sense of shame, a sense that it wasn't right to cage these beautiful and clearly intelligent animals for human entertainment.

The juxtaposition of motherhood and captivity brought to mind again the peril of her own situation, but she tried hard to dismiss the notion from her mind. She had to stay positive, she knew, she had to stay strong mentally as well as physically if she were to elude her pursuers.

She looked down at Fiona, fast asleep and blissfully unaware of the troubled world into which she had been born, and she steeled her resolve. She *would* come through this, no matter what. Her spirits rising again, she turned away from the chimpanzees and looked out across the lake. The waters sparkled in the bright May sunshine, and she shielded her eyes against the sun, taking in the pathway skirting the opposite shore of the lake and behind it the llamas, grazing contentedly in their enclosure.

She looked along the shoreline, then suddenly

started. A hand had tapped her shoulder, and spinning around, she saw before her a smiling man wearing dark glasses and a baseball cap. For a second she was confused, then she felt her stomach tightening in terror as she recognised her assailant from the workshop.

"If it's not the lovely Mary Adams," he said, moving in closely, and, still smiling, slipping his arm around her shoulder.

Deep in the woods, Dave sat with his back against a tree, restless and nervous despite the beauty and solitude of his surroundings. The woodland glade was dappled with sunshine, and the air was full of birdsong, but he was too caught up in all that had happened to appreciate the setting.

He had bought food in a supermarket on the outskirts of Romanshorn, and his lunch was spread before him now – a picnic seeming a plausible explanation for his presence should anyone come across him in the woods – but he found that he had no appetite whatsoever.

Despite his being well off the beaten track he was fearful that Carrow and Mathieson might have persuaded the Swiss police to comb the countryside for him. He found it hard to gauge how likely it was that the Swiss would engage in that much effort, but it did at least seem possible, and the passivity of having to stay put until nightfall heightened his fears of the net closing upon him.

He attempted to put it from his mind and thought

instead of Mary, and where she might be at this stage of her journey to Ballyard. Assuming all had gone well – and he had refused to allow himself the despair-inducing thought of things not going well – she should be getting close to the Beara Peninsula around now.

He imagined her safe and secure in the rambling old farmhouse with Tom and Jenny, and he experienced an intense longing to be there with her. He fought against the sense of isolation that rose within him, but he couldn't shake the despondent feeling of being alone, and hunted, and a long way from home.

For a moment he felt the despair overwhelm him, then he gritted his teeth and pounded the grassy bank with his fist. To hell with self-pity, he thought. He was in battle with those arraigned against him, and if he wanted to win he had to be stronger.

He remembered a conversation he had once had with his father, who had flown with the RAF during the Korean War.

His father had been a good-humoured, outgoing man who rarely talked of his war-time experiences, always playing down the romantic association others attributed to being a fighter pilot, but once, on being pressed by Dave, he had spoken about being shot down behind enemy lines.

When Dave had asked what enabled him to evade capture and to make his way back, his father had answered in one word. Determination. He had said it without any sense of boasting, explaining that the will to continue despite fear, despite hunger, despite cold and exhaustion, *that* was the difference between capture and escape. He explained that he had sworn he would get back to see again Dave's mother, his family and his friends, and he said something else that had lodged in Dave's memory. "Survivors live in the here and now."

When Dave had asked him what he meant he had said that although it was a desire to get back to his unit and ultimately his loved ones that had kept him going, while actually being hunted on the ground by the North Koreans he had lived on a minute-by-minute basis, shutting out all thought of family, friends, or colleagues.

Dave had been intrigued as his father explained that it was vital to accept that in such circumstances you were on your own, no one else could help you, and thoughts about friends and loved ones only acted as a distraction. So to survive, you accepted that the only reality was the moment being lived, the river to be swum, the patrol to be avoided. It was about putting wishful thoughts regarding those you loved out of your head, the better to be able eventually to get back to those very people.

His father had never again spoken with such candour about his war experiences, but the conversation had made a deep impression on Dave. He recognised now the similarities between his own position and what his father had faced, and he determined that he also would be a survivor, he too would block out all thoughts of Mary and his unborn baby if that was what was needed ultimately to rejoin them.

445

People had always told him as a kid that he was like his father – well, now was the time to prove it. His resolve renewed, he looked at the picnic, decided that he would need all the energy and strength he could muster, and despite his lack of appetite, he reached for the food and began eating with determination.

"Don't scream or I'll kill the baby!"

The zoo was full of people, and Mary wanted to cry for help, but she forced herself not to, terrified that Fiona would be harmed. The truly frightening thing was that this man who had introduced himself so smarmily as Thomas Franklin yesterday morning had remained smiling as he made the threat, and Mary knew from his behaviour in the workshop that nothing would be too evil for him to contemplate.

He drew nearer, kissing her on the cheek as though in greeting, and she was struck by the smell of aftershave mixed with sweat. She went to recoil, but Franklin's grip bit into her shoulder.

"Smile as though you're greeting me," he said. *"Smile."*

Mary tried for a smile, forcing her jaw muscles.

"Now look down," he said, the phoney grin still on his face.

Mary did as she was told and saw a flash of reflected sunlight as Franklin twisted a metal object in his hand.

"Stiletto; razor sharp," he said. "Give me the *slightest* trouble, and I'll pierce the baby's heart."

"Please . . ."

"Look in my eyes. Look in my eyes!" he demanded, the venom in his voice bizarrely contrasting with the smile he still managed to maintain for the benefit of passers-by.

Mary swallowed hard, then forced herself to look into his eyes, from which he had lifted the dark glasses. The watery blue eyes were as cold as ever, but they were bloodshot now, and it chilled Mary further to think that he had probably been up all night hunting her.

He stared at her, their faces close together, and for the first time he allowed his smile to vanish.

"If you so much as blink the wrong way, your brat will be dead ten seconds later. Understand?"

The intensity of his gaze was overpowering and Mary felt instinctively that he meant every word he said.

"Understand?" he insisted.

"Yes. Yes," she nodded, unable to endure eye contact any longer.

"Good," said Franklin, slipping on the glasses again, and with them his smile. "Now we're going to take a stroll, arm in arm. If anything you do – *anything* – gives an impression that we're other than a family out for the day, I promise you the baby dies. Got that?"

"Yes . . ." Mary managed, her breathing shallow and her heart pounding uncontrollably.

"Good," said Franklin, his arm still draped about her shoulder. "Now take the brake off the buggy, put a contented mother's look on your face, and stroll with me."

447

Mary reached out her foot, disengaged the brake, then turned to Franklin.

"Look happy," he warned.

She tried for a smile despite her terror. "Which way?" she asked.

"Oh I think towards the exit," he responded mockingly. "Let's go . . ."

The van jolted, hitting another pothole, and despite trying to brace herself, Mary's knee banged against the floor of the vehicle. She reckoned that they must be travelling on little- used back-roads past the outskirts of the city but, locked in the darkened rear of the van, which had no windows, she couldn't tell what direction they had taken.

On leaving the zoo they had walked to the parked van, then at Franklin's command they had entered the rear of the vehicle, Franklin closing over the door after him. He had handcuffed Mary, forcing her hands behind her back and looping the connecting chain of the cuffs through a bracket in the floor, then he had ordered her to lie down. Despite her pleas he had taken Fiona from her, his "guarantee of good behaviour" as he had smilingly explained. He had covered Mary with a blanket, then exited from the rear of the van, taking the sleeping baby into the front seat in her detachable carrycot.

Mary had found the claustrophobia of being manacled under the blanket to be unbearable and had kicked off the covering as soon as he had started the engine, but she knew better than to cry for help or draw attention to the vehicle in any way. She had no doubt but that this man would carry out his threat to Fiona, yet she knew too that if she did nothing the final outcome at his hands would also be appalling.

The horror of Franklin having her defenceless baby at his mercy and her terror of what lay ahead for herself had paralysed her into a despair such as she had never known before, but after a while she had regained some of her composure and forced herself to think. The reality was that she hadn't got the information that this man wanted; but he hadn't believed her when she had told the truth in the workshop, and he wasn't going to believe her now either. The option of telling him what he wanted to know – even had she been prepared to endanger Dave by doing so – simply didn't exist. Instead she had to take some course of action and lying here petrified with fear wasn't going to help.

She looked about the gloomy interior of the van, wondering if there might be a screwdriver or some other tool lying about with which to try to prise the chain of her handcuffs from the retaining bracket, or, failing that, that she might be able to hide, for use as a weapon. *And then what?* Even supposing she were to surprise Visser when he came to release her, would she really be able to stab someone with a screwdriver? Yes! she told herself. *She would have to*. He was threatening her baby's life. She couldn't afford reservations. She couldn't think or act like a victim.

She felt around the van's interior as best she could with her hands, but nothing lay on the floor within the radius that the handcuff chain allowed her. She tried to think clearly of what her impressions had been when she had first entered the van. She had seen the blanket on the floor, there had been a faint smell of turpentine, there had been a wicker picnic basket at the far wall. A picnic basket . . . a picnic basket might contain a knife, she thought. And if she stretched out her leg fully she might be able to drag the basket within reach.

She probed with her right leg, the handcuffs biting into her wrists as she leaned forward as far as possible. Just then the van hit another pothole and the jolt sent a wave of pain up her strained arms. She braced herself for further jolts, then the van slowed and veered around a corner. She stretched out her foot again and was rewarded by contact with a solid object. It had to be the basket, she told herself, there had been no other large object evident when they had entered the van.

She stretched again, grimacing as the cuffs bit into her wrists, but while she made contact with the basket she couldn't hook her leg around it to pull it towards her. She paused a moment, realising that no matter how much she strained she wouldn't get her leg further around the basket. Supposing she pushed it to the left with her right foot, then to the right with her left foot? That way she might be able to work it gradually towards herself. *Provided she didn't kick it out of her reach. And provided Franklin didn't reach his destination while she was doing so.* She gave a tentative push with her foot to see if the basket would move readily, but it was heavier than she expected and only moved slightly. She pushed again and the picnic basket shifted slightly. OK, she thought, this was going to take time, and there might be nothing useful in the basket, but it was all she could think of.

She shifted position, stretched out her left leg this time, and tried to inch the basket forward . . .

Visser's eyes darted from the road to the surrounding countryside, all the while seeking out the right kind of location. He had been driving along the back-roads north-west of the city, but much of the land here was given over to stud-farms whose open pastures didn't provide the combination of cover and remoteness that he wanted for his interrogation of Mary Adams.

He wished he could have had the luxury of a prolonged interrogation, such as he had had in the dockland warehouse with Aksor, but there had been no time to make such arrangements since his arrival in Dublin the previous afternoon. He had been on the go virtually non-stop ever since, as evidenced by an encroaching wave of tiredness, with last night's upper wearing off. He would take another pill when he was finished with Adams, he decided. That would help him to concentrate while orchestrating his next moves.

He knew he would have to get answers from her quickly, but using the baby would loosen her tongue. Then he could call Reinholdt, whose frustration at not having been contacted would be offset by the information gained from Adams. Knowing the American, there would be protests over killing Adams, but it would be a *fait accompli*. He would claim that he had no choice, and the CIA, not wanting any publicity, would accept the situation and pay up – especially if the information from the Irishwoman led to Walker's capture, as it should.

Although he would never admit it to the CIA man, Visser knew that his animosity to Adams had gone beyond a professional level. It was a combination of her blinding him with the turpentine and making him feel foolish by her escape, compounded by causing him difficulties with Reinholdt, that made him react to her on a personal level, something he rarely allowed to happen. Certainly on most assignments he wouldn't have adopted as visible a profile as he had in Dublin, but he had been desperate not to allow her to escape again. Besides, he could always disappear back to the Far East if he were linked to Adams and there was any heat.

In any event he wasn't planning for Adams' body to be found when he had finished with her. A shallow grave in a remote spot and it could be years before the remains were discovered, if they were ever discovered. He had come prepared, packing a folding shovel in the picnic basket along with a paint-can full of turpentine. He knew that the stiletto would be a quicker and cleaner way to end things, but there would be a poetic justice in dousing this troublesome bitch and letting her blaze.

He came now to a T-junction and paused a moment, then turned left, figuring that would take him west, and deeper into the countryside. He drove along, gratified to notice that there was less habitation around here.

What he wanted was a thick copse of trees well removed from the road and any farm buildings, and although so far there were still occasional farms along this route he was pleased that he seemed to be moving into a sparsely populated stretch of countryside.

In the distance he saw the road ascending towards what looked like a stone bridge, its sides partly covered in a thick coating of creepers. He slowed down as he approached, then realised on looking over the bridge that an abandoned railway line ran below it. The old track bed was heavily overgrown and it stretched across the expanse of surrounding countryside like a long pointing finger of green. *Perfect*, he thought.

He drew ahead off the crown of the bridge and pulled in to the right where a gate led into a large field that the track bed traversed. There was no traffic anywhere in sight or within hearing, but nevertheless he wanted to get to the shelter of the railway line quickly and unseen. He turned off the engine, picked up the sleeping baby in her carry-cot, then got out and made his way towards the rear door of the van.

Mary heard Franklin's footsteps approaching, and her heart began thumping alarmingly. She tried to calm herself, but the fear he engendered couldn't be overcome by act of will alone. Any second now he was going to open the rear of the van, and she was still helpless, still handcuffed to the floor. Despite all her efforts she had been unable to work the picnic basket over as far as her hands, and so she now quietly pushed the basket as far away as possible with her right foot, not wanting her captor to know that she was thinking of resistance. Much better to let him believe she was in terror of him to the point of paralysis, a role that wouldn't be difficult in view of how frightening he genuinely was.

The rear door was suddenly pulled open and Mary blinked as the van was flooded with sunlight. Franklin placed the carrycot on the floor of the vehicle, and Mary was relieved to see that Fiona was still sleeping soundly. The picnic basket lay about halfway between Mary and the far wall, but Franklin seemed not to notice its being shifted by a couple of feet and instead he approached Mary. She drew back instinctively, then he was on his hunkers beside her, the whiff of aftershave and sweat again hitting her nostrils.

"Turn around," he ordered, taking a key from his pocket.

Mary did as instructed, and he reached down, unlocking and removing her handcuffs. "Take the baby and get over to the gate – quickly."

Mary got to her feet and took up Fiona's carrycot, glad to have possession of her baby again.

"Move it," said Franklin.

Mary stepped out of the van and looked around. They were in an isolated stretch of countryside with no houses to be seen, and she wondered what had made Franklin stop at this particular spot.

"Put the baby down at the gate and climb over," he ordered, closing the van door with one hand and carrying the picnic basket in the other.

Mary hesitated, fearful of being separated again from the baby, and Franklin quickly approached and without breaking stride smacked her face with the back of his hand. Mary staggered, almost dropping the carrycot. Then he gripped her arm, his bloodshot eyes only inches from hers.

"Do *what* I say *when* I say. Right?"

Mary's face stung, and the combination of shock and pain was such that she could only nod her understanding.

"Get over the gate. I'll hand the child to you," he snapped, and Mary obeyed him immediately this time, scaling the five-bar gate despite still being sore from childbirth. As soon as she was safely on the other side Franklin handed Fiona over to her, then he quickly climbed the gate himself and jumped down beside her. "Let's go," he said, making for a thick corridor of trees and shrubbery that cut through the broad field and stretched away into the distance.

Her mind racing, Mary took in her surroundings as they walked, and she tried to figure out exactly where Franklin was taking them. She saw a weathered stone bridge and reasoned that the straight line of greenery must be the former track-bed of an old railway line. They reached the thick shrubbery, then Franklin instructed her to walk parallel to the heavily wooded track bed. Mary did as instructed, risking a glance back towards the road, but there was no traffic, and it was clear that Franklin had chosen an out-of-the-way location.

There was no escaping the logic of it, and she found herself wanting to be sick as the reality hit home. He had been interrupted during his questioning of her in Harrogate, and this time he was taking her someplace where he *wouldn't* be interrupted. The thought was terrifying, the more so because even when she had told him the truth in her workshop he had refused to believe her. She tried to think of how she might convince him, tried to think of some telling detail she might add to make her story believable. The problem had been his assumption that Dave had acted for some group or agency, and how could she give him information about such people when they didn't exist?

They plodded across the field, her head spinning as she tried to find some way out of her dilemma, then Franklin stopped.

"OK, this will do," he said.

Mary looked about, but there was no farmhouse in sight, no habitation at which they had arrived. She looked back and saw that they were several hundred yards from the road, then Franklin's hand was on her shoulder.

"In there," he said, pushing her towards the densely wooded track bed.

She did as instructed, moving with difficulty into the middle of the trees and bushes. It had obviously been many years since the railway line had closed, for the trees and shrubs were mature and quite closely packed, providing an oasis of coolness and shade after the heat of the open field.

They picked their way along a portion of the track bed, then reaching the edge of a small glade, Franklin ordered a halt. "Nice and private, isn't it?" he said with his creepy smile, indicating the surrounding foliage that completely shielded them from view. "Put down the baby and have a seat. You must be tired," he said with mock solicitude.

Mary didn't answer, realising that Franklin hadn't been heading to a pre-arranged location but had simply wanted somewhere isolated. Someplace where she couldn't be heard – where there would be no point screaming. The thought sent a shiver up her spine, and she swallowed hard, trying to keep her sense of panic at bay.

"I said put the baby down and take a seat," said Franklin, his voice suddenly hard and cold.

Mary looked around, then sat with her back against a tree at the opposite side of the small glade, carefully placing Fiona's carrycot on the ground beside her.

Franklin sat about eight feet away, also leaning against a tree trunk. He had been carrying the picnic basket in his right hand and the van keys in his left, and he laid them both on the ground, then took off his dark glasses. "I want to be able to see your face" he explained, "when I show you our picnic," he added, undoing the hinges on the basket.

Mary knew from his mocking tone that something awful lay within the basket, and remembering his instruments of torture from the workshop, she felt her skin crawl. She knew that Franklin was enjoying this and she tried not to respond as he watched her face while taking the first item from the basket.

"Folding shovel," he said, laying it on the ground. "For digging a grave – your grave. I doubt if it will ever be found . . ."

Mary felt her blood run cold. It was one thing to fear the worst, but to have it actually confirmed . . .

"And here's one you'll like," said Franklin, taking out a large sealed can.

Mary frowned, then Franklin removed the lid.

"Recognise the smell – it's your old favourite, turpentine! And finally . . ." he said, slipping his left hand into the pocket of his trousers, "cigarette lighter . . ."

Mary stared at him, her mouth dry and her breathing becoming shallower.

"Though I suppose the correct sequence would actually be turpentine, lighter, and then shallow grave . . ."

"No!" cried Mary.

"Oh, yes," said Franklin. "You've led me a merry dance. And troublesome fucking bitches who do that pay dearly."

"I've done nothing to you. I just . . ."

"You've done nothing to me? You blind me with turpentine. You lock me in your workshop. You cause me endless trouble . . ."

"I just wanted to get away. I'm sorry if . . ."

"You're sorry?" Franklin laughed harshly. "You've no idea what sorry is. But you will have when I'm finished. Just count yourself lucky I haven't as much time to work on you as I'd like."

"Please, I don't want . . ."

"Shut your stupid fucking mouth. You'll talk when I tell you! Now here's the deal. You're going to die anyway, but if you tell me everything, I won't kill the baby too."

Mary lowered her head, and despite herself she began to sob.

"Stop the snivelling and answer the questions if you want to save your brat!"

Mary swallowed hard and forced herself to look up.

"Where is the rendezvous with your husband?"

Mary hesitated, then seeing the flash of anger in Franklin's eyes, she answered quickly. "Ballyard."

"Where's that?"

"A – a village on the Beara Peninsula." She felt sick at betraying Dave but she had to give Fiona a chance to live. Dave would understand, she thought. Dave would *want* her to tell.

"Why Ballyard?"

"My – my brother has a house there."

"Who did your husband take the film for?"

"No one. This was all an accident, I swear it. I swear it on my mother's grave!"

Franklin breathed out and shook his head sorrowfully.

Mary knew she had to come up with something, and her mind raced as she tried to think how to find a way to satisfy her captor. "If I knew – if I knew where you were coming from on this," she said, trying not to babble. "If you could tell me who you represent, I'm sure we could prove our innocence."

Franklin rose and crossed the glade, then crouched beside her. "*You* want to know who *I* represent?"

"Yes, I'm sure we could convince . . ." Mary was stopped in mid- sentence by a stinging blow to the face.

"I ask the questions, bitch!" said Franklin. "Now for the last time, who was your husband working for?"

"Please, oh Jesus, you must believe me. He's an

459

advertising man. He just went to school with Nigel Gatenby, that's all . . ."

Franklin produced the stiletto and Mary screamed as he swiftly buried it inside the carry-cot.

"No use screaming. You won't be heard," said Franklin.

Mary looked with horror into the cot, then realised that the knife was embedded in the side wall. Fiona whimpered, then turned in her sleep, and Franklin withdrew the gleaming weapon and showed it to Mary.

"I'm going to start carving your brat into pieces."

"No!"

"Yes! And once I start there's no stopping. I'll kill her even when you tell me everything."

"No! Jesus, no! She's just a baby!

"She'll be a *fillet* when I'm finished! So, last chance. I'll ask you one more time, then I start carving her up. Only you can stop it."

Mary felt paralysed with horror, her stomach sick, but something in the words Franklin said struck home. *Only she could stop it.* She looked into his bloodshot eyes and her fear combined with a surge of fury, a sense of outrage that this filthy creature would harm her defenceless baby. He was right. She *had* to stop it, and before she knew what she was doing she screamed at the top of her voice, a scream in part of anguish, but more so a scream of anger; a piercing scream of primal fury. She saw Franklin starting back instinctively, his eyes widening in surprise, and she remembered something she had once read in a self-defence manual.

While Franklin was still thrown she jabbed her thumbs into his eyes, pushing as hard as she could.

This time it was Franklin who screamed as he stumbled backwards, clutching his eyes. Mary clambered to her feet and made for the far side of the clearing and Franklin careered blindly after her, tripping over the empty picnic basket. Mary stooped down and in one quick movement grabbed the opened tin of turpentine and threw the contents into Franklin's face. He roared again, flailing blindly at her but missing, and she emptied the rest of the turpentine over him.

Even in his pain he must have realised what she intended, for he drove screamingly towards where he had left down the cigarette lighter.

Mary got there first and fell to her knees, grabbing for the lighter. Franklin's lunge knocked her off balance however, and she fell to the ground under the momentum of his assault. She reached out desperately with her right hand and felt it closing on the metal lighter. She swung about, flicking on the flint as she did so, and Franklin screamed, with a cry almost as primal as her own of a moment before.

He flung himself backwards, recognising the sound of the lighter being struck. He landed back on the turpentine-soaked ground but the flash of flames that he had tried to avoid never came.

Mary looked at the lighter in horror. It hadn't ignited. She could see Franklin rubbing his eyes as he lay on the ground. He was thoroughly doused in turpentine, but if she couldn't get the lighter to work her only achievement would have been to infuriate him.

She saw Franklin beginning to get up and she moved quickly to place herself in the centre of the clearing, blocking Franklin's route to Fiona. She held the lighter out from her, her hand trembling, and flicked it again. The lighter continued to shake in her hand, but this time a strong flame was emitted.

"No!" screamed Franklin, his eyesight obviously recovered enough to recognise his peril. "No!" he cried, drawing back. "No!"

Mary saw the fear in his eyes.

"Don't!" he cried. "Don't!"

"You bastard!" she screamed.

"I wasn't really going to kill you! It was only to scare you into talking!"

"No!" she screamed. "No!"

"I *swear!* It was just interrogation technique!"

"No, not another word!"

"OK! OK!"

"Stand up," said Mary. "Stand up!"

He rose tentatively, his eyes wide with fear.

Mary could see the terror in his face and she found herself savouring it.

"I wasn't really going to harm you or the baby," he said.

"Liar! One more word and you're in flames!" She looked into his eyes, and something primitive within her said use the lighter, rid the world of this evil creature. She remembered what he had said in the workshop. *Pregnant women always talked when he started on the foetus.* And just now he had said he would make a fillet of Fiona. Anyone who could be so evil, who would abuse a baby – who would abuse *her* baby – didn't deserve to live.

She stood staring at him, the flame strong and unwavering from the lighter, neither of them moving. Time seemed to stand still, and she felt removed from what was about to happen. She stared into his frightened eyes, gripped the lighter even tighter and steeled herself to do it. She hesitated for an instant and then, somehow, the moment passed. She realised that she couldn't kill him in cold blood, couldn't just set fire to another human being, even one as hideous as this one.

She let the lighter flick closed but remained staring at Franklin. She wasn't sure how long she stared wildly at him but after a while she became aware that he was now returning her stare.

As if aware of her inability to kill him in cold blood, he moved a little towards her, holding out his hands in appeasement.

"Don't move!" said Mary, placing her thumb again on the striking mechanism.

"Take it easy," he said. "We can talk this out."

"I said don't move!"

"OK, OK. Just take it easy."

He was looking at her appraisingly and Mary realised that his tone had become more confident.

"Look there's no point in making this more unpleasant than it has to be," Franklin said reasonably, then he started to lower his hands.

"Keep them up!"

He partly raised his hands again. "I'm not going to harm you . . ."

"Damn right you're not!"

"And I never really was. And neither, I think, are you going to harm me."

"Don't bet on it!"

"Look, let's just . . ."

"Don't come any closer!" Mary cried as he advanced slightly.

"Put the lighter down and let's talk," he said.

"Don't make me do it," said Mary, her voice quivering as she realised that she wasn't sure if she could really set him ablaze.

"I don't think you're that kind of person, Mary . . ."

"Stay where you are!"

"You're *not* that kind of person."

She reckoned that another couple of steps would put him in range to grab the lighter. "Stay where you are!" she roared, but he came forward slowly. Although her hand was wet with perspiration she could feel the striking mechanism beneath her thumb, but the moral values of a lifetime prevented her from pressing it, and instead she stepped back, keeping out of reach. "I warned you," she cried. "I don't want to do it. Don't force me!"

"Put down the lighter and let's talk," said Franklin, moving towards her.

"I'll do it!" cried Mary, backing away, yet aware that she mustn't allow him within grabbing distance of Fiona. "I'll do it!" she cried again.

"No . . ." he said, then smiled. He moved steadily closer, then lunged at her.

It was the smile that did it. She flicked the lighter on and jumped sideways just as he grabbed for her wrist. There was a searing flash, and Franklin screamed as he was engulfed in flames. Mary stumbled back in horror as he collapsed howling onto the ground, frantically flailing at himself as the flames took hold. A sickening smell of burning flesh filled the air, and Mary turned away as his skin, clothes and hair burned ferociously. She ran to Fiona and knelt trembling by the carrycot, her head in her hands, then, after what seemed like an eternity, the screaming stopped. She rose gingerly and looked at the dead but still burning body. Revolted, she grabbed the keys to the van from the ground, took up the carrycot, and rushed to get away, stunned by the enormity of what she had done.

"Cheer up, Penny. Might never happen," said Thompson as he approached from the bar with the drinks and sandwiches that constituted their delayed lunch.

The pub wasn't busy early on a Saturday afternoon and they had found a quiet corner where they could talk without being overheard.

Penny smiled and took the food and drink. "Thanks, Chief. This looks good."

"If you wouldn't get a nice pint of Guinness in Dublin, where would you, eh? Cheers."

"Cheers."

They both drank, then Thompson sat back and looked at her. "You think we've lost Adams, don't you?"

Penny grimaced. "It's a quarter to three now. The

road-blocks have been in place, the stations watched . . ."

"She mightn't be making her move till tonight."

"Why would she hang about all day?"

"Who knows? But remember, Penny, sometimes simply waiting is a crucial part of police work."

"Don't misunderstand me, Chief. I'm worried she may have escaped, but I know the value of patience."

"Not everyone does."

"I suppose it depends on your nature. Like . . . my father or my brothers would be hopeless policemen. Dad and Keith are engineers. Paul's a draughtsman. They're used to seeing results for their labour. They'd never cope with police work where you can't measure achievement."

"You've obviously given a lot of thought to your career."

"Yes, it means a lot to me."

Thompson drank from his pint, then leaned back. "What made you want to be a police officer?"

Penny thought, then smiled wryly. "This probably sounds really sanctimonious, but I'd say a passion for justice. And there aren't many jobs where you get to right wrongs – and actually get paid for your efforts."

"Righting wrongs, is that how you see police work?" asked Thompson.

"Well, at its most basic, yes. I mean you're a traffic warden, first aider, amateur psychologist, all sorts of things . . ."

"Too bloody true," said Thompson with a smile.

"But basically you're there to protect the citizen and prevent crime."

Thompson nodded. "Aye. Tall order nowadays."

"I'd say it always was. Life's always been unfair; a lot of crime stems from social conditions."

"Doesn't justify it, Penny. Don't make that mistake."

"No, it doesn't justify it, but I think if you better understand the criminal's background, you can better understand the thinking behind a crime; then you've a chance to prevent it or solve it." She smiled suddenly. "Sounds good in theory; in practice your quarry's likely to be as resourceful as Mary Adams."

Thompson looked at her. "You half-admire her, don't you?"

Penny hesitated. "I suppose . . . yes, I suppose part of me admires her style, her guts in going through childbirth alone while on the run. I daresay I shouldn't . . ."

"No, it's understandable," interjected Thompson. "In spite of the dance she's led us, I find myself feeling the same way. But let me give you a bit of advice, Penny. Whether you're sympathetic to someone's plight, or appalled by what they did, don't become judge and jury. Our job is to catch them. Let others decide how right or wrong their behaviour was. OK?"

"Fair enough."

"Right, lecture over," said Thompson with a grin. "Let's enjoy our lunch – and hope Ms Adams makes her move soon."

Penny raised her glass. "I'll drink to that."

Mary sat tensely behind the wheel of the van, trying to concentrate on the road as she negotiated the busy city streets. Her thoughts had been a jumble since she had fled the abandoned railway line, and she had driven in a daze along the back-roads of the Dublin/Meath border, eventually finding her way back into the city via the Phoenix Park.

The horror of what had happened with the man who called himself Franklin had made analytical thinking really difficult but she had realised that whoever he was, he wasn't Thomas Franklin. In the van she had found a pouch containing a Canadian Driver's Licence in the name of James Wilson, along with a copy of a rental agreement for the van. Whoever he had been, he had clearly used aliases to protect his real identity, and despite her agitated condition Mary had realised that such a person would have a professional background, though whether in espionage, or terrorism, or straight-forward crime she couldn't tell. It seemed likely though that he might be working for those for whom Nigel Gatenby had stolen the microfilm.

The priority now, she knew, would be to lie low until her rendezvous with Tom, ensuring that the trail linking her to Franklin – or whatever his real name was – would be untraceable.

She tried to think coherently as she drove along, and in spite of the residue of terror and disgust that remained with her from earlier, she had reasoned that it was most unlikely that Franklin's body would be found in such a remote spot as the impassable railway line. And even if it were found the remains would be charred beyond recognition. Also if Franklin were as professional as he appeared to be, then she reckoned he probably wouldn't carry any identification on his person – unlikely as it was that any ID might have survived the conflagration.

No one had been about when she had entered the field with Franklin; no one had been about when she had run, distraught, back to the van. There was nothing linking her to the death. The one place her fingerprints might have been found was on the can used for the turpentine, but it too had gone up in flames and would now be no more than a burnt and shrivelled piece of tin.

Thinking of it all again caused Mary's stomach to become queasy, and she gripped the steering wheel more tightly, trying to shut out the horrific images. She would have to concentrate on the present, she knew, have to gather herself so as not to make any mistakes that might bring her to the attention of the authorities. She would make sure to wipe the steering wheel and door handles when leaving the van. She would also wipe the floor in the back of the vehicle lest there be any prints where she had been handcuffed. She would separately dump Franklin's wallet and the spare clothes he had kept in the van . . .

Suddenly her train of thought ground to a halt. The slow-moving traffic had become slower still as she had driven outbound along Amiens Street, and now she could see why. Up ahead was a checkpoint, manned by uniformed police officers. *Oh Jesus, no*, she thought, *not now . . .*

Don't panic, she told herself. They could simply be checking for road tax and insurance. *Or they could be looking specifically for me.* Her heart pounding, she looked about to see if there was any way of escaping.

Turning about against the busy flow of traffic was out of the question, but a few yards ahead on her left was a lane. The checkpoint was about fifty yards ahead, and she considered the possibility of turning the van into the lane when she drew level with it. If the Guards on the checkpoint saw her doing so however it might well result in the alarm being raised. On the other hand if she drove ahead to brazen it out she might be delivering herself into the hand of her pursuers.

The cars in front moved forward, and Mary found herself opposite the lane. She hesitated, undecided, then she realised that she couldn't bear to offer herself up meekly if they were after her. Without pausing any further she turned left, not using her indicators lest they catch the eye of one of the Guards on the checkpoint. She resisted the temptation of looking down the road to see if she had been spotted, instead she turned at a moderate speed as though the lane were her actual destination. Once in the lane and out of sight of the checkpoint she immediately accelerated. The lane curved to the right, and she drove speedily along until it linked up with another major thoroughfare, then she pulled out, turning left, and immersed herself in the busy Saturday-afternoon traffic.

She kept glancing at the rear-view mirror, fearful of seeing the flashing blue lights of a Garda car in pursuit, but none materialised, and she took the first right turn she encountered, anxious to leave the area as quickly as she could.

She would have to get rid of the van as soon as possible, she knew, and considering it now, she realised that she should have done so as soon as she had reached the city centre. In her state of shock after the encounter with Franklin she hadn't been thinking clearly enough, for despite her resolve to break any link joining her to Franklin she had remained in the van, the most tangible link of all. Her original notion had been to abandon the vehicle en route to her rendezvous with Tom but now she had a better idea. The address of the leasing company would be on the agreement form that she had found, so she would discreetly abandon the van within a few yards of their premises and leave the key in the glove compartment. That would minimise the likelihood of fuss about Franklin not returning the vehicle, a far better scenario than police enquiries regarding Franklin were the van reported as missing.

Driving in a loop back towards the city centre, she reached under the carrycot propped next to her in the driver's compartment and found the copy of the rental agreement. She slowed to a halt at a red traffic-light and looked in the rear-view mirror while braking, to make sure there was still no Garda pursuit. Satisfied that there was none, she studied the address on the rental form. It was on the opposite side of the river but not too far away, and she knew Dublin well enough to get there. She thought about the route she would take and what she might do after leaving the van. As she was doing so the light turned to green and she pocketed the rental docket, let off the handbrake, and accelerated back towards the city centre.

36

Carrow pushed aside the coffee cup and drummed his fingers on the table. The dipping sun was beginning to turn golden, but he had no eyes for the beauty of the summer night. He had just finished dinner with Mathieson in a sidewalk cafe near the police station in Rorschach and was feeling totally frustrated at the lack of progress in finding Walker.

"What the hell is that all about?" he said as a cheer came from the interior of the café.

"Lively game of *Jass*," replied Mathieson, looking back into the bar.

"*Jass?*"

"Local game, played with thirty-six cards . . ."

Carrow breathed out exasperatedly. How did Mathieson always seem to know these things? *Jass, Schwingen, faultless French* . . . and always displayed with effortless urbanity, he thought irritably.

"They use four different colours," Mathieson started to explain.

472

"All right, I'm not planning on taking it up!" snapped Carrow.

The intelligence officer remained unruffled. "You did ask, old man . . ."

"Sorry. Sorry, Colin, I'm just pissed off. We've been here seven hours, the Swiss police are running round in circles, and we're still no nearer to catching Walker."

"Hell of a lot of boats and ferries to check," said Mathieson.

"I know, but they've scoured the town and combed the waterfronts. Where's the bastard gone?"

Mathieson shrugged. "I'd nearly say that buying the ticket to Rorschach was a red herring, except he bought it *before* going to the bank, when he didn't know we were in Zurich."

"Exactly."

"The other thing is, he may have changed his plans. Clever chap, Walker, he may have reasoned that we'd check all ticket sellers at the stations, strike it lucky – as we did – and come after him."

"It's possible, I suppose, but – hang on, hang on!" Carrow rose to his feet as he saw Superintendent Vincenz approaching briskly. "Well?" he asked hopefully.

Vincenz shook his head. "Still questioning ferry staff and searching the ships. There's a call for you though. They're holding it at the station."

"A call?"

"From a Detective Inspector Powell in Leeds. Says it could be important."

"Right!" Carrow quickly peeled some notes from his wallet and shoved them under the bill on the table, then started up the street, followed by Mathieson and Vincenz.

"In here," said Vincenz, leading them into a large office when they reached the station. The Swiss detective issued some instructions to the policewoman on the desk, then he closed the office door and the call was routed through.

Carrow sat at a table to answer the phone, and Vincenz flicked a switch so they could all hear via wall-speakers.

"Hello, Mr Carrow?"

"Yes."

"DI Powell here, Leeds."

"You've got something on Walker?"

"I may have. I spent a while yesterday in United Advertising's office, in case Walker came back from Sheriff Hutton. To kill time I was browsing through some postcards, and something clicked with me tonight."

"What?"

"When you reported in from Lake Constance, the name rang a bell. I've been back to the United Advertising office in Leeds and I found the postcard."

"Postcard?"

"Picture of a harbour on Lake Constance, sent by Walker to his secretary."

"The harbour in Rorschach?"

"No, that's the point. It was a place called Romanshorn. Just struck me that if he was familiar with a different harbour, maybe your search was concentrated on the wrong area."

"Right, thank you very much," said Carrow. "Anything else?"

"No, I just thought the Romanshorn thing might be pertinent."

"It might indeed. Thank you again. Goodnight."

"Goodnight."

Carrow hung up and faced Vincenz.

"We've already checked the Romanshorn ferries," said the Swiss policeman, "but maybe we should search the town a bit more thoroughly. We could be there in fifteen minutes."

"Good," said Carrow, rising from the chair. "Let's do it!"

Dave's apprehension grew as he entered the streets of Romanshorn. Dusk had finally passed and the street-lamps glowed brightly against the darkened summer sky as he made his way towards the harbour.

He had stayed under cover in the woods all day, eventually relaxing when it became clear that no one was likely to discover his presence there. He had done some woodland sketching with a pencil and paper, to explain his being there should anyone pass by, and although he had seen nobody in almost nine hours, the sketching had been therapeutic.

He had dozed for a couple of hours, eaten well of the food, and finally – and to his surprise – in the quiet isolation of the woods he had experienced some of the sense of peace he often got when alone in the mountains.

There was nothing further he could do to advance his plans, he had realised, and much as he would have liked to ring Ballyard to check Mary's safe arrival, he couldn't, and so he had rested, savouring the sounds and smells of the pine-scented woods.

Now, however, it was time to find a ferry and stow away under cover of darkness. If his purchase of the ticket to Rorschach had gone undetected he reckoned it should be possible to climb onto one of the steamers, hide in some cranny, and later emerge on the German side of the lake. The problem would be if the authorities knew about his ticket to Rorschach. It wouldn't take a genius then to work out what his plan might be, in which case security would be increased in all the lakeside towns.

As if to underline how perilous his position was he turned a corner to see a police car in the distance, heading in his direction. He kept his pace a sauntering one, but immediately turned left onto another side street. He could feel himself breaking into a sweat. Then he heard the vehicle pass by the top of the street and continue on its way.

He stepped into a shop doorway and paused a moment to try to steady his nerves. The police car could be simply a coincidence, he told himself; then again perhaps it wasn't, but either way he couldn't stop here. Hands trembling slightly, he forced himself to carry on towards the harbour. Being a Saturday night there were lots of people on the streets, and he mingled gratefully with the other strollers.

He remembered the town's layout from his United

Advertising trip, and he followed the route to the waterfront and cautiously approached the area where the steamers docked. He kept close to the walls of the buildings and walked slowly along the pavement to within about eighty yards of the terminal. Then he stopped and put down his two bags in the shadow of a tree.

Earlier he had changed into a dark tee-shirt, black jeans and a baseball cap to reduce his visibility, and now he stood stock-still under the tree and scanned the area around the steamers. To his relief there was no sign of any police activity. Perhaps the patrol car was simply the local police making their presence felt on a Saturday night.

He waited a moment, pretending to be rummaging in his bag, but actually keeping a close watch on the ferry area. Everything looked normal, and he stepped out of the shadow of the tree and started forward. He had strolled about fifteen yards when he saw the parked car. It was pulled in unobtrusively across from the berthing area, and Dave felt his blood chill when he saw two men sitting unmovingly in the front seats.

He stopped immediately and stood flat against the wall. He found himself holding his breath in fear, but the men were looking towards the steamers and after a moment Dave realised that they hadn't observed him.

He flirted with the idea that they might be civilians, but something about the way the car was tucked away and their watchful demeanour convinced him otherwise. He started to back slowly away when a movement in the car caught his eye. One of the men raised something to his mouth, and staring hard, Dave realised that the man was talking into a radio.

Don't panic! he told himself. Stay absolutely still. The men hadn't looked in his direction, and he reasoned that they were probably just checking in on the radio. But there was no doubt in his mind, he had nearly walked into a police trap.

Keeping to the wall, Dave moved slowly backwards until the car was out of his line of vision, then he quickened his pace and took the first turn away from the waterfront.

He knew now what he had feared all along; they were wise to the ferry angle and he couldn't use it. He walked away smartly, aware that he had had a very near miss, and anxious to get out of Romanshorn. Moving as quickly as he dared, he left the town centre and headed for the outskirts.

Mary wished fervently that Fiona would stop crying. She had deliberately sat at the back of the bus to be as inconspicuous as possible, but now the baby's cries were drawing attention. She had cuddled the child and tried discreetly to breastfeed her, but to no avail. She probably needed a nappy-change, Mary realised, but she could hardly do that on the seat of a public bus.

It was almost ten in the evening now and Mary knew her energy was rapidly dwindling. She had been tempted to take one of the speedy DART trains to her destination of Howth, a village on a picturesque peninsula about eight miles from Dublin, but she had reasoned that the train stations might be under police surveillance and instead opted for the public bus.

Several of the bus passengers had glanced back, their looks mostly sympathetic, as Mary tried to soothe the crying child. Not much further now, she thought, as the bus rounded the corner opposite the entrance to Howth Demesne. They passed a church shielded by thick green foliage, then Mary saw ahead the squat mass of the yacht-club building at the new marina.

The bus pulled to a halt at the stop opposite Howth railway station, and Mary alighted with the other passengers, quickly opening her lightweight buggy with one hand while cradling the still-upset baby with the other.

She laid Fiona down in the buggy, picked up her carrier bag, and moved off. The baby was crying loudly now and in spite of her own exhaustion Mary pushed the buggy as fast as she could, hoping the motion might soothe the upset child.

She crossed the busy road and made for the nearby Maritime Hotel. There was no let-up in the baby's distress, and reaching the door of the Maritime, Mary manoeuvred the buggy up the steps and into the narrow foyer. The small reception desk was unmanned, and she went ahead, passing the bar on her right and the restaurant on her left as she followed the sign indicating the first-floor ladies' toilet.

She unstrapped Fiona, took her in one arm and the buggy and her carrier bag in the other, then plodded wearily up the stairs and into the toilets.

To her relief the toilets were unoccupied and, laying

the baby down beside the sink, she quickly changed her into a clean nappy and redressed her. Powdered and dry, the baby nestled against Mary's face, the earlier cries dying down to an occasional whimper as Mary leaned against the wall, fighting off exhaustion.

She wished she were safe with her brother Tom, wished she knew what was happening to Dave, wished she had never got involved in this nightmare. She leaned against the wall, sore, drained of energy and fighting back a rising sense of despair. She could feel tears beginning to well up but gritted her teeth. No! she thought. She couldn't give up after coming this far. She just had to find the strength to hang on for a while more.

She remained slumped against the wall, willing herself to continue, then slowly she stood up straight. She kissed Fiona gently, picked up her carrier-bag and folding buggy, then cradling the baby, she turned and made for the stairs.

Penny felt guilty at taking a degree of pleasure in the bad news, yet she couldn't help herself. She was in the communications room of the embassy with Thompson and Dewsbury, and they had just been briefed from Leeds on Carrow's lack of success in apprehending Walker at Lake Constance.

As a police officer she felt an instinctive disappointment in a suspect escaping, but in this case it was tempered by her dislike of Carrow, and more importantly, by the fact that failing to recapture Walker took the spotlight off Thompson's failure to catch up with Mary Adams.

It was after ten now and the missing actress still hadn't been sighted. Penny was keeping up a hopeful front for her boss's sake but privately she feared that their quarry had either gone to ground or escaped from the city.

Despite the laboriousness of the task, she had earlier suggested a rechecking of all the guesthouses and hotels, but Thompson had rejected the idea. If Adams were from Dublin Thompson felt that she would be staying with friends or relatives, whereas if she were from the country there would be no reason to stay overnight in a city in which she knew she was being sought.

Thompson was counting on her making her break during the next few hours, when darkness would be on her side, a theory against which Dewsbury was arguing.

"My dear man," he assured Thompson, "I'm not unreasonable. Far from it, I think any neutral observer would agree. But this use of our staff for observation purposes . . . it's having a detrimental effect on the smooth running of the embassy."

After being challenged the previous night, Dewsbury had dropped his flirtatious-charmer persona, but Penny could see that Thompson was still having trouble suppressing his irritation with the diplomat's style.

The big policeman leaned forward now. "The purpose of an embassy is to support our national interests, right?"

"Naturally," answered Dewsbury.

"Well, that's what your people watching the stations

are doing. It may not make for 'smooth running', may not be as glamorous as attending receptions, but it needs doing."

"But for how long, Inspector, that's my point? It's five past ten now. When do we acknowledge that the woman has eluded us?"

"When I genuinely believe that to be the case. I promise, I won't tie up your staff a minute longer than I have to, but it'll be dark soon and that's when . . ."

"Sorry, just a second," interjected Dewsbury as the phone beside him rang.

Penny and Thompson looked round expectantly, knowing it was the line kept open for reporting sightings. The diplomat reached out quickly, lifting the phone and pressing a button to channel the call into the wall speakers. "Dewsbury . . ."

"Chris Sutcliffe, sir," said a man's voice excitedly. "I've just sighted our friend!"

"Good show, Sutcliffe. Where are you?"

"Howth, sir. "

Dewsbury turned to Thompson. "That's a village about seven or eight miles . . ."

"I know where it is! Let me speak to him please!" Before Dewsbury had time to demur, the policeman had taken the phone. "DCI Thompson here, let's have the details, please!"

"I was outside Howth station, sir, and heard a baby cry. I saw from behind a woman with the baby but she had curly red hair, so I thought it wasn't our friend. Then she turned around and I saw her face really clearly."

"You're sure it was her?"

"Pretty sure. There were lots of people getting off the bus, so I was able to get near for a close look. I reckon she was wearing a wig, Inspector, but the face matched the photograph."

"Where is she now?" asked Thompson.

"In the Maritime Hotel. I followed her in and she went upstairs into the Ladies' toilet."

"Do you think she saw you follow her?"

"No, I don't think so."

"Where exactly are you now?"

"In a callbox just up the road from the hotel."

"What!"

"My mobile was giving trouble and the Maritime's phone booth was occupied, so I nipped out for a minute to report in."

"Get back fast!" cried Thompson. "Check the immediate vicinity to make sure she hasn't just left. If there's no sign of her, go back in and watch the toilet. If she comes out and orders something in the bar or restaurant, you do the same, unobtrusively. Likewise if she's already in the bar or restaurant. If she leaves the premises, follow discreetly and ring immediately with the reg number if she rendezvouse's with a car. Got all that?"

"Yes, Inspector."

"Good man, now back there fast!"

There was a click as the line went dead. Then Thompson put down the phone and rose excitedly. "I *knew* she'd make her move tonight!"

"So what do we do?" asked Dewsbury.

"Get to Howth in record bloody time!" said Thompson, making for the door.

Carrow and Mathieson looked up questioningly as Chief Superintendent Vincenz came into the room. They were in an office in the police station in Romanshorn and the stocky Swiss detective shook his head in answer to their unasked question. "No contact as yet," he said. "All the steamers are being searched, we're combing the town and we're watching the berthing areas."

"It's only eleven," said Carrow. "He could easily be waiting till later."

"I've arranged for the watch to be maintained all night," said Vincenz. "I've also organised a police launch to patrol the lake – on the off-chance that he tries crossing in a small craft."

"Thank you very much, You've been most thorough," said Mathieson.

"My pleasure," answered Vincenz easily. "Now if you'll excuse me, I must check in with Zurich."

"Of course."

Mathieson waited until the Swiss detective had left the room, then turned to Carrow. "Can't fault them for effort, eh?"

The Special Branch man looked him in the eye. "No; but you don't really believe we're going to catch Walker, do you?"

Mathieson shrugged. "If we don't, there's still the possibility of locating him via the wife."

Carrow made no effort to keep the disdain from his voice.

"Rely on Thompson and his chums in the Irish police?"

"Could do worse," answered Mathieson, "though I wasn't suggesting *relying* on them. Just a fallback position if Walker evades us."

A nightmare position, more like, thought Carrow. It would be unbearable for them to lose Walker and for Thompson to pick up the trail via Mary Adams. "No!" he said, more vigorously than he intended. "No, we've got to get this bastard ourselves. I'm convinced he's somewhere on the lakeside, waiting to make his break. We've got to sit tight and keep our nerve."

"Quite. Just that it's rather a large lake."

"Nevertheless he has to leave from somewhere, then land somewhere. The Swiss are watching every port, and Vincenz has the Germans and Austrians watching their shorelines too."

"Yes. Painstaking man, Vincenz, he even notified the police in Liechtenstein."

"Really? Is that near here?"

"Maybe twenty-five miles down the road. Tiny place, bordered by the Rhine; Walker would hardly regard it as a refuge but Vincenz alerted them anyway."

"All we can do is wait then," said Carrow. He poured himself a coffee from the percolator on the desk. "Liechtenstein . . . famous for stamps, aren't they?" he mused, filling Mathieson's proffered cup.

"Yes. Stamps – and being the last country in Western Europe to allow women the vote."

"Good for them," said Carrow, leaning back and drinking his coffee.

"You're not serious?"

"Aren't I? All these women muscling in . . . used to be a man's job in the force, now we have the Penny Harts of this world being groomed for stardom."

"What's wrong with that?"

Carrow snorted. "The day I report to someone like her is the day I quit."

"That's – that's a little behind the times, Len."

"Then I'm behind the times. Who'd want to be up with the times, the way the world is today?"

"Has been progress too . . ." said Mathieson gently.

"Progress? Terrorists blowing the centres out of cities, people not safe to walk the streets, villains thumbing their noses at the police."

"I meant broad progress, society in general."

"Society's moving backwards, not forwards. When I started as a copper pounding the beat it was different. Before so-called progress, minority rights, bleeding-heart liberals tying the hands of the force. You knew where you stood then, and so did the villains. Mess about on your turf and they faced a good hiding."

"You liked it that way?"

"Yes, I did, and I'll tell you something. There was more stability, life was better then, society was better."

"Provided of course you were male, property-owning, and a White Anglo-Saxon Protestant . . ."

Carrow looked at him searchingly. "Isn't that what you are?"

"Oh yes," agreed Mathieson sarcastically, "a true

WASP, sent to a good public school by Tory-voting parents. I just think those who don't fit that particular bill should have equal rights."

"Are you trying to tell me – " Carrow started, but Mathieson rose and held up his hand, stopping the policeman.

"We shan't agree, Len, so let's agree to differ. I'll be outside getting some air if there's any news."

Carrow felt his temper rising as the intelligence officer left the room. He should have known that Mathieson would be a bloody liberal – it was always the ones born to privilege who could afford the luxury of disdaining it. Probably identifies with Walker as one college boy to another, he thought angrily. Well, he'd show them both. He wouldn't rest until David Walker was a handcuffed prisoner, and then he would give him the kind of grilling he would never forget.

Reaching for the percolator, he poured himself another coffee, determined to stay awake for whatever the night might bring.

Dave felt the pain most acutely in his shoulders and arms, but his back hurt too, and with his hands getting tender, he stopped for a break.

He shipped the oars of the small rowing-boat, then looked back across the lake towards the distant lights of Romanshorn. He reckoned he was a little more than halfway to the German side, but he was unpleasantly surprised at how much the rowing had taken out of him. He knew he had good levels of fitness and stamina

487

from hill-walking, but his aching shoulders and arms testified to a different set of muscles being required for rowing. Arching his back, he stretched the muscles, then lay out on the seats, rocking gently with the boat's motion in the water.

He had stolen the rowing boat from the boathouse of a lakeside villa, a mile or so outside Romanshorn. It had seemed a perfect choice of craft – too small and low in the water to show up on a radar screen, yet sturdy enough to cross the seven-mile expanse to Friedrichshafen.

Despite his urgent need to escape, he had been surprised at how guilty he had felt about stealing another person's property. The lakeside villa had been occupied, and along with fear of being caught Dave had experienced the distaste of feeling like a sneak-thief.

Now however, he had to concentrate on getting safely to Friedrichshafen. He could see the lights of the German town, and he planned to row in their direction before veering west towards a darkened stretch of shoreline outside the town. With no moonlight and the boat unlit, he reckoned his chances of landing unseen must surely be good.

Resting in the boat, he looked up the lake, remembering how magnificent its waters had once appeared to him when lit by the moon. On his fourteenth birthday his father had arranged for him to travel on a British Airways flight from Trieste to London, and as the senior pilot he had allowed the excited boy to sit in the cockpit for much of the trip. Dave had never forgotten the splendour of crossing the moonlit Alps, nor his first sight of Lake Constance, its placid surface illuminated by a full moon.

He could still recall how good it felt being there with his father, who seemed at that moment an almost heroic figure, good-humouredly explaining the rows of instruments that he confidently controlled to keep the plane aloft. Unbidden, Dave now found himself reminiscing about the flight and remembering how his mother had laughed, affecting mock boredom as Dave had enthused for days afterwards about the moonlit journey. It was over twenty years ago, yet he felt a sudden pang of loneliness. How safe and secure everything had seemed then, and how vulnerable he was now, hunted and alone on the middle of the lake!

No, he told himself, thinking like that wasn't on. He had a wife, and soon they would have a baby, and if he wanted to join them in Ireland he had to stay focused. Leaning forward, he reached for the oars and was about to lift them when a sound reached his ears. It was a distant, droning noise, and with a shock he realised it was the motor of an approaching launch. While he had been gazing up the lake and reminiscing it must have been travelling from the eastern end.

Before leaving Romanshorn he had seen a police motor-boat cruising parallel to the coast with a spotlight trained upon the water, and he had postponed launching the rowing-boat until it had departed eastwards. He had reckoned that by the time it patrolled all the way to Rorschach and back he would be well away from the shore but seeing the distant spotlight he now realised that its return journey was being made several miles out from the shoreline.

The engines were getting louder, and Dave quickly

BRIAN GALLAGHER

lay flat in the bottom of the boat, hoping that his craft would be so low in the water as to avoid detection. He felt the water in the bottom of the boat seeping into his clothes, but he lay unmoving, resisting the urge to look over the bow.

The engines continued to grow louder, and Dave felt his fingernails digging into his palms. Think rationally, he ordered himself. Sound travels far at night in an open space, maybe they're not as near as it seems. Also if they were going up the middle of the lake they would probably train the spotlight on the water between there and the Swiss shore.

He lay there, breathing shallowly as the engine sound grew louder, then to his intense relief there was a gradual diminution in the noise as the boat passed and continued westwards up the lake.

Dave lay flat until the sound had died down considerably, then he cautiously raised himself and looked at the lights of the departing motor launch. As he thought, it was travelling up the centre of the lake, its spotlight scanning towards the Swiss shore.

In case anyone might be looking back from the stern he forced himself to wait until it was well into the distance, then he quickly engaged the oars, turned the boat towards the lights of Friedrichshafen and began to row with all his strength for the German shore.

"Well?" asked Thompson, as Penny came out the door of the Maritime to join him in the car park.

She shook her head. "Not in the toilets, I checked

every cubicle. There's a rear window however, also a fire escape on the first floor – she could have got out either."

"Damn!" said Thompson.

On arrival they had unsuccessfully checked the restaurant and the crowded bar, then Thompson had despatched Dewsbury and Sutcliffe in the latter's car to cruise the roads around the village. If they failed to spot Mary Adams they were to extend the radius of the search to the rest of the peninsula.

Despite driving at speed, it had taken more than twenty minutes to get from the embassy to Howth, and Thompson turned now to Penny. "What do you make of it?"

"I reckon she used the loo and came out again while Sutcliffe was at the phone booth. Either that or she realised she was being followed, knew the Ladies was one place a man wouldn't go after her, and got out the back window – or maybe slipped down the corridor and out the fire escape."

"He should never have left her out of his bloody sight!" said Thompson.

"Absolutely. Though in fairness, Chief, he's had no training for this kind of work."

"I know, I know. The thing is though – why did she come out to Howth in the first place?"

"Maybe she has friends here."

"Maybe. But if it was someplace she was going into hiding, she'd hardly have waited till ten at night to go there."

"I suppose not. Unless . . . perhaps the other person

couldn't be there any earlier. Maybe it's a rendezvous point. There must be hundreds of houses out here – could be they agreed on one, and someone is travelling from a distant part of the country to collect her."

"Possibly," agreed Thompson, "though really there's no saying what she's up to."

"So what do we do, Chief?"

"Show me the map there," he said, indicating the folded Ordinance Survey map on the dashboard of their parked car.

Penny handed it over and he opened it, then pointed his finger at a particular spot. "Sutton," he said. "The peninsula of Howth is almost an island. All traffic coming off it has to use this narrow strip of land at Sutton, passing through Sutton Cross or else along this Lauders Lane."

"So if they were both sealed off . . ."

"Exactly. Let's get back there. You drive. I want to ring Superintendent O'Reilly."

Penny reversed carefully, then pulled out of the car park as Thompson spoke on the phone. She left the village and was driving back along the Howth road to Sutton, her eyes still on the road when Thompson turned to her, putting away his mobile phone.

"We really owe the Irish Police on this one, Penny."

"I take it he's providing the roadblocks?" she said.

"Checkpoints for road tax and drunk driving – for official purposes," answered Thompson with a smile. "He's a good lad, is Tim O'Reilly."

"You must know him pretty well."

"Met years ago at a police conference and hit it off.

Kept in touch. I'd visit here, he'd visit the UK, we'd play a few games of golf. Then Alice and I entertained Tim and his wife when they came to the Dales. Alice and Breda became friendly too, so now there's a close tie."

"Luckily for us," said Penny.

"Aye. So there's a tip. If you get married, Penny, have a hospitable husband – you never know when it'll pay off."

"I'll bear it in mind, Chief," she replied with a smile. "Looks like Sutton Cross ahead."

"OK. You and I'll watch it and Lauders Lane till Tim's people arrive."

"Let's hope Adams hasn't already left the peninsula," said Penny.

"Let's hope not. But assuming she's not moved that quickly, this is where we'll get her!"

37

Bob Reinholdt woke with a start. Despite all his years in intelligence work, the CIA man still found it a shock to the system to be woken by a ringing telephone. The glowing digits of his bedside clock showed five twenty, and he reached out for the phone, anxious to still its ringing before Janet woke properly.

"Hello . . ."

"Sorry to ring so early but there's been a development."

Recognising Marty Schulman's voice, Reinholdt found himself quickly becoming alert. "OK, I'll take this in my study," he said, keeping his voice low. He hung up and swung out of bed, replaced the covers about his wife, then donned his dressinggown and swiftly descended the stairs.

All day Saturday his team had been in Harrogate, but there had still been no sign of Visser; now at last it seemed that Schulman had discovered something.

Reinholdt entered his darkened study and pulled

back the heavy drapes to let in the dawn light, then sat in his swivel chair and lifted the electronically scrambled telephone on his desk. "OK, what's happened?"

"Still no sign of our missing friend . . ."

"So what's the development?"

"We've been monitoring the calls of the local uniforms and we heard something about our actress."

"Yes?"

"The locals have scaled down their operation at the bungalow, but we picked up a gossipy call to a guy on duty there. Seems she's thought to be in Ireland by now."

"In Ireland? Where exactly?"

"They don't know. The Brits are trying to trace her there."

"What about her husband?"

"Wasn't mentioned. He never came home though, so I guess they're after him too . . ."

What the hell had happened? thought Reinholdt. Might the husband have somehow stumbled onto Visser? Maybe the South African had been torturing the wife – despite Reinholdt's orders against coercion – and the husband had come home suddenly, perhaps killing Visser in the ensuing fray?

"What do you want us to do?" asked Schulman.

Reinholdt thought a moment, then made his decision. "Call off the observation."

"From the bungalow or the hotel?"

"Both. Pull out and return to London. Whatever's happened to our subject, hanging about any longer risks linking us to him."

"Whatever you say."

"I appreciate your efforts. Pass that on to your guys and emphasise again that this assignment never took place."

"Will do."

"OK, see you when you return."

"See you then."

Reinholdt hung up and sat gazing out at the dew-covered lawn. The birds were singing noisily, but his mind was focussed on what had happened in Harrogate. First Visser had vanished, then Mary Adams had fled to Ireland. The question was, had Walker gone with her? And more importantly, had they the SMORTAR plans?

Reinholdt was worried, so much so that yesterday he had broken all established rules and tried to contact his M15 source, only to be told that he was "away on business". It had left him with little to report to Pete Krucowski that evening, and the Deputy Director had left him in no doubt of his disappointment.

Reinholdt now rose from his desk, deciding to make a cup of coffee before formulating how best to present the latest intelligence to Krucowski. He left the study and was crossing the hall when the early morning quiet was again disturbed by the jarring sound of the telephone.

Quickly recrossing to the study, he lifted the handset.

"Hello . . ."

"Good morning," said a man's voice, and Reinholdt slowly sat down.

He recognised the voice as that of his source in M15.

Reinholdt listened intently to what the man had to say, then breathed out heavily when the short conversation ended. "Jesus Christ!" he said, putting the phone down. "Jesus H Christ!"

Mary awoke, unsure for a moment where she was. The hotel curtain let in the dawn light however, and looking about, she recognised her surroundings. She reached out and switched off the alarm, then checked her watch. Five thirty exactly, the self-setting hotel alarm had been accurate.

She sat up in the bed and looked over at Fiona, fast asleep and curled up in her cot. The room was a quiet one at the back of the hotel, and apart from the disruption of Fiona's feeds at one and four-fifteen, both the baby and Mary had slept well.

She had been exhausted on checking in the previous night, and after a quick bath had been in bed by ten thirty. Although she still felt sleepy she had now had about seven hours' rest and was sufficiently recovered to climb out of the bed. She stretched gently, her mind already beginning to race.

The next hour or so would be crucial, she knew, but she felt strong enough for what lay ahead. She was still sore from the birth, and her nipples were slightly tender from the breastfeeding, but otherwise she felt in good condition. Another hot bath would help, she decided, and she crossed to the bath, put in the plug, added liquid soap and ran the water.

Stepping back into the bedroom, she laid out her clean clothes and checked Fiona again. The baby had been fed at four-fifteen, so with any luck she should sleep for the next hour or two – by which time they should be checked out of the Maritime and on their way to Ballyard.

Mary went to the wardrobe and took down the curly red wig. She had worn it the previous night when she had booked the room and she would have to wear it again on leaving. Laying the wig on the bed, she slipped off her nightdress, then entered the bathroom.

She used the toilet, splashed water on her face and brushed her teeth. By then the tub had filled sufficiently and she lowered herself into the hot soapy water. The temperature was just right and she leaned back savouring its warmth. Ten minutes, she would allow herself. That would still give her time to dress and cross from the Maritime to the fishing harbour in good time.

Her brother Tom had reckoned it would take about twenty hours to bring his trawler, the *Kingdom Maid*, from Kerry to Howth, and so they had arranged a 6.00 a.m. rendezvous for the quayside. She had been tempted to go over to the harbour sooner, in case he made good time, but had decided against it. No point drawing attention by hanging about the quayside with a baby, she had reasoned; better to arrive shortly after he docked and descend immediately to the safety of the *Kingdom Maid*.

She wished the time were now, wished she and

Fiona were on board with Tom, safe and untraceable, no longer needing to worry about checkpoints or police surveillance.

Safe, she thought, what a marvellous feeling that would be. It seemed like an age since she had felt that way. Not much longer now though, she thought, then she lay back in the bath, warmed and relaxed by the hot soapy water, and glad beyond measure that at last the end was in sight.

"Wake up, Colin!" cried Carrow. He burst into the back room in Romanshorn police station where Mathieson lay asleep on a camp bed. "Wake up," he cried, shaking the intelligence officer by the shoulder.

"What – what is it?" said Mathieson, coming to faster than Carrow expected.

"A rowing-boat's been reported stolen!"

"Yes?"

"From a house just outside the town. There last night, gone this morning. It's Walker, I just know it!"

"Not necessarily," said Mathieson, sitting up and wiping the sleep from his eyes.

Carrow felt a surge of irritation. Just once, he thought, just once he would like the M15 man to show a bit of enthusiasm. "It's Walker all right!" he snapped. "Vincenz says that kind of theft is very rare here. For a boat to be stolen exactly when Walker needs one is too much of a coincidence."

"Maybe," conceded Mathieson, rising from the camp bed. "So now what?"

"Vincenz is ringing the Germans this minute, then we get over to Friedrichshafen, fast."

"I wonder . . . there's no guarantee that's where he'd make for."

"It's the nearest town on the German side!"

"Quite. Doesn't necessarily mean though – "

"Look, it's a bloody long row just to get to Friedrichshafen. He's not going to want to add to his journey."

"Perhaps, but maybe we should wait here, pending Walker or the boat being spotted."

Carrow gritted his teeth, not trusting himself to reply immediately. He couldn't recall ever before working with someone so contradictory in approach. The intelligence officer had been subtle and skilfully devious when questioning Walker, yet now he was reluctant to cross Lake Constance in pursuit of him; he had taken the liberal stance regarding women when they had argued about equality, yet Carrow knew Mathieson's wife had divorced him; he had been commended for valour in Borneo and Oman, yet now he was shying away from going into Germany after a fugitive. Carrow decided he couldn't afford to indulge contradictions and ifs and buts right now, and he kept his voice reasonable but locked eyes with Mathieson. "If you want to stay here, Colin, that's up to you. I want to be already on the German side when Walker or the boat is spotted. Vincenz is organising a speedboat to take us to Friedrichshafen, and I'm leaving the second it's ready. Are you coming, or do I head the British end of this alone?"

Mathieson thought a moment, then returned

Carrow's gaze. "You don't head it alone," he answered easily. "So if Vincenz has a speedboat ordered, I suppose we'd better do some speeding."

"Right," said Carrow, "let's go then!"

Dave studied himself carefully in the mirror of the Gents' toilet in Friedrichshafen train station. After washing and shaving he had changed into a new navy tee-shirt. With his black jeans and the dark baseball cap that he now donned he looked clean and trendy; certainly there was nothing in his appearance to suggest someone who had slept rough.

He had spent the night in a wood after reaching an isolated spot on the German side of the lake at about one in the morning. He had beached the boat, offloaded his carrier bags and the oars, then made a hole in the boat's hull with a sharp rock before sliding the vessel back into the lake. He had used an oar to push it out into sufficiently deep water, and with the lake's waters pouring in through the breached hull the boat had sunk in less than a minute.

He had walked to a nearby wood, lain down and fallen into an exhausted sleep, then on rising he had hidden the oars in the thick undergrowth and walked into Friedrichshafen to catch an early-morning train.

Thanks to the German propensity for early rising there had been quite a few passengers about, so that he hadn't felt unduly conspicuous on entering the station. There had been no uniformed police, nor anyone among the passengers who gave the impression of a plain-clothes officer on the lookout for him.

Still, there could be no telling for sure, and now as he prepared to leave the toilet he was overcome by anxiety. He stood immobile, aware that he would be walking into danger when he crossed to the ticket office. He felt paralysed, unwilling to risk being caught now, after all his efforts. Come on, he told himself, hang around like this much longer and you'll draw attention *and* miss the train. He dallied for several more seconds, then stepped out of the toilet and walked towards the ticket booth. Nobody appeared to pay him any particular attention, and he approached the ticket window, queuing behind an elderly woman and a young Catholic priest.

Both of the other customers bought local tickets with the minimum of fuss, then Dave found himself at the window. The ticket-seller was a heavily built middle-aged man and he nodded curtly in response to Dave's friendly "Guten Tag."

"I wonder if you could help me," said Dave.

"Where do you want to go?"

Dave wondered if it was his English-accented German that grated, or whether the ticket clerk was grumpy with everybody, but he smiled at the man anyway. "I want to get to Le Havre, but I'm not sure what's the quickest way regarding connections."

"Le Havre?"

"Yes, the French port. It's on the Normandy coast."

"I know where Le Havre is!" snapped the man.

"Sorry . . ."

The German consulted a map, then turned back to Dave. "You take the seven fifteen from here to

Strasbourg, changing in Singen and Offenburg. Change in Strasbourg for Paris, change in Paris for Le Havre."

"Any idea how long it would actually take to reach Le Havre?"

"You arrive at Strasbourg at ten thirty. It's up to the French to provide you with times from there to Le Havre."

"Thank you. How much is that, please?"

"Thirty deutschmarks," answered the man, taking the money and pushing forward the ticket.

"Thank you for all your help," said Dave, but if the German recognised the sarcasm he ignored it, looking instead at the next customer as Dave picked up his bags and walked away.

Moving across the concourse, Dave could feel his nerves tingling, but there was still no sign of the police, and despite the risks ahead, he began to feel that his plan was going to work.

Thompson lay in his hotel bed, restless in spite of the comfortable surroundings. Penny had organised rooms for both of them in the Marine Hotel, next to Sutton Cross, and at midnight they had retired to bed, disappointed at Mary Adams's failure to show up at either of the checkpoints.

Thompson had just woken now after a fitful night's sleep and was trying to convince himself that all might still be well, yet logic dictated that with each passing hour the likelihood of catching their quarry diminished.

His musings were disturbed by the bedside telephone, and he instantly reached out for it, excitedly thinking that a call at two minutes to six meant developments. "Thompson," he said, sitting up in the bed.

"Good morning, Chief Inspector. Roger Dewsbury here. Sorry to bother you so early . . ."

Thompson's heart sank. He had been hoping to hear from the Garda checkpoints, now instead he would have to deal with this irritating diplomat. He wasn't in the mood for any further moaning about the seconded embassy staff and he deliberately made his tone brusque. "Yes, Mr Dewsbury, what is it?"

"I've been thinking about that business last night – when Sutcliffe lost our friend . . ."

"So well you might. It's caused us a hell of a lot of grief."

"I dare say, but that's not what I meant."

"Well what do you mean?"

"It's only in retrospect that it's occurred to me, but I think in the heat of the chase we overlooked one possibility."

"Yes?"

"We thought Adams probably left the toilet when Sutcliffe went to use the phone – which is why we rushed off to scour the adjoining roads . . ."

"Well?"

"The other theory was that Adams spotted her tail and escaped through the toilet window or the fire escape."

"I know all this, Mr Dewsbury. What's your point?"

"My point is – supposing she did neither? Supposing she'd no idea she was being followed and did the other thing people do in hotels. Supposing she checked in?"

There was a long pause, then Dewsbury spoke again. "Inspector?"

"Yes, I'm here . . ."

"We were so anxious to catch her we ignored the possibility that she wasn't running any further."

"Christ!" said Thompson. "How did we overlook it?!"

"Heat of the moment, desperate to catch her; we assumed she was equally eager to keep running . . ."

"Damn, I wasn't thinking of the place as a hotel! Mentally I was treating it as a bar and restaurant. Now that I think of it, I've a vague notion of seeing some kind of reception desk. It wasn't manned then, or I'd have asked about her."

"Small place, Inspector. The receptionist may have been gone for a few minutes, may even have been showing Adams to her room. If, that is, my theory is correct."

"You haven't rung the Maritime to check?"

"No, this whole thing's just occurred to me. Shall I ring and enquire discreetly?"

"No," said Thompson, swinging out of bed. "I'll go there myself. It's just down the road from here. And Mr Dewsbury . . . good thinking, very good thinking."

"Thank you. Sure you don't want me to give a ring, might save you an unnecessary journey?"

"No way!" answered Thompson. "Do nothing that

might alert them; in ten minutes we'll know if she's there or not . . ."

Refreshed by her bath, Mary finished dressing, then placed the red wig atop her head and carefully adjusted its tresses before the mirror. She quickly packed Fiona's requisites in her holdall, then looked around the hotel room to make sure she had left nothing behind. Satisfied that she had everything, she gently lifted the sleeping baby and laid her in the buggy, then wheeled it to the bedroom door. She opened the door and stepped out into the corridor to pull the buggy through, then quietly closed the bedroom door after her and headed for the stairs.

Looping the strap of her holdall round her arms, she lifted the lightweight buggy, making sure not to tilt the sleeping baby, then she gingerly descended the stairs.

Bathing and dressing had taken a little longer than she had planned, so she now moved smartly towards the reception desk, keen to pay her bill and reach the quayside as quickly as possible.

The night porter looked up with interest from behind his desk and smiled at her approach. He was a thin, grey-haired man, his red-rimmed brown eyes myopic-looking behind thick glasses.

"That's an early start," he said in a wheezy Dublin accent.

"Yes," replied Mary, smiling back as she placed the room key on the counter. "I'd like to pay my bill, please."

"No problem." He leaned forward conspiratorially.

"Makes a break for me from the reading. Although I have to say, this is a smashing book – have you read it?"

Mary glanced at the paperback. "No, I'm afraid not. I was in room 7, for one night." It was almost three minutes past six by her watch, and she was anxious to get to the harbour, but the porter was in no hurry.

"Smashing book – all about the Warsaw Ghetto. Travelled around in the sewers, they did . . ."

"Really?" She took out her purse, eager to shift the conversation to a business footing. "I'll pay cash," she said.

"Fair enough," said the porter. "I'll just note the payment." He reached into the inside pocket of his jacket and slowly took out a biro. "Now, what was the room again?"

"7."

"OK," he said, laboriously entering the details into a ledger.

Come on! thought Mary. She didn't want to hurt the feelings of someone obviously seeking a little human contact, but she was already late for her rendezvous.

"Right," said the man, "that'll be twenty-four pounds, please."

Mary quickly handed over the money. "Thank you very much."

"Oh just a second, just a second." He took up the pen again.

"Have to write out your receipt . . ."

"That's all right," said Mary with a smile, "I won't be claiming it for tax relief. Good morning."

"Oh . . . good morning . . ."

Swinging the buggy round, Mary nodded pleasantly to him, then went swiftly out the front door, and into the fresh air of the summer morning.

Before the speedboat came to a halt Carrow was climbing the steps to the quayside at Friedrichshafen, leaving Mathieson to thank the Swiss boatmen and follow him ashore.

"Chief Superintendent Carrow?" The questioner was a youthful-looking man in a well-cut suit, behind whom stood two uniformed policemen.

"Yes, I'm Carrow."

"I'm Inspector Walther Junger, Friedrichshafen police. Chief Superintendent Vincenz briefed me to expect you and Mr Mathieson." The man's English was perfect, and he smiled as he held out his hand, which Carrow shook briefly.

"Thank you for meeting us, Inspector," said Mathieson, moving forward to shake hands also.

"My pleasure."

"Let's get down to business, shall we?" said Carrow, suspecting from the presence of a relatively junior officer that the Germans weren't treating the case as a top priority.

"Of course, sir."

"Any sighting of Walker or the boat?"

"Not yet," answered Junger.

"You're checking the shoreline, I presume?"

"Yes, I have two craft doing it, one heading east, one west."

"How long have they been gone?"

"One's gone ten minutes, one fifteen. I arranged it as soon as I finished speaking to Mr Vincenz. We're in radio contact. They'll call in if anything's spotted. I've also sent patrol cars along the coast road in either direction."

"Good. What about the train and bus stations?"

"They're next on our list."

"Next?! You mean you haven't been yet?"

A hint of hurt showed in the German's eyes as he answered Carrow. "It's only twenty-five minutes since Superintendent Vincenz called," he said. "I've had to organise patrol craft to search for the boat."

"That was fifteen minutes ago. The stations should be staked out!"

"Ten minutes ago, actually. And with respect, Mr Carrow, it is not possible in ten minutes to despatch officers to every possible departure point. Walker could have made for Lindau, Bad Schachen, Wasserburg, Nonnenhorn, Langenargen, Immenstaad . . . we cannot possibly have every train station and bus stop covered."

"All right, all right, but the ones here in Friedrichshafen could be done."

"Yes, sir, and as your speedboat was approaching, I waited a moment to extend you the courtesy of directing the operation."

"Thank you, Inspector," said Mathieson. "We do appreciate your co-operation."

Carrow picked up on the glance shot him by the intelligence officer and he forced himself to keep his impatience in check. "I'm sure you've done everything you thought necessary, Inspector," he said pleasantly, "but time is precious, and we must move quickly in case Walker's in Friedrichshafen. Can we go to the station immediately?"

"Bus or train?"

"Train, first," answered Carrow. "More anonymous for someone on the run."

"This way, please," said Junger, ushering them to a parked black Mercedes and opening the rear door. He barked a command to the uniformed officers, who ran to their patrol car. Then the German detective jumped into his own vehicle, strapped on his seat belt, and set off at speed towards the station.

Carrow stood unmoving in the early-morning sunlight, his hopes rising when he saw the ticket seller nodding and returning the photograph to Junger. The two men had a brief conversation, then the detective thanked the clerk and crossed to Carrow and Mathieson.

"He recognised him!" said Junger, trying to keep his excitement in check.

"Positive ID?" asked Mathieson.

"Certain. He sold him a ticket about half an hour ago!"

"Can he remember where Walker's headed?" asked Carrow.

"Yes, Le Havre, via Strasbourg."

"Le Havre? Jesus!"

"That is significant?" queried Junger.

"Probably," answered Mathieson. "It's the chief French port for the car ferries to Ireland."

"Devious bastard!" said Carrow almost admiringly. "Devious fucking bastard! It's the one way he can join his wife without having to buy a ticket!"

"Surely one needs a ticket for the ferry?" said the perplexed German.

"Not if you find a sympathetic driver who's booked one of these special offers. The driver can carry up to four people, he already has his ticket, and you simply travel in his vehicle. Walker could hitch a ride or split the cost, then travel on board as a vehicle passenger!"

"But the French police?" said Junger.

"The French police were notified that he's *left* France," explained Mathieson. "They wouldn't be expecting him to enter and exit France again."

"What time does the train arrive in Strasbourg?" asked Carrow.

"Not till ten thirty. We can easily have him picked up," said Junger.

"No," said Carrow, shaking his head, "not this guy. What time did the train leave here?"

"Seven fifteen," answered the German.

"It's only seven thirty-five now," said Carrow, checking his watch. "Could we overtake a twenty-minute head start?"

"Oh yes," replied Junger, his features breaking into a grin. "It's quite a slow train – and I've a very fast car."

Carrow sensed the younger man's enthusiasm and nodded assent. "OK," he said, "let's see just how fast."

Dave turned away from the carriage window as the

train pulled into the station. He reached for his carrier bags, then rose and made for the door as the engine came to a halt.

Other travellers on the early-morning train from Friedrichshafen were also disembarking, and Dave awaited his turn to alight, then walked confidently along the platform. He no longer wore the baseball cap and jeans, but had changed into his best outfit of black shoes, slacks and shirt. He also wore his gold-rimmed reading glasses, and his blond hair was neatly combed.

Reaching the end of the platform, he stopped, put down the bags and looked up at the large timetable notices. He scanned the numerous arrival and departure times, noted the appropriate platform for his connection, then took up his carrier bags and continued on his way.

Despite the early hour the station was quite busy, but on reaching his platform he found an empty bench and sat down gratefully to await the next train.

Crossing his legs, he leaned back, pleased with how smoothly things had gone. The connection times had worked out well, and assuming normal German punctuality he would be speeding eastwards towards his destination of Munich within a few minutes, while Carrow and Mathieson should be speeding in the opposite direction on the false trail towards Strasbourg.

That was assuming, of course, that they were actually on his trail. The rowing-boat theft might not have been discovered, but if it had then the tenacity of Carrow and Mathieson's pursuit so far strongly suggested their crossing to Friedrichshafen. They would certainly check the bus and train stations there, and Dave was confident that he had been sufficiently irritating to the ticket clerk at Friedrichshafen for the man to remember him and his questions regarding Strasbourg/Le Havre connections.

Having paid the Strasbourg fare, Dave had then gone about getting his ticket for Munich. He had remembered a maxim from his first journalistic job that if you ask a favour directly, people will do almost anything to avoid the embarrassment of refusing. Choosing carefully, he had approached a pleasant looking middle-aged woman, and in fractured German, made worse by a convincing and severe stutter, he had indicated that he wished to travel to Munich. With a combination of sign language and stumbling words he had proposed that she take his money and buy the ticket for him, and sensing his embarrassment with the stutter, she had agreed, while he waited out of sight of the ticket office.

After thanking her when she returned with the booking, he had quickly re-entered the toilets, changed into his present outfit and taken his place on the north-bound train to Ulm.

Now as he sat on the platform of Ulm station he reckoned that at last he had shaken off his pursuers. Of course he still had to get to Ireland – no easy task with his passport number on the computer lists of every police force in western Europe. Still, he had chosen Munich for a reason, and although his next scheme depended on several imponderables, he did at least have a plan in mind.

He started to go over it yet again, seeking any flaws he might have missed, then he heard the rumbling of an approaching engine. He looked up, saw it was his train approaching, rose from the seat and gathered his bags. He was looking forward to ringing Mary as soon as he got to Munich, and as the engine halted he quickly moved forward, wishing to board the east-bound train and be on his way.

Penny and Thompson drove at speed around the final bend and into the village of Howth. There was no traffic abroad at such an early hour, and Thompson swung the car hard across the main road to pull up at the Maritime. The risen sun was sparkling on the harbour waters, churned up by the fishing boats as they prepared to take advantage of an easy tide, but the two police officers had no eyes for the fleet as they swiftly made for the hotel entrance.

"Good morning," said the night porter, laying down a paperback novel at their approach.

"Good morning," said Penny pleasantly. "We're hoping you can help us. We're trying to contact someone we think may have stayed here last night."

"That's easily checked," said the porter, reaching for a list on the desk. "We can go through the names together . . ."

"Actually it's a missing person's case. She may not be using her real name."

"Is that a fact?" said the man, clearly delighted to be involved in something out of the ordinary.

"This is the woman," said Thompson, handing over a photograph of Mary Adams, "and she'd have had a new-born baby with her. Probably wearing a curly red wig too."

"Begod," said the porter, staring at the picture and shaking his head, "would you ever be up to them?!"

"Do you recognise her?" asked Thompson.

"Recognise her?" The man gave a little laugh. "Certainly I recognise her – no mistaking that face, wig or no wig. Room 7, no doubt about it."

"Bingo!" said Penny excitedly.

"Well when I say room 7, I should really say . . ." he checked his list, "Ms Susan Campbell. It's a habit you get into, referring to the guests by their room numbers."

"You're quite certain of the identification?" persisted Thompson.

"Oh yes, new baby and all. Sure I'm after just been talking to her . . ."

"When was this?" interjected Penny.

"When she was checking out . . ."

"What?!"

"I was just goin' to tell you. She checked out of the hotel, and – "

"How long ago?" said Thompson.

"Less than five minutes."

"What direction did she go?"

The porter looked nervously at Thompson and shook his head. "I don't really know. You see, I went back to me book – "

"Right! Thank you," said Thompson, already making for the door.

515

Penny followed immediately, then stopped outside where Thompson had halted. He stood looking about, but there was no sign of Adams in any direction.

"We passed no cars or pedestrians on the way here, Chief," said Penny. "She must have gone into the village."

"Maybe. Call the checkpoint and ask them to leave someone in Sutton Cross, but get a squad car up here fast."

"Right," said Penny, reaching for her walkie-talkie and quickly passing on the message. Turning back to Thompson, she was surprised to find him gazing into space. "The car's on its way, Chief. Aren't we going to search the village?"

"We lost her last night, Penny, because we didn't stop to think things out. Instead of running round in circles we need to try and work out what she's at."

"OK," said Penny. "Well, even though she checked out, no car has come out here to collect her, because we would have passed it going back."

"Yet she didn't walk either – we would have seen her," said Thompson.

Penny shrugged. "I can't see why she'd want to go deeper into the village on foot, but it seems the most likely answer. The good part is we know now she's here in Howth, our roadblocks are still in place, and this being a peninsula, she has to travel the narrow strip of land at Sutton."

"Wait now . . . wait now . . ." said Thompson thoughtfully. "A strip of land . . . Jesus, that's it! *Land*. She's not travelling by land at all! It's been staring us in

516

the face." He pointed at the boats. "She's travelling by sea. She's meeting someone all right – here in the bloody harbour!"

"God . . . yes!" said Penny. "It all makes sense now. There are so many boats though, between the marina and the trawlers . . ."

"But she's only a few minutes ahead of us. And we don't have to catch her – we've only to spot which boat she boards and have it tracked."

"Right! "

"OK," said Thompson, "you take the marina; I'll take the fishing piers. Let's go!"

Mary walked briskly, surreptitiously checking those trawlers still moored two and three deep along the quayside. Numerous boats were preparing to leave for the day's fishing, but the crews were busy with their preparations, and to Mary's relief little attention was paid to her as she headed down the West Pier.

She had decided that pushing a buggy along the quayside might draw attention, and wanting to leave nothing linking a woman and a baby with a trawler bound for Kerry, she had gone behind a warehouse near the end of the pier and slipped the folded buggy into a rubbish-filled skip.

She now carried her holdall on her shoulder, and even someone encountering her close-up would have difficulty seeing the sleeping baby nestled inside the folds of her loose-fitting cardigan. She was beginning to get apprehensive, being well down the pier and having checked numerous trawlers without spotting the *Kingdom Maid*. Surely as seasoned a sailor as Tom wouldn't have miscalculated the journey time from Kerry to Howth, she reasoned, yet she also knew that good weather on the east coast didn't necessarily mean good weather in the south-west; despite the sunny morning he could have been delayed by bad conditions. And if he were late, how long could she remain here before becoming conspicuous?

She looked back up the harbour at the smaller number of boats moored near the marina end, trying to see if perhaps Tom had been forced to dock there instead.

"Miss Adams!"

The voice startled her and she swung round. The sun shone into her eyes, and she raised her hand to shade them, then her heart lifted, and she ran towards the comforting arms of her smiling older brother.

"Oh, Tom," she cried, dropping her holdall and embracing him with one arm while supporting Fiona with the other. "You've no idea how glad I am to see you!"

"You too, Mary. You too," he said as he smilingly held and kissed her."

"Oops, careful, you don't want to crush your new niece!"

Mary stood with her back to the quayside, then opened the cardigan to reveal the sleeping baby.

"God," said Tom in wonder, "she's beautiful. A little dote."

"You won't say that when you hear her screaming for her grub . . ."

Tom looked up and smiled as he touched Mary's wig. "Sure I nearly screamed myself when I saw the hair!"

"That's going the minute we're on board. Talking of which, where are you berthed?"

"At the very end. Full house this morning."

"I was getting worried when I didn't see the *Kingdom Maid*."

"I was getting worried when the world's most punctual sister wasn't waiting on the quayside – so I started down to find you."

"Sorry," said Mary with a grin, then her face clouded as she heard the sound of a siren approaching at speed along the coast road. They both turned to see the flashing blue lights of a Garda car come into sight, then the vehicle screeched to a halt.

"Oh Jesus," said Mary, "it's stopping at the Maritime – that's where I stayed last night!"

"Let's go!" said Tom, taking the bag from the ground and turning to start down the pier.

"Don't run, Tom. Just walk briskly," said Mary, joining him and keeping in step, bewildered as to how she could have been traced to the hotel – assuming the dramatic police arrival had to do with her. She kept going, praying not to hear the police car coming down the pier, then suddenly she saw the berthed *Kingdom Maid*, its letters clearly outlined on its freshly painted hull.

Tom swiftly climbed down the quayside ladder and jumped on board. Mary climbed down after him, then, satisfied that Fiona was safely wedged in the front of the cardigan, she allowed him take her weight

519

and swing her safely from the ladder onto the deck.

"Right, out of sight below!" he cried, "then let's get the hell out of here!"

Carrow watched the train pull out of Singen station, picking up speed as it headed west towards Strasbourg, then he turned away, smashing his fist against a hoarding in frustration.

"Steady on, old man . . ." said Mathieson.

"That bastard," said Carrow, "that devious fucking bastard!"

Mathieson nodded. "It does seem our Mr Walker's rather Machiavellian . . ."

"Oh for Christ's sake, Colin, he's not 'our Mr Walker'!" Carrow turned away, knowing even as he spoke that his anger had little to do with Mathieson's phraseology and everything to do with being wrong-footed by Walker.

They had driven at speed with Inspector Junger, hurtling through the Wurttemberg countryside and arriving at Singen station just two minutes before the train. Junger had radioed ahead for support, and with uniformed officers sealing the station and covering all exit doors from the train, Carrow had eagerly led the search. He had savoured the prospect of seeing Walker's face as the advertising executive found himself cornered, and instead had suffered the humiliation of being out-manoeuvred, when an exhaustive search of the carriages had revealed no sign of their quarry.

Junger was now busily directing units to the area

between Friedrichshafen and Singen, but despite having put on a good face for the German, Carrow found it hard to remain optimistic. "Realistically, Colin, do you think Walker might have got off earlier?"

"Unlikely," answered the intelligence officer. "Let's face it, we've been had. And the red herring is all the more perfect if it draws attention to a train he never boarded in the first place."

"You sound almost admiring. Doesn't being taken for a ride bother you?"

Mathieson shrugged. "Sometimes a spot of fatalism isn't amiss . . ."

"Fatalism my arse! You're not telling me you don't want to lay hands on Walker?"

"There are questions I'd like answered, though as I said before, I think most of what he told us in Paris was true."

"That ballsology!?"

"Oh he was lying to cover the wife, naturally, but I think the rest was basically true."

"No subversive aspect, just an innocent civilian?"

"Probably."

"Why chase him halfway across Europe if you believed that?"

"Just the off-chance that he'd betray a link to subversives. One covers all options, standard practice in the business . . ."

"And that's all it is to you – business?"

"What else would it be?"

Carrow looked hard at Mathieson, his clothes still somehow suggesting an air of elegance, despite having been slept in, and he felt the old familiar irritation. "Where the hell is your pride?" he snapped. "Is there nothing personal about it when a villain wipes your eye?"

"No, actually," replied Mathieson, his manner still infuriatingly languid. "Tends not to make for good intelligence work . . ."

"Then I'm bloody glad I'm in police work!"

Mathieson paused a moment, then spoke conciliatorily. "Look, Len, I *can* understand your frustration, but what's the point? You and I have done our bit. The Germans are checking the stations; surveillance will be maintained at bus depots, ferry points, airports. But unless Junger comes up with something – which I greatly doubt – then it's over for us. Let it go. *C'est la vie . . .*"

Carrow turned away. *C'est la vie!* Soft bloody git, he thought angrily. Well, maybe Colin silver-spoon-in-the-mouth Mathieson could afford the luxury of throwing in the towel, but not Len Carrow. He hadn't gone from a Barnsley backstreet to a Georgian house in Surrey by being a quitter, hadn't risen to Chief Superintendent by letting villains off the hook, and he wasn't going to start now.

He looked along the platform, scene of his recent humiliation, and his resolve strengthened. Walker still had to get out of Germany, he thought. He had given them the slip for now all right, but as far as Len Carrow was concerned, the game wasn't over yet.

"There must be something we can do, Chief!"

Thompson stood on the pier's end, watching the

fishing fleet disperse as they left the harbour. Then he turned to Penny. "We did everything possible."

Penny looked in frustration at the fishing boats, all her instincts insisting that Mary Adams must be on one of them. "We can't just let her get away . . ."

"She mightn't be on a trawler at all," answered Thompson quietly. "Look at the marina, Penny. There are scores of yachts, each one private property. The Gardai have been really co-operative, but we can't request that they get warrants to board every one of them."

"It's not the yachts; it's one of the trawlers, Chief, I'm sure of it."

"More than likely," agreed Thompson, "but we didn't spot her boarding any particular one."

"Aren't their movements monitored in any way?"

Thompson pointed at the departing vessels. "See for yourself; once outside the harbour, they split up and head off in all directions."

"No, I meant boats leaving Howth and landing in other ports – would there be some record of what boats were here this morning?"

Thompson smiled crookedly. "I already asked that very question. Irish trawlers don't have to register in Irish ports."

"Damn! Could – could the fleet be traced with radar? We must have navy or RAF bases on the Welsh coast."

"Out of the question, Penny. These are Irish territorial waters. Besides, even if we had permission, there are fishing ports all along the Irish Sea. There'd be nothing to distinguish the Howth trawlers from all the others."

"Isn't there anything at all we can do?"

"Not here there isn't. But we'll work with the Gardai to unearth what part of Ireland Adams hails from. And we'll be hoping, of course, that Carrow and Mathieson pick up Walker's trail again."

"How likely is that, Chief?"

Thompson thought a moment. "Unlikely, I'd have to say."

"Walker and Adams – they're going to beat us, aren't they?"

"Not necessarily. The Gardai may very well track them down. It's pretty hard for two adults and a baby to just vanish into thin air."

"They've been clever and inventive all along," said Penny. "They'll go to ground in such a way as to cover their tracks."

"Easier said than done. As soon as we get back we'll make a formal request to the Gardai regarding Walker. It's not over yet, believe me."

"OK . . ."

Thompson looked at her. "There's something I want to say."

"Yes?"

"Even if it's a thing we don't get Walker and Adams – though I still think we will – but even if we lose them, I want you to know your contribution to the case has been excellent. Really first class. You're the best young detective I've worked with in some time."

"Oh . . . well . . . thank you, Chief. I – I'm really flattered."

"No need to be. It's the simple truth." Thompson

smiled. "You're still a cheeky young bugger, mind, but like the song says, now that I've found you I can't let you go. I reckon we make a good team."

"Thanks, Chief . . . thanks . . ."

Thompson nodded, then looked out at the sparkling blue of the sea, as the trawlers steamed off towards the horizon. They stood together, watching in silence for a moment, then Thompson faced her. "Well, Detective Hart, I don't know about you, but I'm famished. What would you say to a large Irish breakfast?"

"How does 'yes, please' sound?"

"Sounds good," said Thompson. "Let's go."

Penny took a last wistful look at the departing fleet, then turned and fell into step with Thompson as they started back down the pier.

38

Dave threaded his way through the packed bar in Munich airport, protecting his tray of schnapps from the boisterous soccer supporters who milled about the tables. His plan was on schedule so far, but he knew he would have to make his decisive move soon, and he could feel his apprehension beginning to grow.

He had rung Ballyard as soon as he had left the train station in Munich, and he was still awed to think that he was now a father. Tom's wife, Jenny, had confirmed that Mary and the baby were fine and safely en route to Kerry aboard the trawler, yet his delight had turned to trepidation. The very joy engendered by parenthood and Mary's successful escape now made his potential loss all the more horrific should he be caught.

His improvised plan for joining Mary had been formulated yesterday, when he had read in a Swiss newspaper that the Republic of Ireland soccer team was playing a friendly international in Munich that night. The Irish soccer supporters were renowned for their almost obsessively enthusiastic support of the national team, and what better way to get into Ireland, he had thought, than surrounded by hundreds of good-humouredly boisterous fellow travellers.

These same fans were thronged about the bar now, the place awash in green outfits, with the supporters dressed in everything from green, white, and orange national flags to shirts, scarves, hats, and even trousers embossed with the Irish team logo.

Shielding his tray of schnapps, Dave made his way to the furthest corner of the bar, then sat opposite a semi-recumbent supporter who gave an expansive but uncoordinated wave at Dave's approach.

"Sound man yourself!" he cried. "Schnapps for Sammy, what? Schnapps for Sammy!"

The man's speech was badly slurred, but Dave smiled and placed the drinks on their table. He had spent some time combing the airport bar before choosing the man he now knew as Sammy Boylan. Boylan was an overweight, ruddy-faced man of about forty, who had been at the bar drinking heavily, and, crucially from Dave's perspective, on his own.

Having engaged him in conversation, Dave had listened to Boylan's proud boast that he never missed a match, no matter where the team played. His usual pals hadn't travelled for this game, it being only a friendly, but not he, no half measures with Sammy Boylan. Talking of which, Dave had said, how about a couple of full measures of schnapps?

That had been almost an hour ago, and they had soon ensconced themselves at their present table. Dave had plied the man with drink, and Boylan, already half-drunk at the start, hadn't noticed how little Dave drank himself.

"There you are, Sammy," Dave now said, handing him one of the glasses of schnapps. The astringent drink had been a good choice, disguising any taste from the sleeping tablets that Dave had bought earlier in a Munich chemist's shop, and which he had crushed and dissolved into Boylan's drinks.

"Down the hatch, Dave, down the bleedin' hatch!" Boylan cried, knocking back the drink in one go. "Schnapps . . . schnapps for Sammy, what? And Sammy for schnapps!"

He laughed at his imagined witticism, and Dave forced himself to grin. He had always hated the slobbering behaviour of drunks, and he inwardly recoiled from his own false bonhomie, but there was no choice, and he lifted a glass as though about to drink from it, then handed another one to Boylan. "Here, Sammy, as you say in Ireland, a bird never flew on one wing . . ."

"True . . . true for ye, pal . . ." His eyes glazed, the man reached shakily for the glass, raised it to his mouth and knocked back the schnapps.

Long queues had already formed for the charter flights when Boylan finally and suddenly succumbed to unconsciousness. Dave had assisted him out of the bar and to the most outlying corner of the departure lounge, and now, his heart in his mouth, Dave looked about to make sure he was unobserved.

With several different charter flights due to depart over the next couple of hours, the airport lounge was drifting towards good-humoured chaos, and he was pinning his hopes on nobody observing his out-of-the-way corner. There was nothing to be gained by further delay, he knew, and nervously biting his lip, he forced himself to action.

Reaching over the prostrate Boylan, he slipped off the man's green hat and scarf and donned them himself. He glanced around, and satisfied that he was unobserved, quickly opened the pouch of Boylan's travelling bag and took his Irish passport and airline ticket. He slipped them into his own bag, zipped Boylan's pouch closed, then reached over the unconscious man as though making him more comfortable. He surreptitiously slipped Boylan's wallet out of his pocket and went through its contents. To his relief there were no credit cards or other addressed items by which the sleeping supporter could be identified, and he quickly inserted four thousand-dollar bills into the wallet to compensate for the loss of the passport and ticket.

He slid the wallet back into Boylan's jacket, buttoned the garment closed, then shoved the man's travelling bag under the seat on which he slept. He glanced about, but was reassured to see nobody looking in his direction.

So far, so good, he thought. Of course he could still come to grief if a ticket clerk decided to check his appearance against Boylan's passport photograph. Apart from a similarity in age, and his blond hair, he didn't look much like the other man, but he was counting on the check-in clerks' anxiety to process the rowdy football fans as quickly as possible, and he reckoned they would hardly do more than check the ticket names against the passport names. Besides, there was no way of getting to Ireland that didn't entail some risk.

He looked around again, then picked up his bags, tilted his Ireland hat at a rakish angle, and set off to queue with the other fans.

The late-afternoon sun shone from a clear blue sky as the *Kingdom Maid* cruised through the white-topped waters off the Cork coastline. Mary stood in the prow, instinctively shifting her balance in keeping with the swell, and breathing in the salt air.

Fiona lay fast asleep in the cabin below, and Mary had come up on deck, eager to savour again the half-forgotten sensation of being at sea in a fishing vessel. A warm breeze buffeted her hair and, closing her eyes, she tilted her face upwards, allowing the sun to bathe her face in its heat as she reflected on her situation.

The best development was that Tom had received a radio message from Jenny to say that there had been a telephone call to Ballyard. Aware that the radio signal could be picked up by others, Jenny had said that the shipping agent had phoned from the continent to say he had collected their order and hoped to effect delivery tomorrow.

Mary had been thrilled to know that Dave was at large and had collected their money, but waiting until tomorrow to rejoin her suggested complications at his end. And Jenny had said he had called from abroad – which meant that he would still have to run the gauntlet before they could be reunited.

She wished there was some way she could help him, and was frustrated to think that although their future would be determined within the next day or so, there was nothing more she could do for now.

At least her own end of things was going smoothly, she comforted herself, with the boat due to reach Kerry at about 2.00 a.m. At that hour they should dock unobserved, so that no one would know of her journey on the *Kingdom Maid*.

On the other hand she mustn't be too complacent about it; she had thought herself safe in The Maritime, and yet the police had somehow traced her. And there was also the matter of Franklin. Even with his features obliterated and his body unlikely to be easily discovered, it was still something of a loose end; and while the Beara Peninsula was a long way from Dublin, there was, she feared, always going to be the fugitive syndrome, the looking over the shoulder, the possibility that someone, someday, might show up seeking her.

Well, she would have to live with that, she reasoned, just as she would have to live with the image of Franklin burning – a horrific sight – no matter how much she had since rationalised about acting to protect her baby, and just as she would have to live with all the other uncertainties involved in fleeing Harrogate and making a new life in a society that she had left half a lifetime ago.

She breathed out deeply, then opened her eyes, and

looking across the blue of the sea at the lush green coastline, her spirits rose. This was the hand she had been dealt, and now she would play it – and count her blessings. Provided of course, that Dave got back safely, which with any luck should be within twenty-four hours.

She leaned upon the rail, looked out to sea again, and wished that it were tomorrow.

"Olé! Olé! Olé! Olé! – Olé! Olé!" The football fans burst into their chant as the plane jolted onto the runway at Dublin airport, and Dave joined in, eager to consolidate his role of enthusiastic football supporter.

Despite a nerve-wracking few minutes queuing at the Munich check-in all had gone according to plan, and the desk clerk had quickly processed his ticket with only a cursory matching of the ticket against the stolen passport.

Dave had made a conscious effort to be one of the gang during the flight, joining in the chat and sing-songs and chants. The apparent incongruity of his English accent whilst wearing a green hat and scarf had been explained easily to his fellow passengers, who readily accepted his story of being born in England to Irish parents – just like half the Irish squad, Dave had cheekily added.

He had entered wholeheartedly into the banter, which had also helped to keep from his mind from the consequences of Sammy Boylan awakening back in Munich. Between the schnapps and the powdered sleeping tablets Dave had reckoned the man would remain comatose for some time, but with boarding in Munich, flying for over two hours, and disembarking in Dublin, there was the risk of Boylan awaking or being awoken and discovering his ticket and passport to be stolen. Everything hinged on Dave safely disembarking in Dublin airport before Boylan became sufficiently coherent to report his loss, and now as the passengers rose to leave the plane, Dave knew he was only minutes from that goal.

Taking his precious hand-luggage, he joined the line of green-bedecked supporters blowing kisses and making mock-gallant bows to the fixedly smiling air hostesses. The line eventually shuffled off the plane, and he could feel his knees beginning to tremble as he started down the corridor towards the arrivals area, knowing that the moment of truth was approaching.

Apart from the risk of the authorities in Dublin being notified of the theft of Boylan's passport and ticket, there was the equally serious worry of Interpol having all European airports on the look-out for him. He told himself again that with the police aware of Mary's flight to Ireland the last thing they would expect would be the sheer boldness of his flying directly into Dublin airport. Still, there would be officials at passport control, and everything depended on his appearing to be part of a fully-booked charter flight of football fans.

Moving down the passage towards the Arrivals Hall, he aligned himself with the group with whom he had been chatting on the plane, forcing a smile onto his lips as they included him in heading imaginary footballs and kicking imaginary goals. Despite his embarrassment, he participated eagerly, especially when he saw the passport desks looming ahead.

The first groups of fans were now reaching the checkpoints, and without appearing to stare, Dave watched closely to see what degree of inspection was in force. Coming to the barrier, all of the supporters held their Irish passports up in the air, and to his intense relief Dave saw the official smile tolerantly and gesture them through as the fans waved their passports like flags, singing "You'll never beat the Irish!".

Making sure his green hat was well down over his face, and with his scarf around his neck, Dave positioned himself in the middle of his boisterous group so that there were others between him and the barrier. He avoided the passport officer's eyes and held up his passport with the others, as they burst into another chorus of "Olé! Olé! Olé! Olé! – Olé! Olé!".

The passport official grinned, indicating for them to go through, and, still heading imaginary footballs, the group passed the barrier and continued towards the baggage reclaim area. Dave hung back while the others walked towards the luggage carousels, unaware of his absence from the group.

He felt a surge of satisfaction at the success of his ploy, but forced himself to remain on guard. He had still to pass through the customs channel, and it was possible that the authorities might be awaiting him in the Arrivals Hall itself, with a view to tailing him and thus capturing Mary also.

Walking at a steady pace, he made for the blue EC

channel, casually holding his carrier bags. He glanced about and his heart lifted on seeing no customs officer – Ireland, he realised, had implemented the new EC regulations radically easing customs restriction between member states.

Controlling his exhilaration, he emerged unchallenged into the busy arrivals area, crowded with families and friends meeting the returned football supporters. He moved towards the exit at a moderate pace, glancing at his reflection in glass panels to see if anyone followed him, then he stopped and fiddled with a bag-strap to see if anyone would stop also. To his relief no one appeared either to be tailing him or paying him any heed, and lifting his bags again, he walked out of the terminal and into the bright evening sunshine.

39

"Goddamn! I can't believe it!"

Bob Reinholdt enjoyed the look of amazement on Krucowski's face as the older man shook his head. They were seated in the study of the Deputy Director's luxury home in Georgetown, and Reinholdt reckoned the journey to Washington had been worthwhile just to see Krucowski's dour composure shaken up.

"Goddamn!" said Krucowski. "The whole operation from start to finish?"

"An elaborate ploy," answered Reinholdt. "The British have surpassed themselves."

"How come your source only told you this morning?"

"He'd only just found out. M15 ran a really tight operation. They'd suspected a mole for some time, and the finger began to point in the direction of this Gatenby guy. He was made second-in-command of security at Browsdale Research Centre, and his immediate superior, Colin Mathieson, came up with this strategy."

"Mathieson – that's the guy who's been chasing all over France and Switzerland?"

"Right. Mathieson contrived to allow Gatenby access to the SMORTAR plans. Except they were phoneys. Highly credible drawings of manufacturing, testing, and firing procedures, but misleading in vital detail."

"And Gatenby went for the bait."

"Absolutely," said Reinholdt. "Beautifully conceived operation; the real data was safe, Gatenby was flushed out, and by seeing who he went to they'd roll up an opposition spy-ring, terrorist group, whatever . . ."

"Goddamn!" said Krucowski, a note of admiration in his voice. "We bust a gut trying to find plans that were a load of crap!"

"We weren't to know that."

"Not when the bastards kept us in the dark."

Reinholdt smiled wanly. "Well, look at it this way, sir. If we'd been mounting a decoy operation, would we have told them?"

Krucowski looked at the younger man, then gave a rare smile. "I guess we mightn't at that . . . so," he said, his tone businesslike again as he straightened himself in his upholstered chair, "where does this Walker guy come into the picture?"

"Walker was the fly in the ointment," said Reinholdt. "Nothing subversive about him, but he'd gone to school with Gatenby, and there was bad blood between them. Their chance meeting screwed up Mathieson's operation. It's the kind of bad luck you just can't plan for."

"Tell me about it . . ." said Krucowski, nodding in agreement. "So where's Walker now?"

"He seems to have shaken off his pursuers," said Reinholdt. "M15 reckon he'll try to join his wife in Ireland. Not that they really care about him now."

"How come Mathieson chased him halfway across Europe then?"

"M15 kept this a very tight operation, sir. The police leading the manhunt never knew about the SMORTAR ruse. I guess Mathieson had to tag along on the chase so the cops wouldn't get suspicious."

"Jeez, Bob, I don't mind telling you I'm relieved," said Krucowski. "The idea of some dickhead zealot getting his hands on a weapon like SMORTAR . . ."

"I know," said Reinholdt. "Doesn't bear thinking about."

"You've been on the ball on this case, Bob. It won't go unnoticed."

"Well . . . thank you, sir."

"Of course there's still the matter of Jan Visser. No word, I presume?"

"Absolutely nothing," answered Reinholdt.

"I take it the Brits have no inkling of his involvement?"

"None at all. And even if they did come across him, there's no link whatsoever to us."

"Good. How much of the three hundred thousand was Visser paid?"

"Only the first fifty thousand."

Krucowski raised an eyebrow. "Then I reckon we've saved Uncle Sam a quarter of a million bucks – 'cause it sure sounds like Visser's been taken out. Question is, who by?"

"I guess Walker's a possibility," said Reinholdt. "His bungalow in Harrogate was the last place we know Visser went.

"I thought Walker was an ordinary civilian?"

"Yes, sir, but if Visser disobeyed orders and got . . . let's say a little physical in questioning the wife, who knows what might have happened if Walker returned."

"No sign of a body though."

"No, and if I had to guess I wouldn't particularly go for Walker. Visser's been plying his trade for years, must have made a lot of enemies. Maybe someone settled an old score."

"Well, once there's nothing tying him in any way to us."

"Absolutely not, sir."

"Then there's no loss, just a saving of a quarter of a million bucks."

Reinholdt looked at the older man, slightly shocked at the callousness of his assessment.

Krucowski caught the look. "I knew him, Bob; he was a bastard. An effective one, for sure – but a bastard. He won't be mourned."

"No, I don't suppose he will . . ."

"So, I guess if Walker goes to ground in Ireland, that's the end of it?"

"I reckon," answered Reinholdt. "I'd say the Chief Constable will be spoken to discreetly, with word coming down not to waste effort on Walker."

"MI5 must be pretty sure he's clean."

"Yes, sir, seems he's just an adman."

"Ex-adman now – he won't know they've stopped hunting him."

"Yeah. He had a good job, kinda hard on him . . ."

Krucowski shrugged. "Winners and losers, Bob, always that way. This time M15 are the winners, this guy Walker's the loser."

"I guess . . ."

"And now, I think we deserve a drink." He rose and came round the desk, then gave Reinholdt a mock punch on the shoulder. "Good to know we have a safe pair of hands in London."

"Thank you, sir. Thank you very much."

"Large bourbon on the rocks for me. How about you?"

Reinholdt smiled, reckoning he had never earned a drink more. "Yes, sir," he answered, "a large bourbon on the rocks sounds just about right . . ."

40

Dave stopped to get his breath on reaching the summit of the twisting laneway. He slipped off his rucksack, then sat on a stone wall and took in the splendour of the panorama before him. Shimmering in the afternoon sunshine, the water of the Kenmare river estuary was a beautiful mass of turquoise, and further west the dark blue of the Atlantic stretched to the horizon. The mountains of the Beara Peninsula rose against a cloudless sky, and the warm air was sweet with the smell of gorse.

Dave sat on the wall, captivated by the view, but also excited by the thought that he would soon be seeing Mary and the baby. One part of him wanted to run ahead and meet them, but another wanted to prolong the pleasure of anticipation, and he sat back for a moment, basking in the sunshine.

He had rung the previous night, after arriving in Dublin by taxi, but Jenny had explained that the *Kingdom Maid* wasn't expected until about two in the morning. Disappointed at not being able to speak to Mary, he had concentrated instead on safely getting out of Dublin.

He had known it was only a matter of time until the theft of Sammy Boylan's passport and ticket would be reported, and even if the authorities didn't link it to him he had reckoned there would be a lookout for him in Ireland anyway. He had avoided using the bus or train stations in Dublin, and aware of the possibility of checkpoints on the main roads, had bought a bicycle in a Sunday market and cycled via back-roads, covering the thirty miles to the County Kildare town of Newbridge.

Posing as an American on a cycling holiday, he had stayed the night in a guesthouse there, then rung Ballyard early this morning. His delight when Jenny had confirmed Mary's safe arrival had been tempered by not getting to speak to her as she was deep in exhausted sleep after her long journey. Dave had opted not to wake her, leaving a message instead that he should be arriving in Kerry early after lunch.

He realised he was probably being obsessive about covering his tracks, but he wanted to leave no trail that could possibly be followed to Ballyard, and after leaving the guesthouse he carefully despatched his bicycle to the bottom of the nearby River Liffey, then walked to the local train station. He had chosen Newbridge for its location on the Dublin-Kerry rail route, reasoning that if the Irish police were looking out for him it would be at the mainline stations in Dublin and the other major cities.

He had boarded the nine o'clock Dublin to Tralee train and travelled without incident, getting off in Killarney and exiting inconspicuously there amidst a throng of other tourists. A local bus had then taken him to Kenmare, from where he had hiked along the scenic route to Ballyard.

He sat now on the loose stone wall, taking in the view and aware that this area would be his new home, yet also aware that he mustn't romanticise it too much, that it would look and feel a lot different on a bleak January morning. Still, right now it was breathtaking, and he took a last look at the vista before him, then rose from the wall, suddenly wanting to be on his way.

He headed up the laneway and turned the bend, bringing him into sight of the bungalow. He picked up his pace, then saw a movement from one of the windows. A couple of seconds later Mary came out the door, and his heart lifted as she started across the lawn towards him, her blonde hair gleaming in the sunlight. He ran forward, then they were in each other's arms. They clung together, kissing eagerly.

"I've missed you so much," he said.

"You too, Dave – God, it's so good to see you!" As he looked into her eyes and stroked her cheek tenderly, she looked up and smiled. "I'm not sure about the hair though . . ."

"Necessary subterfuge," he said with a grin. "Besides – Blondes Have More Fun . . ."

She smiled back and lingeringly kissed him again. After a while they parted, and she looked at him seriously. "I wondered if we'd ever be together here."

"So did I, honey, so did I. But when I came up the lane and saw you, it felt like coming home."

"Oh, Dave . . ." she said, squeezing his arm. "We've been so lucky. And Tom and Jenny have been wonderful."

"Where are they?"

"Inside, waiting to see you."

"I want to see them too, but even more I want to see my daughter."

"She's beautiful, Dave, just . . . just beautiful."

"In the genes," he said grinning. "All the Walkers had great bone structure. Jenny said you'd called her Fiona."

"I had to give her a name – Fiona was one of the twenty-three on our shortlist."

"Sounds fine to me."

"Good . . . Fiona it stays then." Mary pointed, indicating the Kerry countryside stretched before them. "So, what do you think?"

"Even better than I remembered it. You know, I've been worried about adapting to a new home, new job, different culture . . ."

"That makes two of us."

"But looking at all this . . . and you . . . and having Fiona . . . I think it's all going to work out."

"We'll make sure it does, Dave." She squeezed him arm again. "We'll just make sure of it. Deal?"

"Deal."

"Come on," she said with a grin, "it's time you met your daughter."

"I'm dying to," he answered smilingly, then they turned towards the house and walked arm in arm across the sunlit lawn.

THE END